Brass
Roots

Brass
Roots
a novel

Jan Tenery

ARCHWAY
PUBLISHING

Archway Publishing books may be ordered
through booksellers or by contacting:

Archway Publishing
1663 Liberty Drive
Bloomington, IN 47403
www.archwaypublishing.com
1 (888) 242-5904

Because of the dynamic nature of the Internet, any web addresses or
links contained in this book may have changed since publication and
may no longer be valid. The views expressed in this work are solely those
of the author and do not necessarily reflect the views of the publisher,
and the publisher hereby disclaims any responsibility for them.

Any people depicted in stock imagery provided by Thinkstock are
models, and such images are being used for illustrative purposes only.
Certain stock imagery © Thinkstock.

ISBN: 978-1-4808-2198-9 (sc)
ISBN: 978-1-4808-2199-6 (e)

Library of Congress Control Number: 2015914205

Print information available on the last page.

Archway Publishing rev. date: 10/2/2015

To him who keeps me from falling

CHAPTER 1

Jeffrey was flat-out booked up. Absolutely nothing, not the smallest obligation, task, or favor, could be shoehorned into his schedule—not even if it were sideways and holding its breath.

Far from being uncharitable, the twenty-two-year-old college student had started his day as he started many winter days there in Baxter, Maine: by shoveling snow from the sidewalks of several neighbors who, because of age or infirmity, were happy to have the voluntary assistance of a big, strong Maine boy. Then he jogged to the college for his morning classes, worked on his thesis for the master's degree in music he was pursuing, practiced his trombone, and by way of telephone, convinced his eighty-three-year-old landlord, Bob, to delay pruning a huge maple tree in the front yard until later that afternoon, when Jeffrey could be there to hold the ladder.

Now, with the college band waiting for him to lead their rehearsal, Jeffrey grabbed his conductor's baton and music folder and was making good progress toward the band room when one of the undergraduates stopped him and said, "Mr. Bowden, there's someone waiting to see you in the band director's office."

"Tell them they'll have to come back another time," Jeffrey said brusquely. "I'm busy right now."

But the messenger was also in a hurry. With an apologetic

wave, he disappeared into a classroom, leaving Jeffrey alone in the hallway with his dilemma.

For a moment, he stood there: a six-and-a-half-foot tower of indecision. Compared to his imposing physique, his face appeared small and was flared slightly at the jaw, looking like the rim of a church bell seen from far below. The cherubic innocence of his blond curls was overshadowed by his heavy eyebrows, a feature which he sometimes used to his advantage on the conductor's podium, along with his tendency to glower.

The tapered end of the baton in his hand wavered like a compass needle seeking true north. From the band rehearsal room, just ahead and to his right, came the dissonant chorus of instruments being brought into tune. The mewling reeds and bellowing horns sounded like a needy flock calling for its shepherd. Directly across the hall, behind the door marked "Band Director," waited Jeffrey's visitor.

Suddenly he saw the obvious solution. Rehearsal would take a full hour; he could dispense with his visitor in less than a minute. Taking strides that would make the college basketball coach cry for the loss, he headed for the band director's office and flung open the door, ushering in a wave of blaring trumpets and thundering timpani coming from the rehearsal room behind him.

His visitor, a young woman in a waitress uniform, jumped off her seat, perhaps thinking that Armageddon was under way and being led by archangels in Brooks Brothers shirts.

Jeffrey silently chastised himself for his rude entrance, then offered an apology and a formal introduction. As a way of indicating that this meeting would be short, he remained standing in the doorway with his hand on the doorknob.

The woman sat down again but continued to look up at him with amazement. To her credit, she didn't ask him if he played basketball, as nearly everyone else did. "I'm looking for someone to tutor my son in music," she said. "My friend's daughter plays in the college band, and she says you're a good instructor. Could you give lessons to my son in our home? The Baxter public schools have been cutting their arts programs because they're out of money, and now they don't offer music at all."

Jeffrey knew, even without looking at his schedule, that he couldn't possibly take on a tutoring assignment. Instead of flatly refusing the woman's request, however, he sought to cushion the blow. "Believe me," he said sincerely, "I'm as concerned as you are about the lack of music education in Baxter. We're already seeing the effect of it here at the college. Many of our incoming freshmen are terribly deficient in the basic skills. That's partly why the college hired me as assistant band director, even though I'm still a grad student." Jeffrey also was performing this function at fractional wages for the financially ailing institution, but his visitor didn't need to know that.

"Here's my main concern," the mom said. "Music is something my son really cares about, and I'm hoping that lessons and regular practice sessions on his own will keep him out of trouble. In this town, there's not much for an eleven-year-old boy to do after school." Looking down in embarrassment, she smoothed the front of her apron and said, "I can't afford a babysitter, and I'm afraid my boy is going to fall in with a gang. There's a lot of that going on in our neighborhood."

Jeffrey knew about this aspect of civic impoverishment, too. During his freshman year at Baxter College, he'd had his car stolen by a gang of armed teenagers. Being relegated to full-time pedestrian status had given him direct experience with the far-reaching effects of the economic ice age gripping the central-Maine city. Every alcove and alley held the makeshift encampments of homeless people. Nearly everywhere, vandalism and the scrawl of graffiti stood as a vivid reminder of the city's idle, misdirected youth. In the downtown area, formerly successful businesses had closed. In their place had risen an array of public assistance outlets, which drew throngs of desperate people who often fought each other for a better place in line. Jeffrey truly sympathized with the young mother before him. He couldn't imagine raising a child in such a place as Baxter.

Yet he knew that dwelling upon the woman's plight would only weaken his resolve. Meanwhile, his musicians were waiting. Their concert was coming up soon, and they were far from ready. "I am well aware of the gang activity in this city," he said, glowering a little, "but you must understand that I'm a full-time student here. I also have several part-time jobs, and I do a lot of volunteer work in my neighborhood. My time is extremely limited." He paused to let the facts of his position make themselves plain. Just as he was about to state the logical conclusion, his brain was roughly elbowed aside by his heart. "How would Monday work for you?" he asked earnestly.

※

"I couldn't just send her away without doing something to help," Jeffrey told Bob later that afternoon as together they addressed the problem of the maple tree. A succession of winter storms had broken many of its limbs, one of which hung precariously over the entryway of the house.

With his stubby legs set in a wide stance, Bob studied the tangle of branches overhead and carefully guided his extension ladder into position. The short, solidly built old gentleman was dressed in his usual winter armor of wool and corduroy, augmented with work boots and safety goggles. An electric chain saw hung from a loop on his belt. "How did you manage to fit her into your schedule?" he asked. "Are you keeping your calendar on an accordion these days?"

"I juggled a few things around," Jeffrey replied. "It's only for a few sessions, long enough for me to teach the boy the basics." He steadied the ladder while the white-haired octogenarian started up the rungs. In his five years of lodging with Bob Cherry, Jeffrey had learned not to underestimate his landlord's capabilities. Though long past the typical retirement age, Bob still worked as a freelance accountant and maintained the big two-story house where he and his late wife had raised their four children. Additionally, Bob built intricate wooden puzzles from his own designs and played tuba with the Baxter Band, an ensemble of amateur musicians who presented concerts in the park during the summer. Jeffrey thought of him as a snow-capped cannonball too busy barreling through life to bother with getting old.

"That was smart thinking on your part," Bob declared, climbing steadily into the tree.

Jeffrey stared up at the lug soles of Bob's boots. "What do you mean?" he asked in puzzlement.

"You're nipping a problem in the bud," the older man explained. "Years from now, that boy could be playing for you in the college band. If you tutor him now, he won't need all that remedial work you're having to give to those other laggards."

"The kid's only eleven," Jeffrey scoffed. "By the time he's ready for college, I'll be long gone."

"Oh?" Bob called over his shoulder. "You're going somewhere? Has the New York Philharmonic made you an offer now that Bernstein is stepping down? Or maybe you're going to replace Ormandy at the Philadelphia?"

Jeffrey rolled his eyes. Both acclaimed conductors had passed away decades earlier, yet they enjoyed immortality in Bob's memory, as well as his record collection.

"Don't misunderstand me," Bob hastened to add. He had stopped climbing and now analyzed the framework of branches supporting the dangerous limb. "You're a gifted musician with a promising future. I wouldn't be at all surprised if you wound up leading a major orchestra, eventually. But you can launch your career right here in Baxter. The ladder of success cannot be climbed in a single step, you know. You've got to take it one rung at a time." Having planned his cut, Bob raised his saw and positioned the blade.

"There's no ladder of success in Baxter, only an escalator going down," Jeffrey shouted, but his words were drowned out by the snarl of metal teeth eating steadily through wood. For the next few minutes, sawdust and severed branches rained down onto the snow-covered ground.

Jeffrey stood out of the way and shivered as a gust of wind with Alberta plates swept past. Winter was far from over, but already he dreamed of his summer job crewing on a pleasure schooner off the coast of Maine. It was hard work, to be sure, but three months of blue skies, ocean breezes, and bonfires on the beach provided a welcome respite from the snowy urban misery he experienced in Baxter during the academic year. After graduation, he wanted no part of this decaying city. He could hardly wait to finish his degree and establish himself in a career someplace far away, someplace with promise, someplace warm.

Before long, the dangerous tree limb had been reduced to a pile of firewood on the ground. Like a sheriff holstering his gun after a victorious showdown, Bob hooked his saw on his belt and capably started climbing down the ladder.

"I have a pretty clear vision of what I want in life," Jeffrey said, gazing up at one of his primary role models, "and I don't see how I can achieve any of it here."

"That's what I thought when I came here as a young man," Bob said. Standing on the ground again, he appeared only marginally winded from his exertions. Years of toting his enormous double-bass tuba across the park to the gazebo, where the Baxter Band performed, had extended his natural vitality into his old age. "But I didn't give up on this city, and neither should you." He tapped his finger against his young tenant's chest. "You're getting a good, solid education at Baxter College. Why stop with a master's degree? 'Jeffrey Bowden, PhD,' has a nice ring to it. If you get yourself a doctorate, opportunity will come knocking for sure."

Jeffrey seriously doubted that Baxter, Maine, appeared on opportunity's delivery route anymore. For the moment, however, he conceded the argument and began gathering up pieces of sawn branches while Bob put away his tools.

As the two headed indoors, Bob said congenially, "I'll bet you're hungry after all that ladder holding. How about an early supper?"

No doubt the invitation included further discourse on the merits of Jeffrey's remaining in Baxter after he graduated, but with breakfast being such a distant memory, he decided it was a worthy tradeoff. He quick-stepped upstairs to the shower, remembering to duck beneath the chandelier at the landing. Beginning in adolescence, he had acclimated himself to his above-average height by studying theater and combat athletics, disciplines which had taught him to control his long limbs with grace and thus avoid the gawkiness which so often plagued tall boys. Even now, at a shade over six feet six, his tallness did not seem excessive but necessary for carrying his athletic frame, in the same way that every inch of a contrabassoon was necessary for expressing the full range of its voice.

The upstairs rooms in Bob's house had been relegated to storage, with Jeffrey's rented space carved out from the happy clutter of family memorabilia. The antique furniture, stacks of photo albums, and steamer trunks full of heirlooms were reminders of similar objects Jeffrey had seen in his parents' and grandparents' homes. He understood why Bob hadn't wanted to move to a senior-friendly apartment or a retirement complex:

his life had happened here, among these relics; he was curator of his own museum. Jeffrey could envision himself doing likewise in his own old age, although in some other city, of course. Significantly, all of Bob's children had found it necessary to pursue their own dreams elsewhere, as Jeffrey intended to do. In Baxter, the only path to success led directly out of town.

After showering and changing into jeans and an old sweatshirt, Jeffrey trotted downstairs with his appetite honed. Cooking was another of Bob's interests, to the extent that he had prepared all the meals for his family. Now widowed and with all four kids out on their own, he had been happy to take a big, healthy college boy into his empty nest. Not only was Jeffrey good company, but also his substantial and nearly constant appetite gave the older man an excuse to cook nearly the same volume of food as he had when the house was full.

Jeffrey strode into the kitchen and found all of the work surfaces in promising disarray. Bags of fresh produce indicated a salad in the works, wisps of aromatic steam rose from a stewpot on the stove, and a dessert of some kind was under construction on the breadboard. Sniffing the complex bouquet of fragrances, he wondered what could be the main course.

Bob closed the refrigerator door and appeared concerned, as if he were missing a vital ingredient. "I talked with ol' Ben Hennessey today," he said. "He's decided to retire this spring. That's going to leave the Baxter Band without a director, and us with our 150th anniversary coming up, too." He set a plastic container on the table and began coaxing off the lid. Warily, he asked, "I don't suppose you'd consider taking the podium for us this summer?"

Jeffrey's reply was quick and unequivocal. "Absolutely not," he said. "You know that I work on the schooner in the summer."

Using a fork, Bob cajoled a few olives into a dish. "Aw, anybody can swab decks and chat up the tourists," he said derisively. "You've got a real talent for music. You're wasting it by doing grunt work when you could be directing the Baxter Band."

"That grunt work is helping to pay for my education," Jeffrey pointed out. "I've got some expensive grad courses coming up." He chewed an olive in thoughtful silence. As an adolescent, he had played under Mr. Hennessey for one season. He remembered the grizzled old director saying that the health of the community band was an indicator of the health of the community. With the city in such bad shape, no doubt the band was suffering, too. Jeffrey wondered why things were so bad in Baxter. Every summer, the schooner was full of passengers from out of state who could afford a summer vacation on the coast of Maine. At last, he said wistfully, "It's hard to imagine the Baxter Band without Mr. Hennessey on the conductor's podium. He used to tell us that the 'BB' on the bass drum stood for 'Ben's band.'"

Bob used a wooden mallet to hammer a few cloves of garlic against a cutting board. In between thumps, he glanced slyly at Jeffrey. "It could stand for 'Bowden's Band,'" he said.

"For that matter, it could stand for 'Bob's Band,'" Jeffrey countered. "Why don't you take on the directorship?"

"They need me on tuba!" the older man barked. He stepped across the kitchen and shoved a pan of rolls into the oven, then picked up a long-handled fork and began prodding something in the stewpot. "You're just what the band needs," he said. "You're young and energetic, and you have a real appreciation for the value of the Baxter Band. You know its history, how it started out as a Civil War band and then later retired into civil service, like most community bands in the Northeast. You could recruit some younger players to replace all us codgers who are dropping like flies. You could explain to the trumpet players why some of them are playing cornet parts. I'll bet you could even rustle up a real live cornet player, one with an honest-to-goodness cornet."

"I am not giving up my summer job for such a low-paying position," Jeffrey declared. "If I can't pay for all my courses next semester, it will delay my graduation." He shuddered to think of extending his residence in Baxter any longer than was absolutely necessary.

Still prodding, Bob asked, "Wilmot pays you for assistant-directing the band at the college, doesn't he?"

"Yes," Jeffrey acknowledged, "but that position is shaky. The college is cutting their budget like practically everywhere else in town. For weeks, Professor Wilmot has been hinting that he might have to eliminate my position. I'm afraid the axe is going to fall on me any day now."

"I've lost plenty of jobs in my day," Bob asserted. "Losing a job just means that you have an open schedule. It's an invitation for opportunity." He gave the contents of the stewpot a final jab.

The ringing telephone in the hallway provided a welcome opportunity for Jeffrey, who had begun to feel as though he should check for puncture wounds on his various body parts. Upon answering the phone, he heard a familiar, authoritative voice bellowing, "Jeffrey? Hugh Wilmot here. From the college." The caller added the last bit in case Jeffrey had forgotten the name of the most powerful man in the music department.

In the ensuing silence, Jeffrey imagined the dreadful sound of an axe falling. Resisting the urge to draw his neck into his shoulders, he replied congenially, "Yes, Professor? What can I do for you?"

"If you're available right now, I'd like you to come to my office," Professor Wilmot said. The tone of his voice indicated that there was only one acceptable response to the request.

Bob came out into the hallway to find Jeffrey hurriedly putting on his overcoat and boots. "What's going on?" the older man asked with confusion. "I thought you were hungry."

"Not anymore," Jeffrey muttered, feeling queasy.

CHAPTER 2

Inside the stately brick building that housed the Baxter College administrators, the door bearing the engraved nameplate of Hugh P. Wilmot stood open. A spirited conversation was under way inside the office.

Jeffrey paused in the doorway while his eyes adjusted to the comparative darkness. A sizable forest had contributed to the paneled walls and furniture. Heavy brocade curtains at the window partially blocked the snowy landscape outside, lending a solemn dimness to the room. For one fearful moment, he thought he spotted an axe on the professor's desk, but the object turned out to be the gleaming rectangular base of a brass lamp.

The professor stood in profile before the window, wringing his hands and bending down to address another man who was seated behind the desk. All during Jeffrey's attendance at Baxter College, but most especially this semester, he had noticed that Professor Wilmot seemed to be physically suffering from the strain of presiding over a financially strapped department. While still retaining the full measure of his authority, the music department's chairperson appeared to be wearing away beneath the weight of his responsibilities. His thinning white hair had slipped down to expose the shining dome of his elongated head, and his shoulders sagged in an ever-worsening stoop. He looked like a melting snowman, though a skeletally thin one.

When at last Jeffrey knocked on the doorjamb to announce himself, Professor Wilmot beamed at him as if he were the fire department arriving just as the drapery was igniting. "Ah, Jeffrey!" he cried. "Come in. Andrew Quigley wants to speak with you."

For a moment, Jeffrey thought this was a joke whose next line would be, "And John Philip Sousa wants to take both of you to lunch!" But he had never known Professor Wilmot to make jokes.

The name Andrew Quigley was one Jeffrey had encountered many times while pursuing his music degree. A nationally known conductor, lecturer, and author, Quigley had established dozens of music ensembles across the country. Over the past half century, he had come to be known as the premier living authority on band music. The magnitude of his accomplishments was undiminished even as Jeffrey now laid eyes on the man himself. Quigley had not been sitting at all; he was merely short. He looked like a walking jack-in-the-box with his red bulb of a nose and outsized head crowned by a mop of springy white curls that bobbed as he talked. Beneath his shaggy fake-fur stadium coat, he wore a garish floral-print shirt and lime-green polyester slacks. Pointedly out of fashion, the ensemble conveyed to Jeffrey the casual indifference of a man secure in his reputation.

As Jeffrey came forward, Professor Wilmot introduced him and then explained, "Mr. Quigley is visiting academic music departments across the country. He has offered Baxter College a generous endowment as well as a commissioned piece for our college band."

"It's a fun composition," Quigley interjected in a nasal bray, "frivolous, perhaps, but a real crowd-pleaser. Calls for lots of percussion and a scacciapensieri." He rolled his bulging eyes toward Professor Wilmot and asked with a challenging grin, "You have one, I presume?"

Professor Wilmot's forehead shriveled with worry. His mouth gaped vacantly as he strained for a reply.

Perceiving his department chair's impending embarrassment, Jeffrey said with confidence, "If we don't, I know where we can get one."

Quigley shot his piercing gaze up at Jeffrey. "Smooth," the little man said admiringly, "very smooth. Now tell me, just what is a scacciapensieri?"

Without hesitating, Jeffrey said, "It's the Italian name for a Jew's harp."

"Good!" Quigley barked, florid with pleasure. "Hughie," he said, "I'm going to get acquainted with your assistant director. All right if we use your office?"

Of course it was all right; Professor Wilmot was all too happy for the details of this exciting benefaction to be worked out within the confines of his private office. He shook hands with Quigley, then walked to the door with Jeffrey, who held the older man's bony elbow in case he fainted from anxiety.

Before leaving, the professor whispered to Jeffrey, "That man just saved the future of the college's music department simply by writing a personal check!"

"Close the door, Jeffrey," called Quigley, who had made himself comfortable in the professor's leather chair. When Jeffrey returned, Quigley pointed to the visitor's chair in front of the desk and said bluntly, "Sit down. This is a job interview."

Before sitting, Jeffrey removed his overcoat and hung it on the back of the chair. Immediately, he regretted the poor impression made by his frayed sweatshirt and worn-out jeans. In resignation, he sat down and apologized for his casual appearance. "Professor Wilmot called me here without much notice," he explained.

"That's all right," Quigley assured him with a dismissive wave. "Assessing your self-confidence in ragged clothes is part

of the interview. How'd you know what a scacciapensieri is?
Even I had to look it up."

"This college has an extensive music library," Jeffrey explained. "As assistant director, I am privileged to have access
to it. I like learning about all aspects of music." The chill from
the room had begun to penetrate his sweatshirt, and he now
wished that he had left his coat on, as Quigley had done. Subtly,
he rubbed his hands together to warm them.

"Tell me, how did you get hired as assistant director?" asked
Quigley, who casually began opening the desk drawers and inspecting their contents.

Although surprised by Mr. Quigley's boldness, Jeffrey answered the question. "The college's budget wouldn't allow for a
full-time director," he said. "They were going to do away with
the concert band altogether, but I offered to direct it for minimal pay with no benefits."

Still rummaging through the desk, Quigley said, "Wilmot
told me that in your senior undergraduate year the college canceled a class which you needed in order to graduate. You proposed an independent study activity, which was approved, and
you graduated on schedule. I find that kind of initiative to be
impressive."

"Thank you," Jeffrey said. Troubled by Quigley's persistent
intrusiveness, he asked, "Are you looking for something in particular? Maybe I can help you find it."

"I'm looking for a box of cigars," Quigley said. "A room outfitted like this wouldn't be complete without one."

"This entire campus is designated as a nonsmoking area,"
Jeffrey said.

"I know that," Quigley retorted. "I can read the signs as well
as you can." From the bottom drawer, he withdrew a wooden
box of cigars and set it heavily on the desk. Looking at Jeffrey,
he said, "Never underestimate the hubris that comes with a

position of power, such as department chair at a prestigious college."

"I won't," Jeffrey assured him. He crossed his arms and tucked his frigid hands underneath his armpits.

"Now, back to you," Quigley said as he began peeling the cellophane from one of the cigars. "I also found out that, aside from receiving some privately funded scholarships, you paid for your own education. Why didn't you save your parents some money by taking a federal grant once in a while?"

"Federal grants come from income tax revenue," Jeffrey said. "I wanted to take money only from people who specifically wanted to give it to a college music major. Also, my parents didn't pay for my education. I did."

Quigley snorted derisively and asked, "What are you, a trust fund baby?"

"No," Jeffrey said simply. "I started saving up for college when I was a kid. Music was my first love, and I knew I wanted to pursue it as a career, either as a director or as a player."

"What instrument?" Quigley asked, interrupting.

"Trombone," Jeffrey said.

Quigley handed him the unwrapped cigar and said, "Continue."

"As soon as I was old enough to work," Jeffrey said, "I did jobs for people in my neighborhood. I mowed lawns, walked dogs, raked leaves, washed cars, cleaned chimneys, moved heavy stuff for older folks, tilled gardens, and painted fences. All winter I shoveled snow for almost everybody on my street, and it was a long street. I saved every penny I could for college."

Quigley, who had begun unwrapping a second cigar, suddenly stopped. Narrowing his eyes suspiciously, he asked, "How'd you manage to go to school while holding all those jobs?"

"I was homeschooled," Jeffrey said. "My mom taught me in the early mornings and evenings."

Alarmed, Quigley blurted, "Homeschooled? Don't tell me you're one of those antigovernment nuts with gold coins buried in the backyard!"

"Oh, no," Jeffrey reassured him. "We kept the gold in the bomb shelter, along with the ammo and dehydrated food." He gave a little smile.

Quigley burst into a prolonged cackle. As his mirth subsided, he nodded in approval of Jeffrey's sense of humor. "Actually, I've heard that homeschooled kids are pretty well educated." He began looking through the desk again, presumably for a lighter this time.

Jeffrey was going to respond by saying that he thought most young people would be pretty well educated if they received one-on-one instruction from a master's degree-holding teacher who also loved them, but he took advantage of Quigley's inattention to discreetly blow into his cupped hands.

"Is Baxter your hometown?" Quigley asked next.

"No," Jeffrey said, "I'm from a little village down on the coast, Cold Harbor."

"Sounds lovely," Quigley said dryly. From deep within one of the drawers, he withdrew a lighter and an ashtray. He struck the lighter and leaned forward to light Jeffrey's cigar, then lit his own.

Jeffrey had no interest in smoking. He was more in favor of using the lighter to start a nice little trash fire in Professor Wilmot's metal wastebasket, but he understood that the cigars were a ritual and, thus, were part of the interview. He puffed the cigar enough to get it going, then sat back in his chair, legs crossed, and rested the hand holding the cigar on his uppermost knee, allowing it to smolder freely and contribute in its small way toward warming the room.

Quigley tossed the lighter back into the drawer and set the ashtray where they both could reach it. Leaning forward on his elbows, he said, "I watched you rehearsing the college band earlier today. Impressive conducting. Excellent command of your players."

"Thank you," Jeffrey said genuinely.

"You coached that oboist through a difficult passage," Quigley said, grinning. "She didn't need to breathe nearly as often as she thought she did."

Jeffrey smiled a little at the memory. "I like helping people play better than they think they can," he said simply.

"You're not bullying, as some directors can be," Quigley pointed out, "and yet you're a strong persuader. You engage your listener, you communicate clearly, and you're not shy about displaying your passion for the music. That's effective with your musicians, of course, but it also goes over well with certain members of your audience, especially people who like to see their names listed in the program booklet as financial supporters." He squinted through a veil of smoke and drew placidly on the cigar. After a moment, he said gravely, "You have no future here, you know. I've been in Baxter less than two days. Already I've seen the unmistakable signs of a city in decline."

With equal seriousness, Jeffrey said, "I've been here five years, and I'm convinced that you're right, not only about Baxter, but also about my lack of a future here. What tipped you off?"

Quigley hesitated a moment and then confessed, "I didn't tell this to Wilmot, but I originally intended to give my dough to the Baxter community band instead of the college. As I'm sure you know, the Baxter Band has a history going back to the Civil War. I hate seeing traditions like that die out. Yesterday I went over to the Municipal Building; spoke to some fellow hiding behind a big desk and half a dozen secretaries. Offered him a nice chunk of change that would have kept the Baxter Band going for another hundred and fifty years. He insisted that the money had to go into a special account so it could be disbursed according to the city's activity-funding ordinance, or some such gibberish. What he was saying, I think, is that he wanted to skim off a portion of my money first before applying it where I wanted it to go. Naturally, I withdrew my offer."

Jeffrey thought the anecdote went far toward explaining the city's current financial difficulties.

Leaning back in the chair, Quigley said easily, "It's just as well. Private money invested in a government enterprise is wasted. Too much of it goes toward lubricating the bureaucratic machine. Altruism is most effective when it goes directly from the donor's pocket to its intended recipient, as with your education grants. I'm sure the college will put my money to good use, seeing as they were smart enough to hire you."

The two men sat in silence for a while, Quigley smoking, Jeffrey not, both of them looking out the window. Snow had begun filtering down from the gray sky, but the sun was making a valiant attempt to burn a hole through the clouds. Shivering, Jeffrey silently cheered it on.

Coming after the long silence, Quigley's next words took on a pronounced emphasis. "I'm putting together my own ensemble," he said, swiveling around to look at his interviewee. "Brass, reeds, and percussion. A concert band." Carefully, he stubbed out the half-smoked cigar.

Jeffrey sat perfectly still and kept listening.

"I need a music director," Quigley went on, "and I've been looking for one as I've been visiting these struggling bands across the country. Sinking ships are a good place to find strong swimmers." He slipped his hand beneath the lapel of his stadium coat and dropped the extinguished cigar into the pocket of his Hawaiian-print shirt, the kind of shirt worn by tourists as well as eccentric, wealthy residents of the islands. Giving a toothy smile, he asked, "Can you swim, Jeffrey?"

Jeffrey felt a surge of warmth as rekindled hope flared up in his chest. "I sure can," he said.

❊

The job Quigley offered was a full-time directorship in Hawaii, Jeffrey explained to Bob later that day. The older man was in his workshop assembling the frame for a wooden jigsaw puzzle he had made. He had just spread glue on the mitered ends of the frame members, but he now abandoned his work to stare up at Jeffrey, who continued excitedly, "It's a huge project with a budget in the millions of dollars. Quigley is building a state-of-the-art performance hall with perfect acoustics. We'll recruit musicians and soloists from around the world, and as music director, I'll have full artistic control. Doesn't it sound fantastic?"

Bob's face was frozen in stunned dismay. Behind the lenses of his magnifying glasses, his eyes blinked a few times as though to clear themselves.

"I'm going to Hawaii, Bob," Jeffrey said with an uncontrollable grin on his face. "Hawaii, where it's warm all year round. I won't have to shovel snow anymore!"

Wordlessly, Bob took off his glasses and wiped the lenses with his handkerchief. He looked as though Jeffrey had just told him someone had died, someone whom he regarded highly.

"I know what you're thinking," Jeffrey hastily went on, "but I'm not dropping out of college. There's a university in Honolulu. I can transfer my credits and finish my master's degree there. Quigley's parent corporation is paying for all of it. That's how much he's willing to invest in me."

Still polishing his glasses, Bob glared up at Jeffrey. "That's not what I'm thinking," he said stiffly.

With a deferential nod, Jeffrey said, "You're an accountant, so I can't blame you for wondering about Quigley's business sense. Let me assure you, he's got a long track record of successful projects like this. Smaller scale, to be sure, but he knows what he's doing. Everything has been carefully planned. He showed me blueprints of the performance hall, detailed time lines, signed endorsements from investors, and healthy financial statements. Naturally, he's financing all of it. He's not asking me to risk any of my own money. Quite the opposite. He's paying me a generous salary, beginning immediately."

Bob held his glasses up to the light and polished them some more. "That's not what I'm thinking either," he said.

Jeffrey's elation had settled into a gloomy fog of frustration. "Can't you see what a great opportunity this is?" he asked. "I'll never get another chance like this. Andrew Quigley is a nationally known figure with a solid reputation. It's a rare privilege to have someone like him helping to launch my career. Bob, you know that leading my own ensemble is something I've always wanted to do."

At last, Bob put his glasses on. Focusing his magnified glare on Jeffrey, he said, "I had hoped you would do that in Baxter."

Jeffrey strained to hold back a cynical laugh, but a little of it crept into his voice as he responded, "You mean the Baxter Band? There's no future for me in that. There's no opportunity at all in Baxter. The public schools have cut their music programs, and the college is bound to do the same. Businesses are failing. Gangs are taking over parts of the city."

"Jeffrey," Bob said sharply, "every problem you just mentioned is an invitation for some bright, energetic young fellow like you to roll up his sleeves and generate some changes around here."

Jeffrey stared in mute astonishment, as if Bob had asked him to fly.

In a stern voice, Bob continued, "There's a reason you came all the way from Cold Harbor to play in the Baxter Band when you were a tyke. There's a reason you got accepted to Baxter

College and have managed to live and work here all these years, earning your degree while so many other people are struggling or giving up altogether and leaving town. Something is drawing you to this city. I think God wants you to settle here in Baxter and start making things right again."

Jeffrey remained silent. In his heart, he thought that God wanted him to go to Hawaii, not as any kind of a reward, but for the opportunity to show that, with all the temptations of money, glamour, and potentially great success, he still could live a moral, responsible, and charitable life, the kind of life he intended to live anywhere he happened to be. Even a tropical paradise could be a crucible, albeit one where it was warm all the time and where he didn't have to shovel snow.

Suddenly, Bob remembered his project and hastily tried joining the frame members, but the glue had dried and the pieces failed to stick. Disgusted, he dropped the work pieces and looked up at Jeffrey again.

While trying to think of what to say, Jeffrey gazed at the tools hanging above Bob's workbench. The workshop was formerly the dining room, near the house's front entrance, and it received good lighting from the big picture window. The tools made a pleasing display with the sunlight glancing off the bright little hammers, tiny-toothed saws, nail punches, and spring clamps. Looking at them, Jeffrey wondered, *What tools does it take to repair a city?*

"I don't know what you expect me to do," he said at last. "I don't know how to fix what's wrong with this city. You need to ask an economist or a politician. All I know about is music."

Bob began scraping dried glue from the frame pieces with his hobby knife. He worked slowly and with complete concentration, as though he were alone in the room, and his extended silence conveyed his disappointment more clearly than any words could have done.

Jeffrey had a mental list of things he urgently needed to do. He had to call his parents, he had to pack, he had to arrange for the transfer of his college credits to the university in Honolulu, and he had to recruit another music major to tutor the boy whose mother had come to see him that morning. At the moment, however, the most important thing he had to do was to make Bob understand why he was leaving, to convince him that he wasn't running away from a challenge but was following a golden opportunity.

At last Jeffrey said bluntly, "I think it's too late for anybody to make things right again in Baxter." He paused to let this assessment stand like a dissonant chord, jarring yet accurate from his perspective, and then continued, "You've seen the boarded-up storefronts downtown, all those homeless people and gangs. You've heard about the muggings on the street, the break-ins of people's homes, the carjackings."

Bob was still shaving the ruined joints of his puzzle frame, patiently correcting his error and preparing for another try. For a moment, Jeffrey silently watched the older man's capable hands working with delicate, precise motions. It was only a jigsaw puzzle, but Bob was putting his very best efforts into it.

"Every day on my way to the college," Jeffrey went on, "I see people lined up in front of the unemployment office and the food bank. They look like cattle, shuffling forward, not talking to each other, not even looking at each other unless one of them tries to cut into line ahead of them. They're able-bodied people with brains full of potential, creativity, and dreams—all of it wasted because there's no opportunity for them here. I don't want to find myself joining them in line. I have to take this job. It's my best chance out of this awful town."

Bob had stopped working and sat with his white head bowed. At last, he said, "Jeffrey, I know things are bad here in Baxter. I guess that's why I wanted you to stay. You're so capable, creative, and hardworking; you're just the kind of go-getter this town needs. We need a whole neighborhood of people like you." He looked up with an expression of deep concern. "But also, I'm worried about this job offer you're describing," he said. "Indeed it does sound like a tremendous step forward for you. Yet I know that too much success too soon can easily lead to a person's downfall."

Jeffrey knelt, put his hand on Bob's shoulder, and said genuinely, "I appreciate your concern, truly." Giving an encouraging smile, he concluded, "But you need to remember that this is a long-term project. There is a lot of preparatory work to do before I have a symphony to lead. Believe me, I am not trying to climb the ladder of success in a single step."

This garnered a nod from Bob, which Jeffrey realized was as much of an endorsement as he could expect, given the lingering worry on his landlord's face.

"Just be careful," Bob urged as Jeffrey rose to go. "You may not climb that ladder in a single step, but you can sure come down that way."

CHAPTER 3

As the wide-bodied jet reached cruising altitude, the thunder of its engines settled into a low, steady roar.

Sitting in a window seat next to his new employer, Jeffrey stretched his legs comfortably before him and enjoyed the rare privilege of having ample legroom on a commercial aircraft. Andrew Quigley had been apologetic about the two of them flying first class to Hawaii, explaining that he hoped to acquire a private jet once Quigley Enterprises began its overseas expansion.

"It's an international endeavor, you see," Quigley said as his white curls quivered beneath the air vent, "not identified with any one city but with the whole Pacific region. That's why I'm calling our ensemble the Pacific Wind Symphony. Eventually we'll have performance halls in coastal California, Japan, and maybe even Australia. I've chosen Hawaii for a home base because it's centrally located among those other places and because, frankly," he said with a grin, "it's not a bad place to work, as you'll discover."

The tinkling of glass announced the arrival of a flight attendant with the wine cart. The two men watched as she uncorked a bottle of red and began filling two crystal goblets. Turning to Jeffrey, Quigley said accommodatingly, "We can get you a soda or something else if you don't drink alcohol."

"I'd love a glass of wine, thanks," Jeffrey said and accepted the glass offered to him.

Amused, Quigley nodded in understanding. "You can live it up now that you're away from home, eh?" he joked.

"Not at all," Jeffrey said. "My parents served wine at home for special occasions, as this certainly is."

After Quigley had taken a glass for himself, the two toasted their collaborative future. Then their discussion lapsed into more casual conversation. "You're not as cloistered as I expected you to be, having been homeschooled," the older man said.

Jeffrey remembered the kaleidoscopic range of educational programs and cultural events his parents had shuttled him to all during his youth, as well as their annual family excursions to some foreign country. With a patient smile, he said, "I hear that a lot." As the flight attendant came by again with the wine cart, he murmured discreetly to her, "You might try decanting that next time. Late reds benefit from that."

Quigley decided to get back to business. From his briefcase, he withdrew a binder with 'PWS' printed in raised gold letters on the cover. "You realize, of course, that I'm asking for a significant investment of your time," he said. "Phase one is strictly development: construction, promotion, attracting ongoing support. It'll be a year before you lift a baton."

"Time well spent," Jeffrey said confidently. "Weren't you tempted to direct the symphony yourself?"

Grimacing, Quigley massaged his right shoulder. "My arthritis is so bad now, I couldn't conduct the *Minute Waltz*," he confessed.

Jeffrey knew that shoulder ailments were common among music directors, but at this early stage in his career, it was only a small worry for him. "Tell me about my role in the development phase," he urged.

"Aside from completing your degree, of course," Quigley

said, "you'll be the public face of the PWS. I want you with me as I visit prospective donors. This is a hungry creature I'm building, and it will need a constant supply of financial fodder. There will be lots of public appearances and media attention. Cameras are everywhere these days. We want to be in everyone's viewfinder, get ourselves on the A-list for every arts and cultural gathering on the islands." Quigley paused to nibble a few macadamia nuts and took another sip of wine before continuing, "I'm sure you're aware that a great many big-name symphonies are struggling these days. I have no intention of presenting this world with another wire choir. By contrast, we're going to offer people the unique voice of the wind ensemble, which you will lead through a wealth of musical repertoires from around the world and throughout human history. You'll control the musical aspect of every part of this project, from outfitting the performance hall to planning the programs to auditioning the players. I want your ideas, lots of them. And I expect you to generate a high level of enthusiasm for those ideas as you speak to various audiences, the first of which will be our own planning committee."

Already, Jeffrey's head was brimming with ideas, but he kept them to himself for the moment. "Will you be on the committee too?" he asked.

"Most emphatically no," Quigley said. "I want a well-balanced team, not one swayed by a family monopoly. I've appointed my wife as committee chair. She's very well connected socially on the islands. She also is our company's treasurer—a CPA, board-certified and licensed."

For the next couple of hours, the two men reviewed the blueprints and other documents contained in Quigley's plan book. They were interrupted only by the arrival of appetizers and a multicourse gourmet meal served on fine china. Everything was first-rate and served in a leisurely, elegant fashion. After finishing a snifter of brandy, Quigley nodded off with his head cradled in the contoured neck pillow supplied by the airline. The plan book began to slip from his age-spotted hands. Jeffrey rescued it before it fell, and took it into his own lap.

Outside the oval window, the sky blazed with jewel-like clarity while another field of blue, the glittering ocean, lay below. Jeffrey gazed alternately at these two realms, feeling the weight of the binder in his lap. He absently rubbed his fingertips over the raised gold letters on the plan book's cover. He felt almost breathless from this sudden change in the trajectory of his life. Before accepting Quigley's offer, he had discussed it at length with his parents, seeking their input as he did with every major decision. They had voiced some misgivings about him attaining at age twenty-three what many music directors would consider to be the zenith of their careers. He had addressed their concerns, and ultimately they had accepted his decision to commit himself to the project. His future, once so clouded and uncertain, now appeared to be a distinct and orderly picture, a ready-made road map to his professional success.

Upon arriving in Hawaii, Jeffrey was assigned his own private office in a penthouse suite occupied by Quigley Enterprises in downtown Honolulu. On his first day of work, he was greeted by Deena, a brisk-mannered, young secretary wearing mostly spandex and costume jewelry. He sat opposite her at the rose-colored Plexiglas arc that formed her workstation while she shepherded him through a stack of paperwork for new employees. He read through everything as she requested, and then signed where directed by her curved, purple fingernails. Andrew Quigley had set up his new music director with a generous compensation package. Even after withholdings for taxes, insurance, and a company-sponsored retirement plan, there were ample funds left for Jeffrey to continue building his own financial safety net and contributing to charity, his long-standing practice, while leaving a comfortable remainder for his own living expenses.

"Okay, Mr. Bowden," Deena said when he had signed the last form, "you're done. Welcome to Quigley Enterprises." She gave him a congratulatory smile.

"Thanks," Jeffrey said, happy to stand up after doing the tedious paperwork. He lifted his suit jacket from the back of the chair and asked, "Do you happen to know of any nightclubs around here that feature live jazz music? I play trombone, and I'd like to pick up a night or weekend gig."

She stared up at him from under her bouffant hairdo. "With the salary you're pulling in, you still want a second job?" she asked, clearly shocked. "Isn't that kind of greedy?"

He let the insult slide for the moment and said, "Andrew told me it would be a few weeks before the planning committee gets rolling. I've got some idle time right now, so I thought, why not work?"

Her smile appeared to have gone off duty, and she now regarded him with suspicion. "The clubs I go to only play techno music," she said. "You know, electronic stuff." As he continued to stand before her, she nervously began gathering the papers he had signed.

From where he stood, he could see her personal things stashed in a compartment alongside her chair. A makeup catalog and a fashion magazine protruded from a large designer tote bag made from textured leather and gleaming brass accents. These items, along with her obvious affinity for jewelry and the absence of family photos on her desk, led him to surmise that she was single and living a carefree life, very possibly paycheck to paycheck. "Do you really think I'm greedy for wanting another job?" he asked.

Embarrassed now, she stammered, "Well, I mean, if you're that crazy about working, I guess it's okay." After a moment, her thoughts cohered, and she said, "It's just that you're making some pretty big bucks here. How much money do you need, anyway?"

"How much?" He fell thoughtfully silent as though pondering the question. At last, he said, "Well, I need enough to cover my basic living expenses: rent, utilities, food, clothing, maybe a car—the usual things everybody has to pay for." With a playful glance toward her, he added, "I might want to buy flowers for my secretary on her birthday."

She gave a puckered little smile. "It's in September," she said. "Just so you know."

"Be sure to send me a reminder about it," he said. Narrowing his eyes and thinking further, he continued, "I need a rainy-day fund for emergencies, in case I get sick or injured, or if, God forbid, the symphony doesn't work out and I'm suddenly out of a job."

"But Mr. Bowden," she interrupted hastily, "there are programs already set up to help you if you become disabled or unemployed."

"Yes, I know," he said, "but I don't want to use other people's money when I'm perfectly capable of building up my own savings."

Vigorously, she shook her head. It didn't exactly rattle, but her words resonated with her ignorance about basic economics. "But you wouldn't be using other people's money," she assured him with a smile. "These are programs set up by the government."

"Programs funded by other people's money," he pointed out. To illustrate the point, he gestured toward the stack of papers on her desk. "Look at all those income withholdings you just asked me to authorize. Those same deductions are coming out of your own paycheck. Where did you think that money was going?"

Her face gradually registered her comprehension. She blinked a few times and looked up at him with a slightly stunned expression. "I don't know," she said. "I guess I thought it just disappeared."

With a laugh, he said, "A lot of people think it does just that." He walked over to the glass wall overlooking the city and stood there, admiring the panorama of busy streets and shining skyscrapers. It was a thrilling sight: all those people working in their own areas of expertise, striving for individual success and, in doing so, playing a vital part in an intricate economic machine, generating income for themselves and their families as well as for their government. "I'm also committed to giving a percentage of my income to charity," he said. "Every city has people who need help, even a place as beautiful as this. Although, I guess if you were homeless, you could always sleep on the beach," he concluded with a shrug.

"No, actually there are laws against that," she said.

He raised his eyebrows in surprise at learning this fact. Gazing through the window, he said, "Well, in that case, I would hope that this city has some charitable organizations that provide shelter, food, and other essentials for people going through hard times. I want to be a regular supporter of places like that, and the more money I make, the more I can give to help them." Turning toward her again, he asked, "Do you happen to know of any reputable, efficiently run charities I could support as a standard practice? I like to make consistent donations, because it helps those organizations plan and run their operations more smoothly."

Her eyebrows went through a series of contortions. She opened and closed her mouth a couple of times like a dying fish as she groped for a reply. "Not really," she admitted at last. "I could find out for you, though."

"I'd appreciate it if you would," he said sincerely.

Deena bit her lip thoughtfully and watched Jeffrey put on his suit jacket. While helping him complete his employment forms that morning, she had learned some of his most personal information. But now she seemed to be seeing into the depths of his heart.

"It's easy to think of Andrew Quigley as always having been successful," Jeffrey said, "but I've read about his career, and I know it has taken him many years to accumulate his wealth and stature. He would have started out at our age when setting his goals and building his empire. My own goals are different from his, but I know I need to start working toward them now. I want a family, a big one if I can afford it. I also want to be able to support myself into my old age, the way Andrew is doing. A lot of people from his generation are relying on Social Security, and I think he takes some pride in the fact that he's not. He's still supporting himself and his wife by using money he's earned himself. I have a great deal of respect for someone who can do that. It says a lot about his regard for other people, as what he's doing leaves more money in the pot for those who are less fortunate."

Deena's brain and facial muscles were still getting a workout as she considered this aspect of her employer. She knew that Mr. Quigley was successful. He had to be, she thought, to be able to pay her the salary she was getting as well as the salaries of all the other staff at Quigley Enterprises. But until just now, she hadn't really considered the magnitude of what he had accomplished over his lifetime. "He's a super boss," she said genuinely. "And you're right: he's a hard worker. He stays busy all the time, even though he's in his seventies."

"Have you thought about what you want to be doing when you're that old?" Jeffrey asked.

"Of course not," she said with an abrupt laugh. Then, with sudden seriousness, she said, "I'll bet you have, though."

With a smile, he thanked her for her help and turned to go.

"Hey," she called after him. "Let me know if you find a job playing trombone. I might want to start going to a new club."

CHAPTER 4

As a way of raising local awareness about his project, Andrew Quigley began hiring small groups of local musicians, such as a brass quintet or percussion ensemble, to play short concerts in various public places. After each of these performances, Quigley told the audience about his plans for the Pacific Wind Symphony while his aides distributed informational handouts, contribution forms, and fee schedules for advertisers and sponsors. These publicity concerts generated waves of enthusiasm among the music-loving public. Subsequent promotional appearances attracted increasingly larger crowds and media attention.

Initially, Jeffrey was assigned the role of observer at these events. To a great extent, Quigley was only articulating the contents of the PWS plan book, which Jeffrey had committed to memory, yet it all seemed magnified somehow when he heard it proclaimed aloud by Quigley the showman. Standing at the back of the crowd, Jeffrey could observe people's reactions to Quigley's smooth yet impassioned delivery, and he became as enthralled as the audience by the presentation.

At one of the concerts, Jeffrey felt someone jostle him from behind. He turned to see a Polynesian man about his own age standing behind him: a bald, bronze Buddha with heavily muscled arms and an egg-shaped torso. The man was wearing a black T-shirt, the frontal logo of which had flaked into unintelligibility. A pair of floral-patterned shorts hung loosely over his stout, brown legs. With a challenging smirk, the man said, "You're a long ways from Maine."

Jeffrey failed to detect anything familiar about the man's moonlike face. "How did you know I was from Maine?" he asked.

"It says so on your driver's license," the Polynesian man answered.

Jeffrey reached for his back pocket and found it empty. A moment later, his wallet appeared on the palm of the other man's extended hand. Jeffrey snatched it back. "What did you take?" he demanded, flipping open the wallet.

"I didn't take anything," the man said. "Our local politicians will do that soon enough through the tax code. I'm teaching you lesson number one about getting around safely in this city: never carry your wallet in your back pocket. What's Cold Harbor like?"

Having ensured that the contents of his wallet were intact, Jeffrey fitted the object into his front pocket. "It wasn't named after a man named Cold, if that gives you any idea," he said. More graciously, he added, "I suppose I should thank you for teaching me where to carry my wallet."

"Forget it," the Polynesian man said with an easy shrug. "I've been following you guys around town for a couple of weeks." He nodded toward Quigley, who was still orating. "I'm trying to figure out what kind of scam he's running. I thought you might be his accomplice, working the crowd while he keeps everyone's attention focused on him, but so far I haven't figured out your part in this. That's why I wanted to look in your wallet."

"This is no scam," Jeffrey assured him. "Andrew Quigley is a straightforward businessman. He's highly respected in his field. What makes you think he's dishonest?"

"He's got the perfect cover," the other man said. "He's appealing, dynamic, a good talker, enthusiastic about his product.

Plus, he looks like a Disney character—and nobody would accuse a Disney character of being a crook. That guy is so adorable that he could get away with murder."

"Well, you've got the wrong impression of him," Jeffrey asserted. "He's exactly what he claims to be. For forty years, he's done nothing but share his love of music and donate money to struggling musicians."

The Polynesian man shook his head, saying, "No, there's something going on under the surface with him. I'm usually good at picking up on scams, having run a number of them myself. It's research for a book I'm writing," he added in hasty exoneration. Extending his pudgy hand, he said, "Nice to meet you, Jeffrey. I'm K, as in the letter *K*."

"Your name is the letter *K*?" Jeffrey asked curiously, shaking hands with the man. He had forgotten his embarrassment about having been duped and now was intrigued by the fellow's smooth patter and engaging personality.

"Actually, it's the letter *K* followed by a long string of vowels and apostrophes," K said. "It's royal Hawaiian, going back a few generations, and if you pronounce it wrong, you gravely insult my family. It's safest just to call me K." Once Jeffrey had nodded in concession, K said, "Do me a favor and don't blow my cover if you see me at another one of these public appearances. But if I catch you with your wallet in your back pocket again," he said, pointing his stubby finger, "I'm going to pick it just to reinforce the lesson." Giving a wink, he turned and started off.

For a moment, Jeffrey simply watched him walk away. From the base of K's bronze skull, a tiny, black braid hung like a decorative afterthought. On impulse, Jeffrey called after him, "What's the personal income tax rate in Hawaii?"

Without hesitation, K reported the rate for each of the three income brackets, adding that residents in Honolulu paid an additional city tax, which he also quoted to a tenth of a percent.

"Good Lord," Jeffrey murmured, impressed not only with the high rates but also with K's precise knowledge of them.

K cocked his head and asked, "Any other questions?"

"Yes," Jeffrey said with a smile. "Have you had lunch yet?"

The two men headed for a nearby bar and grill that K recommended. While making their way through a carnival of vendors offering everything from Hawaiian T-shirts to shark's-tooth necklaces, Jeffrey said, "I want you to explain to me how you came to memorize the income tax rates for this state."

"Oh, I just made up those numbers to impress you," K admitted with a sheepish grin. "But I would bet I'm pretty close."

Amid the jumble of sidewalk kiosks and souvenir-seeking tourists, a legless old man sat on a skateboard-like contraption, strumming a ukulele. His instrument case lay open on the ground where his legs would have been.

Reflexively, Jeffrey started to reach for his wallet. His hand had barely twitched when K said in a low, firm voice, "Keep walking."

"I just want to give that guy a few dollars," Jeffrey said.

"Keep walking," K insisted, jabbing the back of Jeffrey's arm for emphasis. "As soon as you put your hand in your pocket, whoever is hiding in that alley will pull you in there and clean you out."

Ushered past the alley at a brisk pace, Jeffrey nevertheless spotted two large, tattooed men in ragged T-shirts lurking behind some garbage cans. A wave of relief washed over him as he and K left the potential danger behind. "How did you know those guys were there?" he asked breathlessly.

"Read my book and you'll find out," K said. "Lesson number two: don't give money to people on the street, no matter how pathetic they look. Too many crooks take advantage of soft-hearted people like you. If you want to help folks, I can steer you toward some good charities."

Having arrived at the small, open-front restaurant, Jeffrey and K settled at a table along an interior wall. K said, "Before we part ways, I'm going to teach you a few tricks, like carrying two wallets: one you can afford to lose, and another one most robbers will never think to look for."

Jeffrey looked up at the waiter who had just brought their menus. "One check," he told the man. Buying lunch for his security advisor was the least he could do, Jeffrey thought.

Midway through their sandwiches, K murmured, "Hey. Watch that action at the register."

Turning his head, Jeffrey observed the waiter standing behind the takeout counter and fitting a plastic lid onto a paper cup of coffee for a customer who stood picking coins from his change purse.

"What do you see?" K prompted.

"Guy buying coffee to go," Jeffrey said.

"Customer's counting out the exact change," K pointed out. "Wants to get rid of his pennies. Now keep your eyes on the waiter."

As they continued to watch, the transaction was completed, thanks were exchanged, and the customer left with his coffee. The waiter walked to the other end of the bar and began washing glasses.

Jeffrey looked at K in astonishment. "The waiter didn't ring up the sale," he said.

K beamed with pride at his new pupil. "Money went right into his pocket," he said. "He's pulled that trick twice since we've been sitting here. Small scale, to be sure, and in part that's why it's so pathetic, because it's petty—on a par with stealing rolls of toilet paper from the employee bathroom. But stuff like that adds up over time, and really it's the principle of the thing. Owner's trying to run a profitable business, already paying big taxes, got his own employee skimming from him."

"Lesson number three: always get a receipt?" Jeffrey guessed.

Scowling, K grumbled, "You're going to know the whole book before I even get it published."

"Don't worry, I'll still buy a copy," Jeffrey assured him. "Is it a guidebook for tourists?"

"Actually, I'm thinking a pamphlet," K said. "Cheap to print, easy to sell on the street or at the airport."

"You really think there's a market for that kind of information?" Jeffrey asked.

K rolled his eyes tragically. "I see so many people get sheared that it breaks my heart," he said. "Old people, young people, people with wealth, people who save up for years for a Hawaiian vacation. They all should know how to protect themselves better. Plus, why shouldn't I make money off my research?" As the waiter came over with the check, K asked him conversationally, "How's business?"

"Good!" the man replied innocently. He took the empty plates from the table and started to walk away.

"Don't forget to ring up that coffee," K called after him.

The waiter looked over his shoulder at him. "What?" he asked with a puzzled frown.

"That coffee with legs you just sold to the guy at the counter," K said with a riveting glare. "The one before him, too. They both gave you exact change. It's still in your pocket."

A wave of expressions ranging from surprise to embarrassment to hatred passed over the waiter's face. Jeffrey thought it was like watching a chameleon change colors.

"I thought I did ring them up," the waiter said stiffly.

"Either your memory is bad or your ethics, my man," K blustered, "but I know what I saw. Do it or else it comes out of your tip and I write about you in the restaurant review I'm doing."

Speechless with fury, the waiter carried the dishes into the kitchen.

Jeffrey regarded K with profound admiration. "You write restaurant reviews?" he asked in amazement.

The bronze Buddha shrugged. "I could always start," he said.

The two men spent the afternoon driving around in K's jeep, touring possible neighborhoods where Jeffrey might find inexpensive but secure lodging. Since arriving in Hawaii, he had been staying at a hotel in town and was anxious to find his own place. The weather was perfect for riding around with the convertible top down. Jeffrey was falling more and more in love with his newly adopted state.

As the jeep climbed into the green hills, K kept up a constant chatter of advice. "Okay, you want to meet girls?" he proposed.

Jeffrey didn't, but for the sake of conversation he said, "Yeah?"

"Buy a roll of numbered tickets," K said, "the two-part kind that are perforated down the middle. Take it to a party and tell people you're running a fifty-fifty drawing, a dollar a ticket. Sell the girl a ticket. You get her name and phone number, plus a buck."

"You are shameless," Jeffrey said, laughing in spite of himself.

"I'm an educator," K insisted. "Girl hands over her money to a stranger like that, she deserves to get taken."

"Who taught you these things?" Jeffrey asked.

"I told you, I do research," K said. "From a young age I realized I could learn lots of stuff just by paying attention. My grandmother runs a general store in Honolulu. She keeps a broom leaning against the checkout counter and rings it up

with every purchase. Most customers never realize they're pay-
ing a broom surcharge. If they do notice, she says very sweetly,
'Oh, I thought you were buying that,' and then corrects the bill.
She must have sold that broom a hundred times."

By the end of the day, Jeffrey had leased a furnished bungalow that was tucked into a quiet, green hillside. He then asked
K, who turned out to be single and living in a back room of his
grandmother's store, to move in with him and split the rent.

K considered the attractive lodgings with obvious approval. "Are you domestic?" he asked. "Or do you plan on hiring
a housekeeper and cook?"

"I'll definitely be hiring somebody to do those things,"
Jeffrey said. "I'm going to be busy working on my career."

"You pay the rent," K proposed. "In return, I'll keep the place
looking good, cook for you, and generally take care of anything
that keeps you from your work. My family is involved in lots of
different businesses, so I can get you a discount on clothing,
haircuts, groceries, dry cleaning, most anything. You get a big
date, I'll rent a tux and a limo and drive you. It impresses the ladies like you wouldn't believe. I'm also good at security, for when
you get to be famous around town, which I'm guessing won't be
very long from now, given the speed Quigley is moving."

Jeffrey found these terms agreeable. Later, he relaxed on a
cushioned chaise lounge on his lanai, which he had learned was
the Hawaiian term for what people in Maine called a porch, and
admired his tropical flower garden while the sun set over the
coconut palms farther down the hillside. An appetizing bouquet of aromas wafted from the kitchen. When K, wearing a
professional chef's apron, came out and set a glass of sparkling
water on the table, Jeffrey asked him, "What's for dinner?"

"Pork and beans," K replied.

The pork and beans turned out to be a fork-tender slab
of braised pork loin garnished with caramelized onions and

pineapple. This was accompanied by crisp, slender green beans in a sweet butter sauce. After his first mouthful, Jeffrey asked in wonder, "If you can cook like this, why haven't you opened your own restaurant?"

"There's an eighteen-month waiting list to get a restaurant license in this state," K told him. "Part of the backlog is that even street vendors have to be licensed by the city. It has cut down severely on that industry. Lots of poor folks used to make a passable living selling fruit and homemade items from carts on the sidewalk or on the beach. They were very popular with tourists. Now they can't afford the license and inspection fees, so they just collect welfare."

"That's pathetic," Jeffrey said before eagerly filling his mouth again.

With an easy shrug, K said, "I'm happy to stay out of the bureaucratic machine and just do what I like to do. You and I can have a private agreement here, a barter arrangement, and we both benefit from it. If I open a restaurant, I've got inspectors from all levels of government checking for dirt under my refrigerator, making sure I hire the correct demographic mix of employees, telling me how much I have to pay them, whether or not my customers can smoke, where I have to buy my ingredients, how much salt and butter I can use in my cooking, and what information I have to print on my menus. I don't want to deal with that many guys with clipboards."

"If you can cook like this," Jeffrey declared, "I don't care about dirt under the refrigerator."

"As if any self-respecting cook would risk making his customers sick," K said, clearly insulted by the notion. He headed back to the kitchen.

Over Kona coffee and gingerbread with pear sauce, Jeffrey gave K an overview of his role in Quigley's grand plan.

"So let me see if I've got this straight," K said. "You're getting a brand-new performance hall with perfect acoustics, world-class musicians, a big salary, and maybe a private jet, all for just standing in front of an audience and waving a stick at some musicians?"

"There's more to it than that," Jeffrey insisted. "I have to study the music, interpret what the composer had in mind, and figure out how to convey that interpretation to my musicians. Then I have to rehearse them until they play it the way I hear it in my head. Only then do I get to stand in front of an audience, and even that isn't as simple as you might think." With solemn authority, he stepped up onto a cement planter. A mild breeze lifted his hair as he stood against the night sky, a rising star against ancient ones. His facial expression became one of composed readiness, like that of a runner on the starting block. Raising his hands to chest level, he cocked his wrists and explained, "I signal my musicians like this. They hold their instruments ready. No one breathes or moves; they make not a sound until I give the downbeat." Both of Jeffrey's hands lightly bounced downward, then wafted up in a slow, measured ricochet. "Woodwinds in unison introduce the melody," he said, drawing his hands through the air. He closed his eyes, concentrating on the sounds he imagined. "The tempo is notated as a steady larghetto, but, in effect, it is the heartbeat of a sleeping muse pulsing in three-four meter." With a slight emphasis of his gestures, he continued. "The reed chorus builds in a subtle crescendo up to the key change." He cocked his head, listening for the proper response from his players and getting it.

K watched from his front-row seat, delighted.

Jeffrey swept his imaginary baton toward a flowering hibiscus, cueing the low brass section. "Tubas and trombones begin a dark, velvety ostinato," he said. "Meanwhile, I do this." He slowly raised his left hand, splaying his fingers above his head and giving a slight rotation to his wrist.

"You unscrew a light bulb?" K asked.

"No-o," Jeffrey complained, breaking the spell to glower down at K. "I pull the English horn through a phrase so lyrical it melts you at the knees." He hopped down from the planter and settled back into his chair. Giving an impatient sigh, he said, "I just have to wait a year until we finish phase one."

K smiled as he studied his new housemate. "You make it all sound exciting, Jeff," he admitted, "and I wish you the best, I really do, but you still haven't convinced me that Quigley is a straight dealer. You obviously want this symphony very badly, I mean, with a passion. It shows in the way you talk about it." Suddenly he fell silent and looked away, reluctant to say anything more.

"Keep going," Jeffrey prompted him.

At last, K looked at Jeffrey again, and this time, his expression was a strange mixture of admiration and fear. "I thought Quigley was a good salesman," he said, "but you've got him beat, no contest. There's weight behind your words. Heat. Energy. Quigley's got fire fueling his delivery, but you've got a nuclear reactor: powerful but quiet, with an integrity that shines through and makes people believe you, trust you. You could sell anything to anybody. You could persuade people to do impossible things, irrational things, things they never dreamed of doing." He paused and gave a troubled frown. "I can't help thinking that Quigley chose you for this job because you're the perfect front for whatever it is he's trying to pull."

"Excuse me," Jeffrey said stiffly, "but I do have some credentials."

"And I, I freely admit, have none when it comes to music," K said, extending his arms in a gesture of surrender, "so please don't be offended by the likes of me. But you wanted to hear what I had to say, and I'm telling you because I'm worried that you're about to get fleeced. It's just a feeling I've developed about you."

Jeffrey's brow furrowed in puzzlement. "Because you picked my pocket so easily?" he guessed.

Rolling his eyes, K said, "Oh, man. My grandmother could sell you the broom all day long."

Jeffrey grew increasingly disturbed as he plumbed the depths of this insult. He hated to think that his new house-keeper was going to have to wash dishes while nursing a black eye. With growing bellicosity, he asked, "So are you saying I'm naive or just plain dumb?"

"Neither," K asserted. "Listen. You're taking this the wrong way." Leaning forward, he said earnestly. "I've got a sense about you, the way you look at the world, the way you interact with other people. I don't know anything about Cold Harbor, but I would bet you're from a good family, raised by people who care about you, who want you to be all you can be, even if you don't actually enlist in the Army."

Surprised by the accuracy of K's assessment, Jeffrey kept listening.

"There's nothing phony about you," K continued, "no dirt you're trying to hide. I know gold when I see it, and Jeff, you are twenty-four-karat. But that makes you a sitting duck for crooks, especially when they dangle in front of you that dream career you've always wanted. I'm afraid you're in for a rude awakening."

Jeffrey offered quick reassurance. "You don't know Andrew Quigley," he said. "The man is totally aboveboard. He hasn't asked me to contribute a dime toward his project. Quite the opposite. He's paying me a very generous salary, basically just for putting together a wish list for the kind of symphony I want. This is not some fly-by-night scheme; it's a project he's been planning for years. Everything is carefully documented. He's shown me blueprints, time lines, written endorsements, finan-cial statements."

"All of which can be faked," K said. "And besides, he doesn't have to ask you for money. There might be some other way he's using you."

Shaking his head, Jeffrey said, "I just can't believe that he is. Quigley's reputation is sterling."

"It could be only silver plated," K said. "Just be careful, is all I'm saying. I don't ever want to have to say I told you so."

CHAPTER 5

Her nose had been carved from ivory or alabaster, or perhaps from unicorn vertebrae, and through some marvelous surgical technique had been grafted to her face. These were
the thoughts running through Jeffrey's mind as he gazed up at
Helen Quigley, treasurer of Quigley Enterprises, who stood at
the head of the conference table welcoming the members of the
planning committee to their first meeting.

In his occasional and tactful observation of beautiful
women, Jeffrey didn't usually take note of their nasal appara-
tuses, but this one fascinated him. It was a Michelangelo sculp-
ture in miniature, remarkable because of its graceful form and
translucence. The very tip was a perfectly round pearl worthy
of display in Tiffany's window. Porcelain wings flared down
from either side to form the nostrils, which were so thin they
could serve as a quality-control index for manufacturers of fine
china. It was most certainly a functional nose, clearly moving
air in and out of Helen's body as she spoke, yet it gave the appearance of being clean and pure, even sterile. This nose was
far too refined to produce mucus or clog up from allergies. Each
delicate nostril was an immaculate little hole, a cozy niche that
you might even feel comfortable crawling into, but you would
be compelled to wipe your feet first.

As Jeffrey stared up at her, she directed her thousand-watt

smile at him and said to the group, "And now it is my great pleasure to introduce our music director, Jeffrey Bowden."

Despite her beaming face and the clatter of applause from
his fellow committee members, Jeffrey's heart sank. Helen
Quigley, treasurer of his future symphony, had mispronounced
his last name.

He pushed his chair back slowly and took his time rising
to his full height as he considered how best to correct her mistake. Seated around the conference table were some of the islands' most influential patrons of the arts: men in designer suits
and silk ties, businesswomen with stiff hairdos and full calen-
dars, dowagers with faceted bits of their inheritances flashing
from their earlobes and fingers. All of them were sophisticated,
discerning people with plenty of other avenues worthy of their
disposable income. It wouldn't do for Jeffrey to embarrass his
boss's wife in front of them. Yet he knew that this was the time
to teach these important people the correct pronunciation of
his name.

"That was a fine introduction, Mrs. Quigley," he said, "and I
thank you. However, I must point out that you mispronounced
my last name."

As her eyes locked with his, he saw them widen with dismay. A blush of embarrassment flooded her smooth cheeks, and
her smile turned icy.

Skating deftly onward, he concluded with gallantry, "But
you say it with such overwhelming charm that I'm seriously
considering saying it that way myself from now on."

The table erupted with delighted laughter.

The skim of ice on Helen Quigley's face immediately melted
in the warmth of her widening smile. She almost wriggled in her
seat like a happy puppy. "Well, Mister—ah, Jeffrey," she said, "by
all means, educate us so we can address you properly."

He said his last name and gave the phonetic reminder, "The

first syllable rhymes with *whoa,* not *wow.*" Having put the issue to bed, he went on to thank the committee members for dedicating their time and other resources to developing the music ensemble that it would be his distinct honor to lead in the near future.

As the group gathered for refreshments after the meeting, Helen Quigley, slim and sleek in her clingy, black dress, appeared beside Jeffrey and took his elbow. "You got me out of a pickle," she said.

"A small matter," he said with a modest shrug, "but it seemed like a good time to set the record straight."

Her eyes sparkled like the wine in her champagne glass. "I have a confession," she said as she motioned for him to come closer. He bent down and felt her lips brush his ear as she said, "I can't stop thinking: *wow.*"

%

Wow was the word K uttered later that day as he stood at the front window of the bungalow and watched the black Porsche pull away from the curb.

"Nice wheels, huh?" Jeffrey said, loosening his tie. Helen Quigley had just given him a ride home from the planning committee meeting. He rubbed his ear as if to erase the memory of her flirtation. It still bothered him.

"Yeah, that too," K said, turning away from the window. "Your boss just went up several notches in my opinion of him. What is she, about half his age?"

"I guess so," Jeffrey said. "But don't hold Andrew in high regard when it comes to women. She told me they're separated, she being wife number four for him. He's set her up in a house way up in the hills, while he stays in a bachelor pad on the beach. That's about as far apart as they can get on a small island." He picked up the newspaper and carried it out to the chaise lounge on the lanai. By the time he had slipped off his loafers and turned to the classifieds, K had appeared with a tall glass of sparkling water garnished with lemon wedges. "As much as I admire Andrew Quigley," Jeffrey said, "he's got a throwaway mentality about women that utterly repulses me." He lifted his drink, toasted his housemate, and drank with evident satisfaction. "One time he said to me, 'Jeffrey, do you know why men pay so much money for divorces? Because they're worth it!' And then he laughed about it." Jeffrey rubbed his ear again.

Deena had warned him about Mrs. Quigley's drinking problem. Two nights a week, Jeffrey worked the admissions desk at a detox clinic run by volunteers from a local church. While the treatment sessions were done by professional therapists, the group found it helpful to have someone of Jeffrey's stature to handle the more physical aspects of shepherding alcoholics and drug addicts into the recovery program. Every time a new recruit spilled through the door, Jeffrey feared it would be Helen. He couldn't help thinking that she knew she was headed for the next exit ramp on the Quigley Highway of Serial Monogamy and was drinking to cushion the ride.

K stood at the hibiscus, carefully pinching off the spent blossoms. Comfortable with his Polynesian heritage, he wore a floral-print sarong and a tank top displaying the muscles he could employ against anyone who had a problem with his wearing a floral-print sarong. After a moment, Jeffrey asked, "K, do you think I'm weird because I don't date women?"

"I think I hear the phone ringing," K murmured. "Excuse me."

"No, no, it's okay," Jeffrey assured him. "I honestly want to know what you think. And don't worry about insulting me, because I've been called all the names: frigid, Victorian, a prude, mama's boy, a closeted gay."

Giving a troubled frown, K responded, "That doesn't leave much for me to say. Why are you asking me about this?"

"Helen asked me why I'm not seeing anyone right now," Jeffrey said. "It reminded me that I'm sort of an oddball in many parts of society, so I wondered what you thought."

"What did you tell her?" K asked, deftly stalling for time.

"It was an awkward moment," Jeffrey admitted. He rubbed his thumb over the outside of his frosty glass. "I could hardly tell her the truth: that, unlike her husband, I want one permanent bond with a woman, not a series of Post-it Notes."

K had finished his pruning and now leaned against a sunny section of the garden wall. His crossed arms looked as though they were covered with gold leaf. With eyes half closed, he waited for Jeffrey to continue.

"When I choose a woman for a partner," Jeffrey said, "I want it to be a lifelong commitment, truly 'til death do we part, just as the vows say. I don't want to go through a bunch of practice runs and get confused by the physical chemistry. That's why I'm holding off on dating, because I'm not ready to make a commitment just yet. But I didn't feel comfortable saying that to someone who is beginning to realize that she is the next Post-it Note about to be discarded."

"So what did you say?" K asked.

"I squirmed around for a while, and eventually we changed the subject," Jeffrey replied. "Now tell me your opinion, as a guy."

K selected his words as carefully as if they were fresh produce at the farmer's market. After a long moment, he said, "Jeff, I get the impression that if a girl dropped a hanky in front of you, you'd think about starting a laundry service." Hastily he added, "But I mean that in a good way. You've got other priorities right now, and there's nothing wrong with that."

"Thanks, buddy," Jeffrey said, reassured. He sucked on a lemon slice and looked at the newspaper again while K went inside the bungalow. Shortly, a tray of hot hors d'oeuvres fragrantly announced its arrival on the table. Jeffrey selected a butterflied shrimp and gave it a thorough dunking in a pungent red sauce.

Noting the automobile ads his employer was scanning, K asked, "Are you in the market for a car?"

"I think it's time I bought one," Jeffrey said. "I can't keep bumming rides from people, and Helen says that a high-end car with good resale value is a practical way of diversifying my investments."

Warily, K asked, "You trust her judgment on that?"

"Andrew is trusting her with his millions," Jeffrey pointed out. "She's a CPA with impeccable credentials." He held up the newspaper for K's approval and got it in the form of a reverent nod.

"Mercedes-Benz," K murmured. "Always a good choice. See if you can get one to match her eyes."

"Wouldn't that look good rolling into the parking lot of Quigley Music Center on opening night?" Jeffrey asked.

"With a uniformed chauffer at the wheel?" K proposed. He struck an erect pose, ready for service.

Jeffrey gave a happy grin. "Maybe," he said. Instantly his expression grew solemn, almost fearful. "This is all happening so fast," he said. "I've got to be careful. I don't want to lose my bearings and turn into an arrogant, unprincipled boor."

"Don't sell yourself short," K said, laying his hand on Jeffrey's shoulder for emphasis. "I see you doing your community service, making your charity contributions, basically living the life of a monk with a better wardrobe. You may be Hawaii's newest rising star, but morally you're still pretty well-grounded."

"It means a lot for me to hear you say that," Jeffrey told him. "I want to stay morally grounded, no matter how successful I get. Andrew has never spoken directly to me about my working at the detox clinic, but I think he's uncomfortable with his music director's being visibly involved with an enterprise like that.

It's just foreign to him. He's used to giving people money and not getting his hands dirty. The financial support is essential, of course, but somebody's got to do the actual work."

"What makes you think he objects to it when he's never said anything to you about it?" K asked.

"Helen came to see me about it one day," Jeffrey said. His expression darkened with the memory. "I think Andrew put her up to it. She said that some of the members of the planning committee found out about me working with drunks and drug addicts. She warned me to be careful about the image I was projecting. She said to me, 'Remember, you are the music director of what is about to become a very prestigious symphony.' I told her I also was an able-bodied resident of this island and that I wasn't afraid of demonstrating that Quigley Enterprises is a responsible member of the community."

"Keep doing the right thing, Jeff," K urged.

"By the end of our conversation, she agreed to persuade the planning committee that I was presenting a good image, PR-wise," Jeffrey said. "I don't think they'll object anymore." He finished his drink and gazed out at the clouds accumulating beyond the waving palm trees; the island was about to get its usual afternoon rain shower. "But I'm the one who's worried now," he said, seeming to look beyond the horizon. "This is a dangerous time. When things are humming along smoothly, it can be very easy to make a mistake. I'm walking a fine line here. As music director, I have an obligation to fulfill my duties with flair and a certain amount of artistic grandeur. After all, people go to the symphony with certain expectations, and I want to give them all the glamour and polish they expect to see. But I want to stay humble, too."

"Sometimes life takes care of that part for you," K said and carried the empty glass to the kitchen.

CHAPTER 6

Remaining humble and adhering to his principles had been at the forefront of Jeffrey's mind upon accepting Andrew Quigley's fabulous job offer. Now, several months into the job, he thought he was managing it fairly well. He routinely contributed to a few carefully selected charities, attended services at a nondenominational church in his neighborhood, volunteered at the detox clinic, and, except for work-related engagements, avoided the social scene altogether. His most immediate and constant temptation came from Helen, as she persistently extended invitations for dinner or drinks at her home.

The pitfalls of visiting a woman alone in such a private setting were immediately obvious to Jeffrey. Yet he viewed each potential meeting with Helen as an opportunity to establish healthy boundaries between them, to cultivate a good working relationship with her as a colleague, and to nudge her toward addressing her alcoholism. While working at the detox clinic, he had learned that people with addictions went through stages of cognizance about their illness and that treatment often was most effective when the client had bottomed out and acknowledged the need for help. Rather than snub Helen's requests for companionship, he responded each time with a counteroffer of his own, safely limiting their meetings to public places and always looking for some sign that she was ready to talk about treatment.

Late one afternoon, he drove home in a blue-gray sedan bearing the trademark hood ornament of Mercedes-Benz. Inside the bungalow, he found K standing at the picture window and looking toward the driveway, clutching his chest dramatically and saying, "Oh. Oh."

"Two more of those *O*'s, and a five in front of them," Jeffrey said, dropping his checkbook onto the table. It still made a pretty good thump as it landed.

"I can't process numbers that big, Jeff. Just tell me the monthly payment," K said.

"The monthly payment is zero," Jeffrey replied.

K stared at him in astonishment. "You paid cash?"

"Helen told me to think of it as a savings account on wheels," Jeffrey said. "The depreciation on that model is negligible. And with the banks paying essentially zero interest, it's as good a place as any to park some extra cash." He dropped into a nearby chair and said with a grin, "Listen to this, you'll love it. I asked Helen to go with me to the dealer."

"So you could pick out one that matched her eyes?" K guessed.

Shaking his head, Jeffrey explained, "I'm trying to get her out of the house more often. You know she's living all by herself in that huge place up in the hills. No neighbors and no companions except for some hired help and her best friend, Smirnoff. I'm watching for any sign that she might be ready for detox. I thought that treating her to lunch was the least I could do in exchange for her financial advice on the car. Anyway, she drives me downtown to the Benz dealer and pretty soon I'm at the salesman's desk, haggling over the terms. Meanwhile, she's slithering around the showroom, looking at all the different models, sliding behind the wheel once in a while, basically auditioning to star in their next TV commercial."

K grinned, getting the picture.

"The salesman starts pressuring me," Jeffrey went on, "at which point Helen comes over and says that she's ready for lunch now and wonders if we could go look at some Jaguars later on. Suddenly, Mr. Hard Sell becomes Santa Claus. What kind of stereo system does she like, what's her favorite color, does she prefer a hardtop or rag? She beams that big smile and very sweetly outlines for him the terms of this deal. He writes down everything like he's taking dictation, then he points out that he's got the very thing she wants right there in the showroom. When he quotes me the bottom line, I ask him if that's really the best he can do for a cash purchase. By the time I pull out my checkbook, he's lopped off enough to pay for lunch almost anywhere in the Western Hemisphere." Once K stopped giggling, Jeffrey concluded, "We settled for a lobster buffet down on Waikiki. In fact," he added, "I won't be wanting any dinner this evening. Why don't you take the night off?"

"Sure, I'd like that," K said. He stood there a moment longer, waiting.

Jeffrey tossed him the keys. "Maybe you could get it washed while you're out," he said.

When K got home later that night, Jeffrey was watching the evening news on TV. Pointing to the glowing fountains of lava spewing across the screen, Jeffrey said, "Look, Kilauea is erupting."

K had brought home a large paper sack of something. He carried it into the kitchen, apparently unmoved by the images of terrestrial upheaval occurring in his home state.

Drawn by the aroma of peanut oil and soy sauce, Jeffrey got up and headed for the kitchen. "I remember studying about this whole chain of islands when I was a kid," he said. "It seemed incredible that they had started out as underwater volcanoes and then rose from the ocean floor over thousands of years, breaking through the water's surface like breaching whales."

K stood in the middle of the kitchen, still holding the sack and looking blankly at nothing.

Jeffrey had sat down at the bar, thinking they were going to eat something, but now his appetite gave way to a growing uneasiness. Cautiously he asked, "What's in the bag?"

At last, K looked at him. He set the parcel down in front of Jeffrey and said slowly, "Very expensive Chinese food."

Puzzled, Jeffrey tore open the sack and discovered an ordinary-looking trove of small white boxes with wire handles. Still puzzled, he asked, "How expensive?"

"We'll know for sure," K said, his voice fading to a shaky whisper, "after you get the estimate for repairing your car." He began to wobble on his feet like a bowling pin about to go down.

Hurriedly Jeffrey got a chair behind K, who sat there for a while rubbing the back of his neck. "Are you okay?" Jeffrey asked, bending down to look into his friend's face. "Do you need me to take you to the hospital?"

Giving Jeffrey a fearful glance, K said, "Let's wait and see if I get any more injuries over the next few minutes." He swallowed, an audible gulp, and then confessed, "Jeff, I wrecked your car."

Urged on by Jeffrey's coaxing, K explained that he had been driving home when another car had run a red light and clipped the rear end of the Mercedes. "I spun around in the intersection," K said, "for about three days, I think. All I could see was headlights all around me, trucks swerving and blasting their horns. At last, the car stopped moving and the police showed up." Looking at Jeffrey, he elevated his chin and pointed at it. "Go ahead and hit me," he urged. "Right here doesn't hurt too bad."

"Don't be ridiculous," Jeffrey said, scoffing, "I'm not going to hit you. I really think you should see a doctor, though. Let's go. I'll drive you in your jeep."

K shook his head and said, "The ambulance guys checked me out at the scene. I'm fine." His face wrinkled in misery as he moaned, "But I wrecked your car, Jeff. Your beautiful, brand-new car. And I had just gotten it washed."

"K, it's just a car," Jeffrey said. "I've got insurance. How did you get home?"

"I drove it," K acknowledged, "very, very carefully."

"Then it can't be banged up too badly," Jeffrey said with a shrug. Encouragingly he tapped K on the shoulder. "Come on, let's eat."

"'Let's eat?'" K repeated, incredulous. "Don't you even want to go out and look at the damage?"

Jeffrey had begun taking boxes from the paper sack and setting them on the counter. "I'll look at it tomorrow," he said. "I want to get at this while it's hot." He opened a box of fried rice. Leaning against the bar, he began scooping the food into his mouth with a plastic fork.

Reluctantly, K stood and selected a box for himself. "I can't believe you're not even a little mad," he said.

"I'm just glad you're all right," Jeffrey said, chewing. "And this food was a great idea, by the way. I was ready for a little something."

K appeared confused and frankly disappointed by Jeffrey's subdued reaction. No doubt he had prepared an arsenal of defenses and felt compelled to launch a couple of them. "You know I'm a good driver," he asserted.

"I wouldn't have given you the keys if I thought otherwise," Jeffrey said.

"And you know that I don't drink," K continued emphatically. "Not a drop."

Jeffrey nodded. "I know that, too," he said. "K, it was just an accident. The same thing could have happened to me while I was driving it home from the dealer this afternoon." He set aside the box of rice and opened another box to find a nest of plump, fried pillows. He bit one to see what was inside. Crab. Superb.

"All those zeroes," K mumbled, "with a five in front of them."
Tentatively, he nibbled an egg roll. After a couple of bites, he
rummaged inside the bag for a tub of sweet and sour sauce.

Jeffrey noted with approval that K appeared to be shaking off his distress. After finishing off the crab pillows, Jeffrey
moved on to teriyaki beef strips threaded on bamboo skewers
and decided to sit down at the bar, where he could get seriously
messy. Using teeth and fingers, he began tearing off shards of
marinated brisket. "Get a couple of estimates," he said, "maybe
three. Any of your relatives do car repair?"

"I'll have one of my sisters marry somebody who does," K
said. "And you can use my jeep as long as you need to."

"Suits me," Jeffrey said conclusively. Having finished eating, he got up and walked over to the sink. With his forearm,
he raised the arced lever of the faucet and washed both hands,
then bent down to scrub his face.

Methodically, K tossed the empty containers into the paper sack and carried the remains of the meal to the trash can.

The volcano coverage was still on the television. Jeffrey
used the remote to turn it off, then headed for the dining table,
where he had spread the score to a Wagner overture he was
studying. Before he could sit down, K appeared beside him and
pointed a finger at his chest.

"Anything you need, you ask me," K said. All of the
toughness had come back into his voice and lava-black eyes.
"Anything. Just let me know."

Jeffrey nodded, then sat down. With his elbows on the table, he rested his chin against his clasped hands and looked
thoughtfully about the room. It was late, Saturday night. He
could hear K moving about in the back rooms. "Busy downtown?" he called to him.

"Usual scene," K replied. "Party hearty."

The calamity was over. Still with his hands together, Jeffrey closed his eyes and silently said a prayer of thanks. It could have been him inside that spinning car, conceivably ending his career before it had properly started. A mere two hundred miles away, the very ground had opened up into a chasm of fire. Yet here he sat, in a place where he wanted to be, doing precisely what he wanted to do. He felt the walls of the bungalow wrapping him in an ascetic embrace, keeping him insulated and focused on his goal. It was far too early for him to claim success; many more challenges and hard decisions lay ahead. But for just a moment, he sat still and savored the progress he had made thus far, enormously grateful for having arrived at this point in his life unscathed by car wrecks and volcanoes.

Ready now for Wagner, he picked up his pencil and scanned the pages of the score, looking for the place where he had left off. The symbols of musical notation communicating each instrument's pitch and duration of tone, and so much more, was a vernacular exceedingly mathematical in its conciseness, where a world of importance resided in a single dot. Almost magically, the patterns of tiny pen strokes overlaying a five-bar staff generated lush, impassioned sounds in his mind's ear. At last, he found his place and studiously began reading through the measures, tapping the eraser of his pencil to establish the tempo, occasionally humming a phrase before pausing to scribble a note to himself in the margin. Lost in the music, he forgot the hellish images of the erupting volcano, unaware that the ground was about to be split by different forces beneath his feet.

CHAPTER 7

The next day, Jeffrey was in his office at Quigley Enterprises reviewing some auditions when Helen appeared at his door, all smiles. "Hi," he said in surprise, removing the earbuds connecting him to his music player. "What's up?"

"I just sealed the deal on that private donation," she said.

"How much?" he asked.

"Three and a half million," she said.

He blinked at her through the blizzard of zeroes that was fogging his mind. After regaining his voice, he said, "I'm just curious. How big of a briefcase does it take to hold that much money?"

"Oh, it won't come in all at once," she told him, "and certainly not in cash. I'll receive a series of biweekly installments beginning next Friday. Why don't you come up to my place for dinner that evening? I'll walk you through the deposit process." With a tilt of her head, she sent a silky tress forward over her shoulder like a baited hook.

Skeptically, Jeffrey raised an eyebrow and asked, "Why do I need to make the deposits, Madame Treasurer?"

"It's a condition of the grant," she explained. "The donor requires the two of us to cosign each of the deposits. Keeps me honest, you know," she concluded with a wink.

"Who is this most generous donor?" he asked curiously.

"That, I'm afraid, must remain secret," she said. "All you will see is the back of the check and the bank receipt, which is enough to assure you that each installment makes it safely into the symphony's trust account."

"How many installments?" he asked.

"Seven, at five hundred thousand each," she said.

Jeffrey sat in stunned silence as the magnitude of these figures registered in his brain. At last, he said, "Helen, I am overwhelmed by the level of support we're getting. With those kind of resources, we'll be able to give the people of this state a musical experience beyond anyone's expectations." He swiveled toward her and continued speaking with growing excitement. "Think of the possibilities—I mean, even beyond the top-quality performances we're planning. We could offer scholarships, a summer music camp, instruments for kids who can't afford them. It won't matter that the state has cut music programs in the public schools; we could establish our own privately funded music academy, offering everything from basic music education to recitals and full-fledged concerts for young musicians. If we fund it completely with individual contributions, we can control everything and make it more efficient than any public arts commission based in Washington. It could be a model for other states to follow." He stopped to ponder the scenario he had just described. The vision pleased him exceedingly, and he smiled a little in wonder as he admitted, "You know, I've always wanted to direct a children's band."

Having watched and listened to him in stunned silence, Helen now mustered a cynical little laugh. "Aren't you even going to ask for a raise?" she asked.

Still engaged in his thoughts, he looked up at her in surprise and said dismissively, "No, of course not. Have you told Andrew yet?"

"Yeah, he knows about it," she said.

"This is fantastic!" Jeffrey declared, bolting from his chair. "I've got to talk to him about this."

She caught his arm as he passed through the doorway. "Don't forget," she said, "Friday night, dinner at my place."

It took a moment for him to remember. "Oh—the deposit procedure," he said at last. He stood in the doorway with her as he thought.

Annoyed by his hesitation, she verbally prodded him. "Jeffrey, we have to do this the right way. Both of us need to confirm each of the deposits. I don't know what you're worried about. When Quig appointed me as treasurer, he expected you and me to work closely together. It's not like I'm doing anything behind his back."

"I understand," Jeffrey assured her. "And don't worry, we'll follow the deposit procedure to the letter. Only, let's choose a nice restaurant and make it a standing date. You name the time and I'll meet you there."

She crossed her arms over the front of her peach-colored silk dress and gave a delicate frown. "Why don't you want to come up to my place?" she asked. "I employ a private chef, you know. It will be elegant." She tossed her hair to one side and waited for his reply.

He looked down at the labyrinth of her ear and the long, slippery slope of her neck. At last, he said with a twinge of discomfort, "I just don't think it's a good idea to visit you alone in your home."

"Jeffrey Bowden," she gently scolded him and began powering up her smile, "are you afraid of me?"

Affecting surprise, he asked, "Afraid of a woman who can pull three and a half million out of a single donor? You bet I am."

※

For the next couple of months, Jeffrey reserved a table at a Japanese grill that both he and Helen liked. They first conducted their financial business and then ate a well-prepared dinner, after which each of them drove home. Only twice, when the waiter had refilled her sake cup too many times, did he feel it was necessary to drive her home himself. On each of these occasions, Jeffrey telephoned her housekeeper and asked her to meet them at the entrance to Helen's mountainside home. While the matronly Hawaiian woman held the door for him, he carried Helen to the sofa and made her comfortable there. Then he made arrangements for one of her staff to retrieve her car the next day. Always, the housekeeper nodded her approval and thanked him as he went out the door.

But when the boss directed him to go up there alone, he couldn't refuse.

After having successfully courted a new investor, Jeffrey and Andrew Quigley had been flying home from the Big Island when the older man asked the flight attendant for an antacid.

"Are you all right, Andrew?" Jeffrey asked in concern.

Quigley grimaced. "Something in that luncheon today didn't agree with me," he said. While his antacid tablets fizzed in a glass of water, he asked, "What have you got lined up for this evening?"

Jeffrey replied that he had no plans.

"The Islands Arts Commission has a fund-raiser tonight," Quigley said, "a dinner cruise of some sort, and I don't think I should go. I'd like for you to take my place. There will be lots of press coverage and likely a two-page photo feature in tomorrow's paper. It would be good for Quigley Enterprises to make an appearance. The event starts at six. Black tie."

"I'd be happy to go in your place," Jeffrey said. "Where is it?"

Quigley drank his stomach remedy and wiped his mouth with a napkin. "Helen has all the details," he said. "We were going as a couple. Pick her up a bit beforehand at her place. She'll give you directions."

Properly attired and on time, driving his newly repaired Mercedes, Jeffrey negotiated the precarious road leading up to Helen's residence. It was a rambling place on the side of a lush, green mountain overlooking the ocean. He had been up there before in the company of other planning committee members. From outside, the house looked like a cozy little condo, but the vast arrangement of rooms inside seemed endless. Helen had explained that the interior of the house was larger than the exterior, an architectural conundrum that was resolved by the place being recessed into the mountainside. Natural waterfalls trickled down slate panels in the dining room, and native trees grew through the ceiling. Mirrored room dividers multiplied the furnishings, giving the illusion of even more space. It was an impressive structure, but Jeffrey thought that she would have been happier renting a place in town, closer to other people and to the beach, which, from up here, appeared merely as lines of surf undulating like long, white ribbons washing ashore after a shipwreck.

Helen met Jeffrey at the door with a slightly dazed look on her face. She was wearing a knee-length party dress with spaghetti straps and no shoes. Her hair was tousled as though she had been napping. Blinking at him through a vodka fog, she said with mild surprise, "Hi."

"Andrew asked me to take you to the fund-raiser in his place," Jeffrey said pleasantly. "He wasn't feeling well this afternoon."

She held the door open for him and made a feeble attempt to straighten her hair. "If I had known you were taking me, I wouldn't have started on the vodka so soon," she said. "Sit down. I'll be ready in a moment." With a whisper of taffeta, she disappeared down a hallway.

Jeffrey elected to remain standing. The situation made him extremely uncomfortable, and he wanted to remain so, as a way of staying on his guard and resisting any disastrous impulses. The trick was to pretend he was standing before an audience, as if in a play, with hundreds of eyes watching him. Befitting his role as escort, he stood patiently by the door. The textured walls seemed to spread out for miles before him. It was a catacomb of sparse elegance, outfitted with Japanese wall hangings, skeletal furniture, a restrained color scheme, and cold, unobtrusive lighting. No wonder she was lonely here, he thought; the place was full of emptiness.

Helen came out patting her face with a shell-pink towel and asked, "How did you get stuck with the assignment of babysitting me?"

Hoping to draw her away from the mire of self-pity where she seemed to be headed, he said easily, "I guess Andrew thought I could use a night out with a colleague. Anyway, I'm always happy to represent the symphony at these sorts of events."

She sat down to put on her shoes, a mere assembly of straps holding the stilettos to her feet. Sunk into the plush chair, with her dress flared around her, she looked like a bonbon in a pleated paper cup. She swung one crossed leg and looked up at him with a sly smile, asking, "Want to skip the party? My cook is off for the evening, but I'm sure we could come up with something."

"We won't get our picture in the newspaper that way," he said. With a coaxing smile, he leaned forward into the abyss of temptation and extended a hand for her to take, then carefully backed away, lifting her off the chair.

She tottered on her high heels and giggled as she fell against him, clinging like a boutonniere to the front of his tuxedo. His first impulse was to take her by the shoulders and push her away, yet he knew that this could invite disaster. The alcohol was no less volatile for having been transferred from the bottle to her stomach. A stern word or blatant gesture of rejection on his part could set up a contentious evening featuring tears, angry outbursts, and all sorts of awkward situations.

Stonily, he shut off his senses to her perfume, her exposed skin, her soft, happy humming, her boozy manner. Affecting paternal concern, he said, "Let me have your brush. I'll tidy your hair, and then we'll be on our way."

"Are you giving me the brush-off?" she whined. Pouting, she rummaged through the contents of her purse.

"Just getting you ready for your photo op," he replied cheerfully. "No need to bristle."

This made her laugh. "You're fun," she said. "So simple. Just a big, blond Boy Scout." She burst into laughter again. Then, abruptly, her tone changed to one of concerned advisement. "Trust me, you'll never get anywhere in this world if you don't develop a few glaring faults and complex psychological illnesses." The last few words came out in a drunken slurry of syllables.

"Oh, I do trust you," Jeffrey said. "You're the treasurer of my symphony, remember?" He hastily smoothed her hair with the brush. "There, that's better. Let's go."

She tucked the brush back into her purse and smirked. "I recognize your kind," she said. "You were always the good little boy, doing whatever Mommy and Daddy told you."

"They kept me in line, all right," he acknowledged. He held out her gold brocade jacket, eager to cover up those shoulders.

Her mood took another U-turn. A choking sob came into her throat as tears brimmed at the edges of her mascara-fringed eyes, threatening to turn her into a raccoon. Just as quickly, she regained her self-control. Contrite now, she lowered her eyes and said with mild resentment, "It must be so easy for you, always knowing what's right. You're never tempted." She turned her back to him and poked her hands into the sleeves.

The lamplight fell upon the bare expanse of her back, which was fully on display before him. Her pale skin draped over the ridges of her shoulder blades and flowed downward to her tapering waist, pulling his eyes over her anatomy. For a brief, incautious moment, he imagined running the palm of his hand over that perfect skin, holding those delicate bones in an embrace, sensing the allegro beating of a feminine heart.

This isn't the one, Jeffrey, he firmly told himself before quickly pulling the jacket up over Helen's shoulders. By the time she turned around to look at him, he had regained his composure. Still, he was shaken to know how close he had come to violating his own boundaries with her. "Oh, I am tempted powerfully," he assured her, "and it is never easy. I question myself sometimes, wondering why I'm being such a holdout, missing all those experiences while the years slip by."

"So why do you?" she asked, adjusting her collar.

The unhappy woman who was asking Jeffrey this question was Andrew Quigley's fourth wife, now living apart from her husband. Jeffrey thought this fact alone should have been enough of an explanation for her, yet clearly she couldn't see it. Standing there and fishing for an answer, he rejected any explanation that might seem critical of either her or her husband. At last, he said, "Right now, this symphony is the most important thing in the world to me. I want to concentrate all my energy on making it a success." He thought it was time they both got out of that house and on the road. "Do you have the directions for this fund-raiser where we're going?" he asked.

She reached into her purse for a printed card and handed it to him, keeping her eyes lowered. Blinking, she pressed her glossy pink lips together.

Don't cry, he thought desperately as he swiftly escorted her to the door; *please don't cry.*

Outside with her at last, he steered her toward the car. "Hey, how about I get you a cup of coffee to drink on the way?" he suggested. "We've got a long evening ahead of us."

"Don't worry," she said dully, "I'll be fine by the time we get there." She sat limply in the passenger's seat of his Mercedes and looked up at him while he fastened the safety belt for her. "I wish I had known you when I was younger," she said as she reached up to lay her hand against his cheek. "I'll bet you could have talked some sense into me."

Gently but firmly, he moved her hand away. "It's not too late to change, Helen," he said.

Her eyes widened a little, and she looked at him almost fearfully. "Oh," she said, "it is far too late."

CHAPTER 8

Wearing boxer shorts and an open bathrobe, Jeffrey ambled into the kitchen the next morning and found K already at work. The chef's small, black braid hung over the collar of an opulent yellow silk kimono, and his child-sized feet were fitted into velvet thongs. Jeffrey poured himself a mug of hot coffee and stood watching a sheaf of green onions being converted into a pile of tiny zeroes on the countertop.

"Crab and tomato omelet today," K said.

"Just right," Jeffrey said approvingly and headed for the sunny lanai. His hair was still wet from the shower. Combed straight back, it lay flat against his head and broke into a light tumble of surf over the collar of his bathrobe. As an afterthought, he said, "A little more of that dill sauce this time."

K called after him, "You and Helen made the newspaper."

"Mission accomplished," Jeffrey said. He settled into a cushioned bamboo chair amid the lush greenery of his garden. On the table, a tropical fruit cup awaited him. He stretched his bare legs in the mild winter sunlight and luxuriated in its warmth, then at last reached for the glass dish holding his breakfast. He spooned up a chunk of something in the color range of pink, orange, and red, and put it into his mouth. Its pungent sweetness sent spasms of pleasure through his jaw. *Forever,* he thought as he chewed. That's how long he wanted to live here.

K came in with the mail and with the newspaper opened to the arts and society page. A spread of photos showed various smiling people in formal dress, drinks in hand, posing on the deck of a handsomely appointed yacht. Using a green onion tassel, K pointed to a photo at the bottom of the page. Jeffrey recognized himself in profile, with his arm around Helen's waist. The caption read: "Jeffrey Bowden and Mrs. Andrew Quigley share a private moment in the shadows. Both represent the Pacific Wind Symphony, which was founded by Mrs. Quigley's husband, Andrew (not in attendance)."

Jeffrey tossed the newspaper onto the table. "That's disappointing," he said.

"Disappointing?" K's voice had taken on a parental sharpness. "What's Quigley going to say when he sees that?"

In an equally well-honed voice, Jeffrey replied, "He'll probably say, 'That's disappointing.'" He began thumbing through his mail and tried to ignore K's persistent glare.

"Did he know you were at this party with his wife?" K demanded.

Jeffrey dropped the mail into his lap and sighed with impatience. "It wasn't a party. It was a fund-raiser," he said with his voice straining like a cello string. "And, yes, he knew. He asked me to attend and to take Helen. K, why are you giving me a hard time about this?"

"Why does a bus make that loud, obnoxious noise when you step out in front of it?" K shot back. He jabbed his forefinger against the newspaper on the table, rattling the spoon in Jeffrey's fruit bowl. "I've got a bad feeling about this, Jeff. This is looking like the setup for a huge sucker punch."

"It was a legitimate work-related event," Jeffrey insisted. "We were there representing the symphony, I as music director and she as treasurer, at least up until her fourth martini. I see no sign of an imminent sucker punch."

"Neither does anyone else who gets hit with one," K pointed out. "Okay, I get it that you were just following orders, but you've got the beginnings of a scandal here. What kind of man asks you to take his wife to an event with drinks and photographers?"

"One who has complete trust in me," Jeffrey asserted with sudden vehemence. "One who knows that I would never behave improperly with his wife, no matter how private the setting." With the handful of mail, he gestured at their surroundings and asked, "Do you think I would risk all this? Look at this place. I live in a sunny island paradise. The weather forecast is always either 'Beautiful' or 'Very beautiful.' I've forgotten what it's like for my neck to itch from a wool sweater. Look at the fruit that grows here." He lifted the glass bowl into the sunlight. The cubes sparkled like immense jewels. "No prim Victorian apples or puckery blueberries," he went on, "but blushing, glistening, luscious things, all of them full of juice and sugar and flavors I can't even name. And, oh yes, I've got this career that's assembling itself before my eyes, with people lining up to invest their money in it. This is what music directors work their whole lives to achieve, and I am not going to throw away this opportunity for anything, especially not for Helen Quigley."

Instantly he regretted the revulsion that came through in his voice. Helen may have been pathetic in her self-destructiveness, but it was not Jeffrey's privilege to judge her. His role was to help her, just as he helped every vomit-stained, needy soul who stumbled into the detox clinic. He mentally groped for some words of reparation, but K had prepared one last volley.

"So explain the romantic pose," K challenged.

"There's nothing romantic about my arm being around her waist," Jeffrey said. "She'd had too much to drink, and the ocean was swelly. I took her astern, away from the cameras, or so I thought. She was hanging over the rail, and I was keeping her from falling in." He grimaced with distaste at the memory.

"I really would rather not talk about it, since I'm about to eat breakfast. I am about to eat breakfast, aren't I?" he asked pointedly, then went back to sorting through his mail.

"I'm worried that this is going to come back and bite you," K said on his way back to the kitchen.

"I can hardly control what reporters do with their cameras," Jeffrey said after him. With curiosity, he examined an envelope bearing the official seal of the City of Baxter, Maine. Expecting a long-forgotten parking ticket or some other bureaucratic loose end, he worked the flap open and unfolded the enclosure. When K returned with his omelet, Jeffrey held up the letter and said, "Look at this. I got a job offer."

K unfolded a pair of wire-rimmed glasses and squeezed them onto his moonlike face. Studying the embossed seal at the top of the page, he said, "Baxter, Maine. Anywhere near Cold Harbor?"

"Inland, where I went to college," Jeffrey said. "The town has a community band. The director has retired, and they're asking me to replace him."

K pointed at the proposed salary. "Is this your daily lunch allowance?"

Jeffrey took back the letter and felt a sweet pang of nostalgia. "Community bands don't have a lot of money to pay their directors," he said with a smile, "not unless they've been endowed by Andrew Quigley." He laid the letter on the table and started with enthusiasm on his omelet. "What do you think, K?" he asked, chewing a mouthful of his personal chef's latest delectable success. "Should I give up this little hillside bungalow, these coconut trees and hibiscus flowers, and go back to Maine, the land of frozen door locks, Alberta clippers, and black ice? It's still winter there, still snowing. The municipal road crew would be running out of road salt right about now." For a moment, he regarded the letter like a mountaineer looking down at the distant foothills where he had begun his climb.

Warily, K asked, "So you're considering the offer?"

"Don't worry," Jeffrey assured him, "I'm not going anywhere. Of course, it's good to know I have something to fall back on, in case this Hawaii gig doesn't work out." He smirked at the ridiculousness of the notion and continued eating.

At the sound of automobile tires braking, they looked through the open patio door to the picture window in front of the bungalow. Helen's Porsche had just pulled up to the curb.

"Were you expecting company?" K asked.

Jeffrey shook his head, clearly puzzled. "We've got a planning committee meeting this morning," he said. "What's she doing here?" He barely had time to close his bathrobe before he heard her heels clicking briskly across the tiled entryway.

She breezed through the living room in her smooth, swift glide and came directly out onto the lanai. In the sunlight, her green dress looked like a pea pod glittering with dew. After settling into the chair which K held for her, she leaned forward, elbows on the table, shielding her eyes with one hand as though the oversized sunglasses weren't enough. Her hair was combed back and tied with a green chiffon scarf. The bow looked like a giant butterfly kissing the back of her neck.

Jeffrey leaned forward to peek under her hand. "You okay?" he asked gently.

"Headache." She uttered the word as though mere speech were painful.

"Want a mimosa? Little hair of the dog?" he asked. Without waiting for her response, he looked at K and held up two fingers, then sat quietly for a moment studying her ghostly skin. She had forgotten her makeup this morning. More likely, her hands had been too shaky to attempt applying it. From the kitchen came the pop of a champagne cork. She winced at the sound. "We made the papers last night," Jeffrey said, hoping to cheer her.

Giving a tiny groan, she said, "Please don't mention last night."

"Okay," he said amiably and began looking for something to distract her from her misery. Reaching for the letter from Maine, he said, "Hey, you'll never guess what I got in the mail today. A job offer." He waited for her to laugh.

K brought their mimosas in champagne glasses. She drank half of hers, then set the glass down and began digging through her handbag.

"I got a job offer," Jeffrey said again, still holding the letter and grinning. "A little town back on the mainland wants me to direct their municipal band this summer."

She flashed him a taut smile. "Yeah?" she acknowledged politely, then drained her glass and looked around for K.

Jeffrey took the glass from her, saying, "That's all, unless you want me to drive you to work this morning. Anyway, it's a community band, all amateurs. They meet in a run-down gazebo in the park and play Sousa marches for folks in lawn chairs. Meanwhile, kids and dogs run around everywhere while homeless people try to walk off with the percussion equipment. After the concert, someone walks around with a tambourine, collecting donations."

Helen had resumed searching through her handbag. At last, she said, "Here it is." She withdrew a slip of paper and held it out to Jeffrey.

He refolded the letter and tucked it into the pocket of his robe. "What's this?" he asked, reaching for the object she handed him. "A bank receipt?"

"Yes," she said. "The check that you and I signed last week was the final installment of the anonymous donation. The full three and a half million is officially in the bank."

"Super," he said and started to slip the receipt into his pocket.

"Look at it first," she said. "Make sure you verify the account number." She handed him the most recent statement from the symphony's trust fund as a reference.

Surprised, he said, "I trust you, Helen. We've been making deposits like this for weeks now."

"Follow the procedure, Jeffrey," she insisted. "Years from now, someone could ask questions. You'll be glad we did this the right way, down to the last deposit."

Obligingly, he compared the account numbers on both documents. "Okay, they match," he said. He kept the receipt and returned the statement to her.

"Deena's filing those for you, right?" Helen asked.

"She files a copy, I keep the original, and you've got the electronic record on your computer," Jeffrey said. "That should cover it."

Helen sat rigidly in her chair and looked at her empty glass. Clearly on edge, she seemed to be waiting for something to happen. She reminded Jeffrey of a musician tacitly counting the measures leading up to her solo.

Jeffrey sighed. He had tried countless times before, but he thought maybe this time he would succeed. Maybe she was too hungover to get angry with him. With extreme gentleness, he asked, "Helen, are you ready?"

Her colorless mouth gaped in what looked like horror. "What?" she asked in a whisper.

"Are you ready to admit that you have a drinking problem?" he asked, looking steadily into her face.

Her head fell forward, and her shoulders sagged as the muscles relaxed.

Encouraged by her evident relief, he said, "The clinic where I work has a great rehab program, very private and with a good success rate. If you agree to give it a try, I'll take you there my-self today after the planning committee meeting."

When she looked up at him again, she was smiling. "Okay," she said.

After an astonished silence, he asked in disbelief, "Really? You'll go?"

"Absolutely." Now displaying her usual composure, she looked at her watch and said, "I'd better go. I've got to run some reports before the committee meeting." She stood and tucked her purse under her arm.

Jeffrey got to his feet, elated but still a bit stunned. "Helen, you won't regret this," he said. He saw that a bit of color had crept back into her cheeks, and he took it as a hopeful sign.

"I'm sure you're right," she said.

After Helen left, K came over to the table to take their empty glasses. "Everything cool?" he asked.

"I think I just saw a ray of hope," Jeffrey said and went to his bedroom to get dressed.

Soon afterward, he came out wearing a pale yellow shirt, a lavender-gray necktie, and gray slacks. On a whim, he had tucked the letter from Maine into his shirt pocket, thinking Andrew would get a kick out of it.

As it turned out, Jeffrey never had a chance to show any-one the letter from Maine. He was too busy watching his world fall apart.

CHAPTER 9

The files stacked on Deena's desk were Jeffrey's first clue that something was wrong at Quigley Enterprises. The long, sweeping arc of Plexiglas was laden with documents, rubber-banded bundles of receipts, and reams of computer printouts. Entire drawers had been pulled from filing cabinets and were stacked on a handcart for removal.

In the suite of offices beyond the reception area, Andrew Quigley's door was closed, yet Jeffrey could hear his boss behind it, bellowing, "I don't care what time the bank opens, I want to talk to the top dog, now! Get him out of bed if you have to!"

The door to Helen's office stood open, although she herself was nowhere in sight. Her chair was occupied by the Quigley Enterprises computer tech, Tim. The gangly, red-haired man sat before Helen's computer monitor, staring at the screen in dismay. Deena stood on tiptoe behind him and reached over his shoulder to jab her finger at the display of icons. "Try that folder," the secretary blurted. "Maybe she moved her files."

Jeffrey burst into his own office to find his desk phone in use by Wally, the company's public relations manager. The nervous Japanese man stood clutching the receiver and worriedly smoothing his thick, expensively styled hair. In a tight voice, he muttered, "There's no answer."

Bald, sensitive Howard, the art director, huddled in the

visitor's chair like a frightened animal. With both hands, he twisted the hem of his black pullover in helpless misery.

Jeffrey noted the empty cavities in his filing cabinet and surmised that those were his records on Deena's desk. "What's going on?" he demanded.

Wally hung up the telephone and glared at Jeffrey. "A thirty-dollar check bounced," he said accusingly.

Baffled, Jeffrey asked, "Why all the commotion over a measly thirty bucks?"

"The check was drawn on the symphony trust fund," Wally said. "There's supposed to be three and a half million dollars in that account."

"There is," Jeffrey asserted. "Helen and I cosigned the last of the deposits last week. She told me the full three and a half million is officially in the bank."

Deena came in saying, "Well, there's no trace of the money now. The account balance is zero, and all of Helen's computer files have disappeared."

In exasperation, Jeffrey asked, "What does Helen have to say about all this?"

"She's not here yet!" Howard whined. "Nobody knows where she is."

Jeffrey nearly blurted, "I just had breakfast with her," but he stopped himself in time. More cautiously, he asked, "Has anyone tried calling her?"

"Of course we tried calling her," Wally snarled, "about five seconds after Deena opened the overdraft notice from the bank. I've been dialing Helen's cell phone constantly, but she's not answering. I'm going to try her home number now." He stabbed at the keypad with his manicured index finger.

"I'm sure she'll explain this once she gets here," Jeffrey said, sounding more confident than he felt. "Check her calendar. Maybe she had a doctor's appointment."

"I checked," Deena said. "The only thing on her schedule this morning was the planning committee meeting."

While Quigley's muted voice erupted like thunder from his office down the hall, Jeffrey stood among his distressed colleagues and tried to think what might have happened to Helen. If she had been in an accident, he would have seen her car on his way to the office. She had said nothing about having another engagement that would cause her to miss the committee meeting that morning. On the contrary, she had mentioned having to run some reports beforehand.

Wally slammed down the telephone receiver and announced, "No answer at her home phone."

"Oh, this is the end of the symphony," Howard moaned, curling forward with his head in his hands. Deena went over and soothingly patted his back.

Looking exhausted, Tim came into the room. "I've looked everywhere for those files," he said. "Her hard drive is wiped clean of them. There should be spreadsheets and deposit records and monthly reports, but they're all gone. Now I'm scanning the whole computer system for a virus."

"Why are my files on Deena's desk?" Jeffrey asked him.

"Mr. Quigley has ordered an audit," Tim said. His voice softened almost to a whisper as he concluded, "It looks like the trust fund has been robbed."

"Jeffrey, how could you have been so careless?" Deena blurted, nearly in tears. "You were responsible for overseeing those deposits."

"I did oversee them," Jeffrey insisted. "All of you need to calm down and think this through logically. You know how it was set up. The money came in a series of seven biweekly installments. The checks went directly to Helen. She and I co-signed each one, just as the donor required, then she made the deposit and gave me the receipt. I verified the amount and the account number each time. Every penny of that donation went into the trust fund account, I'm sure of it."

"Well, it's gone now," Deena said through her sniffling, "all of it!"

"Helen's gone too," Wally said, hanging up the phone. Everyone turned to look at him. "I just talked to her house-keeper," he went on. "When she came on duty this morning, Helen's car wasn't there and her wardrobe closet was empty. Even her luggage was missing."

"I can't believe this," Jeffrey whispered. Barely an hour ago he was sitting with Helen in his garden, comforting her and making plans for her rehabilitation. A fearful thought occurred to him. "I'm going to drive out to the airport," he said as he started for the door.

Wally grabbed his arm and stopped him. With undisguised suspicion, the PR manager said, "I think you'd better stay right here. We don't want any more people disappearing until we find out what's happened."

Jeffrey stared at his colleagues, all of whom now regarded him with distrust. Irritated, he shook free from Wally's hand and asked the group incredulously, "Are you accusing me of having something to do with this?"

"How do we know you aren't meeting her somewhere?" Deena asked with an accusatory glare. "We all saw that nice photo of the two of you in the paper this morning." Quigley bellowed for Deena to come into his office and she scurried out.

Suddenly weak-kneed, Jeffrey sat on the edge of his desk as though pushed there by the collective weight of the other men's stares. "This is unreal," he said, baffled and deeply hurt. These were his colleagues with whom he had worked for the past year with nothing but mutual trust and respect. "I can't believe you'd suspect me of taking money from my own symphony."

"Knock it off, Jeffrey," Howard snarled. "It's obvious to

everyone that you had an especially close relationship with Helen."

Jeffrey was doubly insulted by the implication: first, that he would compromise his moral standards, and second, that he would choose such a pathetic and vulnerable partner. "This was my future career," he said angrily. "Why would I sabotage that? And if I had been conspiring with Helen, why would I have come to the office today? Why wouldn't I have skipped town with her if indeed that's what she did?"

From down the hall, Quigley roared, "Jeffrey! You're next."

Heading toward Quigley's open door, Jeffrey saw that Deena had gone back to her workstation. He stepped into his boss's office and suddenly stopped.

The little man stood behind his desk at the window, facing toward the city. With his hands raised, he leaned forward. For a horrifying instant, Jeffrey forgot about the pane of glass in the window and thought that the ruined millionaire was about to pitch himself forward over the ledge. Quigley was merely leaning his hands against the transparent glass, yet Jeffrey could easily imagine that a man who had lost such a sizable fortune might be driven to any desperate act, even suicide. "Andrew," Jeffrey said from across the room. "What's happened to us?"

"It's all over," Quigley said in a thin, miserable voice. "The Pacific Wind Symphony was supposed to be the crowning achievement of my career, and she's ruined it."

Jeffrey struggled to hold back his frustration. With slow, calm certainty, he said, "I verified every one of those deposits, Andrew. You must know that."

Turning toward him, Quigley waved off his concern with impatience. "Of course, of course, I have no doubt about that," he insisted. "This isn't your fault, Jeffrey. It's strictly a family matter." The older man regarded his protégé with a pained expression and continued gravely, "But you've got to bear the consequences along with everyone else." He sank into his chair and slumped forward to cover his face with his hands. In a muffled, shaky voice, he said, "Quigley Enterprises is dissolved as of today. Deena will make the announcement at this morning's planning committee meeting." He drew a deep breath like a sob and concluded, "I'm sorry, Jeffrey. I can't employ any of you any longer."

Jeffrey came over to him and knelt as though comforting a child. With gentle persistence, he asked, "What can I do to help you? Couldn't we start over?"

Quigley lowered his hands and brusquely shook his head. "This will be international news," he said gravely. "My reputation is ruined worldwide. No one will support an effort with the name Quigley on it ever again." Turning his reddened eyes toward Jeffrey, he said shakily, "But I will not allow my failure to tarnish your name. That is why I'm terminating you along with the others. If you're connected with this scandal in any way, it could spoil your chances of any future appointment. You know how the press operates. Even if the facts exonerate you, the mere hint of involvement in something like this is enough to ruin a reputation. Very soon, this office will be swarming with reporters. I want you to get off the island before some newshound latches onto you and starts using creative journalism to link you with this. I'll try to keep your name out of it as the investigation proceeds. That will give you a chance to make a new start somewhere else."

Jeffery stood as if to go, but then he hesitated. Uneasily, he said, "I feel like I'm running out on you."

"I'm firing you, Jeffrey," Quigley pointed out. "Besides, there's nothing further you can do for me. If your records are in order, as I have no doubt that they are, then from here on out it's a job for lawyers and private investigators. I'll find her if it's the last thing I do, but that could take years." The little man got up and led Jeffrey to the door, insisting, "You've already given me a year of your life. I don't want to ruin the rest of your career by dragging down your name along with mine." Pushing Jeffrey into the hallway, he urged, "Leave the islands today. I'm confident you'll find another position somewhere else. Normally, I would be happy to give you a reference." His voice faltered and broke as he concluded, "But under the circumstances, I doubt you'd want one from me." Quigley's curly white head bowed beneath the weight of his disgrace. Unable to offer so much as a handshake of farewell, the ruined man closed the door between them.

Jeffrey stared at the paneled teakwood door for a long, indecisive moment. At last, he turned and walked out into the reception area. Deena sat behind her desk, weeping.

"There's no money, Jeffrey," she wailed. "None of us will get so much as a final paycheck. Oh God, what'll I do? I have bills to pay!"

Howard, carrying a cardboard box full of his personal possessions, stopped at Deena's desk on his way out. "Don't worry, Dee," he said easily. "You'll qualify for unemployment. We all will."

"But it can take weeks to start getting unemployment checks," she tearfully told him.

Howard looked briefly surprised and then shrugged. "Guess I'll move in with my mother for a while," he said. "She's got a place on the Big Island." With a casual nod, he went out the door.

Resentfully, Deena said, "My mother doesn't have a place on the Big Island."

Jeffrey pulled out his wallet. "Here, Deena," he said, taking out most of his cash. "This should come pretty close to your last paycheck."

She stared breathlessly at the handful of currency he

offered, then waved it off, insisting, "Oh no, Jeffrey, you don't have to do that. Not after all those horrible things I said to you in there!"

"It's all right," he assured her as he pressed the money into her hand. "We all were pretty emotional. Take it. It'll tide you over until you get another job—and you will get one, you know."

She compressed the money in her fist and said in a shaky whisper, "I've never been fired before. I've always counted on a steady paycheck coming in." Suddenly she looked up at him with a guilty expression. "I know you told me I should start a rainy-day fund in case something like this happened. Now I wish I had taken your advice."

Jeffrey wished the same thing, but he saw little point in saying so now. Kneeling, he looked into her face and told her, "Deena, it isn't your fault that you've been fired, and you need to remember that your condition is only temporary. There are countless opportunities out there waiting for you. You may have lost your job with Quigley Enterprises, but you've still got your skills, your knowledge, your potential. And you don't have to limit yourself to being a secretary, you know. Now you're free to become anything you want to be."

Still frightened but listening, she looked at him with glassy eyes.

"Think of it this way," he said, giving a little smile. "You've just got an open schedule right now."

She laughed through her tears and said, "Good old Jeffrey the optimist." Somewhat calmer, she asked, "But what will you do? You've lost more than any of us. The rest of us can get jobs with another firm. You've lost your career."

He stood up, which was a monumental effort in light of the truth of her statement. "I'll just have to find another ensemble to direct," he said.

During the elevator ride down to the parking garage, Jeffrey considered his options. The most immediate employment opportunity had arrived in that morning's mail from the City of Baxter, Maine.

Maine. Just thinking about it made his neck itch.

✄

At home, K was shattered by the news. He slumped in a wicker chair in Jeffrey's bedroom while his departing employer hastily filled a suitcase. "This can't happen to you," K said weakly. "You did everything right. Obeyed the rules. Lived according to your principles. It's not fair that you should lose everything."

"I haven't lost everything," Jeffrey said with quiet insistence. Inwardly, he too was shattered, but there was no time to bemoan his misfortune. "I still have my savings and my trombone, and if I can get off the island before some reporter corners me, I'll still have my reputation." He dug through a drawer of T-shirts, polos, and Bermuda shorts, all of them wholly inadequate for late winter in Maine. In a fit of impatience, he demanded, "Where do I keep my dress shirts?"

Raising a flaccid arm, K pointed at the chest of drawers. "Third drawer down," he said.

Jeffrey took out a couple of dress shirts, the only long-sleeved ones he had. Fresh from the laundry service run by a branch of K's extensive family tree, the garments were still carefully folded around cardboard inserts, sheathed in tissue paper, and tied with colored raffia. This attention to detail, which at first had seemed excessive and silly, he now regarded as a charming signature flourish of the native islanders running the laundry. The ordinary act of taking out a clean shirt was like opening a present. It was just one more thing he was going to miss about this lovely place. He tossed the shirts into his suitcase and closed the drawer. "Andrew promised to keep me out of the investigation as much as possible," he said to K. "He knows I had nothing to do with this, that it was all Helen's doing."

Looking through the sliding-glass door, K extended a hand toward the lanai. "She was sitting right there," he said, "drinking your champagne and sucking up all that sympathy from you. And all the time, she had her luggage in the car." His fingers contracted around an imaginary neck and closed tightly into a fist.

"I honestly can't see how she did it," Jeffrey admitted, stuffing a few more socks into the suitcase. "Andrew oversaw everything. The planning committee reviewed the trust-fund statements at every meeting. I cosigned every check, verified every deposit. She fooled us all."

K watched Jeffrey zipper the suitcase shut. In a jumble of emotions, none of them pleasant, he blurted, "I just want to point out that I haven't once said, 'I told you so.' But I really, really want to."

Jeffrey hefted his luggage and started for the door, saying, "Come on, I need you to drive me to the airport."

"Where are you going?" K asked, following him out.

"To accept a job offer," Jeffrey said, "the only offer I've got at the moment." He stopped at the coat closet and grabbed his windbreaker off the hanger.

K's mouth fell open in disbelief. "Maine?" he asked.

As the two men walked out to the Mercedes, Jeffrey insisted, "It's only temporary, just until I can find something more substantial." He then said emphatically, "And don't tell anyone. I don't want any reporters tracking me down. I don't want anyone else to know about this whole mess." He loaded his suitcase and trombone into the trunk, then got into the passenger's seat and waited for K to start the engine.

As he headed to the airport with K, Jeffrey gazed through

the side window at the coconut palms waving against the blue sky. A warm breeze caressed his face and ruffled his hair, like the hand of a woman he had hoped to meet here. Another opportunity lost. As they drove along the boulevard through the business district, passing bright towers of commerce with flags flapping from their distant pinnacles, he thought of the rainbow of souls on this island whom he had wanted to serenade with a brass- and ebony-throated chorus driven by a percussive heartbeat. Addressing K, he said miserably, "You were right. It was a scam all along. The only part you got wrong was the person running it." He shut his eyes against the unbearable beauty of the adopted home that he now was leaving. "Go ahead and say it," he urged. "Say 'I told you so.'"

Staring unhappily at the road ahead, K mumbled, "I don't want to anymore."

They traveled in silence the rest of the way. At the airport, K pulled the Mercedes alongside the curb in front of the terminal and stood by while Jeffrey lifted his luggage from the trunk. Dutifully, K said, "I'll take care of terminating your lease on the bungalow. Now tell me what to do with the car. Ship it? Sell it?"

Jeffrey looked with disinterest at the vehicle and shrugged. "See what you can get for it," he said, "and don't forget to keep 15 percent for yourself."

K's face brightened. "Hey, thanks," he said. "Where do I send your 75 percent?"

As an afterthought, Jeffrey reached into the glove compartment and withdrew a small notepad. Handing it to K, he said, "Let me have a mailing address where I can reach you. I'll be in touch when I get settled."

K said he would be returning to his grandmother's store and began jotting down the information.

Jeffrey watched while he did so, taking one last look at the bronze Buddha, his exotic friend, cook, housekeeper, and so much more. At last, they shook hands. With his suitcase in one hand and his trombone case in the other, Jeffrey headed into the terminal toward the ticketing area.

As he stepped onto the escalator, a minor detail, one that he had glossed over a moment before, now resounded in his consciousness like a cymbal crash. He looked at the slip of paper K had given him and then turned in astonishment. Just before the escalator carried him out of view, he called down to K, "Your name is Kenneth?"

CHAPTER 10

At the Honolulu airport, Jeffrey used his credit card to purchase a seat on the next flight to the mainland. Bailing out Deena that morning had diminished his cash supply, which was not altogether a bad thing considering the perils of traveling with a full wallet (lesson number four in K's handbook for tourists). He also thought that a credit card statement would provide his new employer with a clear record of his travel expenses and thus facilitate his reimbursement.

While waiting for his flight, he called the Human Resources representative for the City of Baxter and said he was coming to interview for the position of music director for the Baxter Band. He was flying standby, he told her, and promised to call with a definite arrival date as soon as he booked the final leg of his journey so she could schedule the interview.

"I hope you still have your parka," the HR rep cheerfully warned him. "We're supposed to get a blizzard tomorrow."

Jeffrey thanked her for rolling out the white carpet for him. She was still chuckling when he hung up.

He had some time before boarding the five-hour flight to San Francisco, and stretching his legs seemed like a good idea. While strolling around the terminal, he was drawn repeatedly to the TV monitors, half hoping and half fearing to catch a breathless reporter announcing the breaking news of the

Quigley Enterprises scandal. Any time now, the media would learn of the disappearance of Quigley's millions and would descend on the ruined music magnate like hungry vultures: prying, posing embarrassing questions, parading all of his troubles for audiences of every news medium from grocery-store tabloids to blogs. Andrew Quigley would be presented as the victim of the theft, yet an untold number of professionals had been affected. With the construction of the performance hall now coming to an abrupt halt, Helen had taken money from the pockets of the building contractors and laborers who might have finished the structure, as well as from interior decorators and manufacturers of seating, staging materials, lighting, wall coverings, and carpeting. Florists, caterers, parking valets, and even ticket-takers had lost the income they might have received had the symphony grown to fruition. And, of course, musicians, composers, and advertising companies had lost out, too. Andrew Quigley was a prime example of how a successful businessman could be a powerful engine driving many fortunes. Now that the entire project had died, Jeffrey wanted no part of the postmortem. He was relieved to hear his boarding announcement before the news story broke. He felt fortunate to get off the island with an intact reputation, as he was going to need it once he attempted to get his own career back on track.

His seatmate on the flight to San Francisco was a fashionably scruffy young man wearing the rugged, travel-friendly attire of a road warrior. As soon as the flight was under way, the man reached for his laptop computer case. Dangling from the handle was a laminated press badge from a TV news station in San Francisco.

Aside from playing possum for five hours, Jeffrey saw no way to avoid conversation with a professional newshound. He hadn't even brought a book to hide behind. Currently, the reporter was busy scrolling through his e-mail, perhaps scanning the latest bulletins from the home office. A press release from Quigley Enterprises, coupled with a casual comment from Jeffrey linking him to the emerging news story, could result in a multimedia news team meeting him at the arrival gate when the plane landed. Impulsively, he located the airline's safety-information card in the pocket of the seat ahead of him and studied the diagram of the aircraft as if he were thinking of buying it. He had just located the nearest emergency exit when the reporter uttered the dreaded word, "Hi."

As a teenager, Jeffrey had learned conversational Italian, and he thought that this might be a good time to lapse into it, claiming, "*No Inglese.*" But his recollection of Italian was sketchy, and he couldn't be sure that the other man didn't also know the language. Speaking as anonymously as possible, he answered, "Hi."

"Quite a mess back there, wasn't it?" the reporter said.

"Sure was," Jeffrey agreed.

"Amazing how something like that can go on for so long," the reporter said, shaking his head in wonder. "Millions of dollars in damage."

"No doubt." Jeffrey returned his attention to the information card and reviewed the procedure for exiting the aircraft via the inflatable slide.

"I'm with KTV in Los Angeles," the reporter explained. "Flew over a few days ago with a film crew. We took a chance on catching a big eruption, as everything pointed that way. After a while, my editor decided he had seen enough lava."

Kilauea, Jeffrey thought with relief, *that's what we're talking about.* The volcano had been spitting lava periodically ever since the night of K's car accident. Relaxing a little, he began leafing through the airline's in-flight magazine.

"What do you do?" the reporter asked.

Jeffrey didn't want to lie. Even a little white lie offended his personal ethics and seemed cowardly. A subtle shading of the truth, however, was merely artistic license. After an interval of silence, he confessed with affected embarrassment, "I'm in between jobs right now."

This earned him a sympathetic nod. "I see a lot of people in that situation," the reporter said. "Tough economy."

Switching to offense, Jeffrey asked, "How's the news business?"

"Cutthroat," the reporter assured him. "An erupting volcano is newsworthy when it first happens, but after a while, people get tired of it. I need an edge on my competitors, a hot tip on some juicy scandal. You know, maybe some kind of grand larceny at the corporate level, involving betrayal by a beautiful woman and with international implications."

Jeffrey smiled. "Good luck," he said as he put on his headphones for the in-flight movie.

％

During his layover in San Francisco, Jeffrey tried to use his debit card at a fast-food place, but the cashier's machine refused the transaction. He paid for the meal with cash, then immediately sought out an ATM to try the debit card there. Repeatedly, he punched the necessary buttons. Each time, the machine responded that no funds were available. A phone call to his bank in Hawaii confirmed that his account had been frozen.

After failing to reach anyone at Quigley Enterprises, he called K, who told him, "The robbery is just starting to hit the news media here, and already it's making a big splash. Regardless of what Quigley may have told you, it looks like you're part of the investigation too."

"Should I come back to Hawaii?" Jeffrey asked.

"Definitely not," K said. "You don't want to be anywhere

near the feeding frenzy that's going on here. They've probably locked everyone's assets as a formality while they audit the books. How are you paying for things?"

"I'm using my credit card for plane fare, and I have a little cash with me," Jeffrey told him. "I should be okay for a while. From what I've heard, I may have to buy a parka when I get to Maine."

"What's a parka?" K asked.

Jeffrey assured him that he didn't want to know.

※

It was snowing when Jeffrey's plane landed in Cleveland just before midnight. The ticket offices were closed, so he spent the night in the airport, shivering in his windbreaker and tropic-weight slacks. He watched a televised weather report of the storm while, outside, the real thing occurred with frosty vehemence. His cross-country flight path was carrying him on the coattails of the blizzard, all the way to Maine.

Sleeping was impossible, so he spent the early morning hours reviewing an endless parade of personal worries, all of them stemming from his torpedoed career and inaccessible bank account, the latter of which likely would be held hostage for the duration of Quigley's audit. It could be a couple of weeks before the city issued his first paycheck, yet immediately upon arriving in Baxter he had to find lodging and some means of transportation. The city's bus service, he recalled, was the pits. Maybe he should have asked K to ship the Mercedes after all. Jeffrey also intended to begin searching for more substantial employment, which would require some creative dressing up of his résumé so that the year in Hawaii didn't look like a complete failure.

By dawn, his incessant worrying had worked up a raging

appetite. He began impatiently watching for signs that one of the airport restaurants was opening for business. He had nearly settled on something from a vending machine when he noticed a thin, gray-haired black woman digging through a trash bin along the far wall.

She wore a baggy warm-up jacket that was ripped down the back and a pair of bedroom scuffs with substantial mileage on them. Her shriveled legs showed beneath the hem of a skirt that might once have been a tablecloth. She almost certainly was homeless, and she was harvesting bits of discarded food as though this was going to be the high point of her day. Chastened, Jeffrey remembered that he had a wage-paying job waiting for him and the more immediate luxury of a pair of intact loafers on his feet. He silently thanked God for these, and for reestablishing his perspective. As hungry as he was, he recalled that his last meal had been a crab omelet and a champagne cocktail. Humility calmed his self-centered anxieties. His irritation vanished. He dug a few dollars from his pocket in case the woman worked her way over to his side of the room.

When the ticketing agents came on duty, Jeffrey put his name on the standby list for the next available eastbound flight. While waiting to be called, he assembled his trombone and began playing a few jazz numbers for his own entertainment as well as for anyone else who happened to be listening.

As a music major in college, he had learned to play all the usual orchestral instruments, from piccolo to kettledrums, but the trombone had always been his favorite. To him, there was a sensual appeal about brass instruments in general. He especially liked the trombone's noble sound and the masculine nature of its effective range. His own horn, a modest professional-quality model, had become a familiar tool for his artistic expression and was so responsive that it seemed almost alive. When he picked it up, the cold brass warmed instantly in his hands. The act of positioning his lips and tongue against the mouthpiece was almost like a kiss, a notion reflected by the technical term, *embouchure*. To help the horn achieve the proper pitch, he breathed warm air into it, and when he began to play, it vocalized all of the emotions that the composer had written into whatever piece he happened to be playing.

At the moment, it was "Variations on 'In the Mood,'" a work he had written for a composition class, transcribing Glenn Miller's jazz warhorse for solo trombone. The lively melody was the perfect wake-up alarm for the cold and cavernous airport terminal. Baggage handlers broke into a rhythmic shuffle as they passed with their cargo. As more travelers began filling the lobby, heads bobbed, fingers patted the chair armrests, and feet tapped on the snow-sodden carpet. Passersby began dropping dollar bills into Jeffrey's trombone case.

As he moved on to a medley of Ellington ballads, the black woman came over and stood a short distance away, nodding to the music and watching him with her heavy-lidded eyes. Her left elbow projected at an odd angle, perhaps a birth defect or an improperly treated injury, and her jacket pockets bulged with the morning's fragrant haul, most noticeably something featuring onions and pepperoni. She may have been homeless, he thought, but she also could be someone's grandmother, sister, or aunt. How had she become detached from her family tree? Were any of her relatives aware that she had been reduced to garbage picking for sustenance?

She knew the words to "Solitude" and began singing along in her wobbly, cigarette-smoky contralto. The effect was that of a Victrola stylus heaving and hopping over a scratched vinyl record, though charmingly. After a few bars, Jeffrey stopped playing and invited the woman to sit down.

The two worked their way through a common repertoire of nightclub standards. She was far from being Sarah Vaughn, but he was equally distant from being J. J. Johnson. They played and sang together for the mere pleasure of the chance encounter, each of them enjoying temporary refuge from their respective troubles under the shared umbrella of music. Immediately he noticed an increase in the rate and denomination of tips being offered. Before long, a small crowd had gathered. The onlookers' smiles and applause after each number evoked a bloom of momentary pride on the homeless woman's acne-scarred face. When it came time to board his flight, Jeffrey gave her their earnings and headed for the departure gate.

✺

Jeffrey continued cobbling together his cross-country journey, charging each leg of the trip to his credit card and hoping for reimbursement from the City of Baxter. At last he staggered, fatigued and jet-lagged, into Baxter International Airport.

Upon entering the terminal, he thought at first that someone must have accidentally bumped the air-conditioning onto its lowest setting, and quite a long time ago. Then, seeing his fellow travelers in their quilted parkas and wool overcoats, he overcame his climatic disorientation and realized that he was seriously underdressed.

Squinting in the harsh fluorescent glare of the lobby, he saw that hundreds of travelers had been stranded by the weather. The PA system blared a continuous litany of canceled flights, both domestic and international. Through the windows draped in frost, Jeffrey saw that taxis, trailing wakes of slush, were pulling up to the curb to discharge even more would-be travelers. A pale sun, anemic and wasted, sank toward the horizon as though too discouraged to look down any longer on the snowbound city. He found it hard to believe that this was the same sun he had seen two days ago in Hawaii. It was all coming back to him: winter.

Wandering through a fog of fatigue, Jeffrey sought out the baggage carousel for his flight and stood shivering amid a crowd of recent arrivals waiting for their luggage. All around him, people expressed their unhappiness in a variety of languages, although he observed that young children, regardless of their nationality, all sounded alike when they cried.

At last, suitcases and garment bags began tumbling from the delivery chute onto the baggage carousel. He missed his trombone the first time around but caught it on the repeat, then continued to watch for his suitcase.

Jeffrey's cell phone rang, and he stepped away to a relatively quiet spot to answer it. A familiar voice sounded unusually serious as it said, "This is Kenneth. You and I will not use any other names during this conversation. Got that?"

"Got it," Jeffrey said. Surprisingly, he still had the energy to be both curious and worried.

"The volcano is still erupting here, if you get my drift," K told him. "Things are blowing apart hugely."

Jeffrey leaned weakly against the wall. "Can you give me any details?" he asked.

"The auditors confirmed that the money in the trust fund is gone," K said. "All of it. And the lady is gone too, as you must know. She flew out of town shortly before you did."

"But what about all those deposit receipts she gave me?" Jeffrey asked in frustration. "The bank statements. Were they all fake?"

"That's the three-and-a-half-million-dollar question," K replied, "although knowing the answer isn't going to put that money back in the bank."

Jeffrey had never known there were so many pain receptors located in his eyeballs. Rubbing his eyelids, he mumbled, "I trusted her. We all trusted her. But what else could we have done? The boss himself appointed her as treasurer."

"This is the part you're really going to like," K said. "Your former boss is telling everyone that you were an accomplice."

Jeffrey was speechless for a long, stunned moment. At last, he stammered, "But how can he say that? He told me himself that he knew I was innocent, that it was all his wife's doing."

"He's building a case that the two of you were a romantic item," K said. "He's claiming that you took advantage of Lady Smirnoff's incapacity and talked her into cooking the books. Remember all those meetings you had with her in restaurants? The times you took her home after she had gotten a little tipsy? That fund-raiser on the yacht? A lot of people had been noticing the two of you around town, and photographs are beginning to surface. Your former boss is using all of it to put you in the legal crosshairs."

"But that's crazy," Jeffrey blurted. "Why would I sabotage my own career?"

"He says there are three and a half million reasons why," K said.

"You tell him," Jeffrey said with sudden vehemence, "that I want to hear that directly from him. I want him to call me at this number today—whatever day this is—and explain to me why he's blaming me all of a sudden."

"That," K said emphatically, "is the last thing you want to do. The man is obviously desperate to drag somebody into court. Since he can't find the lady, he'll be happy enough to pin this on you. You have no chance of defending yourself while your bank account is tied up. If you're going to court with him, you need big lawyers, and that takes big money. Now listen to me. I strongly suggest that you lie very low until it stops raining lava here or until you've got the money to hire a legal pit bull equal to his."

Jeffrey gasped just then and whispered, "Oh, God. Helen—"

Furiously, K shouted, "Will you forget about her? She's prob-ably in Switzerland by now!"

"No, she's right across the lobby from me," Jeffrey said and disconnected.

CHAPTER 11

Helen had put together an effective disguise, shrouding her hair in a scarf and hiding her face behind oversized sunglasses and the upturned collar of her white wool coat. But there was no disguising that smooth, swift glide.

Jeffrey watched her moving along the far wall, and within seconds, he was convinced of her identity. He started after her, using his trombone case as a wedge to pry his way through the sea of people and luggage that lay between him and Helen Quigley, the woman who had robbed him of his symphony.

She was headed for the exit and making good progress. Hoping to gain the slightest advantage in the chase, even at the risk of alerting her to it, he took a chance and shouted, "Helen!"

The tactic worked. She hesitated a step and shot a nervous glance around the terminal.

Her momentary pause gave him the edge he needed. In that brief interval, he halved the distance between them. As she resumed her brisk pace, he pushed desperately through the crowd and appeared to be maintaining the ground he had won. Then he heard his own name coming through the overhead speakers.

"Jeffrey Bowden," blared the announcer, "meet your party at the information desk. Jeffrey Bowden—"

As though physically prodded, Helen broke into a run for the exit.

The electronic doors swung open just then to admit a new batch of arrivals. A conglomerate of luggage-bearing men wearing bulky overcoats stood blocking the doorway, stomping snow from their shoes and staring in surprise at the jam-packed lobby. Unencumbered by luggage, Helen slipped easily through the incoming travelers. Jeffrey was only steps behind her but found himself hopelessly blocked.

In desperation, he ran to the window alongside the doorway and hurriedly wiped away the frost in time to watch the white wool coat disappear into a taxi. For one fleeting, insane moment, he considered smashing through the glass with his trombone case and jumping into the vehicle with her. Instead, he merely watched while she shut the door. The taxi pulled away, and in a whirling eddy of snow, she was gone.

He gave a groan of despair and rested his forehead against the cold glass. Then, as another taxi pulled up to the curb, a flicker of hope flared up in his chest. With rekindled energy, he started for the exit with the intent of pursuit.

"Jeffrey Bowden!"

This time he heard his name coming not from the PA system, but from a compressed ball of dynamism in the form of a woman. Short, stocky, and middle-aged, she came at him with her wide jaw thrust forward like a bulldog's and her fists pumping back and forth like the driving rods of a locomotive.

She charged up to him, beaming with an effusion of cheeriness that seemed utterly out of place on this miserable afternoon. "Hi," she trumpeted, then grabbed his hand and pumped it as if inflating a tire. "You don't have to tell me," she said. "I know for a fact that you're Jeffrey Bowden from Hawaii. No one else would have a tan like that in Maine in the middle of February. I'm Terri Turcott from the City of Baxter Municipal Building." While Jeffrey's brain sluggishly processed this information, the woman hurried on to say, "I heard that they just closed the airport. No more flights in or out for twenty-four hours. You were lucky your plane landed when it did. You might have had to go back to Hawaii!" She rolled her eyes in mock horror and laughed, a chirruping flourish of chimes.

"I'm sorry, ma'am," Jeffrey said, already having forgotten the woman's name, "but I've got to meet up with someone. I just missed her, but if I can grab a taxi, I might still be able to catch her." He took a hasty step to one side.

The woman's quick little feet mirrored his maneuver, effectively pinning him in place. "You found her," she asserted happily. "I'm the person you're looking for. Terri Turcott, from the City of Baxter Municipal Building."

"No, no," he insisted, "you don't understand. I'm talking about someone else, a woman I have to speak with." Again he tried dodging her, and again he was unsuccessful. For a while, the two danced from one side to the other as Terri repeatedly matched Jeffrey move for move, blocking him like a miniature football lineman.

"I'm the one, Jeffrey," she insisted with her tenacious grin. "I'm the one you needed to meet."

Giving a sigh, he abandoned his plan to pursue Helen. It would be impossible to follow her now. Resigned to the attentions of his escort, he rallied his strength and pulled his mouth into a polite grimace, the closest he could come to a smile. Tentatively he asked, "Ms. Turcott, is it?"

"Oh, please!" she cried dismissively. "Call me Terri." She grabbed his arm with one hand and his trombone case with the other, then pulled him toward the exit, saying, "I would have been here sooner, but I don't get off work until four thirty. Mr. Geegan doesn't allow us to leave the office early, not even by a minute."

At this point, Jeffrey understood that this kind lady had come to meet him on her own time. Humbled and embarrassed by his ungracious attempt to abandon her, he now thanked her for her trouble.

"Oh, no problem!" she crowed. "I was glad to do it. In fact, I volunteered!" She released his arm and preceded him through the doorway. Frizzy, gray hair foamed out from beneath her wool cap like jet exhaust.

Outside, an icy blast of wintry air penetrated Jeffrey's windbreaker and sent a shock wave of shivers through his body. He stepped off the curb into ankle-deep slush, which immediately filled his loafers. His numbed feet then churned the melted ice as he waded after the figure darting through the parking lot. With her quilted overcoat billowing behind her, she looked like a party balloon in a high wind, bouncing and careening off the parked cars.

At last, she stopped at the rear of an old VW minibus and fumbled through a handful of keys. Jeffrey drew up alongside her in relief, then noticed the cluster of high-rise hotels looming nearby. Each one featured a grid of warmly illuminated windows. Helen could be in one of those rooms, he realized, no doubt in a luxury suite with room service bringing her the most expensive items on the menu. It was tempting to think he might still be able to find her. "Terri," he said, "you don't have to bother driving me. I'll just take a taxi to my hotel."

Her mouth fell open in hearty laughter. "Hotel?" she repeated. "With all those canceled flights? There won't be a vacant hotel room in this town, you can be sure of that. You're coming home with me." Definitively, she loaded his trombone case into the back of the VW and closed the hatch. When he began to protest, she insisted happily, "No problem! We've got a room that's practically all ready for you. Plus, you and I can ride to work together in the morning." Pointing at the passenger door, she said, "It's unlocked. Jiggle the handle and it'll open."

Encouraged by the arctic wind sweeping across the parking

lot, Jeffrey hurriedly opened the door and clambered inside. The VW's interior was as cold a tomb and nearly as dark given the blanket of freshly fallen snow covering the windshield, but he was relieved to be out of the wind and in a place where he could shiver in relative comfort.

Terri had settled into the driver's seat and now looked over at him, clearly amused by his slow-wittedness. "There's an ice scraper in the glove box," she prompted him.

It would have been a joy for him to find a pair of gloves among the jumble of road maps, sunglasses, combs, and screw-drivers, but no such luck. Upon locating the ice scraper, he dutifully climbed outside and began clearing the windshield. The VW's engine coughed weakly in response to Terri's repeated cranking. The parking lot was emptying fast. As Jeffrey moved to the driver's side to continue scraping, he asked her, "Should we call a tow truck?" He imagined getting one with a big, well-heated cab.

"No, no, I'm sure it will start," she sang gaily, tapping the windshield to indicate an icy spot he had missed.

Eventually, the engine grumbled to life and settled into an erratic whine. With the windshield sufficiently clear, Jeffrey climbed back inside and sat on the hard vinyl seat. There was snow in his ears and down his shirt collar, and his feet felt like blocks of ice. He pressed his frozen fingers against the miniature heating vent in hopes of the slightest breath of warm air. Meanwhile, Terri muscled the VW into gear and started off, using a combination of driving and sledding to maneuver through the ice and rutted snow while clenching her small teeth in a determined grin. Her expression appeared almost rapturous, like a half-mad explorer striving for the South Pole. "After all that monotonous sunshine you had in Hawaii," she said, her breath steaming in the cold air, "I'll bet you were ready for a good old-fashioned New England snowstorm!"

Several terse responses jostled to be the first to leap from his mouth in vehement denial, but his jaw muscles were too busy making castanets of his teeth to offer a reply.

The main street through town lay deep in snow, which apparently had accumulated for the duration of the storm. Up on Hillside, the street leading to Baxter's higher-end residences, a rotating yellow light signaled the dutiful efforts of a city snowplow. Likely it was the only one operating on behalf of the entire municipality.

Traffic was light in the poorly lit downtown area, where economic stagnation had preserved the same gloomy desolation that Jeffrey remembered from a year ago. Countless streets of wasted real estate stretched left and right, from the failing business district to the utterly defunct manufacturing district to the bleak riverside apartment buildings standing as the last defense against complete abandonment. Nearly every wall was embellished with coarse graffiti. In the alleys and vacant lots, an occasional dim glow revealed huddled figures sharing the meager warmth of a barrel fire. Occasionally there came the distant wail of a police siren. Evoked by this diorama of misery, a flood of remembrance came rushing back on Jeffrey like a crashing wave. He remembered how much he despised this city and how desperate he had been a year ago to leave it. Now, barely off the plane that had brought him back here, he was determined to start job-hunting right away. There was no future for him in Baxter.

The city apparently had initiated a wide-reaching effort to help the unfortunate. Lighted billboards along the roadway, similar to those which might have promoted manufactured products and private businesses, touted a wealth of social programs ranging from child care to elder care. Assistance was available for the unemployed, the uneducated, the uninsured, and the childbearing unwed. A food bank offered help for the underfed, and a weight loss program promised help for the overfed. There even was a billboard promoting a hotline for reporting graffiti, although an offensive phrase had been spray-painted over it. According to the credits at the bottom of each billboard, all of these programs and services were affiliated with or supported in some way by the city. Looking over at Terri, Jeffrey asked, "What kind of work do you do for the city?"

"I used to be part of the secretarial pool," she answered, "but now that you're taking over the Baxter Band, I'll be your administrative assistant. You know, a personal secretary."

Skeptically, he asked, "Why do I need a secretary? All I'm doing is directing a municipal band."

"Oh, you'll be doing lots more than that," she assured him. "You're also a department manager. That means you'll have to make budgets, write reports, attend committee meetings—"

"Whoa," he interjected. "It sounds like I'm in way over my head. I'm not qualified to do any of those things. I'm just a music director."

"No problem!" she said. "I'll help you every step of the way. You'll be sharing an office with me at the Money Building. That's where the city's administrative offices are located. Its real name is the Muni, or Municipal, Building. But everyone calls it the Money Building."

"Because that's where all the tax money goes?" he guessed.

"See?" she said with a proud smile. "You're catching on fast."

Learning to be a bureaucrat for the sake of directing a municipal band was exceedingly low on his list of interests, somewhere after undergoing dental surgery, and he wondered how he could tactfully break this news to her. As they stopped for a red light, he pointed out, "You know, Terri, the city hasn't officially hired me yet. I'm only here for an interview."

Reaching over, she pinched his wrist between her thumb and forefinger to feel his pulse, then gave him an affirming nod and said, "You just passed the interview."

They had entered the residential section of the city's outskirts. Here the streets had been spottily cleared, as if the snowplow had chosen its course at random or by some obscure method of prioritization. "I think it's only fair to warn you," Jeffrey said, "I may not last long at this job. If I get a better offer somewhere else, I'll probably take it." He lurched against the door as the tires caught in deep snow, pulling the VW toward the shoulder.

Giving a yank to the steering wheel, Terri brought the vehicle smartly back onto the road. "You're going to like working in Baxter," she said confidently. "There's lots of great people here, and tons of opportunity for growth."

"Regardless of that," he responded, "I have to think about my résumé. It's still early in my career. I don't want to have to explain an essentially idle summer spent leading an amateur ensemble. Besides, I hate cold weather." He grabbed for the dashboard as the VW drifted to the shoulder again.

Terri straightened the vehicle's trajectory with a firm hand on the wheel. "Winter's almost over," she said brightly. "You'll be so busy learning your new job, the months will fly by. Then it will be summertime and beautiful, and the band will be putting on concerts. At that point, your résumé won't matter, because once you work with the Baxter Band, you won't want to work anywhere else." He prepared to launch another protest, but she cut him short, saying, "Big hill coming up. Hold on." She gunned the engine for momentum and barreled up the incline.

Pressed back in his seat, Jeffrey felt the VW fishtailing as its tires struggled to maintain traction. The vehicle crested the hill at a snail's pace, then headed down the other side, where the road had been plowed clear to the pavement. A sharp bend at the bottom of the hill shone with a pool of glare ice directly in their path.

"Don't worry," Terri said as they began to pick up speed. "I make this curve almost every time."

They swept around the turn at a breathtaking twenty miles per hour while the headlights' beam provided a thrilling close-up of the massive trees lining the road.

When their path had straightened again, Jeffrey gasped for breath and said, "Hey, how about I buy you dinner someplace? We could relax over a hot meal, and maybe by the time we're finished eating, the roads will be better."

She shook her head and said, "No, I need to get home. My husband, Tommy, will be waiting for me to fix his supper. He doesn't cook," she added, "and he gets very worried when I'm late like this."

"It would be my pleasure to treat both of you to dinner," Jeffrey insisted, reaching for his cell phone. "Go ahead, call him and put his mind at ease. Ask him to meet us at your favorite restaurant, any place you want."

She glanced at the device he offered her, but she shook her head again. "Tommy doesn't drive," she said, "and besides, we don't have a phone at home."

Surprised, Jeffrey asked, "Do you live that far out of town?" He hoped they weren't headed for some primitive little cabin deep in the woods.

"No, we live in town," she assured him, "but we disconnected our phone service about a year ago. Tommy never talked on the phone much anyway, and the extra money really comes in handy," she concluded with a stubborn smile.

In trying to imagine what kind of man might have married this human dynamo, Jeffrey never would have pictured one who was housebound and perhaps incapacitated in some way, yet indeed that was the impression he was getting. More than ever, he hated to impose on the Turcotts, but he saw no alternative.

In compensation, he thought he might be able to help them out in some way once he got a better idea of their needs.

Unprompted, Terri offered, "Tommy's unemployed right now, but he used to be a manager for the Baxter Shirt Company."

"I remember hearing about them," Jeffrey said. "They used to be a big employer in town years ago, didn't they?"

"Yes," she affirmed. "Then the whole business suddenly closed down. It happened almost overnight because of some kind of top-secret decision by the company's CEO. It was especially frustrating for Tommy because he had been in charge of their most productive work team. They won awards every year, primarily because of his leadership. He was a real management genius."

"That's too bad," Jeffrey muttered in genuine sympathy. "How long has he been unemployed?"

"Five years," she said.

They had entered a residential area interlaced with a network of winding, unplowed streets lined with modest but sturdy-looking homes. Most appeared unoccupied, and many were posted for sale. It was a safe assumption that the occupants had been driven to seek their livelihoods elsewhere.

Terri braked before a dimly lit house whose driveway had been shoveled only partly, and badly at that, as though the job had been attempted by a child.

"I'd better clear that snow for you," Jeffrey said, "before we get stuck."

"We'll make it," she assured him. "No problem." Taking a wide turn with its engine roaring, the VW lurched and bucked its way toward the open door of the attached two-car garage. "Oh, there's Tommy now," she said.

Inside the garage, a slump-shouldered man leaned wearily on a snow shovel with one hand and held the other against his lower back. The VW's headlights illuminated a tragic mask of misery and pain. Upon seeing a large male figure in the passenger seat of his wife's car, however, the man's expression instantly turned to one of alarm. As the VW rolled into the garage, the two men stared at each other with mutual suspicion.

"He's looking pretty chipper this evening," Terri noted happily. "It must have been a good day for him."

The VW pulled into the garage alongside an economy-model sedan and then nosed up to a wall of stacked cardboard boxes whose sides were scrawled with such labels as, "Coats," "Shoes," and "Books." A collection of garden tools stood among bicycles, golf clubs, and the paraphernalia of various other hobbies.

"We have a yard sale every weekend," Terri explained, killing the engine. "The extra money really comes in handy."

Jeffrey climbed out of the VW to find Tommy standing at the rear bumper. The heavy-jowled, unsmiling man stared at the new arrival like a rottweiler awaiting orders.

Standing on tiptoe, Terri kissed her husband's unshaven cheek and said, "Hi, Tom-tom! Sorry I'm late. This is Jeffrey Bowden, the new director of the Baxter Band and also my new boss. He just flew in from Hawaii. Isn't that exciting? All the hotels in the city are booked up because of the storm, so I invited him to stay with us." She opened the VW's cargo hatch and said, "Bring in his trombone case, okay, big guy?" Her happy chatter suddenly stopped, and she stared wide-eyed at Jeffrey. In a fearful voice, she asked, "Did you have any other luggage?"

Jeffrey then remembered his suitcase, which he had abandoned after K's phone call and the ensuing excitement of Helen's appearance. He looked at Terri, still with her coat on and holding her car keys ready. They had met only an hour before, but already he knew that if he asked her to, she would drive him in an instant over those snowy roads again to fetch his bag. Then he looked at her husband, for whom he had caused a delayed dinner and a disrupted household for the next twelve hours or so.

Summoning what little strength remained in his travel-weary body, he shrugged. "I can get it tomorrow," he said with a thin smile. "No problem."

Terri bounced into the house with Tommy trudging along behind, carrying the trombone case. Jeffrey followed them and stepped into a living room that was utterly devoid of furniture. Even the walls had been stripped of photos and artwork, leaving only the less-faded rectangles of newly exposed wallpaper.

Tommy set the trombone case on the floor next to a spacious coat closet holding an impressive collection of empty hangers. While lacking Jeffrey's height, Tommy nevertheless was a big, well-built man of about sixty years, not fat, but broad and solid. His flat, unfeeling expression was that of a man who had taken a beating for so long that he now was simply enduring it with neither discomfort nor hope. He pulled off his stocking cap to reveal a bear-like skull bristled with silvery brown stubble, then carefully stored his outer garments in the closet. Turning to address Jeffrey, he said, "You can sleep either on the sofa or on the recliner." He gestured at the dimples in the carpet that suggested where these pieces of furniture once had stood. "The recliner is more comfortable," he suggested.

"Tommy, you can be such a rascal," Terri chided him with a grin. "Don't worry, Jeff, there's a bedroom upstairs just waiting for you. We sold some of our furniture," she explained, taking their guest by the arm, "just a few pieces we didn't need. The extra money really came in handy." She led him from the empty living room into a conventional-looking kitchen, saying, "Now just make yourself comfortable, and I'll whip up some supper for us." She reached into a cupboard for a can of soup and set it on the counter along with three bowls. "Sit down, sit down," she urged as she began rummaging through a drawer for a can opener. "This'll be ready in a jiffy."

Tommy slumped in a chair at the kitchen table, nearly co-matose with despair.

After two solid days of travel, Jeffrey was ready to fall forward onto any horizontal surface. "Terri," he said, "I don't mean to seem ungrateful, but I am absolutely bushed. All I really want right now is to get some sleep."

"No problem!" she chirped, dropping the can opener. "Come on, I'll show you to your room."

Carrying his trombone case, he followed her upstairs to a small bedroom where a bare light bulb in the ceiling shone down on the metal frame of a single bed. The mattresses leaned against a wall that was papered with images of cartoon rocket ships and floating astronauts. After helping his hostess position the box spring and mattress onto the bed frame, he assured her, "I don't need sheets. Go on downstairs and enjoy your dinner."

She wouldn't hear of it. "Don't be silly," she said, "I've got them right here." From the closet she withdrew an armful of folded sheets printed with red and blue dinosaurs. She also grabbed a few dinosaur-themed towels and placed them in the adjoining bathroom.

Obligingly he helped her cover the mattress with the bed linens. Eager to join the stegosaurs in their repose, he said pointedly, "Thanks. Good night."

"Now I'll just scare up a pillow for you," she said and slipped out of the room before he could stop her.

When she reappeared with the pillow as well as a chair, Jeffrey took the items from her and insisted, "Terri, this is perfect as it is. You've already done much more than I could expect." She cheerfully ignored him and went out again, returning this time with a blanket. He took it from her and tossed it onto the bed. Holding her by the shoulders, he said sternly, "Terri, your husband is waiting for his dinner. I want you to go downstairs and fix it for him. I have everything here that I need for the night. Now go on. I'll see you in the morning."

Reluctantly, she wished him goodnight and left him alone, closing the door softly behind her.

The click of the latch echoed in the empty bedroom like a jailer's key in a prison door. After two days in crowded airport terminals and the cramped seating compartments of commercial aircraft, Jeffrey stood alone, locked inside his bleak new reality with nothing to distract him from the plain fact of his complete and abject failure.

The room was as cold and quiet as a tomb, and he realized that indeed a death had occurred. His future career in music—a career that had been teeming with possibilities, not merely for his own personal gain, but also for the benefit of countless generations of aspiring young musicians—had suddenly and cruelly been snuffed out.

He tossed his windbreaker toward the chair, missed, and disinterestedly allowed the garment to lay where it fell. Next, he kicked off his soggy loafers and had better luck directing these items onto the floor, where they lay weeping onto the low-pile carpet. He fought the temptation to emulate them and instead sat on the bed to peel the socks from his feet. Jet lag and exhaustion had numbed his brain beyond the point of rational thinking. His whole body begged for sleep. The logical course of action was to get under a hot shower and then into bed, but instead he sat looking down at the tan lines left by his long-absent sandals. He already missed his adopted home, the warm and beautiful place he had come to love, the place from which he now was exiled. He knew the room was cold, but he didn't feel it. Ironically, what he felt was a stockpile of anger igniting and spreading through his torso, a blaze of resentment and embarrassment at having been duped, at having the great promise of his directing career vanish like a rug yanked out from under him by Helen Quigley.

Impulsively, he pulled out his cell phone and called K's number. While waiting for the connection, he closed his eyes, wanting to see once more, if only in his imagination, waves tumbling endlessly onto glittering white sand beneath a generously blue sky.

Ever prescient, K greeted him by saying, "I saw your weather on TV. If it makes you feel any better, it's raining here."

Eyes still closed, Jeffrey felt an almost physical longing as he imagined tropical rain: warm, misty rain seeping into the rich volcanic soil, trickling down the grooved hides of rotund pineapples, running down the open throats of hibiscus. Yes, he thought; in Hawaii, even a rainy day was beautiful. At last, in a voice strained with frustration, he said, "I almost caught her. She was at the airport here in Baxter when my plane landed. I tried to catch up to her, but she got away from me."

"Lucky for you," K said bluntly. "You'd be a dope to turn her in. Don't even think about calling the police. Believe me, I understand what you've lost, but you'd only be making things worse for yourself by stepping into this legal mess."

"This isn't just about me," Jeffrey insisted. "She committed a crime and I want her to pay for it." Anger fueled his rant as he continued talking over K's attempts at logical rebuttal. "The airport is closed because of the storm, so she's probably staying in a hotel somewhere," Jeffrey speculated, "but she'll have to come back eventually to continue her flight." His mind raced with possibilities. "I could camp out in the terminal and wait for her," he said. "Better yet, I could call the police and initiate a dragnet. Surely they could find her. The newspapers could put her picture on the front page—"

"With your mug shot right alongside hers," K interrupted firmly. "Snap out of the revenge mode, Jeff. She'll take you down with her by claiming that you helped her set it up. No jury will believe that you both traveled to the same city by coincidence. It looks too much like a planned getaway for two."

Ultimately, Jeffrey had to admit that K was right. His rage quickly subsided. He thanked his friend for his good advice and ended the call. Shivering on the edge of the bed, he helplessly accepted the grim reality of his situation. Helen had robbed him not only of his career, but also of any possibility of bringing her to justice. He had to let her go. He had to let his anger go, too. It wasn't warming him; it was consuming him.

The worst of it was knowing that he himself was largely to blame for his misfortune, as he had ignored warnings from all the important people in his life, people whose advice he always had valued. Sitting in this room where apparently a child once had slept, he realized that he felt very much like a child himself for having blundered so badly. He should be thankful he didn't catch Helen; otherwise, he could be spending the night in a jail cell, one with far less attractive wall decorations.

Except for the bed and the things Terri had brought in, the room had been stripped bare of everything, no doubt sold at the weekly yard sale—with the extra money really coming in handy, as she would say. He felt mildly resentful that he couldn't even work up a good case of self-pity when his obliging hosts were themselves so obviously destitute. God forgive him, he hated this city and what it did to people.

Weariness and despair weighed down on his slumped shoulders. All of his strength was gone. Hope and confidence, usually ever present in his nature, had fled. From his sitting position on the bed, it was a natural—even welcome—progression to slide forward. Before the thought could register in his brain, his knees hit the floor in an attitude of prayer. Circumstances had brought him down a few notches, cut him down to size, and now he bent his spine forward in abject humility before a higher, wiser authority. Stripped of ego and ambition, he was reduced to his essential belief that there had to be some purpose for his existence even though he had momentarily lost his bearings. It was too cold to unclench his teeth, so he spoke the words in his mind.

God, is this really the path You intended for me to take? If not, where did I go wrong? If I had turned down the job in Hawaii, I would have spent the past year in Baxter, no farther ahead than I am now. This is a city in need, without question, but what can I do to change anything? Is directing a community band really the best work I can do for You?

At last, he stopped asking questions and waited for a response. It came in the form of a blurted apology.

"Oh—sorry." Tommy stood in the doorway, holding something under his arm. Making an awkward gesture, he stammered, "The latch doesn't always close right and the door swings open. Sorry to interrupt."

Jeffrey realized how foolish he must have looked, and for a moment he considered claiming to have lost a contact lens. Instead, he hastily got up and said dismissively, "It's okay."

For an instant, a strange warmth glowed faintly in Tommy's eyes, like a flame kindled from dead ashes. Blinking, he said slowly, "I brought you another blanket. It can get pretty cold in here at night. We don't heat the upstairs anymore."

Jeffrey caught the rolled-up blanket tossed to him. "Thanks," he said with sincerity.

"If I seemed unhappy earlier," Tommy went on, "it's not because of you personally. I like to know ahead of time if company's coming, so I can prepare." He raised his slumped shoulders in an apologetic shrug. "I'm still getting used to us not having a phone."

Jeffrey nodded. "That's understandable," he said. He watched while the older man gazed around the room, perhaps still seeing the absent furniture. Jeffrey waited, half expecting to be invited to use the bureau, the dresser, the little desk and chair.

Looking at Jeffrey again, Tommy asked with genuine concern, "Are you going to be all right in here? You need anything else?"

"Believe me," Jeffrey assured him, "this is perfect. I'd be sleeping in the airport terminal if it weren't for your wife's hospitality."

The muscle in Tommy's right cheek twitched, his best effort at a smile. "Terri's got a big heart," he said. "She's very excited to have a new boss. She's worked for the city for five years, ever since I got laid off from my job. To be honest, she hates it, but it's our only income." He fell silent for a moment, studying his guest before appearing to deem Jeffrey worthy of hearing more. "After I lost my job," Tommy continued, "I was qualified to receive unemployment benefits, but I couldn't bring myself to apply for them. For me, it would have felt like admitting I was licked, that I had given up on myself. I kept thinking I would find another management job somewhere. As the years went by, I began to see the strain I had placed on Terri because of my stubbornness. This week was especially bad for her. She almost quit, but then she heard that you were coming to take over the Baxter Band. You are the first thing that has made her hopeful in a long time."

Jeffrey fumbled for words. "Really," he said at last. "Well, I hope I can do a good job. She gave me an overview of my responsibilities, but I'm only a musician. Serving as a department manager is going to be a completely new experience for me. I might be looking to you for some advice."

Tommy pulled in his chin as a gesture of puzzled surprise. "Why me?" he asked.

"Terri described you as a management genius," Jeffrey said.

The shroud of gloom returned to Tommy's face. "A management genius who can't find a job," he said in disgust, "and who didn't have the sense to apply for unemployment benefits when I was eligible. It's too late now."

"Did Terri ever ask you to apply for them?" Jeffrey asked.

"No, of course not," Tommy said.

"Then, clearly, she never gave up on you finding work again," Jeffrey pointed out. "As for you being unemployed at the moment," he said with a shrug, "that just means you've just got an open schedule right now."

As Tommy considered this new perspective, his face went through a series of small spasms as if working out the kinks from muscles he hadn't used in a very long time. Slowly and gradually, in spite of his efforts to suppress it, a small grin appeared on his face. Then he began to laugh, just a chuckle at first, which rose like an echo from within the empty barrel of his body. His chuckling grew in volume until at last he stood there in the doorway, shoulders shaking, and belly laughed.

Quick footsteps sounded on the stairs. Terri's worried face appeared at her husband's side. "Tommy, what's wrong?" she demanded. "What are you doing?"

"I'm laughing," Tommy said to her.

Her expression of concern was unabated. "I can see that," she said. "Are you feeling all right? You never laugh. Jeffrey, what did you do to him? This isn't the husband I know."

Still chuckling, Tommy turned and went downstairs, leaving Terri staring in disbelief at Jeffrey.

"I can hardly wait to see what you do at work tomorrow," she said.

CHAPTER 12

For twelve solid hours, Jeffrey slept, blissfully insulated from his troubles. Only the sound of his name being spoken and a gentle, persistent rapping at the door brought him gradually awake. For a groggy moment he thought it was K announcing breakfast, and in his imagination, he was back in his island home with its abundance of simple pleasures: the warm breezes wafting through the bungalow, the tropical flowers brightening the garden, his Mercedes-Benz brightening the driveway, a multimillion dollar career in the making.

"Jeff? You awake?"

The voice coming through the door was male, but it didn't sound like K's. Jeffrey cracked open his eyes and blinked a few times, gradually resolving the images of spaceships and astronauts on the wall. At last he remembered: Maine. *Oh God.* "Yeah, I'm awake," he said grimly, pushing aside the blankets.

"Time to get up, son," Tommy said. "I'm going to start breakfast."

Jeffrey promised he would be right down.

He showered in the adjoining bathroom, then finger-combed his hair, palm-ironed his shirt and trousers, and digitally brushed his teeth. The mirror reflected the healthy crop of wheat-stubble beard that had sprouted on his face over the past couple of days. No doubt Tommy would loan him a

razor if he asked. On the other hand, if he got arrested for embezzlement that day, a beard would look appropriately criminal in his mug shot.

Standing alongside the bed, he put on his windbreaker and
gathered up the items he had laid on the chair overnight. The interior of his wallet was a dismal sight. He still had enough cash
to worry about being robbed, but not nearly enough to secure
an apartment. Likely it would be a week or more before he got
his first paycheck, meager as it was, from the city. His stomach
filed a noisy complaint of neglect. Oh yes, and there would be
the problem of buying food.

His shoes had dried during the night and now were mis-
shapen and stiff. The insoles had developed a permanent wave;
wearing them would be like walking on a corrugated roof. He
tried kneading the leather to loosen it, and while he did so, the
soles began coming apart at the seams.

Outside the window lay a Siberian ocean of drifted snow.
Gazing at it, he tried to remember whether he had packed another pair of shoes in his suitcase, and then he desperately
hoped he would find that piece of luggage waiting for him at
the airport. Buying a new wardrobe was out of the question,
as his bank account was as frozen as that landscape out there.

With his assorted worries firmly established at the forefront of his mind, Jeffrey tucked his shoes under his arm, picked
up his trombone case, and headed downstairs. He wondered if
the airport crowd in Baxter would be as receptive to an impro-
vised jazz performance as the Cleveland audience had been. If
he could pick up a rhythm section, he might make some real
money.

In the kitchen, something fragrant was baking in the oven.
Tommy stood at the sink washing a mixing bowl. Sunshine
poured through the window onto his hands and reflected off the
splashing water, making it look as though he were scrubbing

the bowl with thousands of tiny diamonds. His gray sweat suit was threadbare at the seat and elbows, and his ancient sneakers appeared only slightly more intact than Jeffrey's loafers. He put away the mixing bowl and turned around, drying his hands, as Jeffrey came in. After the two men exchanged greetings, Tommy said, "I just started the coffee. Breakfast is in the works."

"Great," Jeffrey responded. He sat at the kitchen table with his shoes in his lap so as to fully assess the damage.

Tommy opened the refrigerator, and Jeffrey immediately saw that this was where his hosts kept their bountiful supply of empty white space. Quickly, he said, "You don't have to make anything for me. I'll grab some breakfast in town."

Tommy came away holding an empty jar of brown mustard and a few shriveled vegetables that appeared worthy of discarding. "Don't be silly," he said. "There's plenty for you." He carried the items to the work counter alongside the stove and reached for a cutting board.

Terri rushed in, still in her bathrobe. "I forgot to make the coffee," she blurted, and then stopped upon seeing the coffeemaker midway through its brewing cycle.

"I made it," Tommy said easily. "No problem." He stepped to the pantry and began gathering a few small cans from the shelves.

"Oh!" she said, clearly stunned. "That's great, Toms. Thanks." She looked in wonder at Jeffrey, who was still sitting at the table with his shoes in his lap. Scratching her wild frizz into further disarray, she said, "I'll get some breakfast started for you guys."

"I'm doing that too," Tommy said with steady confidence, taking some plates down from a cupboard. "You go have your shower."

For a moment, Terri stood watching her husband as if caught in a dream. At last, she said, "Okay, I will," and gave one last look at Jeffrey before turning away, blinking in disbelief.

Tommy brought the plates over to the table. "Problem with your shoes?" he asked Jeffrey.

"They got wet in the snow last night, and now the soles are coming loose," Jeffrey said, setting the useless things on the floor.

"I've got some old shoes in a box in the garage," Tommy said. "You might find something out there that would fit you."

Wondering how he would ever repay these people for their kindness, Jeffrey walked through the empty living room and went into the attached garage. The light from the overhead bulb fell short of illuminating the area where the boxes were stored, so he lifted the bay doors to admit some daylight, and there before him lay the partially cleared driveway. The remaining snow glistened in the morning sun: brilliant, beautiful, beckoning.

The garage floor was ice-cold under his sock-clad feet, but he barely noticed; his attention was entirely focused on his mission. Digging through the box of shoes, he found a pair of galoshes that were snug but tolerable. Further excavation produced a pair of gloves with not too many holes in them. Thus outfitted, he grabbed the shovel from the corner of the garage and began clearing the driveway.

The act was primarily a gesture of thanks toward his hosts, of course, but he also had a selfish motive. He had suffered a professional disaster in Hawaii and, by returning to Baxter to lead the community band, was taking a huge step backward in his musical career. Additionally, he was worried about living up to his responsibilities as a department manager for the city; it could be a whole new area for him to prove his inadequacy. What he himself needed to see, immediately and vividly, was some degree of competence. Heaving a shovelful of snow was something he could do quite well.

It had been a year, but his muscles quickly remembered the routine. He shoveled with vigor, exuberantly, even joyfully, grateful for the work and the satisfying appearance of bare pavement in his wake. No doubt he would be sore the next day—already he felt a pinch in his right shoulder—but whatever the repercussions, he knew the activity had been worthwhile when he started back toward the house and saw the expression on Tommy's face.

The older man had come out to the garage looking for him and now stood staring openmouthed at the cleared driveway. "Wow," he said as Jeffrey strode past. "Thank you."

Jeffrey returned the shovel to the corner of the garage, then headed for the door leading into the house. Breathless as much from exhilaration as exertion, he paused to kick off the wet galoshes and to glance one last time at the cleared driveway. "My pleasure," he declared triumphantly and headed indoors.

Tommy followed him into the kitchen, where something fragrant was sizzling on the stove. "Coffee's ready. Help yourself," Tommy said as he hurried over to stir the contents of the skillet. "I think I fixed your shoes," he added.

Upon inspecting his loafers, Jeffrey saw that the soles had been glued in place and their interiors outfitted with new insoles. On the kitchen table was a jar of contact cement as well as a rubberized rain slicker and a tweed suit jacket. Each garment bore holes that precisely matched his shoe size. "You cut up your clothing to fix my shoes?" he asked in disbelief.

Tommy shrugged. "Why not?" he responded. "I don't need the jackets anymore, and you'll get a few more miles out of those loafers."

Jeffrey tried on his refurbished shoes and gave them a test drive as far as the coffeemaker. "Nice," he said approvingly and poured himself a cup of coffee.

The oven timer dinged. While fitting an insulated mitt on his hand, Tommy said, "I've given that treatment to all my shoes. Sure makes them last longer." He swung open the oven door and lifted out a pan of freshly baked rolls.

Jeffrey's stomach roared its approval. It felt like days since he had eaten anything. He sat at the table with his coffee and watched while Tommy filled one of the rolls with the concoction in the skillet, then served it to him on a plate. The finished product had a substance and flavor that somehow surpassed its humble beginnings. Jeffrey devoured it.

"Want another one?" Tommy asked. He was wearing a little smile tentatively, as if it were a new garment he was breaking in and starting to get used to.

"Don't go through any trouble," Jeffrey murmured. But his eyes said, "Yes, please."

Tommy made two more. Jeffrey ate them both.

Terri came in, dressed for work, and saw Jeffrey licking his fingers while Tommy stood by displaying his newly adopted grin.

"This is more fun than feeding alligators at the zoo," Tommy said.

"Have you ever thought of selling those things?" Jeffrey asked him.

"Not until just now," Tommy said and returned to the stove.

Terri eased cautiously into the chair next to Jeffrey as though unsure of her surroundings.

Tommy placed a sandwich on her plate and advised, "Keep your hands away from his mouth."

"I just put a huge dent in your food supply," Jeffrey confessed.

She shrugged and said, "Looks like we're still doing okay. He hasn't opened the beans yet." She directed Jeffrey's attention to a row of canned beans on the top shelf of the pantry and explained, "That's our poverty barometer up there."

Tommy divided the last of the coffee among their three cups and joined his wife and their guest at the table. "After I lost my job at the shirt factory," he explained, "I bought those beans because I thought that was all we could afford to eat from then on. Yet here it is, five years later, and somehow we have managed to get along without them."

"Five years on only one income is quite an achievement," Jeffrey said. "You should give advice to others who are struggling. Share your survival skills."

"Me, giving advice?" Tommy asked. He gave a short, cynical laugh. "In addition to selling sandwiches, right?" His doubtful expression gradually faded as the idea appeared to take root. Thoughtfully silent, he watched Terri enjoying her breakfast. Then, looking at Jeffrey again, he said, "I guess you'll be looking for a place of your own today, huh?"

Taking the cue, Jeffrey hastily assured him, "Oh, absolutely. I'll grab a newspaper this morning and see what's available." Gloomily, he remembered his meager supply of cash.

Tommy asked, "What are you looking for, a house? Apartment?"

"An apartment," Jeffrey said, nodding thoughtfully. "Someplace small, not too expensive." Maybe a cozy little ATM vestibule, he thought, or a cheap motel room somewhere, just him and the cockroaches. Of course, getting arrested for embezzlement would put a roof over his head too, at least for the duration of his jail term.

Terri dawdled over her sandwich, taking smaller and smaller bites as though wanting it to last as long as possible.

After a moment, Tommy said, "You know, Jeff, you're welcome to stay here another night or longer, if you need to. It's certainly no trouble for us. You and Terri could ride to work together until you find a place of your own."

The breath that Jeffrey had been holding came out as a long, quiet sigh of relief. Humbly, he said, "Thank you. You have just solved a huge problem for me. The truth is, it cost me a lot of money getting here from Hawaii. I can't afford to rent an apartment until the city starts paying me. I'm pretty low on cash."

He felt his muscles relax as though a physical burden had been lifted from his shoulders.

Terri popped the rest of the sandwich into her mouth and dusted off her hands. "Well," she said brightly, "I guess we'd better head for work."

Jeffrey followed her to the front door and waited while she put on her coat.

Suddenly, she gasped and said to him, "I just remembered your suitcase! We won't have time to get it this morning. The airport is clear on the other side of town from the Money Building."

Tommy came up behind them, saying, "Let me have your claim ticket, Jeff, and I'll pick it up for you." He smiled at his wife and said, "I'm going out to buy groceries anyway."

CHAPTER 13

That morning, Jeffrey and Terri commuted to work under far more favorable conditions than those of the night before. The city snowplow had finished its route overnight, and a tentative sun illuminated the pothole-ridden, frost-heaved pavement of the road leading into town. Still, a low bank of gray clouds loomed at the horizon, poised to sweep overhead with the gift of more snow. Winter was far from over.

Terri drove in uncharacteristic silence. Only when she braked for a red light did she speak, and then it was as though she were talking to herself. "He hasn't made coffee in five years," she murmured. With a puzzled frown, she stared at the road ahead. "I thought he had forgotten how."

Downtown Baxter looked just as bad as Jeffrey remembered. Lines of people already snaked along the sidewalk in front of the public assistance offices flanking Main Street. Meanwhile, in the buildings' upper floors, the windows of abandoned commercial offices reflected each other's blank stares. He wondered about the people who used to work in those offices. By some ironic twist, any number of them could be standing in line at the ground floor of the same buildings where, years ago, they had earned a living. But what happened to their skills and intelligence, their creativity and ideas, their ambitions and competitiveness? Did those qualities die on the vine like frost-killed tomatoes overlooked at harvest time? Or were they merely dormant, waiting to be revived by some vibrant, inspiring leader? He couldn't imagine any such person coming to this cold, bleak city.

Shortly before nine, they arrived at the Municipal Building, a well-maintained two-story structure with its name emblazoned in gold letters over the front entrance. Terri drove around back to the employee parking lot. There she found a vacant space next to an orange City of Baxter snowplow with its blade resting on the ground, like the head of a weary workhorse after its labors. Indeed, the lot had been thoroughly cleared, which made for an easy hike to the snow-free sidewalk at the back of the building.

While heading toward a door marked "Employees," they passed a set of stairs leading down to the basement. At the bottom of the stairwell, a stooped, crooked-legged man in a blue fisherman's cap used a heavy iron shovel to dig out the snow that had collected there. Each time he filled the blade, he paused to gather his strength before heaving the snow up onto the ground-level sidewalk. Jeffrey pitied the man for his onerous labors and was about to offer assistance when, with a sudden clang, the shovel's blade fell off.

"Short day for you, Cap," Terri called cheerfully as they passed.

Jeffrey was startled upon recognizing the wrinkled, scowling face that glowered up at them. In a low voice, he asked Terri, "That's Cap Ordway, isn't it? He was the equipment manager for the Baxter Band when I played with them years ago. I'm surprised he hasn't retired by now."

"I don't think he wants to retire," she said. "He's having too much fun complaining about work."

Once inside the building, they followed a carpeted hallway toward a pair of beautifully carved and polished mahogany doors. Each was mounted with ornate bronze hardware and flanked by panels of etched glass.

"Nice offices," Jeffrey remarked with genuine admiration.

"That's the administrative wing through there," Terri told him, then continued on to a plain metal door leading into a stairwell. "Our office is upstairs."

"Administration?" he repeated, stopping to peer through the etched glass. Several ghostly figures moved among an orderly arrangement of desks. "Would Mr. Geegan's office be in there?" The city's mayor, Arthur Geegan, had signed the letter offering Jeffrey the band director's job.

"Yes," Terri affirmed, "but he sees visitors only on Mondays. That goes for employees, too."

Jeffrey followed her through the metal door and into the stairwell. "I just want to ask him about getting reimbursed for my travel expenses," he said.

"That ought to give him a good laugh," she said.

The cement-block walls and frugal lighting of the stairwell eased their transition to the second floor. Here, the decorators apparently had run out of carpet, polished hardwood, and etched glass. The purely functional second-story hallway featured a gritty linoleum floor and industrial-beige walls punctuated at regular intervals with mysteriously unlabeled doors, all of which were closed.

Terri led Jeffrey to a door at the end of the hall and into a room jammed with office furniture. Sitting at the nearest desk, behind a crenulated barricade of stacked paperwork and overflowing in- and outboxes, a husky, red-haired young woman clutched a telephone receiver in her freckled fist and said, "Mm-hmm. Mm-hmm. Okay, I'll get that right over to you." After hanging up the phone, she rested her chubby arms on the desk and beamed at Jeffrey. "Oh boy," she said eagerly, "a new cellmate."

From behind a filing cabinet, a tall, bony wisp in a purple dress looked up from the papers she was filing. Her lank, shoulder-length pageboy accentuated the thinness of her face. Both forearms were fitted with orthopedic braces. Mournfully, she asked, "Terri, is this the new director for Ben's band?"

"It sure is," Terri answered. She tossed her coat onto a nearby table and pulled Jeffrey forward like a prize calf at a 4-H auction. "Guys, this is Jeffrey Bowden. Jeff, this is Randie."

The copper-haired desk jockey gave him a casual salute and leaned comfortably back in her chair with her hands folded upon her ample stomach. Her telephone rang, but it didn't seem to disturb her.

"And that's Violet," Terri concluded.

The sad-faced file clerk offered a feeble wave.

Terri led him through a maze of cluttered worktables to a pile of secretarial accoutrements with a desk partially visible underneath. "The first thing I want to do is brief you on the status of the band," she said.

The first thing Jeffrey wanted to do was look for another job. He was quivering with the desire to escape from this foreign territory. After only a year's absence, he thought he might be able to reclaim his position as assistant band director at good ol' Baxter College. The wall clock read a few minutes past nine. Professor Wilmot likely was settling behind his desk right about now, perhaps checking his supply of cigars. It would be a good time to call.

"I'll clear off a chair so you can sit down," Terri said and began gathering a stack of computer printouts from the seat of a metal folding chair that apparently served as an extension of her desk.

Jeffrey didn't want to sit down. He wanted to find a quiet stairwell where he could make a phone call. "I don't need a chair," he told her. "Band directors are used to standing up. Let's keep things simple and just stick with what Ben had in place last year," he said. "Same musicians, same music programs, same performing venue."

"Jeff, have a seat," Terri urged. "This is more complicated than you think."

"No," he insisted, "it's really very simple. All we need is some musicians, some music, and a place for our concerts. Since the band played last season, those things must be already in place, right?"

"Not really," she said. "The band has been losing members over the years, and we're down to about twelve players. Also, the city condemned the gazebo in the park, which is where they used to have concerts. Last summer they played in the school auditorium, but attendance was extremely low. Here's what's left of our music library." From under her desk she dragged out a deteriorating cardboard box. "When people dropped out of the band, they didn't always return their music, so we're missing a lot of parts."

He pawed briefly through the torn and tattered scores. Many of the pieces dated from his own days of playing with the band, a decade or more ago. "Let's just toss this old stuff and buy all new music," he said. "A few patriotic songs, a couple of Sousa marches, an old Broadway tune or two. That ought to do it."

"You'll have to get approval from the budget committee before we can buy anything," Terri advised him.

With growing irritation he said, "I just want to buy a few pieces of music. For that I have to go through a committee?"

"Sit down," she said patiently, "and I'll explain how things work here. Didn't you have a budget committee in Hawaii?"

Stubbornly remaining on his feet, he said, "No, I had a treasurer with a checkbook."

"Well, here you have to get the committee's approval for all expenditures," she said. "That's why you need me as your assistant, to help you with the meeting schedules and agendas and budgets and expense reports and all the other details I haven't even told you about yet. And we have to work fast, because the band's first concert of the season is traditionally held on Memorial Day."

The growing oppressiveness of the task began to weigh down on Jeffrey. In frustration, he cleared an edge of the worktable behind him and leaned against it, telling himself that he still wasn't technically sitting down.

Across the room, Randie relaxed in her chair and appeared highly entertained by this session of new employee orientation. Violet was still at her filing cabinet, diligently working a crossword puzzle.

Addressing Terri, Jeffrey said in a tight voice, "I don't see why this has to be so complicated. It's just a community band, a bunch of amateur musicians who want to get together and play music."

With a patient smile, she told him, "It's not that simple, Jeff. You see, the Baxter Band is a municipal activity, funded by the city. We have to abide by their rules. After all, the band's expenses, including your salary and this music you want to buy, are paid for by the taxpayers. We can't just do whatever we want. We have to be accountable."

"Sure, I can understand that," he conceded, "but the band will never be ready by Memorial Day if I have to go through a committee for everything."

"No problem!" she cried gamely. "You just tell me what you want done." She rummaged through her desk drawer and pulled out a steno pad. After flipping past several pages of grocery lists, tic-tac-toe games, and lunch orders, she found a blank page. "Okay," she said, holding her pen ready. "Fire away."

He rapidly enumerated the list of items that came to mind. "We need musicians," he said, "the full complement of band

instrumentalists. Music stands. Folding chairs. Also the instruments typically supplied by the band: drums, tubas, and the
usual assortment of percussion instruments."

"You mean the little jangly things?" she asked.

"Yes," he affirmed. "Also, we need someone to haul all that
stuff to and from rehearsals and concerts. Does Cap still do
that?"

"No," she said. "After Ben left, Mr. Geegan assigned Cap to
the athletics program."

"Okay, so we need an equipment manager," Jeffrey said,
sensing the beginnings of a headache. "We need to sort through
that box of music and take inventory, see what parts are missing, and try to find replacements. We'll have to ask the budget
committee to approve some new music, and we need a place to
rehearse in the evening. Why did the city condemn the gazebo?"

"There was an ongoing problem with vandalism," she said.
"The city's maintenance department couldn't keep up with repairs. Finally it got so rundown that it became a safety hazard,
and now it's just a gang hangout."

Jeffrey considered all this in silence. He knew that band music was meant to be played outdoors. The gazebo had been the
perfect place to play in the summer. People brought picnic bas-
kets, spread blankets on the lawn, and had their supper in the
park. It was a nice, low-cost outing for families. Kids had plenty
of room to run around and play, and the adults socialized with
their neighbors while enjoying the music. Abruptly, he cleared
off the folding chair and sat down. "This is already sounding like
an impossible task," he muttered. Looking out the window, he
blurted in disgust, "I can't believe it's snowing again!"

Terri sprang up and pulled down the window shade. "Now
don't worry, Jeff," she said, "you just leave everything to me. I'll
get started on this list right away."

The office door opened. Instantly, Violet slipped her

crossword puzzle into the top drawer of the filing cabinet. Randie snatched up the telephone receiver and said, "Mm-hmm. Mm-hmm. Okay, I'll get that right over to you."

In the doorway stood a slender, taut-featured young woman with platinum hair drawn back into a tight little bun. She wore a tailored suit that was all business, and her blood-red mouth was as short and straight as the minus sign on an accountant's spreadsheet.

"Hi, Darla," Violet crooned from behind her filing cabinet.

Darla scanned the room like a hawk taking inventory in a chicken coop. Upon spotting Jeffrey, she headed directly toward him. With each step, her spiked heels ripped into the carpet. As she came nearer, Jeffrey noted that the severity of her outfit had been softened by the addition of a bow at the collar; the pressed edges looked sharp enough to draw blood. She stopped abruptly before him and pinned him with her gray eyes. "Mr. Bowden," she said dourly.

With a slight nod, he returned her cold glare. He was not in the mood to be bullied by a professional paper shuffler, no matter how nattily dressed.

"Miss Diamond, executive secretary to Mr. Geegan," she said in an obsidian voice, then handed him a stack of paperwork. "These are employment forms for you to complete."

Accepting the hefty pile, he snapped insolently, "Is there a test at the end of it?" He thought if he could get himself fired before his initial interview, he could start job hunting right away.

Without blinking an eye, Darla responded, "As a matter of fact, there is."

Oh, she is good, he thought; *her wits are sharp enough to draw blood, too.*

"As a city employee," she explained, "you are required to take a drug test."

"Drug test?" he repeated, raising his eyebrows in alarm.

She turned up the intensity of her glare. Cocking her head, she asked, "Is that going to be a problem for you?"

"That depends," he shot back. "Which ones do you want me to try?" He no longer was annoyed; now he regarded her as a challenge. Looking up into her precisely rouged face, he knew there was a smile in there somewhere, trying to get out. He showed her a small example himself, just to get her started.

Her mouth remained rigid with not a twitch of emotion. She blinked her thickly lashed doll's eyes and said dully, "Welcome to the City of Baxter," then turned and stabbed the carpet with her heels on her way out.

Randie hung up the phone and checked her watch. "Who's ready for coffee break?" she asked.

"Me," Violet sang, heaving the file drawer shut.

"Me too," Terri chimed in. "Come on, Jeff."

"You three go ahead," he said. "I'd better get these forms filled out." He fished a pen from the container of writing instruments on Terri's desk and dutifully began working his way through the questions. Terri grabbed her purse and followed her cohorts out the door.

The instant they had gone, Jeffrey dumped the employment forms onto the floor and dug out his cell phone. Professor Wilmot's office number was still in his list of contacts. He hastily dialed it. Upon hearing the familiar voice, Jeffrey announced himself to the music department chairperson and heard what sounded like a horrified gasp on the other end of the line. Worriedly, he asked, "Professor, are you all right?"

"Uh, yes, I'm fine," the other man stammered. He gulped and then asked in a fearful whisper, "Jeffrey, why are you calling here?"

Jeffrey had been wondering how to account for his return to Maine. For the time being, he decided to be cagy. "I'm taking a break from my ensemble in Hawaii," he said lightly, "doing a bit of traveling across the country. I thought I might stop by the college to see you."

"Oh no!" the professor gushed with breathless anxiety. "I don't think that would be a good idea, not at all. That is, under the circumstances."

"What circumstances, Professor?" Jeffrey asked. "Please tell me what is going on."

After a brief pause, Professor Wilmot said, "Andrew Quigley called here earlier looking for you. I really don't think I should be talking to you, because he made me promise to contact him if I heard from you. He said there was some sort of financial trouble in Hawaii."

"I'll level with you," Jeffrey said soberly. "Our plans in Hawaii have come to a sudden halt. It looks as though our treasurer has run off with all our funds."

"That isn't what Mr. Quigley told me," Professor Wilmot responded. "He said that the initial investigation pointed to you as the culprit. He's been trying to locate you in order to charge you with embezzlement."

"Professor," Jeffrey pleaded softly, "I hope you will believe me when I tell you that I had nothing to do with the loss of the symphony's money."

"I do believe you," Professor Wilmot said in a voice that resonated with sincerity. "In all the years I have known you, you always were a highly reputable and trustworthy young man, remarkably so, in fact. But for some reason, Mr. Quigley is convinced that you were responsible for his financial ruin, and he means to make you pay for it. When I was on the phone with him, I told him I didn't know where you were, which of course was truthful at the time. But I would feel very uncomfortable if you were to come here. If he called back, I wouldn't know what to say."

Jeffrey replied that he understood and had no intention of

causing any moral dilemma for the good professor. He thanked Wilmot and then hung up.

Sitting amid the clutter of office equipment and secretarial accouterments, Jeffrey felt like an alien. Through a tear in the window shade, he saw the snow coming down even more heavily. After a year's residence in Hawaii, he couldn't stomach another winter in Maine. It was only February; there were months of cold weather ahead.

Scrolling through his contact list, he came across the number of Ray Greenleaf, a semiprofessional trombonist he had met while playing a jazz gig in Honolulu. Ray had complimented Jeffrey on his playing and invited him to look him up if he ever got to San Diego, where Ray was putting together a chamber wind ensemble.

San Diego, Jeffrey thought; on the southern coast of California. Sun, sea, warm weather; it sounded like Hawaii with longer highways. He dialed Ray's number and was pleased when he not only answered but also remembered Jeffrey. They exchanged pleasantries, then Jeffrey explained that he was no longer in Hawaii and was looking for work on the mainland. "How's your chamber group coming along?" he asked.

"It's undergoing some reorganization right now," Ray said. "It could be a few months before we're ready to sign on anyone new, but if you can be patient, I'll call you if things work out the way I'm hoping."

Jeffrey gave Ray his cell number and said he would wait to hear from him.

"What are you doing now?" Ray asked.

"Directing a community band in Maine," Jeffrey answered.

"Maine, wow," Ray said with a laugh. "San Diego will be quite a change from that."

"I sure hope so," Jeffrey said.

After hanging up, he felt cheered by this new possibility.

Employment with Ray's group was still highly iffy, but he had planted a seed of opportunity and now only needed to wait for it to prove its viability and grow to fruition. In the meantime, he realized that Baxter might be a safe place for him to lie low, since Andrew Quigley had already failed to locate him there. Directing the Baxter Band might be a fun way to pass the summer. He would have Terri round up some players and schedule a few rehearsals. From that box of old music, they should be able to scrape together some marches and patriotic warhorses, a few throwaway tunes from Broadway musicals of the previous generation, things the old folks could sing along to. He would cobble together a few concerts, enough to take them through the summer. With luck, he could be heading to San Diego by Labor Day.

He had made scant progress through the stack of employment forms when his officemates returned from their coffee break. Terri almost bounced across the room to her desk. After she had sat down, Jeffrey felt compelled to warn her, "Terri, I hope you realize that my employment with the city as band director could be only temporary."

"From what I've seen, Jeff," she said with a happy smile, "everything in life is temporary. Now listen. I just saw Cap Ordway, and he told me he's got some band instruments stored in the basement. If you want to go look at them now, I'll finish those employment forms for you."

"You would do that for me?" he asked in surprise.

"Of course," she said, relieving him of his burden. "A lot of these forms are repetitive. I'll use the information you've already provided as a guide for filling out the same questions that show up elsewhere. If there's anything I can't answer, I'll check with you later. Most of the questions are pretty standard, anyway. You're not a convicted felon, are you?"

"Not yet," he affirmed.

She giggled and said, "What a kidder. Now go downstairs and tell Cap to show you those instruments. The band may be closer to being ready than you thought."

On his way to the basement, Jeffrey stopped by the administrative department, thinking he might bevel Miss Diamond's rough edges and negotiate a brief meeting with Arthur Geegan.

Standing before the imposing wooden doors was a petite, elderly woman wearing a doll-sized designer suit and sensible high heels. Her steel-gray hair hung in a well-behaved pageboy. In one hand she clutched a rolled-up computer printout, and with the other she pounded her bony fist against the door. Jeffrey thought she could have cut her way through the glass with the substantial diamond on her left hand. Peering through the etched glass panel, the woman shouted, "I see you in there, Darla. Open up! I need to find out whether the municipal grand emperor has completely lost his mind."

A key scraped in the lock, and the door opened just enough to reveal a shoulder pad worthy of stopping an NFL lineman. In her practiced monotone, Darla said, "Mrs. Roosevelt, today is Thursday."

"I read my calendar this morning, thank you," replied the gray-helmeted firebrand, who managed to push the door open a few millimeters. "I know all about King Arthur's silly rule limiting visitors to one day a week. That's a cowardly way for an elected official to avoid unhappy constituents. The budget committee meeting is tomorrow, and I want an explanation for this quarter's financial report." She shook the papers gripped in her jeweled fist.

"Mr. Geegan is very busy at the moment," Darla said and dutifully began to apologize when, behind her, a dark-suited man suddenly appeared with both arms spread in welcome.

"Rosie! How nice to see you," the man cried in a robust tenor voice. "Darla, why didn't you tell me Mrs. Roosevelt was coming in today?" A vigorous man of about fifty, Arthur Geegan swept forward to meet his visitor. His rich brown hair displayed just enough silver highlights to project an attitude of maturity and trustworthiness. The lapel of his suit jacket was laden with a near-military display of pins and ribbons denoting his association with various civic organizations and special-interest awareness groups.

Mrs. Roosevelt shook the rolled-up computer reports at him as though he were a naughty puppy. "Arthur, you shifted funds again," she said accusingly. "What's the point of allocating money for a specific budget item if someone else can grab it for their own pet project?"

Geegan took the unhappy lady on his arm and escorted her into his office, crooning sympathetically, "Now don't you worry, my dear, I'm going to take care of that problem." From behind his closed door, her agitated voice sounded like a muffled jackhammer as she continued her complaint.

Darla blinked her thickly lashed eyes as if to clear them of smoke. Turning to close the main door again, she discovered Jeffrey standing just inside. "No visitors until Monday," she said firmly.

"I just wanted to take a look at your newspaper," he said, pointing toward the publication which lay on the coffee table in the waiting area. "May I?"

"Only for a moment," Darla said. She secured the door behind him and returned to her desk.

Jeffrey carried the newspaper over to the window and scanned the national headlines. Fortunately, his Hawaii troubles hadn't made the local news. Looking through the window, he watched snow falling on what he assumed was Mrs. Roosevelt's Cadillac parked at the curb. A uniformed driver passed the time by brushing snow from the windshield. Jeffrey guessed that Mrs. Roosevelt was one of Baxter's dwindling number of high-tax-bracket elites; that would explain Geegan's willingness to meet with her.

Jeffrey dropped the paper onto the table and scanned his surroundings. For a city in financial decline, Baxter had some cushy administrative offices. The waiting area offered an assortment of plush chairs upholstered in a classy gray suede. The textured white walls featured several large, nicely framed prints. Ornate planters of lush greenery filled every corner and niche. A generous supply of warm air gushed down from the heating vents near the ceiling, while the inoffensive strains of a piano trio seeped from speakers tastefully hidden away somewhere. All six secretaries were busy at their computers and telephones. From the hallway leading to Geegan's office, Mrs. Roosevelt continued her harangue.

Jeffrey approached Darla's desk and asked her, "Any chance of me getting five minutes with him, since I'm already here?"

With an irritated glare, she said, "That is very unlikely. It's almost eleven o'clock, and he goes to lunch at eleven." She looked down at her work again.

Jeffrey stood watching the seemingly endless snow falling outside the window. "Ever been to San Diego?" he asked.

"No," she said resentfully.

Mrs. Roosevelt's extended diatribe continued from behind Geegan's door. After a moment, Jeffrey said to Darla, "Tell him his eleven o'clock appointment is here."

"You don't have an eleven o'clock appointment," she dryly pointed out.

Undeterred, Jeffrey said, "I'll bet he would jump at the chance to give me one."

Darla narrowed her eyes in a sneer of admiration, then pressed a button on her phone and informed Geegan that his eleven o'clock appointment was waiting for him.

A moment later, Geegan's door swung open and the harried

mayor shooed his visitor into the hall. "I'm so sorry to have to cut you short, Rosie, but I must give preference to my scheduled appointments," he said.

"I want this discussed at the budget committee tomorrow, Arthur," Mrs. Roosevelt demanded. "I intend to hold you accountable for what happens to the citizens' money."

When the elderly lady had left, Geegan turned to his secretary and beamed his perfect white smile. "Darla, that was a brilliant scheme," he said. "I never would have gotten rid of that gray-haired dragon if it weren't for you. I'm going to lunch now."

"Hold on," Jeffrey said. "I'm your eleven o'clock appointment."

Before Geegan could ask who he was, Darla introduced Jeffrey and explained, "Mr. Bowden is replacing Mr. Hennessey as director of the Baxter Band."

"Oh yes, taking over Ben's band," Geegan said with an approving nod. "Nice to have you here, uh, Jerry." He straightened his suit jacket and turned to go.

"I just wondered," Jeffrey said quickly, "whether I might get reimbursed for my travel expenses getting here."

Terri had been right. Geegan laughed all the way out the door.

%

After leaving the administrative wing, Jeffrey headed for the stairwell leading to the basement and encountered two women in conversation who stood blocking the door. One of the women clutched a box of file folders; the other gripped the handle of a wheeled cart holding interoffice mail. "Excuse me," he said, wanting to pass.

The mail deliverer, thinking he must be a visitor in need of directions, advised him, "That doorway leads to the basement. Nothing down there except maintenance."

"That's where I'm headed," Jeffrey said. "I want to see Cap Ordway."

The woman smirked. "He's downstairs, all right," she said. "I was just there delivering his work orders. Caught him sitting down, whittling, and eating a sandwich."

"In the middle of the morning?" the other woman cried and rolled her eyes. "Must be nice. Some of us have to work."

Addressing both of them, Jeffrey asserted, "Cap worked all morning plowing the employee parking lot while the rest of us were still having breakfast. Now, excuse me." He stepped between the women and started down the stairs. At the first landing, he looked back and saw their surprised faces framed in the window of the door.

Compared with the esthetic qualities of the first floor, the basement of the Municipal Building was completely utilitarian in design, with concrete floors and stark florescent lighting. Instead of nicely framed prints, the dull yellow walls bore mysterious stains, gouges, and patches of exposed drywall where obsolete fixtures had been ripped out. There were no potted plants here, only an occasional patch of mold. The mood music was a weird industrial opera featuring a grating chorus of machinery noises highlighted by random metallic shrieks, clangs, and compressed-air thuds. While the first floor presented a clean-scrubbed, shining face to the public, here in the basement were the working guts of the facility. Exposed pipes, electrical cables, and ductwork snaked in all directions. A huge, rumbling furnace sent warmed air to the offices upstairs, which returned the favor by sending its effluent drainage down here for disposal.

Jeffrey walked along the corridor, which he saw as a long, narrow exhibition of mishap and mortality, reminding him of all the things that could go wrong in a public facility. On display were fire extinguishers with neatly folded hoses, canisters of deicing salt for slippery sidewalks, orange cones for demarking wet floors, and electrical boxes with high-voltage warnings. Beneath a red emergency wall telephone hung a poster listing poison control guidelines and a hotline number. Beside every doorway was posted a diagram of the evacuation route for that area. While the workers on the first floor dealt in the esoterica of committees, schedules, and public relations, the basement crew discreetly preserved the structure from disaster, saw to the comfort and safety of the building's inhabitants, and stood by, ready to save lives.

At last he stopped at a wedge of light spilling from an open doorway. Cap Ordway, the city's maintenance man also in charge of athletics, sat behind a gouged wooden workbench, shaving a small chunk of wood with his pocketknife. The detached blade of his snow shovel lay before him while the wooden handle stood vertically gripped in the vise of his knobby knees. Also on the workbench lay a half-eaten tuna sandwich on a greasy brown paper bag. Jeffrey had made the acquaintance of enough hardworking men to know that the ones who ate lunch at a quarter to eleven in the morning did so because they had work to do during their designated lunch break.

Cap had weathered badly from the days when Jeffrey remembered him hauling equipment for the Baxter Band. At sixty-five, Cap was a withered old man with bony shoulders and a stooped posture that spoke of weariness and chronic pain. All of his cushioning had been worn away, leaving nothing but hard angles on a rigid frame. A few wisps of gray hair poked out from beneath the faded blue fisherman's cap that seemed to be glued to his head. His mouth was set in a grim attitude of stubborn endurance. Not quite an expression of determination, it was more the look of a long-suffering animal bitterly awaiting the next inevitable blow. Ignoring the tall young man in the doorway, he concentrated on hewing the piece of wood and stopped periodically to check its fit between the shovel's handle and blade stem.

Jeffrey said hello, introduced himself, and politely asked for a few minutes of Cap's time.

"I'm on my lunch break," Cap snarled. He still hadn't looked up.

"Then stop working and eat your lunch," Jeffrey said.

"This is the only chance I got to fix this shovel," Cap said, continuing to work. As an afterthought, he allowed, "The sandwich ain't that good, anyways." Patiently, repeatedly, he whittled and tested the shim until at last he achieved the exact thickness and slope he needed for a snug fit. Using a small hammer, he tapped the wooden chip into place. "It's gettin' to where I have to fix this shovel every winter," he said.

"Why don't you buy a new one?" Jeffrey asked.

"New ones are plastic," Cap explained. "They'll break eventually, too, but I can't fix plastic. Wood and metal, I can fix." At last, he grasped the repaired shovel by the handle and shook it. The blade remained firmly in place. The maintenance man bared his teeth in a brief, satisfied grin, then propped the tool against the wall and turned his attention to his visitor, as though assessing him for needed repairs. His small eyes were as washed-out blue as his headgear and were so deeply set that they appeared to have been hammered into his face. "Bowden," he said gruffly with an intensified scowl. "I remember you."

A knot of fear tightened in Jeffrey's stomach as he waited to hear just how much Cap remembered.

"You played in Hennessey's band a few years back," Cap said.

"That's right," Jeffrey acknowledged, then swiftly took the reins of the conversation. "You were hauling the band's equipment back then, but I hear you're not doing that anymore. Why did you stop?"

Cap wasn't ready to give up the reins just yet. "After Ben announced his retirement," he said, regarding Jeffrey through narrowed eyes, "I heard talk about some young punk takin' his place."

"I would be the young punk in question," Jeffrey confessed.

A cloud of dread shadowed Cap's face as the overworked maintenance man deduced what would be asked of him next. The sag in his shoulders worsened as though already bowing under the newly added burden. Wearily he said, "The city's athletics program gets bigger every year. We've got municipal teams for basketball, softball, Special Olympics, soccer, you name it. Each time they add something new, I put in a requisition for more help, and every time it gets turned down. Geegan says, 'It's just one more event, Cap. You can handle it.' They pile on straw after straw, until this camel's back is about broke. Well, go ahead and add your straw." With a defiant glare, he warned Jeffrey, "But I don't work for free. If you want me to set up for band concerts, it's overtime. Very expensive overtime."

"The Baxter Band won't have any concerts if I don't pull things together first," Jeffrey said. "Right now all I want to do is look at the instruments you've got down here."

Cap snatched a ring of keys from a wall hook, eased himself onto his feet, and shuffled away, favoring his left leg. To Jeffrey, who followed him through the workshop, the old man didn't look strong enough to carry a piccolo. Cap stopped before a door stenciled with the word *Storage*. While fitting a key into the lock, Cap reached back with his free hand to rub the muscle at his belt line. "Just when I had my back pain under control," he muttered.

Jeffrey's inventory of the band equipment revealed a few banged-up music stands, a dented tuba, a bass drum with the letters *BB* painted on its head, and a box of percussion instruments, the little jangly things, which looked more like a collection of scrap metal. He also found a box containing a few musty uniforms that appeared worthy of display in an antiques museum.

As they walked back to the workbench, Jeffrey said, "Now I want you to take me to look at the gazebo. Afterward, I'll buy you a better lunch than what you have there."

Cap dumped the remains of his sandwich into the trash can and took his jacket down from a wall peg. "You goin' like that?" he asked, indicating Jeffrey's windbreaker. "It was twenty degrees outside last time I checked."

"This is all I've got for a jacket," Jeffrey replied. "I've only been in town for a day."

"Where'd you come here from?" Cap asked as they walked out to the parking lot.

"Hawaii," Jeffrey said.

"Couldn't take all that good weather, huh?" Cap said derisively.

"I wanted to come back and direct the Baxter Band," Jeffrey insisted, trying to sound sincere.

They had reached the orange City of Baxter plow truck. The maintenance man gave Jeffrey a disbelieving look and headed toward the driver's side, saying, "Uh-huh."

Jeffrey opened the passenger door and climbed up into the cab. "The Baxter Band has a great historical importance, you know," he said as Cap settled behind the wheel. "It was started over a hundred and fifty years ago as an infantry band."

"I bet they carried their own equipment back then," Cap said and started the engine.

CHAPTER 14

With Jeffrey riding in the passenger seat, Cap drove to the municipal park, a vacant, snow-covered field with the gazebo tucked into one corner. The big City of Baxter truck plowed easily into the snowy parking lot, climbed the curb, and carried them efficiently up to the gazebo, where a prominent sign warned that the structure was condemned.

"Sit tight a minute," Cap instructed Jeffrey. Before long, he had plowed a pathway around the structure so they could easily walk its perimeter.

A stand of ancient, shaggy conifers formed a natural backdrop for the gazebo and ran the length of the park, separating it from an adjoining residential area. Jeffrey climbed down from the truck and stood in the shadow of the trees, shivering as their familiar forms stirred a long-buried memory.

Even after all this time, he could see her clearly in his mind: a dark-haired nymph wearing a dress made from bright, fluttering scarves. Petite and pixie-like, she sat off by herself under a tree, listening to the band and applauding after he performed his solo. That summer, he had thought of her as his own personal groupie. Now, standing beside the gazebo where he had played with the band twelve summers ago, his gaze followed the line of trees all the way to the rail fence and ultimately to the duck pond at the far end of the park. The intervening years seemed to evaporate, just as the water had evaporated from his body after he emerged from the pond one warm August night after a canceled rehearsal. The girl had darted ahead of him, pushing through the reeds. He had no choice but to follow her; she had stolen his heart, his sensibilities, and all his clothing.

Cap said, "I thought you wanted to look at this."

Jeffrey snapped out of his reverie. The vividness of the re-emerging memory left him shaken, as if he had suddenly unearthed a corpse. He stared blankly at the gazebo, not really seeing it. His mind still reeled with images of the naked girl slipping like a nighthawk through the dusk while he pursued her with all the naive enthusiasm of a satyr attending his first bacchanalia, and then, the most disturbing image of all: a city maintenance man shining a light on them and yelling.

At last, Jeffrey found his voice and asked Cap, "Is it salvageable?" mostly as a way of stalling for time while his mind reestablished itself in the present. He hoped beyond hope that Cap had forgotten the incident from years ago.

"Not hardly," Cap declared. "Snow's covering up the worst of it. Don't step inside. The flooring's gone in places." He pulled a long-handled squeegee from the truck and reached over the railing with it, working around the perimeter of the gazebo and scraping away the snow to expose the warped and broken planks of the flooring.

The railing was smashed away in one corner, and every one of the lattice panels skirting the gazebo's perimeter had been broken, perhaps kicked in by some thug's Doc Martens. The roof was falling in, and strips of tar paper dangled through the gaps like somber-toned banners. All the flat surfaces of the structure had been knife-gouged or else spray-painted with graffiti of the most vulgar kind. The gazebo was a three-dimensional compendium of coarse language, profanity, and obscene insults. Jeffrey wondered why successive generations of kids imagined that using these shocking words somehow made them appear grown up. As a grown-up himself, he felt only embarrassed and irritated by the display. He hoped the San Diego economy was healthy enough to keep its youth more usefully engaged.

When Cap had finished clearing away the snow, Jeffrey said, "All right, let's talk specifics. Forget for the moment that we don't have the money to do what I'm about to propose. But if we were going to rebuild this thing, could we salvage some of the lumber?"

After a sweeping, squint-eyed assessment of the visible boards, Cap allowed, "Some of it might be worth saving. The flooring looks pretty solid from here over to the F-word. Beyond that, they got a little warp to 'em, especially there at the S-word. But we might could use those for understructure." He pointed a gloved hand and continued, "The railing's still good, except for that corner where it's insulting somebody's mother." Then he looked at Jeffrey and cautioned, "But working with salvaged lumber is risky. If I miss pulling a nail from one of those old boards, it could cost me a saw blade. We ought to use all new material."

Giving a nod of agreement, Jeffrey said, "As long as we're wishing for the stars, let's ask for the whole galaxy. I'd like to give Geegan an estimate of what it would cost to rebuild the gazebo in time for the band's opening concert on Memorial Day. While we're here, why don't you go ahead and take some measurements?"

"Don't need to measure," Cap said. "I've still got the plans I drew up."

Jeffrey looked at him in astonishment. "You built this gazebo, Cap?" he asked.

The maintenance man looked up at the defiled structure one last time before turning away. Quietly, almost inaudibly, he said, "Yep."

Neither of them said anything as they got back into the truck, but Jeffrey's conscience, which up to then had been focused on dreams of San Diego, now got up on all fours and shook itself awake. He sensed that this withered old man could be one of the few remaining souls who cared anything about this town. Something more than a gazebo was at stake, Jeffrey thought. While he was waiting for Ray Greenleaf to call, he might as well do something useful.

As Cap drove them out of the parking lot, Jeffrey remembered the promise he had made to Cap earlier. "How's the food at that coffee shop across the street?" he asked.

"Not nearly as bad as the coffee," Cap said and drove them directly there.

They were the only customers. A waitress sat behind the counter playing solitaire on her computer, ignoring a near-empty coffeepot that was scalding on the burner. Seeing the new arrivals, she called, "Hey, Cap, what gives? Two lunches for you today?"

"That sandwich you sold me this morning was moldy," Cap complained as he and Jeffrey settled onto a couple of stools at the counter.

"Why didn't you bring it back?" she asked.

"The mold was the best part," he shot back. He went on to suggest that if the waitress found herself with some free time on her hands anytime soon, she might make them a fresh pot of coffee. Reluctantly, she did.

"Couple of pieces of pie," Cap added as a smile crept onto his face, "with a slice of rat cheese on mine."

Jeffrey opted for rat cheese as well. As they began eating, he asked, "Cap, why is there so much vandalism in this town?"

"Oh, you know how it is when parents let their kids run wild." The older man focused his steely beam of derision on Jeffrey, who winced, although he knew very well that the

incident in the park twelve years ago was entirely his own fault
and not his parents'. "Kids need more than just feeding and
watering," Cap continued. "They need a role model to show 'em
what they ought to be aiming for. There's not enough examples of worthy men around here for boys to copy, so they run
in gangs, and that just means trouble." In between mouthfuls
of pie, he elaborated. "One boy by hisself has got one brain. But
you get two boys together, they got half a brain between 'em.
Three boys, a third of a brain. Any more than that?" He shook
his head. "No brains. The fact is, kids in this town don't have
enough to keep 'em busy."

"But you told me the city increases the athletics program
every year," Jeffrey said.

Cap's response was sharp and irritated, as if Jeffrey had
touched a sore spot. "Maybe not all kids care about sports," the
older man said. "Maybe they're too clumsy for athletics. Maybe
their friends talk them into making trouble just for the thrill of
it. Maybe their mothers are too busy working two jobs to raise
'em proper."

Jeffrey understood that Cap was not speaking in gener-
alities but with specificity. Cautiously, he asked, "How do you
know all that?"

"I ain't blind, and I'm only half deaf," Cap said. He scraped
his empty plate as if there might be more pie underneath.

Watching him, Jeffrey was thoughtfully silent. After a moment he said, "I want to rebuild that gazebo." He was surprised
to hear himself say it, but it was true.

"Soon as you do, it'll get sprayed again," Cap said.

"So if that happens, we'll paint over it," Jeffrey asserted.

"No you won't," Cap declared with sudden vehemence. "Not
if you want to keep your job."

Confused, Jeffrey asked, "What do you mean?"

"The city has a special department, Graffiti Abatement,"

Cap said. "It's their job, and theirs alone, to paint over graffiti in this city. That's what they do and that's all they do, and nobody else better do it for them. There's a strict ordinance about it."

"That's crazy," Jeffrey scoffed, reaching for his coffee cup.

"Welcome to Baxter," Cap said.

"I still want to rebuild the gazebo," Jeffrey said. He swirled the remaining liquid in his cup. There was something swishing around at the bottom, but he decided against determining what it was. In disgust, he set the cup down and pulled out his wallet. "What this place needs is some competition," he said.

Cap gave a short laugh and asked rhetorically, "What fool would open up a new business in this town?"

Jeffrey thought he knew the answer to that question, but it was far too early to say for sure. "Don't buy your lunch tomorrow," he said to Cap. "I'm going to bring you the best sandwich you've ever had."

As the two men headed out to the truck, Cap's attitude became conciliatory. "Find me some help," he said, "and we'll commence tearing down that old gazebo."

"I'm not sure I can get approval for your overtime," Jeffrey warned.

With a dismissive wave toward the park, Cap said, "I'm sick of looking at that profane pile of scrap wood. It'll be worth putting in a few nights and weekends just to get rid of it. I won't charge you for it, and I'll get Geegan's okay to take the thing down."

Jeffrey promised to round up a volunteer work crew. He and Cap climbed into the truck, and the big engine rumbled heartily to life.

As they headed out onto the street, Jeffrey had to have one last look; he couldn't help himself. He leaned forward so he could see across the cab, beyond Cap's profile. Through the driver's-side window he gazed once more at the park, the rail fence, and the duck pond. The truck gathered speed, carrying them along. Jeffrey watched through the back window as the scene of his youthful indiscretion disappeared into the distance. Turning back in his seat, he noticed Cap glaring at him.

He remembers, Jeffrey thought, sinking into his seat with dismay.

※

When Jeffrey got back to the office and learned what Terri had done in his absence, he was so astonished that he had to sit down.

"The band's first rehearsal is scheduled for next Wednesday night at seven," she told him, "at the music room in the high school. They don't have a music program anymore, but they do still have their band equipment, and they said we can use it for rehearsal. I'll go with you and help set up everything. The night watchman will open the doors for us and lock up after we leave. I'm taking the music library home with us tonight so I can get it organized. Here's a list of musicians coming to the first rehearsal. I found everything but a tuba player."

He took the sheet of paper she handed him and held it limply while blinking with disbelief. "I could give you a crash course in directing and you wouldn't need me at all," he said.

She laughed and said, "Of course we need you, silly. This is your band. Oh, and here's your employment forms." She handed him the stack of paperwork that Darla had given him earlier. "Just look them over to be sure I got all the answers right. Then sign them."

He was silent for a long moment as he stared at her in awe. *All that initiative,* he thought, *just waiting to be tapped.*

Across the room, Violet had pulled a chair up to Randie's desk. In addition to her wrist braces, the emaciated file clerk wore ACE bandages on both legs. She now leaned forward eagerly while Randie read to her from a medical dictionary.

"Listen to this one, Vi," the burly redhead said. "'Bilateral tendon paralysis. Sporadic and unpredictable.'"

"Ooh, that sounds good," Violet crooned. "Tell me the symptoms so I can practice."

It was like discovering an oil field, Jeffrey thought, one pocketed with vast reserves of crude.

As he and Terri left for the day, he carried the box of band music downstairs. His shoulder still ached from shoveling snow that morning, and he was looking forward to a hot shower. As he followed Terri across the parking lot, freezing rain pelted his windbreaker like buckshot.

"You really should buy yourself a winter coat," she said as they climbed into her VW.

"It's almost spring," he argued, trying to still his chattering teeth. He didn't see any point in spending his dwindling cash on a winter coat, especially since he might be going to San Diego in a few months. While waiting for Terri to start the engine, he dredged up his memories of spring's timid and halting appearance in Maine. "In a couple of weeks," he said, "the ground will start to thaw, just the top half inch or so, and it will be as slippery as walking on overcooked spinach. We'll start getting rain mixed with snow, which will make clearing the driveway feel like shoveling wet cement." Through the windshield, he watched a long rod of ice drop from a power line. He hoped that no one had been walking beneath it.

Terri, ever hopeful, dutifully cranked the engine.

Accompanied by the strains of a cold, reluctant car engine, Jeffrey continued his soliloquy. "About a month from now, there will be green grass and flowers," he said. "Not here, of course, but somewhere south of the fortieth parallel. Here in Maine, there will be mud everywhere, and where there isn't mud, there will be thick, gray fog that freezes on the roadways. After that, we'll start seeing robins and green buds on the trees, which will mean only a few more weeks of sleet and freezing rain." He decided to start playing his trombone regularly in the evenings in order to get his embouchure in shape. When Ray Greenleaf called him to audition in San Diego, he wanted to be ready to hit the airport tarmac running.

While Terri drove them home, Jeffrey told her about his and Cap's intention to rebuild the gazebo in time for the band's Memorial Day concert.

"But where will you get the money for materials?" she asked.

"I thought I'd make a proposal to the budget committee tomorrow," he said.

"Ben never had any luck with that group," she warned. "The city has a lot of problems to address, and the band is a low priority. Don't forget, you also want to ask for new music and an equipment manager. Adding a construction project will put our department way over budget."

He gazed through the window at the vacant office buildings and boarded-up storefronts on Main Street. Interspersed were billboards promoting the city-sponsored public assistance programs. He wondered if he was the only person in town who saw a direct cause-and-effect relationship. "There's just never enough money, is there?" he asked rhetorically.

"Let's just hold the band concerts in the high school auditorium, like we did last year," she urged. "Nobody cares about that old gazebo anyway."

"No," he said with quiet determination. "I want to rebuild it."

"But why?" she asked.

He had been asking himself that question and at last had come up with the answer. "I owe somebody a favor," he said.

They arrived home to find the Turcotts' driveway packed with passenger-filled vehicles beginning to back down toward the street. Slowing the VW, Terri rolled down her window and stared in puzzlement at these people whom she identified to Jeffrey as neighbors, friends, and casual acquaintances. A few of Tommy's former coworkers from the shirt factory also were among the departing crowd. "Hey, guys," Terri called to the waving occupants of the nearest car, "what's going on?"

The jumbled chorus of responses was unintelligible; still, jubilant excitement was evident on the people's flushed faces and in their ongoing conversations.

Terri turned to Jeffrey in wonder. "Did he say 'revolution?'" she asked.

Mystified, he could only shrug.

Upon entering the house, Terri and Jeffrey saw that Tommy had hosted a party. Folded card tables and metal chairs stood propped against the living room walls. A trash bin near the door held a large number of soiled disposable plates and paper napkins. In the kitchen, Tommy stood at the sink, drying the rack of dishes he had just washed. He greeted them with a broad smile and announced, "I'm starting a neighborhood support group for people with open schedules."

Terri had begun removing her coat, but now she let it hang forgotten from one shoulder as she sat down to listen. Jeffrey set the box of band music on the table and stood beside her, waiting to hear more.

Tommy said, "Jeff, you gave me the idea this morning when you suggested that I peddle my sandwiches and poverty survival tactics, but the ball really got rolling when my friend Levi came over with a big sack of frozen shrimp to give us. His son is a fisherman from downstate, and occasionally he brings a truckload to market up here, with extras for his family and friends. It was far more than we could use, so I started making sandwiches and inviting people over. Pretty soon, the house was buzzing with conversation about the problems we're seeing in our community. It started out as a gripe session over lunch, but then I suggested that as experienced businessmen we should use our skills to come up with ways to improve things as well as to teach people about economics in a free society."

Having finished drying the dishes, Tommy began preparing dinner while smoothly continuing, "People from the business world understand the forces that enable success. They know the joy that a man experiences when he gets paid for doing something he's good at and loves to do. They know how to fix problems using limited resources. In fact, it is precisely the condition of working within limitations that pushes them to be creative and cooperative."

He tossed a handful of shrimp into a hot skillet. The eruption of steam punctuated his monologue like a shimmering, ringing cymbal. "You should have seen this house!" he cried exuberantly. "Our living room was filled with enthusiastic, chattering people. I got out my old presentation easel and magic markers and turned the conversation into a brainstorming session. The city has set up lots of programs that are well-intentioned but overwhelmed or poorly managed or simply not working well. Some of them operate on erratic schedules, for example, or are inefficient and frustrating to use. We listed tons of things that need fixing, but when everybody started to get discouraged, I told them to think of each problem as a puzzle to be solved, the way I used to do with my team at the shirt factory. It was like a science lab in here, the way everyone was dissecting and analyzing things and proposing solutions."

Pausing only long enough to stir the shrimp and turn down the heat under the rice, Tommy immediately resumed his happy tirade. "Everything was on the table," he declared, spreading his hands for emphasis, "neighborhood security, child care, vandalism, illiteracy, transportation, you name it. We discussed some very promising solutions today, and everyone went away with an action plan and a clear idea of how he could use his particular talents and resources to help people in the neighborhood. Oh, and my sandwiches were such a big hit today, I got my first order. One of my former golf buddies wants a whole tray of them for his son's birthday party tomorrow."

Later, as the three sat down to a beautifully prepared meal, Terri exclaimed, "Tommy, I am so proud of you for taking the initiative!"

Tommy, who hadn't stopped grinning, said, "It's Jeffrey I have to thank. I never realized I could help anybody else. I always thought I was the one who needed help. Many of the people here today said the same thing about themselves. It was a real thrill to see so many folks excited and engaged, being creative and using their own individual expertise in some way. Every one of them had something to offer but had been sitting around getting rusty and maybe even lazy. That's a good way to lose your self-respect. It was rewarding to see them realize that new jobs aren't going to magically appear. We all understood that if we want new jobs, we have to create them ourselves." Abruptly, Tommy fell silent, and his face collapsed into its former expression of sadness.

Alarmed, Terri asked, "Tommy, what's wrong?"

"Nothing's wrong," he said mournfully, rubbing his cheeks. "It's just that my face hurts from all this smiling."

CHAPTER 15

The next morning, while Tommy prepared sandwiches, Jeffrey sat at the kitchen table and prodded his host for advice.

"I've got a budget committee meeting today," he explained, "and the management aspect of my job is totally foreign to me. The city hired me to direct the band, but they're not giving me the resources I need in order to do it. It's not like I'm asking for Carnegie Hall; we just need a few basic things. The gazebo is unusable and needs rebuilding. Our music library is outdated, and the athletics program stole our equipment manager."

Tommy stood at the counter chopping vegetables. "I can sympathize with you," he said, "but even big corporations have to deal with resource problems. What makes them successful is figuring out how to solve those problems in a financially responsible way. One reason publicly funded programs are so ineffective is that they try to solve their problems politically, by lobbying for more funding, for example. They never look at the efficiency of their operations and ask how they can cut expenses, redesign processes, or improve productivity. An unending flow of money is poison to a private enterprise. It encourages overspending, wasteful practices, redundancy, and bad management decisions like hiring too many people who don't have enough to do."

"Are you're saying I should just work with what I've got?" Jeffrey asked with growing despair.

"Not at all," Tommy assured him. Having filled a platter with assembled sandwiches, he pushed his forefinger through a bowl of radishes, selected a few choice ones, then took up a paring knife and began carving radish roses. "See if you can find a sponsor to finance your gazebo reconstruction in exchange for free advertising at the concert," he said. "Same with the new music you want. Open the phone book to the yellow pages and select a few targets. Approach the manager of each one yourself, in person, to make your proposal. Try any business that has to worry about competition: plumbers, doctors, auto repair shops. If they think you might approach their competitor next, that could motivate them to make a deal with you."

Jeffrey had found a piece of scrap paper and was furiously making notes. "Keep going," he said. "This is helpful."

One of the radishes split under Tommy's knife, spoiling the rose effect. Calmly, he popped the mistake into his mouth and started on another radish. "Here's how you can get an equipment manager," he said. "Propose to the budget committee that the city hire a part-time assistant for Cap."

"Hiring somebody is out of the question," Jeffrey interjected. "Even I know that. There's simply no money for it."

"Follow me on this," Tommy said patiently. "Cap's overtime is expensive because he's been there forever and he's worked his way up the pay scale. For a veteran employee like him, time-and-a-half amounts to some big bucks. Have Terri run the figures for you, then show Geegan in black and white that it will cost the city less money to give Cap's overtime work to a part-timer at starting pay. Also, impress upon him that an overworked, retirement-aged maintenance man is a high risk for a work-related accident. That'll get his attention."

"Masterful," Jeffrey said, adding to his notes.

"Make sure you've got all your backup data at your fingertips before you go in to committee," Tommy said, pointing the paring knife like a saber. "Remember: if you find yourself in a fair fight, you've come unprepared. And just so you know who you're dealing with, if you confronted Geegan with the fact that 50 percent of the city's population is below the median income level, he would declare it an outrage and vow to change it."

✼

Jeffrey purchased one of Tommy's sandwiches to take to Cap, as he had promised, and went down to the basement to deliver it shortly before lunchtime.

Sitting behind his workbench, the maintenance man had just answered the telephone. His face was creased a bit more than usual as he listened intently to the caller's request.

While waiting for Cap to finish his call, Jeffrey leaned on the workbench and surveyed the array of tools on display. A wall rack held the full range of hammers, from a tack hammer small enough for a child's toy box to a hefty framing hammer that could put up a house or tear it down, depending on the manner of application. Screwdrivers hung in graduated sizes like the pipes of a church organ, along with bubble levels, a steel framing square, auger drills, files, rasps, and handsaws. The old-fashioned implements were an admirable testament to their owner's adherence to tried-and-true ideas as well as to the confidence that comes to a man working within his realm of expertise. In this workshop, there were no laser levels or electronic gauges, no complicated gadgets with fussy attachments—nothing more modern than a rechargeable hand drill.

At last, Cap told his caller, "Hold on. I think I got that on my computer." He laid down the phone receiver and swiveled in his chair. On the floor behind him was a brand-new desktop computer still in the box, which he apparently was using as a shelf. He picked up a metal box of index cards he had set there, flipped through the cards until he found the one he wanted, then turned back to the phone to relay the information requested. After hanging up, he looked at the sandwich Jeffrey had placed before him and said, "This ain't from that coffee shop across from the park."

"Terri's husband, Tommy, made that," Jeffrey said. "He's thinking about starting his own catering business." He watched Cap sink his teeth into the sandwich.

As the older man's jaws worked, his small, tired eyes slowly lit up with excitement. "This is one fantastic sandwich," he said and took another large bite to make sure.

"Do you want another one tomorrow?" Jeffrey asked.

"You bet I do," Cap said.

Jeffrey held out his hand. "Three bucks," he said.

"Make it two," Cap said.

Shaking his empty hand as a prompt for cash, Jeffrey insisted, "The price is three dollars."

"I mean, make it two sandwiches." Cap pulled six dollars from his wallet and handed them over. "Grab a chair," he said. "I found my plans for the gazebo. Thought we might make it a little bigger, give the bass drummer more swing room."

"Go ahead and change the plans however you want," Jeffrey told him. "I'm on my way to budget committee now to get you a part-time helper."

"My eye," Cap snarled.

Jeffrey nodded with certainty. "Say good-bye to your overtime, Cap, and let's build us a gazebo," he said.

As he headed out the door, he thought he had cut the intensity of Cap's glare by half.

%

It had been a perfect night for skinny-dipping. And despite what Cap might have surmised that August night in the park some twelve years ago, skinny-dipping was the extent of what had occurred between Jeffrey and the girl up to that point. In the hormonal frenzy of the moment, however, Jeffrey had been convinced that he was in love with her. As she had suggested the next course of action toward deepening their relationship, he had found himself at a perilous crossroads. Among the other impulses flashing in his thirteen-year-old brain were the warnings his parents had implanted there about the ethical behavior they expected of him, his responsibilities as a young man, and the dangers he faced from imprudent behavior: diseases rendered in clinical detail, the commitment he must make if a pregnancy resulted from his actions, even the possibility of a rape accusation from the girl's parents if she was a minor. Oh, they were masters, his parents, able to douse the most ardent romanticism with the cold water of reality. All through adolescence, he had sat through their lessons attentively but with an undercurrent of long-suffering impatience. While he respected his parents, it was clear to him that they had never been in love.

Their teachings were nearly lost in the moral amnesia of that August night as he and the girl emerged naked from the pond into the deepening twilight. With the darkness about to fall over them like a blanket, he tried hard to convince himself that the risks his parents had detailed didn't pertain to him, that it would be okay just this once. His effort failed. The lessons had been too firmly ingrained for him to ignore them now.

She knew a place they could go, but he knew that already he had gone too far. Apologetically, he told her he thought he had better get dressed and call his mother to come take him home, at which point the girl had grabbed his clothes and run away. The subsequent chase had been captured in Cap's spotlight and thus halted. Jeffrey's embarrassment was a small price to pay for being given the opportunity to end his misadventure.

He could have gotten away with it; his parents needn't have known. But after he got home, he told them both what he had done. His mother had cried a little with relief and pride, before grounding him for the rest of the summer. His father had shaken his hand and told him he was growing up to be a fine, upstanding young man; then he promptly made arrangements for Jeffrey to spend the remainder of the summer hauling canvas on the schooner.

It was just as well. Mr. Hennessey's band programs had been musically less than challenging. By putting to sea in the tourist trade, Jeffrey began making substantial money that went far toward financing the college education he wanted. His passion for the girl in the park cooled with surprising quickness. True love, he understood then, would have a more lasting effect on him. He buried his romantic impulses like a coal banked in ashes, conserving its heat until the time when he could take it out, rekindle it, and let the flame erupt brightly, boldly, unashamedly.

⁂

Approaching the conference room, Jeffrey faced the next woman to enter his life. She was ninety pounds of refined, pure tenacity wearing sensible high heels and a Chanel suit. Every gray hair of her pageboy lay obediently in place as she stalked the hallway outside the conference room. Sunlight flashed from the facets of her jewels.

He estimated that Mrs. Roosevelt was in her seventies. The supple, tender years of her youth had faded into dim memories, and now she was as gnarled, bristly, and unbreakable as a fibrous root. Already she seemed familiar to him; he had half a dozen great-aunts just like her. They all came to Maine from their homes in Connecticut and Manhattan to summer at their cottages in Christmas Cove or Boothbay Harbor, and to shop at L&L Bean, as they laughingly called it. These grand old ladies spent the long days of June, July, and August playing golf, tending their roses, or scouting the art galleries for an original Marin or Wyeth for the dining room. They wore discreet whiffs of expensive perfume and sometimes a dab of lipstick and face powder, but they also wore the medals of honor that came with advanced age: the network of lines, the sharpened bones, and the wry glint in their skin-draped eyes, all of which they had acquired over three-quarters of a century spent attending regattas and learning to drink good whiskey on the best balconies in Kennebunkport. They knew their way around a tennis club and belonged to at least one arts or historical society, but they also knew how to haggle with lobstermen at dockside for the best prices.

As Jeffrey approached, Mrs. Roosevelt's ice-blue eyes gleamed at the prospect of confrontation. "Who are you?" she demanded eagerly.

"Jeffrey Bowman, director of the Baxter community band," he replied, giving a slight bow.

Her mouth twisted into a smirk. "I suppose you're coming to the budget committee to plead for more money," she said.

"On the contrary," he said. "I want to propose receiving a bit less."

"Are you being impertinent with me?" she demanded, straightening up to her full fifty-eight inches of height.

"I am being completely honest with you, Mrs. Roosevelt," he said. "While I am grateful to be employed by the city, I prefer for my band to be funded by direct contributions from my audience and sponsors. The less money they have to pay the city in taxes, the more they'll have available for supporting my band."

Her expression remained skeptical, but she relieved him of further scrutiny as Darla unlocked the conference room door and invited her inside for coffee and pastry.

Expecting Terri to come along soon, Jeffrey lingered in the hallway and thus presented a physical barrier to an approaching throng of budget committee members just arriving. Roughly they elbowed and shouldered their way past him to get into the conference room.

One man gruffly said to him, "This is a private meeting for department managers only."

"I am a department manager," Jeffrey asserted.

"Oh! In that case, come in," the man said. "I thought you were just somebody off the street."

"Somebody off the street who pays your salary?" Jeffrey blustered, but the public servant didn't hear him, as he had hurried into the room before all the best pastries were gone. Deciding that Terri must not be coming, Jeffrey went in too.

The conference room was decorated in administrative-department fashion, with plush carpet, recessed lighting, and tasteful artwork on the glossy white walls. The ceilings, which he estimated at eighteen to twenty feet, easily accommodated an enormous arched window framing a gray, wintry sky. Dominating the center of the room was a massive, round mahogany table comprised of pie wedges forming a sunburst. Shiny as glass, it was utterly empty, holding not even a floral centerpiece or a pencil. Meeting attendees sitting around the circumference held their croissants on plates in their laps, eating with one hand and holding their coffee with the other. Darla had placed the meeting agendas and other printed matter on narrow tables along the walls.

"It is forbidden to put your coffee cup, or any earthly thing, on the Round Table," said a voice at Jeffrey's elbow.

He looked down and saw Mrs. Roosevelt standing beside him.

"That," she said with a nod toward the table, "is a revered altar. Although it appears to be a table, it does not serve that function. Rather, it is a symbol of the city's philosophy that appearances are more important than actual utility."

"Thank you for the information," he said.

"The standard meeting format is as follows," she continued. "Darla prepares a lengthy agenda, which attendees glance at just prior to the meeting. Then our imperious leader rushes in to present us with the crisis of the day. The agenda is shelved while this most recent fire is fanned for a while, for the sheer pleasure of generating heat and distracting attention from other matters. Maybe a sinkhole appears in a main thoroughfare, or code violations are discovered at the newly constructed firehouse. Responsible parties will be conveniently unavailable. Committee members will waffle and whine, then someone will propose a task force or study group to give the appearance of concerned action. In case you're wondering why they don't just fix the problem, they always need to study it first; these things are complicated, you see. Their ultimate response will be to create a new subcommittee or review board to stand guard over the problem and watch it die from neglect."

Jeffrey said, "I'm beginning to think my band is a tiny speck on the city's windshield."

"It is," Mrs. Roosevelt said with an arched eyebrow, "if you're lucky."

Darla came up to Jeffrey, looked at his empty hands, and demanded, "Where's your Friday report?"

"What's a Friday report?" he asked.

In complete seriousness, she said, "It's a report that is due on Friday."

Jeffrey stammered, "I'll go back to my office and get one."

"There's no time for that now," she snapped. "The meeting starts in five minutes." She continued to glare at him, demanding a better response.

After a torturous moment of mental groping, he said, "Maybe Terri will bring it to me. Is there a phone in here I can use?"

Darla directed him to a beige wall phone with an accompanying panel of instructions.

He began reading the elaborate procedures for dialing in-state, out-of-state, and international calls. With growing dismay, he murmured, "I just want to call my office," and then realized that he didn't know his office telephone number. Looking around and failing to spot a phone directory, he suddenly remembered that he had loaned Tommy his cell phone that morning. *Tommy would know Terri's office number,* he thought with certainty. He lifted the receiver of the wall phone. The buttons were small and narrow, like almond slivers. Squinting to read the numbers, he pressed them carefully as he dialed the number of his cell phone. Failing to hear a connection, he tried dialing 9 first. Still no luck. "How do I get an outside line?" he asked the man closest to him.

"Dial 21-day," the man responded.

"Day?" Jeffrey repeated in confusion. "D-A-Y?"

"No, the day of the week," the man explained. "It's a security code. Changes every day."

"How is that secure if everyone knows the code?" Jeffrey asked in exasperation.

"It's to prevent anyone but city employees from making a call," the man said.

"What citizen in his right mind would come in here to make a phone call?" Jeffrey muttered. He required further assistance to help him understand that the day of the week was represented not alphabetically but numerically, and that Friday was not the sixth day, as he had always thought, but the fifth, as the city's workweek began on Monday. With his head aching, Jeffrey dialed 215, achieved a dial tone, and successfully connected with his cell phone.

"Hello?" Tommy said.

"Tommy, it's Jeff," Jeffrey cried exultantly.

Tommy waited a few seconds and finally asked, "What do you want?"

It took a moment for Jeffrey to remember. "I need my Friday report," he said.

"Where did you leave it?" Tommy asked. "I don't see it anywhere."

"I need Terri to prepare it for me," Jeffrey explained, perceiving from Darla's steady glare that the meeting was about to start at any moment. "What's her office telephone number?"

"Aren't you at work now?" Tommy asked, confused.

"Yes, but I'm not in the office," Jeffrey said in hurried desperation, "I'm in the fifth circle of hell, and there's no phone directory here."

There was no time to obtain the report, Darla sternly informed him; Mr. Geegan was on his way.

Dejected, Jeffrey hung up the phone and found an empty chair at the Round Table, where already the other department managers were conferring together with grim faces, their low voices trembling with the weight of their discussions. He sat back in his chair, being careful not to touch the polished mahogany disc and hoping that no one would ask to see his Friday report. As he studied each of the twelve other people at the table, he tried to imagine the important functions they held, what large operating budgets they controlled, and the massive responsibilities they took home with them at the end of the workday. How did they sleep at night, he wondered, knowing that thousands of citizens relied on them every day for services ranging from garbage removal to disaster preparedness? How could these public servants be sure they were putting the taxpayers' money to its best use? When they made decisions, did they pause to consider how they were affecting real people, people with families to support and businesses to run, elderly couples trying to get by on their retirement incomes, unemployed men desperate to regain their sense of worth and ability? Where did a person study to become a public servant? Where was their training ground?

"We've got to disintermediate that process before we begin to consider moving forward," one man was saying to another. "I'll get our outgrowth regional director to connect with our goals planner and start generating some feedback options."

The other man nodded, not only in comprehension, but also in agreement. "That's the quadrant I'm in now too," he said.

Jeffrey's gaze drifted to the arched window. As he watched a clump of wet snow slide down the windowpane, he took a moment to reflect on his own personal collection of worries that huddled at the back of his mind. These ranged from his fear of being charged with embezzlement to his lack of money for his legal defense and then to the warm beacon of a potential job in San Diego, a prospect which seemed to offer his best chance for restoring his musical career. And yet at the forefront of his concerns was the Baxter Band, at this point still a disjointed and vague assembly. Sitting in this room full of municipal magnates, Jeffrey felt insignificant, his concerns laughably small. All he wanted was a couple of pieces of new music, someone to carry the band equipment, and a bit of lumber to rebuild the gazebo, yet he needed the committee's approval for all of it. Idly, he cleared his throat.

All conversation around the table stopped. Twelve pairs of troubled eyes shifted expectantly in his direction.

He felt like a child interrupting the grown-ups, but now that he had their attention, he seized upon it. "Good morning," he said, mentally groping for something to say next. "I'm Jeffrey Bowden, director of the Baxter Band."

The attendees began leafing through their agendas, looking to see how this topic of discussion had escaped their attention.

"As you might know," Jeffrey said tentatively but with growing confidence, "Ben Hennessey has retired and the city has hired me to ensure that the band continues its long history of providing the people of our city with live music." Everyone appeared to be listening, so he kept talking. "Traditionally the band concerts have been held in the municipal park, although the gazebo there is badly deteriorated. I plan to recruit volunteer labor to tear down the old structure and build a new one in time for the band's opening concert on Memorial Day, but I need this committee to approve the cost of building materials. Additionally," he said, really getting into his quadrant now, "the band's equipment manager, Cap Ordway, is busy taking care of the athletics program. He's already working a significant amount of overtime and can't handle any more. Cap is sixty-five years old. I'm concerned that by our asking him to work beyond his capacity, he's likely to have a work-related injury, which would be a great expense for the city. I propose hiring a part-time maintenance man at the starting pay rate to relieve Cap of his overtime."

"New hires? In this economy?" cried a man seated to Jeffrey's right. The man's eyebrows arched above his horn-rimmed glasses like leaping gazelles.

From across the table, Mrs. Roosevelt said, "Mr. Bowden, I would be interested in knowing exactly how much the city pays Mr. Ordway for his overtime. Could you obtain that figure for us?"

"Certainly," Jeffrey said and reached into his shirt pocket for an index card. Reading from it, he quoted the amount for her.

Not yet sufficiently impressed, she queried, "And what would a newly-hired part-time worker cost, comparatively, including both salary and benefits?"

He flipped the card over and read her the information.

The faces around the table grew thoughtful, although several people continued shaking their heads.

"New hires are absolutely out of the question," muttered the man next to Mrs. Roosevelt. "Mr. Geegan himself said so."

"The bottom line is a cost savings to the city," Mrs. Roosevelt said to him. "You can't argue against that."

This appeared to sway the committee's opinion in Jeffrey's favor.

Addressing the group, Mrs. Roosevelt said, "I move that we recruit a part-time worker to absorb Mr. Ordway's overtime work." Casting her steely gaze around the table, she concluded, "Unless anyone here thinks we should continue paying premium wages for work that could be done much more cheaply by an entry-level person?"

No one appeared ready to challenge her. Someone seconded the motion, and a show of hands indicated unanimous approval.

"Thank you," Jeffrey said, giving a nod toward the gray-haired lady. "Now, what do you say about the materials for rebuilding the gazebo?"

"How much do you need?" someone asked.

"Enough to buy some lumber, nails, and paint; perhaps two hundred dollars," Jeffrey said. "Purchased from the local hardware store, of course, to keep the money in the community."

The man to his left leaned over and murmured, "You can get it cheaper from across the border in New Hampshire. No sales tax there."

Discussion ensued, but in the end too many heads were shaking no. Rebuilding the gazebo would require a different source of financing, Jeffrey realized. Still, he was batting 0.500, which was not bad for a rookie.

At that point, Arthur Geegan rushed in. "Table the agenda, Darla," he blurted. "We have a crisis to deal with."

"Protocol, Mr. Geegan," Darla murmured as a reminder.

"Yes, of course," Geegan hurriedly responded. "Whatever business has been discussed up to now, deem it so," he said. He then went on to inform the committee of the new concern that had just come to his attention.

From across the polished plain of mahogany, Mrs. Roosevelt caught Jeffrey's eye and gave him an arthritic thumbs-up.

CHAPTER 16

Terri looked up from her computer as Jeffrey came into the office. "How did it go at the budget committee?" she asked eagerly.

"Mixed results," he said, sitting down in the folding chair. "We got our equipment manager, thanks to Mrs. Roosevelt. But the committee balked at paying for the gazebo reconstruction. We'll have to scrounge up two hundred bucks from somewhere else." He sipped from the paper cup of coffee he had brought from the meeting.

"Why don't you ask Mrs. Roosevelt for the money?" Violet suggested. "She probably carries that much cash around in that Gucci handbag of hers."

"Did you see that new car she's riding around in?" Randie added. "It's bigger than the one she had before. What a show-off, buying a new car every year and hiring someone to drive it for her."

"I get the impression that Mrs. Roosevelt isn't very well liked," Jeffrey said. *Except perhaps by handbag salesmen, a certain car dealer, and one dedicated chauffer,* he thought, smiling behind his coffee cup.

"She's always prowling around the Money Building and giving them a hard time over in administration," Randie said. "She votes against every new program the city tries to put in place, and she's always complaining about taxes. You'd think it was coming out of her own pocket."

Jeffrey thought it was time his officemates learned Economics 101 and was just about to offer a short introduction when Terri said to him, "Jeff, Mrs. Roosevelt might be the answer to our problem. She's one of the wealthiest people in town. She's known for giving money to lots of charities, and she might be willing to pay for the new gazebo."

Shaking his head, Jeffrey said, "I don't want to ask her."

"But all we need is two hundred dollars," Terri argued. "I'm sure she can afford it. She hires lots of people to work for her—cooks, maids, a chauffeur. She even has her own private tailor. Anybody with that kind of money can afford to pay for a measly little gazebo."

"No," he said firmly. "In situations like this, wealthy people are the first ones to get hit up for contributions."

"They're the ones with all the money," Terri said, as if this should have been obvious.

"They're also the ones who get a constant stream of requests from every charity in the book," he said. "People like Mrs. Roosevelt are already supporting a substantial part of this city's economy through the taxes they pay and the people they employ. They're also expected to donate generously to hospitals and universities and the arts. There is no end to the number of hands extended in their direction."

"But if someone is lucky enough to have that kind of money, they should be expected to hand over some of it," Terri maintained.

"And they do," Jeffrey said, "to the extent that some of us take for granted all the things those people pay for, things as basic as this building we all work in, your desks and computers, even your pencils and paperclips. But the main reason I don't want to ask Mrs. Roosevelt is that I don't want only rich people supporting this band. Rich people support the symphony, and generally they're the only ones who get to attend symphony concerts. A community band plays for everyone, even the homeless people hanging around in the park. It should be supported by everyone who thinks it is a worthwhile activity. Almost everyone can afford to drop a couple of dollars, or even a dime, into our collection plate."

Giving a puzzled frown, Terri asked, "Do you mean it's a kind of charity?"

"Yes," he acknowledged, "in the sense that whatever money we get is given voluntarily and not taken forcibly through the tax system. We could put together a fund drive right now and let people begin showing how much they want this band."

"That means it's only going to survive if people support it," she said somewhat fearfully.

"It also means that the people who do support it will feel a sense of ownership and perhaps be motivated to stay involved," he pointed out. "Charity benefits the giver as well as the recipient. It feels good to give away some of your hard-earned money."

"Not if you don't have a lot," Randie interjected. "Then it hurts."

"I agree, it hurts sometimes, too," Jeffrey said, "but that just shows how much you value the thing you're supporting. Instead of having someone like Mrs. Roosevelt write us a big check, I would be far more grateful to receive a few dollars from lots of people, those who truly want to support what we're doing." He drained his coffee cup and set it down, saying definitively, "No, Mrs. Roosevelt is off the hook for this one."

Just then, Darla came in with a delivery of interoffice mail.

"Mm-hmm, mm-hmm," Randie said into her phone receiver. "Okay, I'll get that right over to you."

To Jeffrey's surprise, Darla walked over to him and handed him an envelope with his name on it. "Nice performance at budget committee," she murmured.

"Thanks," he replied, then watched her stab her high heels across the carpet and out the door. Miss Diamond's attitude appeared to have come down a notch or two on the Mohs scale, he thought, maybe as far as garnet. The envelope she had given him was marked, "Hand Delivery." He worked it open and examined the contents.

Across the room, Randie and Violet had begun sorting through the office mail, searching for uniquely formed paper clips and tossing aside the mail itself to deal with later. "Here's an overlapping spiral," Violet murmured with delight.

Randie studied the object and declared it a structural marvel. "That'll look great in your collection, Vi," she said.

Jeffrey had been staring at his mail in silence. At last, Terri's curiosity got the better of her. "What is it, Jeff?" she asked.

He suddenly stood up and put on his windbreaker. "Terri, may I borrow your car?" he asked.

"Of course," she said, reaching for her purse. "Where are you going?"

"To see Mrs. Roosevelt," he said with a conflicted frown, "and return this personal check she just sent me."

※

Mrs. Roosevelt's street address had been printed on the check, making it easy for Jeffrey to locate her residence. The neighborhood contained Baxter's oldest and stateliest mansions dating from the era when multiple generations lived together, often with a large staff of hired help.

The house was just what he expected: immense and immaculate, an imposing brick structure surrounded by a substantial wrought-iron fence. He parked alongside the curb and approached the gate, which he found to be unlocked. Seeing no warnings of patrolling guard dogs, he proceeded up to the house.

It was a long walk, one that gave him time to reflect on the number of people employed by the owners of such houses as this. Beneath that cloak of snow, he was sure, lay a vast lawn and gardens requiring skilled maintenance. If there was a swimming pool in back, that would be another small industry. A window-washer could work here nearly in perpetuity, given the multitude of glass panes reflecting the sky. In addition to the cooks, maids, chauffer, and tailor already noted by Terri, there would be bookkeepers, financial advisors, and estate lawyers. Far from hoarding her wealth, Mrs. Roosevelt was putting money into the pockets of countless individuals, feeding and clothing their families, financing their children's educations. *Why are such people criticized as privileged elites,* Jeffrey wondered, *when they should be lauded for helping in such a large way to sustain their local economies?*

A uniformed maid showed Jeffrey into a spacious hallway. He waited while the maid walked toward an arched doorway leading into a room at the end of the hall, where he saw two seated figures silhouetted before a blazing fireplace. Judging by the coldness of the hallway where he stood, the house was being minimally heated.

Mrs. Roosevelt came out wearing a handcrafted shawl over her Chanel suit. She greeted him pleasantly, then said, "Good heavens! Is that all the coat you wore? Come join us by the fire."

He followed her to the end of the hall and into the sitting room, which was only slightly warmer than the hallway and sparsely furnished. He doubted that they held yard sales in this neighborhood, but it was easy for him to imagine that a fair amount of the furniture had been sold off, with the extra money really coming in handy.

The maid had set out a chair for him. The other person seated before the fireplace was a much older woman in a wheelchair. She took no notice of his arrival. A glimpse at her face revealed the placid expression of minimal awareness. Her shrunken body was shrouded in a cocoon of blankets and knitted shawls, and a metal tray attached to the wheelchair held a plate of soft foods.

"Please excuse me for intruding," Jeffrey said in a low voice to Mrs. Roosevelt. "I won't keep you long."

"That's all right," Mrs. Roosevelt assured him. "I've done all I can with her. Sarah, why don't you take over? She won't eat for me."

Sarah the maid repositioned the wheelchair, turning it slightly away from the visitor, and began coaxing the old woman to eat.

"My mother," Mrs. Roosevelt confided to Jeffrey as they settled into their chairs.

He smiled in understanding, having seen many of his older relatives cared for in their homes. "It's good you have staff to help you with her," he said.

"Indeed," she agreed. "The convalescent homes are so crowded these days. You can't buy a room, even with private money. In previous summers, I've taken her down to our cottage in Damariscotta. That's south of here, on the coast," she explained.

"I know where it is," he said with a nod. "I'm from Cold Harbor." He held his hands toward the fire, savoring its warmth, and saw that the fireplace had been modernized. Its masonry inserts efficiently directed the heat into the room while still offering the cheerful, crackling flames of the open firebox. While inadequate for heating the entire room, it offered a cozy warmth for those seated before the hearth.

"You know, then, the restorative nature of the Maine coast in the warmer months," Mrs. Roosevelt said. She paused to watch the maid's meager progress with the balky invalid, then continued, "But travel is becoming increasingly hard on Mother. If we can't get down to 'Scottie this year, we might spend the summer in town. I think she would be just as happy staying here, and it would give my staff more work to do. I want to keep them employed as long as I can. Some of them have been with me for decades." She fell silent, mulling over some private, nagging worry.

Not wanting to further impose upon her, Jeffrey said, "I'll get to the point of my coming here today." He reached into his shirt pocket for her check and handed it to her. "I'm sorry," he said, "but I can't accept this kind of money from you."

Without a word, she took the check, crumpled it, and tossed it into the fire. A sheepish smile crept upon her face. "I suspected you wouldn't, but I had to try," she said.

"Please don't think I'm ungrateful," he hastened to add. "Believe me, your offer was very tempting. A generous benefactor like you could solve all of the Baxter Band's financial problems. But it is a community band, after all, and I think its support should come from the community at large, through small, private donations."

Another staffer emerged from the kitchen with a tea service and set it before them.

"You'll join me for lunch, I hope?" Mrs. Roosevelt asked her guest.

"You're very kind to ask me," Jeffrey said as he started to rise, "but I don't want to inconvenience you."

"It's no inconvenience at all," she assured him and laid her hand on his arm. "Please stay. You've gone through the trouble of coming here, and I confess I've been wanting to chat with you."

He couldn't think of a better place to linger on a cold February afternoon. With gracious thanks, he settled back onto his chair. There in the comfort of the fire, Jeffrey and Mrs. Roosevelt drank tea and ate small sandwiches and other finger foods that were easy to consume without utensils or fuss.

Studying his teacup, Jeffrey said, "This stoneware is from a ceramics shop in Georgetown, Maine, isn't it?"

"Yes. I like the potters who work there," Mrs. Roosevelt said. "I try to patronize local artisans whenever I see good-quality work. My accountant says I overdo it, but I think it is the duty of someone in my income bracket. Poor people can't support such industries."

He watched her delicately nibbling her sandwich, a dowager rabbit. Risking impertinence, he said teasingly, "I'll bet you over-tip waiters."

"If the service is good," she admitted. "Waitresses, especially. So often they are the sole providers for their families." She pressed a linen napkin to her mouth and then asked, "How did you guess? About my tipping practices, I mean?"

"My mother is the same way," he said fondly. "I never saw anyone get so much satisfaction from rewarding an attentive waiter or giving some artist a good sales day."

"I'm not surprised to learn that your family has money," Mrs. Roosevelt said, watching the fire. "People don't live in Cold Harbor unless they can afford the property taxes." Her gaze crept toward him again, and she said in muted wonder, "And here you are, trying to scrape up two hundred dollars to build a gazebo in the municipal park."

With quiet firmness, he said, "I respect my parents too much to ask them to bail me out of my financial difficulties, and they respect me too much to offer to do so."

She nodded in understanding and contained her admiration behind a stern countenance. "I want to clarify that by giving you that check, I wasn't trying to buy your band," she said stiffly. "As you might have guessed, my own sources of income have dwindled along with everyone else's. I've looked around for good places to invest what money I have left, and right now I think the Baxter Band is worthy of my support, however much of it you will accept. Mr. Bowden, you appear to have a good understanding of the importance of that band, an understanding which, frankly, your predecessor lacked. I learned that you yourself are a musician. Did you ever play for Ben's band?"

"Only briefly," Jeffrey said and quickly steered the conversation toward safer waters, lest she begin recounting an amusing incident involving the duck pond, Cap Ordway, and two naughty young people. "Mrs. Roosevelt," he said, "please understand that by returning your check, I don't mean to discourage you from supporting the community band. I welcome contributions from everyone. If you find yourself in town this summer, I would be honored for you to attend some of our concerts. We'll have some arrangement for collecting donations there."

"I suppose you'll program the same pieces that the band played under Ben's direction?" she asked with a noticeable lack of enthusiasm.

"We have an established music library to draw upon," he told her, although this was stretching the truth a bit, considering the paltry contents of the cardboard box beneath Terri's desk. "However, I am looking into ways to expand our repertoire. What did you think about the concerts Ben offered?"

She hesitated before answering. Finally, she grimaced and said, "Ben seemed to think the band was getting to be old-fashioned, and he started having them play more modern songs, ones the young people would know. I suspect Arthur Geegan was behind that change, as he seems to have his fingers in every pie. I have to tell you, the new music didn't go over very well. We old folks missed hearing the pieces we were familiar with, and the young people didn't want to hear their pop music played by clarinets and tubas and such things, especially in a school auditorium."

Having finished his tea, Jeffrey placed his empty cup and saucer on the serving tray. "Like you," he said, "I am in favor of the band playing music that is in keeping with its tradition. I also feel strongly that the band concerts should be given in an outdoor setting again. I'm determined to have that gazebo rebuilt in time for the opening concert on Memorial Day."

While the maid took away their empty dishes, Mrs. Roosevelt sat in contemplation and then suddenly appeared to have made a decision. Turning to Jeffrey, she said, "Before you go, Mr. Bowden, I have something else to offer you. It's in the front hall, on your way out."

She walked out with him and opened the door to a coat closet. Pointing to an old-fashioned leather book satchel on the floor, she said, "That's it, there. Perhaps you'd lift it out for me."

He picked up the satchel, which was surprisingly heavy, and set it on the narrow table she indicated. At her direction, he unbuckled the leather straps and opened the flap. The satchel was stuffed with sheaves of stiff, heavyweight papers that turned out to be handwritten music scores.

"You'll want to examine them more closely at your leisure," she said, "but essentially what you have there are the unpublished manuscripts of band music written by my great-grandfather shortly after the Civil War."

Carefully, Jeffrey began leafing through them, and soon he found his attention being torn between listening to her narration and reading the yellowed documents in his fingers.

"As a music scholar," she said, "you will have learned how these community bands got started in New England. The Baxter Band's original mission was to lead the Maine infantry into battle during the Civil War. Some of the enlisted men were musicians, and the ones who survived the war came home and formed brass bands that played in the town square for civic functions as well as for the people's entertainment. My great-grandfather was among those lucky survivors. He spent his later years writing music for the Baxter Band. Some of his pieces were published, but many, such as those you have there, were set aside and forgotten. Eventually they were passed on to his daughter—my grandmother—and she in turn gave them to me."

After reading the composer's signature on the music, Jeffrey looked at Mrs. Roosevelt with amazement. "Your great-grandfather was R. B. Harte, the cornetist and composer?" he asked.

"I'm surprised you know of him," she said. "He doesn't get so much as a single line in most music encyclopedias."

"He's in the more comprehensive ones," Jeffrey said. "Sousa himself performed one of Harte's compositions in Paris around the turn of the century. Did Ben Hennessey know about these scores?"

Her expression hardened as she said, "Ben wasn't trustworthy, in my estimation. When I broached the subject with him, I immediately saw that he wouldn't value those compositions the way you apparently do. Ben thought the military history of the Baxter Band was outdated, irrelevant, even embarrassing. I also was afraid he would let Arthur Geegan talk him into handing those manuscripts over to the city."

Jeffrey failed to see why the city would have any use for such historic documents, but he said simply, "Well, I am honored that you would show these to me," and then closed the satchel, intending to return it to the closet.

She stopped him, saying, "I want you to take those with you and read through them. See if your band can use any of that music in your programs this summer. I also want to clarify that I am giving those manuscripts to you personally, Mr. Bowden, and not to the city. Most emphatically not."

Stunned by her gesture, he stared at her while struggling to come up with an adequate response. "These are unpublished scores," he said at last. "They're irreplaceable. Are you sure you want me to have them?"

Her gaze was unwavering as she said, "Mr. Bowden, in the short time I have known you, you have earned my confidence. There's an integrity beneath your surface, built into your bones. It isn't a matter of you coming from a similar station in life as I do. I like and trust you, Mr. Bowden, not because you come from a wealthy family on the coast, but because you come from a wealthy family on the coast and are living and working here in Baxter, trying to make things right again." With a gesture toward the satchel, she said, "I think those documents are safest in your hands."

"More so than in the state museum?" he asked.

She rejected that option with a definitive shake of her head. "That music doesn't belong in a museum," she said. "It should be played by the band it was written for. The Baxter Band is on the brink of fading into obscurity. If these compositions are not performed under your direction this summer, I fear they will never be heard."

She motioned for him to take the satchel, which he did, and then she shooed him toward the door. Seeing her lowered gaze, he guessed that her emotions were getting the better of her.

He stood in the doorway with the satchel clutched securely under his arm and said, "Mrs. Roosevelt, this gift of yours is more valuable than that check you tossed into your fireplace. You are one of the most generous people I have ever known."

She had recovered her composure as well as her crusty veneer. With a scowl, she said gruffly, "Well, for heaven's sake, don't tell anyone."

※

When Jeffrey returned to the office, he set the leather satchel in front of Terri and said, "If you own a pair of kid gloves, now is the time to put them on." He hurriedly cleared the worktable and began emptying the case of its precious contents.

"These are original conductor's scores," he told her, handling each yellowed page with its due reverence, "unpublished and irreplaceable."

Seeing the dates, she gasped and said, "These are a hundred and fifty years old!"

"And yet look how legible they are," he pointed out as he continued to lay out one handwritten gem after another. "Thanks to someone's thoughtful care, they are very well preserved. Mrs. Roosevelt's great-grandfather, R. B. Harte, wrote these pieces. They are literally priceless, and yet she's entrusting them to us so they can be performed by the Baxter Band."

"I never heard of R. B. Harte," Violet said. Curiosity had drawn her and Randie over for a look. "Who is he?"

"He's been described as the John Philip Sousa of Maine," Jeffrey said, "yet he's largely unknown outside the tiny world of band music." By now, the worktable was covered with compositions along with a sprinkling of tiny brown shards that had crumbled from the brittle pages. Surveying the wealth of new material, he said in awe, "There's enough music here to fill the band's programs for the whole summer. Look at this cornet solo," he blurted, holding up an ornately annotated page. "That will sound fabulous in an open-air concert!"

"Careful!" Terri spread her hands to catch the shower of confetti drifting down from the paper's ragged edges. Confounded, she cried, "How can we possibly use these? They'll fall apart if you handle them much more."

He studied the manuscripts for a thoughtful moment, then said, "They need to be copied, maybe even by hand, note by note, the way they were written."

Randie spoke up tentatively. "My kid brother has a computer program for writing music," she said. "He enters the notes on his keyboard and prints everything out, with the staff lines and everything."

"That sounds promising," Jeffrey said to her. "I'm not very good at typing, though. Would your brother be willing to transcribe one of these pieces for me?"

The chubby redhead had turned suddenly shy. "I could do it," she stammered uncertainly.

Shaking his head, he said, "Randie, this is a big project, and I'm sure you have plenty to keep you busy all day. Mr. Geegan won't be happy if your own work goes neglected because of me."

Her cheeks turned as red as her hair. "No," she said softly, "I mean, I'll do it at home after work. On my own time. You know, as a volunteer."

Violet gave a small gasp of surprise.

For a moment, Randie herself appeared shocked by her offer, but as she stood trembling before the astonished stares of her officemates, her hesitancy tiptoed into the realm of conviction. "I could do that," she said with growing surety. Then she licked her lips and asserted, "Sure, I'll do it as a volunteer. Why not? I mean, if Jeff will trust me with one of those, I could take it home with me tonight and give it a try. It sounds like a fun challenge, to tell you the truth. If you like the way it comes out, I'll go through the whole shebang for you, one at a time."

"You would do that for me?" he asked in amazement.

With an emerging grin, she said, "Hey, you guys are having way too much fun with this band thing. You've got to let the rest of us get involved, too. Do you know how boring it is to sit around every day, holding down a desk and watching the clock until it's time to go home? It might be fun to do some real work for a change."

Jeffrey selected one of the pieces for Randie's experiment, then he explained that he would need an individual part printed for each instrument in the band. All during their conversation, Violet had looked on wistfully as though wanting to do something too. Jeffrey had been thinking of asking the queen of crosswords to help Terri with the band's advertising when it came time for their first concert, but his cell phone rang just then. Seeing K's phone number on the display, he excused himself and stepped into the hallway to answer the call.

"Update from the islands," K said. "Remember, no names."

"Right," Jeffrey said. "Is it still bad there?"

"Yes and no," K said. "The intended lawsuit against you is falling apart. I have inside information on that. It doesn't look like you'll be wearing the striped pajamas after all."

Leaning against the wall, Jeffrey closed his eyes and breathed a long, relieved sigh. "That is fantastic news," he said. "You are my hero."

"Thanks," K said, "you're my BLT. But this is not as fantastic as you might be thinking. In fact, you're in more danger now than before."

The office door opened as Violet and Randie left for the day. In the crook of her chubby arm, Randie cradled a sturdy brown envelope which no doubt contained the trial manuscript for her computer transcription project. Jeffrey returned their waves of farewell and then whispered worriedly into the phone, "Why is it more dangerous for me now?"

"Your boss is very frustrated with our legal system," K said. "He was counting on nailing you for your lady friend's crime, seeing as how he can't find the lady herself. But even the best lawyers he can buy are telling him he has no case. So he has taken the matter into his own little Mickey Mouse hands."

Jeffrey groaned. "I don't like the sounds of this," he said, covering his eyes with his free hand.

K continued, "If you can possibly lie any lower than you currently are, I suggest that you do so. No utility bills, no new credit cards, no charge accounts at the Apple Store, nothing that could be used to trace your location. Seriously, don't even think of filing a change of address with the post office. In case you haven't already figured it out, I've been handling your personal mail here. Your mother sends her love. Uncle Lou is in the hospital, but they think they got all the kidney stones."

Jeffrey managed a weak smile. "I'm relieved to hear that," he said.

"Also, your credit card statement arrived," K said. "You sure racked up the airfare getting there. Is your new boss reimbursing you?"

"Have you seen any flying pigs lately?" Jeffrey asked rhetorically.

"That's what I thought," K said. "Well, don't worry, I paid the bill for you."

"Thank you," Jeffrey said. "I'll repay you as soon as I can."

K said, "Forget it. I'll take it out of the proceeds when I sell the Benz. You've got serious problems to worry about. Some local thugs I know are getting job offers and instructions to buy parkas. They don't know what they are, either, but they're willing to find out. These are bad men with guns and baseball bats."

Jeffrey was stunned into silence for a long moment. At last, he asked incredulously, "Are you saying he means to kill me over this?"

"Oh no," K reassured him, "at least, not at first. More likely he wants you to bleed, internally and out, for a long, long time. After that, he'll probably kill you." When Jeffrey began to protest his innocence, K interrupted him, saying, "You don't seem to understand how thoroughly this man has been ruined. It's not just the trust-fund money that's gone. The whole project is washing out to sea. You might recall that quite a few people had their fingers in this pie, very powerful people who now have had their multimillion-dollar feelings hurt."

"Why aren't they going after the missing lady?" Jeffrey demanded with sudden anger. "She's the one with the money!"

"They probably are," K said. "I'm sure they have enough bullets for both of you."

After shutting off his phone, Jeffrey leaned against the wall while building up a good, healthy case of paranoia. He tried to think whether anyone else besides K might know his whereabouts. Professor Wilmot, bless his balding head, had unwittingly deterred Andrew from looking for Jeffrey in Baxter. By what other means might he be traced? Was his air travel itinerary discoverable somehow? By using his cell phone, was he betraying his geographic location?

His head was pounding, and he thought he might be coming down with a cold. What he needed was a dose of warm weather, the kind they probably were having in San Diego at this very moment. Gloomily, he slipped his phone into its case and headed back into the office.

Terri was just getting her coat on when he came in. Seeing his face, she said, "Hey, sad sack. Look what we got." She pointed at the edge of her desk.

At first, Jeffrey saw only the coffee cup that he had brought out of the budget committee that morning, but upon closer inspection, he noticed that the words "Gazebo Fund" had been written on the side in black marker. "Oh," he said, "good idea, asking for donations."

"Look inside," she urged.

He did and saw two lovely portraits of Andrew Jackson held together with an overlapping spiral paper clip.

CHAPTER 17

The threat of being attacked by Andrew Quigley's hired thugs weighed like an anvil on Jeffrey's mind. As Terri drove them home from work, he sat rigidly in the passenger seat and stared worriedly at the dirty snowbank into which he feared he might have to throw up at any moment. K's phone call had spawned a thriving hatch of anxieties, and now they all were having a party in his stomach.

Terri noticed his gloomy attitude. Assuming that his primary concern was the same as hers, she said, "Don't worry, Jeff. Everything will be ready for the band's first rehearsal. The only thing I have left to do is to find a tuba player."

With a concentrated effort, he pulled himself out of his morose self-obsession and scratched through his memory. At last, he said, "Try calling Bob Cherry. He played tuba with the band for years and years."

"I did call him," she said, "but he said he was still too sick to play. You see, he didn't play all last year. It sounds like he's doing poorly."

Jeffrey looked at her in surprise and said, "Bob? Sick? That doesn't sound like him. I rented a room from him all during college, and he was absolutely robust. When I left for Hawaii, he was still renewing his hobby magazines five years at a time."

"That's the funny thing about life," she said. "It's full of quirky little surprises like unexpected illness. Since you know him, why don't you borrow the car tonight and go visit him? He'd probably like to see you."

Jeffrey wasn't so sure. Bob hadn't been very happy with him for accepting the job offer from Andrew Quigley. Coming back a year later to report the catastrophic failure of that venture was hardly the basis for a pleasant reunion.

He looked out the side window again and resumed brooding over his potentially imminent assault. The streets had grown shadowy in the twilight. Every pedestrian appeared to watch Terri's VW as it passed, and every car reflected in the side mirror seemed intent on following them. Furtively, Jeffrey pressed down the lock button on his door.

"Did you just lock your door?" Terri asked.

"You should always lock your doors," he argued defensively. "Crime can happen in any town." He turned up the collar of his windbreaker and slouched a little in his seat, wondering if he should dye his hair or grow a beard as a disguise. Then he realized how little those actions would help when there was no way to disguise his height, except perhaps to chop off the lower half of his legs. His murderous pursuers might very well do that for him, he realized with a shudder.

He had a poor appetite at dinner and excused himself for it by saying he thought he was coming down with a cold. If only Ray Greenleaf would call, he thought; that would solve all his troubles. No one would trace him to a chamber ensemble in San Diego.

Later that evening, the members of Tommy's neighborhood support group began arriving for a meeting. The formerly empty living room quickly filled up with folding chairs, card tables, and lively conversation. Tommy was building a customer base for his homemade sandwiches, with the hope of starting a small-scale catering service. Other members of the group were pooling their individual talents and resources to remedy certain deficiencies in the city. Most of the plans were still in the early stages, but already the group's activities were having a noticeable effect on its members. Most were retired gentlemen, although a few were still of working age, like Tommy, and had lost their jobs. All appeared to relish the social nature of the gathering and the atmosphere of free expression. Shortly, the room resounded with impassioned declarations.

"Just because the government offers a program, you don't automatically have to take it. Remember, somebody else is paying for it."

"Every time we ask the city to fix our problems, they have to raise taxes. We're killing the few businesses we have left in this city. Then, everybody suffers."

"Who needs another bureaucrat? Let's just figure out a way to do this ourselves!"

The high-spirited atmosphere temporarily diverted Jeffrey's mind from his worries. He was amused and heartened to see these grizzled citizens hobbling around and talking together with such communal purpose.

A sudden pounding on the door, however, startled him into his prior state of anxiety. Instantly, his imagination was gripped by a nightmarish image of armed, vicious thugs bursting through the doorway and terrorizing these gentle souls, looking for the tall, blond guy. The caller, however, was only another neighbor arriving to participate in Tommy's event.

Weary of being in constant fear, Jeffrey told Terri that he had decided to visit Bob, as she had suggested. "I'll call a taxi," he offered.

"Don't be ridiculous," she said, pulling her keys from her purse. "We're happy for you to borrow the car. You're practically part of the family."

Tommy happened to be within earshot and came over

to give Jeffrey's shoulders a fatherly hug. "Going out, Jeff?" he teased. "Got a date and need to borrow the car?"

Accepting the keys from Terri, Jeffrey mustered his best smile and thanked the couple before heading for the door.

"Don't forget curfew, son," Tommy called. He and Terri shared a hearty laugh.

Jeffrey sat in the darkness of the car's interior and listened to the babble of happy voices resonating from inside the house. The softness of the sound, muted by distance, seemed to illustrate how far removed he himself was from the condition of being happy. Not only had he come back to the miserable city he had sought to escape, but also he now had a target on his back. However blameless he might be, it appeared that he was destined to pay the price for the demise of Quigley's dream. Nervously, he locked the car doors before backing down the driveway.

The light was on in the workshop at Bob's house. After parking at the curb, Jeffrey sat in the car for a while, looking at the steeply pitched roof and the craggy old maple tree in the front yard. Their familiar, enduring outlines stirred fond memories of his residence there, and for a moment, he was tempted to inquire whether his old room was available for rent. Immediately he dismissed this possibility. He already had taken too many steps backward. He hadn't thought of his college years as being particularly happy ones at the time, but now they seemed vastly preferable compared with what he was currently experiencing. He hated to think he was missing the high points in his life by not paying attention. Was nostalgia coloring his memories or clarifying them?

A shadow moving along the sidewalk suddenly caught his attention. In the dim streetlight, he discerned the figure of a man in a hat and trench coat walking slowly toward the car. Although partially hidden by the snowbank along the curb, the man obviously held his right hand clenched at his side, as if gripping a gun.

With fumbling fingers, Jeffrey tried to reinsert the car key into the ignition, readying himself to flee. At that instant, the man stopped, as though waiting for his prey to make the first move.

Jeffrey remained still and continued to watch, all the while calculating the best course of action. Should a hail of bullets come through the windshield, he might improve his chances of survival by cowering inside the car rather than trying to drive away.

The man took a few more steps forward, then paused again. At last, he came to a cleared area in front of the car. His right hand jerked a little, urging along a Chihuahua on a leash. The dog had been lifting its tiny leg every few feet along the snowbank.

Feeling enormously foolish, Jeffrey let out the breath he had been holding. It was absurd for him to be suspicious of every stranger and to be jumping at shadows, like a character in a murder mystery film. His would-be assassins probably hadn't even gotten their black hoods on yet.

He walked up to Bob's door and knocked several times until at last it opened a crack. Bob peeked out and in a thin, soft voice, he said, "Why, Jeffrey! Hello! Sorry, I was taking a nap. Won't you come in?"

"A nap?" Jeffrey repeated in surprise. "Bob, I've never known you to take naps." He stepped through the doorway and was alarmed by his former landlord's apparent deterioration. Once dynamic and robust, Bob now appeared fragile and fearful. He stood hunched over, as though trying to hide from some unseen foe. In one short year, he had lost a significant amount of weight. His skin was pale, and his white hair was an untidy feathery cap. Instead of his usual wool shirt and rugged trousers, he now wore the easy-on wardrobe of an invalid. His loosely fitting ny-lon track suit was embroidered with the logo of InfinitiCare, a health-care company that Jeffrey vaguely remembered being discussed at the budget committee.

Additionally disturbing was Jeffrey's discovery that the older man's workshop had been transformed into an in-home hospital room. The workbench and tools had been cleared out and replaced with a cushioned recliner surrounded by an ar-ray of medical equipment. Along the wall stood several large metal cabinets with illuminated dials and flashing buttons, all of them beeping and humming with mysterious importance.

In a voice that was nearly a whisper, Bob invited his vis-itor to sit down. He gestured to a molded plastic chair whose cushioned backrest bore the InfinitiCare logo. Meanwhile, Bob ensconced himself in the recliner and elevated the footrest. His standard lug-soled footwear had been replaced by hospi-tal-style slippers with nonslip nubs on the bottom.

Before Bob could ask what brought him back to town, Jeffrey explained, "Things didn't work out in Hawaii quite the way I expected. I came back to Maine to direct the Baxter Band this summer." He watched in puzzled fascination while Bob strapped on a Velcro wristband, tethering himself via a jumble of colored wires to a machine that looked like a small refriger-ator standing next to the recliner.

While driving over, Jeffrey had prepared himself for a dose of ridicule and smug assertions of, "I told you so." But Bob was preoccupied with what appeared to be his new hobby. The re-frigerator-like machine beeped and spit out a strip of paper from the side into a wire collection basket. Bob reached over, looked at the paper, and noted something on a small notepad.

Baffled by the change, Jeffrey said with concern, "Terri told me you've been sick, Bob. What happened?"

"Oh, I've had a terrible time," Bob declared, "starting last spring. I thought I was having indigestion, but my doctor said he heard a pitter-patter in my ticker." He tapped the left side of his chest to remind Jeffrey where this particular organ resided.

"Isn't your ticker supposed to go pitter-patter?" Jeffrey asked.

"This was something out of the ordinary," Bob explained. His face was gray with worry at the recollection. "Everybody seemed very concerned about it. They put me on medication. Then InfinitiCare showed up and set me up with these monitors, just to keep track of things. They're a great outfit," he added reassuringly. "They sought me out. I didn't even need a note from my doctor. Their representative came right to my door and enrolled me in a nifty home-care program. I've got my oxygen machine, cardiac monitor, medication dispenser, the whole setup. The nurse comes in faithfully once a week to see how I'm doing."

Jeffrey couldn't believe that only a year ago this man was fearlessly climbing ladders, cooking multicourse meals, and building ingenious puzzles from scraps of wood. "So did they determine that you had a heart attack?" he asked.

"Not yet, thank God," Bob said, "but I could have one anytime now. That's why we're keeping track of it. Got a little EKG device running here. See the printout?" He tapped the wire basket that held an ever-accumulating length of tape. "I keep a logbook of all the readings. Blood pressure, oxygen levels too. There's all kinds of things that can go wrong." He rested his hands on his lap and tapped his fingers together nervously.

"That must keep you pretty busy," Jeffrey said.

"It sure does," Bob affirmed and fell into a gloomy silence.

"It must be reassuring to have all those InfinitiCare people taking care of you," Jeffrey said. "Do you think it's helping?"

"Oh, definitely," Bob said. From a nearby table he picked up a handful of colorful brochures, all of them bearing the

InfinitiCare logo. "They've been teaching me all about my various illnesses. Every time my nurse comes around to check on me, she finds something else to monitor. See, they want to catch things early, before they become a problem. My nurse says I might be at risk for developing a potentially incipient condition. We have to be on the lookout for that."

Jeffrey nodded with growing comprehension. He looked around the room and asked, "Where's your tuba?"

Bob appeared stymied by the question, as though he had forgotten he had ever played the instrument. "Oh," he said at last, "after I got sick, I realized I couldn't play anymore, so I put it away. It's around here somewhere."

They both fell silent for a while. The machines stood about the room with imposing authority, dutifully beeping and humming.

"The truth is," Bob admitted, "I don't want to play it anymore, Jeffrey. I'm afraid it might be too stressful. My nurse seems so concerned about me, I think I'd better just take it easy from here on out." He folded his hands in his lap and looked down at them like a reprimanded child trying to be good.

Looking at the sleek, smooth-running machines with their authoritative logos and imposing buttons and dials, Jeffrey thought that something almost criminal had occurred here. He suddenly stood up and declared, "Bob Cherry, I can't believe what has happened to you. This organization is supposed to be helping you, but they've bullied you into becoming an invalid."

Bob stared up at him in mute surprise.

"I'd like to pull the plug on each one of these machines and push them out the door," Jeffrey declared. "No doubt you have medical problems, but your nurses shouldn't forget that you're also very capable and independent, or at least you used to be. I can't believe you're going to give up doing the things you love to do just because you're afraid to take risks."

"That's easy for you to say," Bob shot back. "You're a young man with your whole life ahead of you. How much longer have I got? Another four years? Two? Six months?"

Considering the threat he faced from Andrew Quigley, Jeffrey wasn't sure whether he himself would have that long. "None of us gets a guarantee," he started to say.

"I'm talking about averages," Bob interrupted. "You know that you've got many more years ahead of you than I do, statistically speaking. So don't go lecturing me about being brave when the Grim Reaper is hanging around my doorstep but doesn't even know you're in town."

Jeffrey fell silent. His opinion hadn't changed, but he wondered just how sick Bob really was. On one hand, the complicated machinery and intensive medical regime suggested a serious condition. On the other hand, when Jeffrey looked at his former landlord's eyes, he thought he saw the old, blustering Bob still in there, trying to get out. "Bob," Jeffrey said in a gentle, coaxing voice, "just think how many times you carried that tuba across the park to the gazebo. You never worried about having a heart attack then. All you thought about was how to play that solo at the opening of the Holst Suite and whether you had packed your valve oil in your case. Bob, I want you to play with the Baxter Band again. We need you, and I think you need us."

Bob looked down at his hands again and remained stubbornly silent.

"I won't ask you to do anything you shouldn't," Jeffrey said, "but I'd sure like to see you playing that tuba again. Would you want to try?"

For a brief moment, the thought appeared to take hold in Bob's imagination. Then he began to fidget as if uncomfortable with the notion. "I don't know, Jeffrey. I'll have to ask my nurse," he mumbled.

As Jeffrey prepared to leave, he said to his old friend, "Whatever you decide about the band, take care of yourself, Bob."

"I'm in good hands," the old man assured him. "InfinitiCare is a caring organization."

But just whom do they care about? Jeffrey wondered.

CHAPTER 18

Driving home, Jeffrey was a little ashamed of himself for his earlier fearfulness. The pep talk he had directed at Bob could have been just as applicable to himself. It might be years before his would-be attackers found him. And in the meantime, Andrew himself could succumb to illness or, perhaps, be distracted by a new, younger version of Helen and forget all about his grudge against his former music director. If Jeffrey was going to live every day in fear of an attack, then he might as well notify Andrew of his whereabouts, confront him, and get it over with.

His homeward route took him past the municipal park. Instinctively, slowed down for a look. The streetlight illuminated the gazebo enough for Jeffrey to catch a glimpse of a shadowy figure moving around the side of the structure.

Curiosity instantly morphed into suspicion and then turned into anger. He wheeled into the parking lot and skidded to a stop alongside a small, unfamiliar pickup already parked there. He caught sight of the figure again as it came out from behind the gazebo and into the beam of the car's headlights. As Jeffrey watched, a stoop-shouldered man wearing a fisherman's cap hobbled forward, shading his eyes against the glare. Jeffrey rolled down the window and yelled, "Cap?"

"What?" the maintenance man demanded.

Jeffrey shut off the engine and got out of the VW. "What are you doing here this time of night?" he asked in exasperation.

"Had to set up for a basketball game couple hours ago," Cap said. "Figured I'd kill some time here before I go back and take everything down again."

"All this overtime will be the death of you," Jeffrey muttered. Shoving his hands into the pockets of his windbreaker, he walked over to stand beside Cap, who had a large tape measure clipped to his belt and was making some calculations on a pocket-sized notepad. For a while, Jeffrey looked up at the gazebo, but its vile appearance caused him to look away again. For him, the destruction effort couldn't start soon enough.

There was little traffic this time of night. From within the nearby houses came the muted clamor of television, the invention that had helped bring about the demise of the community band. Every one of those houses had an attic, which in Jeffrey's imagination contained old trumpets, clarinets, and other instruments that were just waiting to be dusted off and played again. Yet he knew that behind the curtained windows, the occupants gathered around the TV or fiddled with their computers, oblivious to the world outside their front doors. He wondered whether there was still a place in this town for a community band when the community itself had changed so much. "How's the search for a part-timer coming?" he asked when Cap had put away his notepad.

The maintenance man gave a cynical laugh. "Nobody wants a part-time job," he said. "It would mean giving up their unemployment check."

"Did Geegan advertise?" Jeffrey asked.

"Yeah, I guess," Cap said. "Nobody's applied, though. I'm all done here. You up for coffee?"

Jeffrey said that he was, and the two men drove their vehicles across the street to the coffee shop.

Cap was in a talkative, congenial mood. Upon learning that the restaurant was out of rat cheese, he shrugged and ordered ice cream with his pie. While digging into it, he told Jeffrey, "During Hennessey's time, the band didn't draw near the crowd it used to. Thirty, forty years ago, I remember that band played all over town for just about every outdoor function you can imagine. Any new business always had a grand opening with the band playing out front in the street, flags flying, red-white-and-blue bunting everywhere. Ladies' Aux would set up tables loaded with all kinds of homemade things." He paused with his fork in the air while his eyes focused on a decades-old memory. "Raisin pie," he murmured, his gravelly croon verging on lust, "with real cream." His concave chest heaved a regretful sigh as he reached for his tepid coffee.

Jeffrey knew the era Cap was talking about, although not from personal experience. He had seen it in photographs in the Music Library at the college, preserved and on its way to being forgotten.

"Politicians used to give speeches from a scaffold or on the back of a flatbed," Cap continued. "Everybody came out to listen. People actually knew who their representatives were. Today, everything is sound bites and websites." He drank some coffee, grimaced, and continued, "You heard the TVs inside those houses across the street. There's a reason Hennessey retired, you know. That band is dying. It may already be dead. Go ahead, rebuild your gazebo, but you'll be playing music for the squirrels. None of the people around here want to go to a band concert in the park."

"Let's not think that far ahead," Jeffrey said. "Right now, the gazebo is my main concern." He reached for his wallet, but Cap said that he would pay this time around.

As they walked out to their respective vehicles, Cap gestured across the street to the neighborhood bordering the park.

"See that?" he said. "There's your audience, inside those houses, behind those closed doors. Everybody's in front of the TV or on the compooper playing video games. You'll never get those people to come out to a band concert. Most of 'em have forgotten all about the park being there. You could run naked through that park and no one would notice."

Upon hearing this, Jeffrey whipped around in surprise, but the maintenance man had stepped down off the curb and began moving toward his truck. It was unclear whether or not the statement had been meant as a provocative ribbing.

Jeffrey heard laughter just then, coming from a distance. It floated across the street from the park, coming from the direction of the gazebo. Cap heard it, too. The two men stood still for a moment, looking and listening some more.

Across the street, three figures huddled near the gazebo, engaged in some shadowy enterprise. The streetlight caught a metallic flash, and a moment later came the recognizable clatter of a spray can being shaken.

Cap broke into a stiff-legged run across the street, moving with astonishing speed. Jeffrey hurried after him, not wanting to be shown up by a gimpy old man. He was game for a fight as long as there was no cutlery involved.

As they neared the gazebo, Cap bellowed, "Hold it right there, Bud!"

Two of the figures melted into the darkness, but the third, the biggest, stayed behind. A slick-headed, tattooed hulk in a zippered warm-up jacket, he was too clumsy and slow-witted to get away. He stood with his soft baby face screwed into a pout. In the streetlight, his ears glittered with studded metal piercings.

Cap went directly up to the thug and batted the paint can from his hand. Then he reached up and swatted the side of the boy's head, just enough to get his attention. "Pretty nice friends you got, running off on you like that," Cap said. "How'd you get permission to stay out past your curfew?"

"Ma's working late," the boy mumbled.

"So when she gets home tonight after working a double shift, she'll have to go out again and pick you up at the police station," Cap said. "Is that what you wanted?"

"I was just trying to have some fun," the boy whined in protest.

"Well, was it fun?" Cap demanded.

"No," the boy admitted. He had lost his tough-guy attitude and now just appeared tired. He sniffed and wiped his nose on his sleeve. "Will you give me a ride home, Grampa?"

Cap bent down to pick up the paint can. In a weary voice, he replied, "Don't I always, Bud?"

The three of them walked back across the street to the diner, the boy shuffling along in his youthful swagger a little ahead of the two adults. Cap explained to Jeffrey, "My youngest daughter's boy. He's a case. Sixteen years old, been through day care, Head Start, peer mentoring, special ed. Now he's in juvie detention, him and his whole gang. Sometimes I think they act up just for the attention."

Jeffrey imagined the hefty kid tearing down an old gazebo, maybe hauling lumber and roofing materials, and spreading paint on some newly erected posts.

"I got the okay from Geegan to tear down that old gazebo," Cap said as they reached their respective vehicles. "Figure I'll start on it tomorrow after work. Did you find me any volunteers yet?"

"I'm finding them one by one," Jeffrey assured him. He had found one volunteer so far, that one being himself. He had a second one in mind too, but the young man didn't know it yet.

※

The next day, Jeffrey stopped by the administrative department and asked Darla how he might find the probation officer assigned to a particular youth who was a frequent troublemaker in the city.

"Has the boy given you problems?" she asked, giving a slight frown. "Are you reporting him?"

"No," Jeffrey said, "I want to try helping him."

She regarded him in surprise for a moment and then wrote down the name and phone number of someone at the police department who could direct him to the juvenile corrections division. "Good luck," she murmured in a warmish voice as she handed him the slip of paper. She didn't exactly smile, but it appeared to Jeffrey that Miss Diamond was getting positively chalky around the edges.

Darla's referral helped Jeffrey find a probation officer named Vince Ferrier. He was a beefy, crew-cut little guy with an easy, confident manner. His smile resided so comfortably on his face that Jeffrey imagined Vince letting it stay there even while he verbally pummeled the insolence out of the toughest of juveniles.

Jeffrey told Vince about the gazebo-rebuilding project and said that he had a particular youth in mind who might benefit from the activity. "I don't have much information to help you identify him," he admitted. "He's a big sixteen-year-old, shaved head and tattoos, lots of ear metal, and he goes by the name of Bud. His grandfather is Cap Ordway, the maintenance man for the city."

Vince grinned and raised his square jaw, revealing a neck between his head and blocky shoulders. "I know who you mean," he said. "Bud's a frequent flier around here. Gazebo rebuilding is about the only thing we haven't tried with him. I guess it couldn't hurt, as long as he's supervised."

"I'm sure his grandpa will keep close tabs on him," Jeffrey said, "and there will be other adults there, too. We'll keep him too busy to get into mischief."

"Raising the bar might be good for Bud," Vince said. "He's been supervised so closely and for so long that he's never really had a chance to find out what he's capable of. You understand that you can't pay him, right? The city has laws against minors working for pay."

Jeffrey hadn't known that fact. As he contemplated it, a memory from his college days emerged. Some of his customers had been overjoyed to learn that he was willing to do a job they couldn't get younger kids to do. It was no wonder he had cornered the market on shoveling snow. The reasoning behind such an ordinance was something to puzzle out another time. "We won't be paying Bud or anybody," he assured Vince. "It's strictly a volunteer effort."

"When are you starting the project?" Vince asked.

"This afternoon," Jeffrey said. "Cap will probably be there right after work. I'm going to pick up some food first so I can feed the crew."

"I'll let Bud know about it and bring him to the park myself," Vince said. "If you can use another pair of hands, I might hang around. I'm glad the city is finally doing something about that gazebo. It's been an eyesore for too long."

Jeffrey told him he would be more than welcome to help out.

"You're not getting your food from that diner across the street, are you?" Vince asked, almost losing his smile.

"No," Jeffrey quickly assured him, "this will be high-quality stuff."

"In that case, I'll definitely stick around," Vince said.

※

Jeffrey had placed an order with Tommy earlier that day. When he and Terri got home from work, he found that Tommy had the sandwiches wrapped and bagged.

"A dozen at three bucks each, right?" Jeffrey asked. He gave Tommy a pair of twenties and told him to apply the excess toward his next purchase. "No doubt I'll be feeding the work crew again," he explained.

Tommy took the money reluctantly, saying, "Jeff, you don't have to pay me every time. You're practically a family member."

"You're not getting your raw materials for free," Jeffrey pointed out. He headed out with his purchase before Tommy became inspired to refund his money.

A noticeable amount of progress had already been made by the time he arrived at the park. The bed of the City of Baxter pickup held several trash receptacles containing broken shingles, ragged strips of roofing paper, and warped plywood from the gazebo's rotting roof. Bud was walking the perimeter of the work area, holding a big magnet on a string, picking up loose roofing nails, and trying hard not to let on that he was having fun. Cap had given him a heavy leather tool belt to wear. The garment seemed to affect his swagger. By the end of the evening, Jeffrey thought the boy was starting to develop a gimpy leg like his grandpa.

The early shift was ready for dinner, so they immediately broke for a tailgate party in the back of Terri's VW, which Jeffrey had driven there. The sandwiches were a great success. Vince took down Tommy's phone number, saying his wife would probably enjoy a break from cooking dinner once in a while.

Jeffrey swung a hammer most of the evening, knocking loose anything that had been nailed together and tossing the lumber into a pile, which Bud hauled one armful at a time to the truck. Toward the end of the work session, Cap came up to Jeffrey and said, "Bud thought that since his probation

officer brought him here, this must be some kind of punishment detail. He asked me what you had done to deserve being
here, too."

Jeffrey grinned. "What did you tell him?" he asked as he
knelt down to knock loose some railing.

"I told him you axe-murdered boys who defaced public
property," Cap said.

"You should have told him I chased naked girls through the
park," Jeffrey said.

Cap broke into a cackle, but he quickly caught himself.
After reestablishing his usual dour demeanor, he said seriously,
"Your father came to see me after that incident. Tracked me all
the way to the basement in the Money Building. Said he wanted
to thank me for stepping in and putting a stop to it before you
got hooked into doing something you regretted."

Jeffrey looked up in surprise. "I never knew he did that,"
he said.

"He told me you had gone right home that night and told
him and your mother about it," Cap said.

"Yeah," Jeffrey admitted. "I was never good at keeping se-
crets from my parents. Guilt always showed up on me like
chicken pox. It was easier just to confess whatever I did wrong,
take my medicine, and get it over with." He laid the hammer
down and rubbed his aching shoulder.

"That's what your pop told me," Cap said. "I've got to
tell you, that changed my mind about you. Most boys would
have thanked their lucky stars that they got away with it and
would've hid it from their parents, maybe thinking they had
earned themselves another roll of the dice with Lady Luck."

"What I earned for myself," Jeffrey said, "was a full-time
summer job at sea, with lots of adult supervision."

"I noticed you didn't play with Hennessey's band any more
after that," Cap said.

Jeffrey nodded. "That was the idea, to keep me busy and away from trouble."

They both watched Bud gathering up shards of splintered wood and dropping them into a pail for disposal. The young man had been a cooperative and useful worker all evening.

In a low voice, Cap said with sincerity, "It's good for that boy to be around men who can show him how to behave, men who can stand as examples for him to copy. Decent men." His eyes flickered toward Jeffrey for an instant. Then he began loading his arms with the lumber that had been loosened. While safely diverted by the activity, he said, "You turned out all right, Jeffrey."

When Cap had stood up again, Jeffrey laid his hand on the other man's shoulder and said, "Even though I'm about a dozen years too late, I think I should thank you, too. You showed up just in time to keep me from going any further."

The older man said with conviction, "That was all the further you were going, and you know it. I just gave you a way out of that situation without losing face. That little dollop of nature you were chasing, she was famous for leading boys into trouble. I caught her playing her tricks plenty of times."

Jeffrey's mouth fell open. "She told me I was the first one!" he cried.

"That's what she told all of you boys," Cap said disgustedly and headed for the truck to discard the old lumber.

CHAPTER 19

All the arrangements were in place for the band's first rehearsal, just as Terri had promised. "But we still have to find a tuba player," she reminded Jeffrey as they followed the security guard in through the back door of the high school auditorium.

The school's band equipment was stored in a closet behind the stage. The guard escorted them there and then left to finish his patrol. Until a part-timer could be found to handle the job, Terri and Jeffrey had appointed themselves as volunteer equipment managers. The two of them transported the assorted drums, cymbals, and other percussion instruments into the rehearsal area, then began setting up chairs and music stands in the traditional horseshoe configuration on the auditorium stage. Until Randie finished her transcription project, the band's rehearsal material would be drawn from a few classics from the Ben Hennessey era.

The first player to arrive was a lanky, balding man about forty years old who sported a dirty-blond goatee. He came in without seeming to notice there was anyone else in the room, then flopped down in the first chair of the trumpet section as though it had his name on it. After taking out his horn, a flashy, silver-plated model from a prestigious manufacturer, he flipped disinterestedly through the folder of music on his stand, then crossed his arms, stretched out his long legs, and waggled his feet impatiently.

Jeffrey went over to break the ice. "Hi," he said, "I'm Jeffrey Bowden. I'll be rehearsing you guys tonight."

"How'ya doin'," the other man said flatly. "Steve."

Jeffrey thanked him for coming and then asked, "Is this your first time playing with the Baxter Band?"

"Yeah," Steve drawled. "Normally I play jazz, but I had some time to kill, so I thought I'd help you guys out."

With a similar lack of enthusiasm, Jeffrey said, "Great." So far, he was unimpressed and wasn't looking forward to dealing with the trumpeter's inflatable ego. Curious to see just how much PSI he could achieve, he asked innocently, "Do you play professionally with an orchestra?"

Steve gave a quick shake of his head as if ridding himself of a pesky fly. "I freelance with a bunch of different groups," he said. "You know, anybody who needs a good front man. Mostly what I'm doing right now is private lessons." He smacked his lips, whipped his trumpet into position, and began warming up by rippling through a series of scales.

Jeffrey took the opportunity to move along to the clarinet section and speak to a couple of new arrivals there.

A sudden clatter drew everyone's attention to the doorway, where someone's instrument case had fallen open, strewing a small horn and its accessories onto the floor. The owner of the case was a large woman who bent over and completely blocked the doorway as she began retrieving the items one by one. Behind her, impatience showed on the faces of the people who were waiting to get through the doorway. At last, the red-faced woman stood up and approached the trumpet section with her eyes shyly downcast. She appeared to be in her early twenties. Her lumpy body was covered with so many layers of loose pull-over sweaters that she looked like a walking sack of potatoes.

The only available seat in the trumpet section was next to Steve, who now was breezing through the "Carnival of Venice" variations, showcasing his speed, style, and proficiency in extended circular breathing. The woman hesitated, then timidly lowered herself onto the chair.

Steve suspended his warm-up routine in deference to his new section mate. "Got enough room?" he asked her with a cruel smirk.

She gave a quick nod and buried her attention in the depths of her instrument case. Her lank hair partially curtained her face, but Jeffrey could see her eyes darting about fearfully as if she were expecting an ambush any time now. With fumbling motions she fitted a mouthpiece into a silver cornet lightly scarred with the patina of age.

"Boy, that's an oldie," Steve said derisively. "I didn't think anybody played those anymore. What is that, a pawn shop special?"

She cleared her throat as if to speak, but she lost her nerve and merely shook her head. Her chalky face grew mottled with embarrassment, and her small eyes blinked repeatedly as if holding back tears.

As the musicians began warming up with their instruments, the room filled with a cacophony of tootles, tweets, blats, and bovine-like lowing. Jeffrey noted it was almost time to start rehearsal. Still, half the chairs were empty. A few old-timers looked to the empty tuba section in the back row and lamented Bob's continued absence.

"Looks like this is it," Jeffrey said and started rehearsal.

Having four players in the trumpet section, he wanted to rank them by ability by listening as they took turns playing a passage from the music. "Steve, you first," Jeffrey said.

Steve played faultlessly through the exercise, then lowered his horn and resumed waggling his feet, appearing as nonchalant as if he had merely sneezed.

"Second chair?" Jeffrey asked as he looked at the large woman with the cornet. "What's your name, miss?"

She worked her mouth for a moment as if the muscles had frozen up from disuse. Finally, while looking at the floor, she whispered, "Fern."

"Okay, Fern," Jeffrey said, "let's hear you play it."

He gave her the downbeat, and she sputtered through the notes with haste, as though wanting to get her turn over with and move on to the next player.

Steve rolled his eyes at the pathetic result.

Jeffrey went on to test the remaining players. Fern clearly was the weakest, but he left her where she was for now. Maybe she would improve with practice, he thought hopefully.

Throughout rehearsal, Terri sat off to one side of the musicians, smiling and tapping her feet in clear enjoyment. Overall, Jeffrey was discouraged by the paltry attendance and the rustiness of the players. Nevertheless, at the end of the session he thanked them graciously and announced the details of the next rehearsal.

As the players began getting up to leave, he saw Fern hurrying for the door and asked her to wait. When she appeared not to hear him, he stepped after her, calling, "Fern, I'd like to talk to you for a moment."

She kept going.

He struggled to pass through the crowd of people who were clogging the doorway. By the time he got outside, Fern was bolting through the parking lot toward a small economy car. He sprinted after her and caught up to her just as she yanked open the door. "Fern," he barked angrily, "I said I want to talk to you."

"There's no need," she said, nearly in tears. "I'm quitting." She flung her instrument case into the front seat and got behind the wheel.

"All you need is a little instruction on your technique," he insisted, grabbing the door to keep it open. A light snow was falling, blowing into the car and onto her lap. "I'm willing—"

She cut him off, saying, "I'm sorry, Mr. Bowden, I've got to go. I'll call you tomorrow," and tried shutting her door. "Let go," she said, "the snow's getting in." He removed his hand from the door, and she slammed it shut. The car's engine roared to life.

If she got away now, Jeffrey knew he would never see her again. Swiftly, he walked around to the passenger's side, taking a chance that the door was unlocked. It was. He opened it and jumped inside the car.

Startled, Fern shrieked at him, "What do you think you're doing, getting into my car?"

In order to fit inside the little vehicle, he was forced to twist his spine into a slight corkscrew, like half a strand of DNA, with his head, eyebrows first, toward her. "We can talk here, or we can go someplace public," he said. "A coffee shop or wherever you want. But I am not letting you quit so easily."

Over the idling engine, he could hear her labored breathing. It was a bellows of misery, almost a sobbing. From within her plump face, her small eyes seemed to be those of a prisoner looking out from within a padded suit.

He raised his hands in a gesture of harmlessness. More softly, he said, "Don't worry, I'm completely trustworthy. I can even give you references." He was shivering from the cold. In his haste to catch her, he had run out without his windbreaker, but he wasn't going back for it now.

Fern had calmed down and now blinked the tears from her eyes. "My car's heater isn't working," she said. "We'd better go someplace." She shifted the car into gear and backed out of the parking space.

Her instrument case had fallen onto the floorboard by Jeffrey's feet. He picked it up and held it in his lap. "The only place I know of is the diner across from the park," he said.

She drove there. In the headlights, the powdery snow looked like white veils wafting over the road.

At the restaurant, Fern and Jeffrey settled into a booth against the back wall of the dining room. He felt as though he should apologize for bringing her to a place where the food was so rotten. "The pie isn't bad," he admitted.

"I can't have pie," she said. "It's not on my diet."

They settled for coffee. He drank his black with sugar, and she doctored hers with a packet of something she carried in her purse. He noticed the packet was printed with the InfinitiCare logo, the same one he had seen on the medical equipment and brochures in Bob's living room.

The air temperature inside the restaurant suggested that the people running the diner were trying to save money on their heating bill. Jeffrey wrapped his hands around his coffee cup to absorb its warmth. He was too cold to waste time on small talk, so he got right to the point, saying, "First rehearsal is always a little rough. It takes a few weeks for everyone to get back into condition again. I don't want you to quit, not before I've had a chance to work with you."

"Wednesdays aren't good for me," she mumbled, looking down at her coffee.

"It was good for you tonight," he pointed out.

"Tonight was an exception," she said.

"Make another exception next week," he said.

"Then it wouldn't be an exception." She gave him a challenging look.

It was his serve. He said, "Tell me what night is better for you. I'll change the rehearsal schedule."

Skeptically, she said, "You wouldn't do that just for me."

Over the brim of his coffee cup, he said defiantly, "Try me." He took a drink, grimaced, and went back to using the coffee as a hand warmer. "What night, Fern?" he pressed her.

"You don't need me. You have Steve," she said.

"I don't want Steve; I want you," he said. "What night, Fern?"

"I'm not sure," she murmured. "I'm busy with a lot of things right now."

Clearly that avenue was blocked, so he tried another. He was determined to crack her shell. "Where did you get that cornet?" he asked. "I never thought I'd be lucky enough to direct a band with a cornet in it."

"It belonged to my uncle," she said. "He left it to me when he died, a few years ago. Recently, I decided to take it up again." Looking at Jeffrey in his thin shirt, she asked suddenly, "Aren't you cold?"

"Yes," he admitted. His coffee had grown that way, too. He gave a pathetic laugh, feeling foolish.

"You ran after me without even putting your coat on," she said.

"I really don't want you to quit band," he said with sincerity. "Please, just give it one more week."

She blinked her tiny eyes as she considered his request. In a near whisper, she said, "I don't know. At first, it seemed like a good idea to play my uncle's horn in a band, but now I'm not so sure."

"All you need is some instruction and more practice," he assured her. "You were already sounding better by the end of tonight's rehearsal. I know I can help you, and I want to. Won't you give me a chance?" He was shivering, so the last word came out as a stuttered, "ch-ch-chance," causing them both to laugh.

"We had better get you someplace warm," she said.

He paid for their coffee and gratefully accepted her offer of a ride.

She had an emergency blanket in the trunk of her car and gave it to him to wear while she drove him home. On the way, they talked about things other than band. He asked her if she knew of any inexpensive apartments for rent, or a boarding-house where he might find a room.

"I just need a place for the summer," he explained. "I'm try-ing to line up a job in San Diego."

"That sounds nice," she said. "Actually, any place other than Baxter sounds nice." She didn't know of any places for rent at the moment, but she promised to let him know if she learned of any.

As they pulled up to the curb in front of the Turcotts' house, Jeffrey saw that his hosts had left the downstairs light on for him.

"Do you live with your parents?" she asked curiously.

For expediency, he simply told her that he did. It was pretty close to the truth, he realized, considering that he had essen-tially moved in as a member of Tommy and Terri's household. Before getting out of the car, Jeffrey said, "Fern, I'm sorry I scared you by jumping into your car. That isn't something I'm in the habit of doing."

She nodded and said easily, "It's okay. I wasn't scared, just surprised. I didn't expect you to care that much if I quit band. You've got a whole section of trumpet players."

"I don't like to see people fall short of their potential," he admitted, "and you must know that technically you're playing in the cornet section. Of all those players, you're the only one genuinely qualified to play there, by virtue of your instrument. By the time our first concert comes around, I'd like to see you instead of Steve playing first chair."

Her disbelief was beyond words. All she could muster was a hopeless sigh and a rolling of her tiny eyes.

"You're out of practice, no doubt about it," he went on, "but there's something special about your playing style. Did you learn to play in public school?"

She shook her head and said, "My uncle taught me. He played in the Army Band."

"That's it," Jeffrey blurted excitedly. "I knew it had to be something like that. You would have gotten some excellent in-struction. Mediocre people don't play in the Army Band." In an instant, he could envision what she might achieve during the intervening days before their next rehearsal. "There are a couple of technical things about cornets that I wonder if you know about," he said and picked up her instrument case. With his fingers on the latch, he asked her, "May I?"

"Sure," she said and shut off the car's engine.

She had parked under a streetlight, which conveniently illuminated the front seat of the car. Jeffrey opened the case and took out her horn, a charming little shepherd's-crook model. Handling the old instrument with due respect, he showed her a few exercises she could use during her practice sessions at home. After a few minutes of instruction and demonstration, he passed the horn to her so she could try the technique. After several attempts and repeatedly passing the cornet back and forth, she began to catch on.

"Listen to yourself," he said encouragingly after a while, "you're already sounding much better." She still had far to go, but there was no doubt her playing had vastly improved. "Between now and next Wednesday," he said, "I want you to make a commitment to practicing for an hour every night."

"Every night?" She had to think for a moment. "I'll have to juggle some other things around, but I guess I can manage it."

"A full hour," he pressed her. "No cheating. Will you do that?" Upon receiving her promise, he added, "If you can get to the school a bit early next week, I'll work with you some more before rehearsal." He realized he could be pushing the limits of his surrogate mother's patience, but he was pretty sure that Terri wouldn't mind going in an hour early.

He unwrapped himself from the blanket and returned it to the trunk of Fern's car. She then offered to pick him up next week, saying, "It's the least I can do if you're willing to tutor me."

He accepted the offer with sincere gratitude. To him, the gesture was more than just a convenience to him; it was assurance of her staying in band, at least for another week.

Jeffrey was relieved to find the front door unlocked. The hour was late, and he hadn't wanted to waken anyone so as to let him in. He stepped into the empty living room and quietly shut the door behind him. Turning, he saw Terri and Tommy sitting at the kitchen table. Both were looking at him with big smiles on their faces.

"What's her name?" Tommy asked. "Does she come from a good family?"

"I hope you behaved like a gentleman the whole night," Terri said.

Jeffrey held back a laugh, nodding in understanding of their little game. "It's not what you're thinking," he assured them. "She's just a band member."

"You run after a girl on a cold night without your windbreaker," Terri said incredulously, "you're gone for two and a half hours, and she's just a band member?"

"What was in the bottle?" Tommy asked.

Confused at first, Jeffrey quickly realized what Tommy had seen, no doubt glinting in the streetlight. "Oh, that was her cornet," he explained. "I was showing her some exercises she could do for next week."

"Oh," Tommy said and gave his wife a knowing look. "We should have used that excuse when your folks caught us sharing that jar of dandelion wine."

Doing her best to keep a straight face, Terri asked, "Was she under the blanket, too?"

Yes, they were his surrogate parents, Jeffrey realized, and they were having an enormous amount of fun at his expense, but he really didn't mind. "I'll be in my room," he told them and headed upstairs.

He heard them laughing with delight even after he closed the door.

CHAPTER 20

Once Jeffrey started getting a paycheck from the city, he began contributing to his hosts' household expenses. Although it took a substantial chunk out of his earnings, he was glad to be paying his way, to some extent, and to give up his freeloading ways. Additionally, a couple of times a week he placed an order with Tommy for sandwiches to feed the gazebo crew.

The project had begun attracting attention. Motorists often slowed down to rubberneck, and many honked their horns in approval as they drove by. Others stopped to inquire about the activity. As word spread that it was a volunteer effort, the work team steadily grew. Some of the nearby residents specifically thanked Jeffrey for reclaiming their park.

"Don't thank me," he corrected them. "Cap is the crew chief. This is his project."

From the juvenile division of the police department, Vince arranged for Bud's two pals, who also were on probation, to participate. They had seen how much fun Bud was having with getting to use carpenter's tools and being allowed to drive his grandpa's pickup to haul away the debris, and they had wanted to join in. Vince put Bud in charge of the other two and gave him the title of Youth Captain. He also gave him an Army-style fatigue cap with an official-looking insignia. Bud quickly adjusted

to his position of authority and kept a close eye on his two subor-
dinates. Realizing that they were looking to him for direction, he
began setting an example for them by behaving more maturely.

As the demolition of the old structure neared completion,
Jeffrey used his wages to set up a debit account at the hardware store in town so Cap could buy supplies as he needed
them. Mayor Geegan had met privately with Jeffrey and approved funds for the gazebo materials, provided they were purchased at the lowest possible cost, which meant buying them
from a tax-free New Hampshire supplier. Jeffrey had thanked
the mayor but declined city funds, saying that he preferred to
pay for the materials himself and buy them from the vendor of
his own choosing.

The hardware store manager in Baxter had been furious to
hear of the city official's purchasing recommendations.

"Those people don't understand what they're doing to the
private sector in this town," the manager complained. "I can't
even get the graffiti-abatement people to patronize my store.
With all the repainting they do, it would really help my bottom
line for them to buy their paint from me."

"Do you know anything about the kids doing the graffiti?"
Jeffrey asked. "Are they coming in here to buy spray cans and
markers from you?"

The manager gave a cynical laugh. "I'm not profiting from
the criminal side of that activity either," he said. "For all I know,
those hoodlums are driving to New Hampshire too. I've already
laid off half my staff because business is so slow. There's not
much more I can do to cut my expenses. If things don't pick up
this summer, I'll be closing my doors before the end of the year.
Then everybody will be driving to New Hampshire."

"You may be the only hardware store in town," Jeffrey said
to him, "but you still need to promote your business and convince people of the importance of your role in the community.

Why don't you sponsor my band concert? We'll be doing some publicity soon, and your name could be all over town on our posters and flyers."

The manager proposed giving Jeffrey a discount on his building materials in exchange for free advertising at the concert.

Jeffrey agreed. Upon returning to the Money Building, he stopped by the maintenance department and told Cap, "Go ahead and buy whatever you need at the hardware store in town. Just tell them to charge it to the Baxter Band account."

From behind his workbench, Cap regarded Jeffrey with overt skepticism. "Construction materials get charged to my department," he said. "That gazebo project will put me over budget."

Jeffrey had gone to the basement not only to speak with Cap, but also to retrieve the box of band uniforms from the storage closet. Sensing an extended argument ahead of him, he set the heavy box on the workbench while assuring the maintenance man, "Your department won't be charged for any of the rebuilding expenses. Whatever you buy at the hardware store will come out of my budget." More accurately, it was coming out of Jeffrey's pocket, but he didn't want Cap or anyone else to know that.

"Your department can't pay for those materials neither," Cap said. "The only item in your budget is salary. Yours."

Skeptically, Jeffrey asked, "How do you know that?"

"All department managers get a detailed budget report for city expenses," Cap explained. "It's so we can envy whoever's getting more than we are."

"Trust me, Cap, my band is paying for those materials," Jeffrey said as he hefted the box of uniforms. "Now stop arguing with me. I've got to take these uniforms upstairs and see if they're still any good." Conclusively, he headed for the door.

"Geegan won't let your band wear those uniforms during a concert," Cap said.

Jeffrey came back and set the box on the workbench again. With impatience straining his voice, he asked, "Why not? I'm the band director. It should be my decision."

"Hennessey bought those uniforms way back before Geegan's time," Cap told him. "The band wore 'em for a few years, then Geegan took office and decided he didn't like the idea of a city-funded band wearing military uniforms."

"But that's absurd," Jeffrey said. "The Baxter Band's origins were in the Civil War. The musicians were out on the battlefield with their fellow soldiers, rallying their courage with their music, all of them fighting to end slavery in America. It's hardly something to be ashamed about."

"I'm just telling you what Hennessey told me," Cap said. He watched Jeffrey closely, waiting for his reaction.

For a moment, Jeffrey silently rubbed his sore shoulder. At last, he vowed stubbornly, "I am not going to become another Dmitri Shostakovich!"

"Attaboy!" Cap exhorted, then asked, "Who's he?"

"A Russian composer who lived during the Stalinist era," Jeffrey explained. "He had to get the government's approval for everything he wrote before it was performed. Every new composition came under scrutiny. And if the authorities decided they didn't like his work, they could pick him up in the middle of the night and send him off to Siberia." Looking at the box of uniforms, he speculated, "So, if uniforms are out, what's next? Am I going to need Geegan's okay on the music I select?"

"That's happened before," Cap said.

"This band is not going to become a political tool for whoever happens to be in office," Jeffrey asserted. "Not as long as I'm here." Again he lifted the box and headed for the door.

"You work too hard for what they're paying you," Cap called after him.

Having no rebuttal to that, Jeffrey kept going.

Halfway up the stairs, he had to stop and relieve his aching shoulder of its burden. With the heavy box propped on the handrail, he groaned with misery while massaging the sore muscles. Between his directing rehearsals and working on the gazebo, his right shoulder ached almost constantly. He desperately wished that Ray Greenleaf would call. This interim position with the Baxter Band was not worth risking potentially severe damage to his body, especially not to something as important as his right arm. There were plenty of things he looked forward to doing with that arm, such as carrying his bride over the threshold on their wedding night, pitching a baseball to his son, and lifting his infant daughter high into the air just to hear her laugh. These images were a clear part of the future he imagined for himself, but they seemed exceedingly remote and unattainable given his currently paltry conditions of employment.

Standing there in the stairwell, he listened to the sound of a distant machine grinding up something, possibly the bodies of department managers who forgot their Friday reports. The cinder-block walls rose around him like a prison; it was an atmosphere of depression and hopelessness. This was the source of many of the problems in this city, he realized, this institution that was supposed to be serving the people. He wondered whether all municipalities operated with ineffective committees, public servants who cloaked their idleness in obscure jargon, and city administrators who maintained locked doors between themselves and their constituents. Although the Baxter Band's municipal status provided vital funding, it also severely limited Jeffrey's options as director. Ever since being hired, he seemed to be fighting with city officials every step of the way. The band uniforms were not a political statement, only a visual enhancement emphasizing the historic nature of the music his band would play. Yet he didn't look forward to locking horns with Arthur Geegan over the matter. If Ben Hennessey had already tried and failed, what chance would Jeffrey have? It would be far easier for him to carry the box back down to the basement storage room and forget the uniforms. His throbbing shoulder voted for that option.

Above him, however, stood the doorway leading to the first floor. He was halfway there. He wasn't in the habit of quitting just because something was hard to do, and yet he wondered if this continual resistance he faced was an indication that he was heading in the wrong direction.

As it turned out, the uniforms wouldn't be an issue of contention. Upon inspecting the contents of the box, he and Terri discovered that many of the garments were badly moth-eaten and that all of them had fallen to pieces, the stitching having rotted away from years of storage in the damp basement. The only bright moment of the afternoon was when he learned that she had some aspirin in her desk.

He slumped in the folding chair, weary and frustrated, while she continued sorting through the pathetic woolen fragments. "Terri, it's hopeless," he said. "Let's just throw them away."

But she wasn't so easily dissuaded. "I think there's enough good material here to piece together one or two complete uniforms," she said. "I want to take them home and see what I can do with them." After repacking the box, she asked him, "Will you carry this out to the car for me?"

Ignoring the wild protests from his shoulder, he said pleasantly, "Of course. I would be happy to." At the end of the day, he lifted the box of uniforms and clenched his teeth against the pain while following her out to her car. "Oh, look," he said as they started across the parking lot, "it's snowing again."

During the drive home, Jeffrey brooded over his predicament. He had come to Baxter only because that had seemed his best option after leaving Hawaii, yet he saw no future for himself there. With the city in such bad financial shape, the budget committee could very well deem the band an unnecessary expense to the taxpayers and he could be out of a job. He was twenty-four. He wanted a family and he thought it was time he started thinking seriously about finding the right partner, yet he couldn't imagine raising children in such an awful place and on such a small salary.

At last, Terri broke his gloomy reverie. "Jeff," she said, "if I can get a complete uniform out of that box, how about having one of the band members wear it for playing a solo?"

"I guess we could do that," he agreed. "Fern's playing has really improved. I've been thinking about giving her a featured part. Those R. B. Harte pieces were written to showcase the cornet."

"That's what I was thinking," Terri said excitedly. "Why don't you have her come over early before your next tutoring session so I can take her measurements?"

He shook his head, saying, "You'd better wait until closer to the concert. She told me she's dieting and that she's dropped a lot of weight. If you make a uniform for her now, it could be too big for her in a couple of months."

"I'd like to start on it now," Terri insisted. "Sewing a custom-fitted garment takes a long time. I've got to fit those pieces together and see that the fabric drapes properly. I also have to make sure there's enough room in the shoulders for when she's playing her cornet. It could take weeks. I think you'd better ask her to start coming over next Wednesday." She paused long enough for him to agree to speak to Fern about it. Then she added happily, "I'm so glad you convinced her to keep playing with the band. She seems like such a nice person. Tommy and I both think so."

After arriving at home, Jeffrey carried the box of uniforms into the house while Terri held the door for him.

"Tommy, we're home," she called before going to hang her coat in the closet.

In the kitchen, Jeffrey was surprised to see that the stove and countertops were bare. Normally dinner preparations were under way by the time the two commuters got home from work. A moment later, Terri came in and also was puzzled.

Hearing a creak on the stairs, they both turned and saw Tommy slowly coming down with a tragic expression on his face. He looked almost as depressed as the night Terri brought Jeffrey home from the airport.

Fearfully, Terri asked, "Tommy, what's wrong?"

Tommy came up to Jeffrey and handed him his cell phone, which he had been using that day. "A guy named Greenleaf called for you," Tommy said in a soft monotone. "He said to tell you that if you're still interested in working for him, you can fly out to San Diego right away and audition. His group needs a trombone player." Tommy blinked a couple of times, then sank into a chair at the kitchen table.

Wide-eyed, Terri looked up at Jeffrey with an expression of utter betrayal. "No, Jeffrey," she whispered, "you can't do this to us. You can't leave now."

Jeffrey felt instantly energized by a flood of relief. At last, his ship had come in. He was going to a warm, sunny place where he could play music with other professionals. There would be no budget committees, no bureaucrats milking the city's few remaining taxpayers, no city administrators telling him how to run his band.

He looked at Terri, who was staring up at him fearfully. Then he looked at Tommy, who was slumped at the table and staring at the floor. Clearly they were disappointed, but Jeffrey was desperate not to let this opportunity slip away. Decisively he said, "I'm going upstairs to pack."

Terri was right on his heels. "You are not leaving," she asserted and trotted after him up the stairs.

Climbing with no loss of momentum, he said, "I'm sorry, Terri. I can't stay in Baxter. This job isn't right for me."

"Oh yes it is," she insisted. "This job is made for you. This job has your name written all over it, embroidered, even."

They had reached his bedroom. He pulled his suitcase from underneath the bed and laid it on top of the dinosaur sheets. He felt like a heel for leaving these two kind and loving people, and yet he knew that Ray Greenleaf's offer was his best chance at restoring his career. He told himself—commanded himself—to remain committed to his course of action in spite of his emotions. "I need a more substantial job than directing a community band," he said. "I've got to think about my future."

"Why don't you think about the people who care about you?" Terri asked sharply. "Those people who have come to rely on you, who have become inspired by you and now are helping you to make Baxter a better place? Can't you see what you've started here? Don't you realize the changes that are happening in this town because of you?"

He sighed loudly and said, "I studied to be a musician, not to spar with bureaucrats all day!" Brusquely, he walked past her to the closet and began tearing his clothes from the hangers.

She watched him with a knowing smile. "That's the problem, isn't it?" she asked. "This job is a lot harder than you expected. You thought it would be a snap, pulling together a dinky little community band, but now you're seeing just how hard it is, and you don't think you can do it."

"Oh, please!" he cried indignantly. His voice resounded off the closet walls. "Don't try to insult me. I'm sure I could put together some nice concerts this summer if I kept working at it, but this isn't what I studied to do." He continued draping his shirts and trousers over his arm, then carried them to the suitcase.

"It doesn't matter what you studied to do," she said. "What matters is what you're able to do. Jeff, you're a leader. People get behind you, and when they do that, you have a responsibility to lead them."

"I'm fighting the city every step of the way," he argued, returning to the closet for more clothes.

"And you're winning that fight, Jeffrey," she insisted. "Why would you want to quit now? Just when you've started to make progress, you're walking out on us. I never knew you were such a quitter. Quitter, quitter, quitter! And after all the support you've gotten from Cap and the whole gazebo crew, not to mention Tommy and me."

Grabbing another armful of clothing, he said, "Terri, you must know how grateful I am for the hospitality you've shown me while I've been here. But I can't sacrifice my career just because you want me to stay. Don't take it personally."

"Oh, I do take it personally, mister," she retorted with venom. "I take it very personally. This is my town, and nobody has made the kind of progress you have in making things better around here. I won't let you quit with the job only half finished. That little community band is just part of the picture. Jeff, can't you see how much you've improved the lives of people around you? Just look at Tommy. I haven't seen him this active and happy in years, not since before our son died."

Jeffrey had started back toward the suitcase with the last of his clothing, and now he stopped. While Terri's words registered in his brain, he looked at the spaceman wallpaper, the dinosaur sheets. This had been their son's room, he realized, their son who had died. He could just about guess the age, judging by the decorations. A teenager would have hung the walls with posters of pop musicians, cars, pretty girls. Their son would have been much younger, perhaps not even an adolescent. A child.

Terri had read his thoughts. "Yes, this was his room," she affirmed as tears welled in her eyes. "And for years after our little boy died, Tommy used to come up here and just sit for hours, not saying anything. He was profoundly depressed. And then you came, and the first night you were here, I saw my husband standing in this room and laughing. Do you realize how big of a change that is? And now, because of you, he's organized a neighborhood support group and started a small business, and he's feeling happy and full of hope about each new day—and it's all because you came and stayed with us. And now you're going to ruin all that by leaving."

Jeffrey flung the armful of clothing into his suitcase and turned to face her. "Oh, lay it on, why don't you?" he urged angrily. "The guilt, I mean. Heap it on me! Do you want a trowel? A shovel? Would a dump truck be big enough?" He realized he was shouting. Trying to tone it down, he continued sternly, "This is not fair, Terri. You can't blame me for the grief you feel over losing your son. I am very sorry for your loss. Truly. But I have to leave Baxter. There's no future for me here."

"Then make one!" she challenged, standing on her toes to hurl the words at him. With her arms flung out, fingers spread, she appeared ready to levitate. "What makes you think things will be any better in San Diego? You might not like it there. You might just hate it."

She was right, Jeffrey realized; he hardly knew Ray, and he was taking a big chance that his new colleague wouldn't be a complete ogre to work for. Staunchly, he said, "I won't know unless I go and find out."

"And if you do go, you won't come back," she said, her voice breaking. The fight was draining out of her, fast. Gasping in between sentences, she gave him all she had left. "I just know it," she said tearfully. "You're going to abandon us, drop out of our lives. Just like our son did. Our little eight-year-old son, Jeffrey."

He stared at her in shock for a moment. Then he narrowed his eyes in disbelief and anger that she would make up such a blatant lie. "You'll say anything, won't you?" he said accusingly. "Anything to make me stay."

But she could say nothing more. Speechless with sorrow, she covered her face with both hands and sobbed.

"Nice try, Terri," he said stonily, "but I'm not buying it. That cannot be true. It is too much of a coincidence that your son and I would have the same name."

He turned back to close the lid of his suitcase and saw that the topmost garment wasn't his. In his haste, he had taken from the closet a tiny warm-up jacket, red satin with ribbed collar and cuffs, barely worn. Over the left breast was embroidered the name Jeffrey.

It was the smallness of the garment that got to him, the image of the tiny arms that would have fit into those sleeves. It was just a sprout of a lad who had been taken from these two dear people, and it broke his heart to see the physical reminder of their loss, which they had kept for an untold number of years. Why had they held on to it? Did they think that, by some miracle or breach of physical law, their boy might come back? Indeed, Jeffrey wondered, recalling his hosts' eager acceptance of him, had the Turcotts' son come back in the personage of Jeffrey Bowden?

Jeffrey pulled Terri into his arms just as Tommy appeared in the doorway. While she sobbed into his shirt, Jeffrey looked over her head at the man whom he had helped simply by accepting their invitation to stay as a guest in their home, to eat their food and borrow their car, to share their lives unwittingly as a surrogate son.

With calm composure, Tommy said to him, "It's okay, Jeff. You can go if you need to. We'll be okay, all of us. We'll get along without you, just like we did before you came."

All at once, Jeffrey decided he wasn't going to fight it any longer. Something was holding him to this city, something aside from the arms of this weeping woman. He thought of all the efforts he had started, the inroads he had made with Cap, Fern, Mrs. Roosevelt, Bob, and others, and he realized he had more work to do with all of them. This was what was holding him, he thought: these loose ends, like strings tied around his finger, reminders of unfinished business. What made him think it would be any better in San Diego? Had it been any better in Hawaii? Was happiness something we pursued and discovered, like buried treasure? Or was it something we created for ourselves in whatever place we happened to be?

With Terri still hugging him, Jeffrey took his cell phone from his pocket and dialed Ray Greenleaf's number. When Ray answered, Jeffrey identified himself and thanked him for his offer. Then he said that he had decided to remain in Baxter after all. By the time he had returned his phone to his pocket, Terri had stopped crying and let go of him.

"Yes, yes, yes," she cried happily, jumping in a little circle and pumping her fists in the air. "I knew you would make the right decision."

Watching her dance of exuberance, Jeffrey struggled to be noble about his sacrifice. Even so, he felt compelled to impress upon her, just a little, how much he had given up. "It was a job in San Diego," he said to her. "San Diego, in Southern California. Do you know how beautiful that place is? It's warm there all year round. No snow, not a flake. There are flowers and palm trees. It's almost like Hawaii." He gathered up the clothing from his suitcase, including the little warm-up jacket, and carried everything back to the closet.

Beaming with joy, Terri assured him, "Don't worry, Jeff. It will get warm here, too. It's just like you were saying the other day. I saw a robin this morning. That means only a few more weeks of sleet and freezing rain."

CHAPTER 21

That evening, Tommy prepared to host another meeting of his neighborhood support group. The membership had expanded, with new arrivals showing up every week. Almost everyone who attended knew someone else who wanted to learn how they could improve their situation, and each week's assembly brought a few new faces. Likely, many of them had been motivated to attend because of the homemade sandwiches Tommy served, but they also sat through the educational sessions and later admitted to being enlightened.

The retired professionals in the group took turns giving seminars on the basic principles of free trade, explaining how capitalism maximized human potential and gave everyone, not just the rich and powerful, the chance to fulfill their dreams.

"When you hold a job, you get more out of it than just a salary," Jeffrey heard a man named Roger say to the crowd one evening. "You learn the discipline it takes to get yourself out of bed in the morning. You learn how to be responsible for something, how to demonstrate to other people that they can depend on you. You learn how to work with other professionals and with your customers, how to negotiate, how to honor a contract. Whatever skills you learn in order to do your job, those skills become a part of you. When anyone asks what you do for a living, you have an answer for them. You can say you're a carpenter or a mechanic. A job gives you a professional identity. You don't get any of those things from an unemployment check."

During the break, Jeffrey said to Roger, "I would swear that you and my dad went to the same business school. I heard that same lecture while I was growing up." Upon learning that the man was a retired physician, Jeffrey asked if they might talk privately for a moment before the group's activities resumed. Roger's comments had caused Jeffrey to wonder about Bob Cherry and the adverse effects of having to give up the occupations that formerly had been such a large part of his life. While the other meeting attendees moved into the kitchen for refreshments, Jeffrey and Roger remained in the living room.

Roger was fifty, much younger than Jeffrey had expected for a retiree. The former doctor explained that he had given up family practice only a year ago. Short and athletically robust, he had a large, round head that was bald on top and flanked by two panda ears of dark brown hair. His eyes were bright and alert behind the round lenses of his glasses.

"I retired early because the regulators were driving me out of business," Roger said in response to Jeffrey's inquiry. "For years I had a nice little practice in Baxter, me and a colleague. Family practice used to be a rewarding field. You understood your patient better by virtue of getting to know the family dynamics, a constellation of data that you could draw upon in forming your diagnosis and prescribing treatment. Then the regulations got tougher. We had inspectors looking through our medical records and telling us what we had to write there and within what timeframe, even what color pen we had to use. They came out with new billing procedures, and we had to hire extra clerks to handle it all. The coding system alone was a nightmare. They had a code for everything, depending on the diagnosis and payer. We had to buy guidebooks and send our billing staff to seminars to learn how to comply with all the new rules." Suddenly, he asked, "Why are you rubbing your shoulder? Does it hurt?"

Jeffrey admitted that it did.

"Have you been to a doctor about it?" Roger asked.

"No," Jeffrey said. "I've just been taking aspirin and resting it when the pain gets too bad." When Roger offered to take a look at it, Jeffrey gratefully agreed.

While palpating Jeffrey's shoulder and upper back, the doctor continued, "Anyway, our reward for jumping through all these hoops for the government was the privilege of receiving a small percentage of what it actually cost us to provide services. People with good insurance plans wound up subsidizing retired folks and the indigent. The problem is, that payment model tends to drive up the price of everything. In the end, everybody suffers."

"Ouch," Jeffrey said.

"Yeah, no kidding. I had to raise my fees, which made nobody happy," Roger said.

"No, I mean my shoulder hurts," Jeffrey said, "there, where you're pressing."

Roger made note of the place, then held Jeffrey's arm at the elbow and wrist and checked his range of motion, moving the arm in various directions and taking note of where movement became painful. "I didn't need somebody from Washington, DC, to tell me I should be charitable to the less fortunate," the doctor went on. "From the beginning of my practice, I always provided free or low-cost services to people who needed it. After all, they were my neighbors. Many of them operated businesses that I frequented."

"How did the regulators get involved in the first place?" Jeffrey asked.

"Somebody passed a law, ostensibly for protecting the gullible public," Roger said. "Some people are comforted by the idea of a big regulatory body watching over all those sneaky doctors. But if people don't trust their own doctors, why should they trust the regulators? Who watches over them? Tell me how you hurt your arm. What have you been doing?"

"Directing a band and building a gazebo," Jeffrey answered. "Up until a year ago, I shoveled a lot of snow."

At last, Roger said, "I think you've got a frozen shoulder. You'd better see a doctor about that."

"I thought I just did," Jeffrey said.

"I'm a retired doctor," Roger corrected him. "That means I'm not licensed to order redundant tests. For that, you need to see a doctor who's still practicing, a licensed physician."

Puzzled, Jeffrey asked, "Why would I want redundant tests?"

"Oh, they're not for you," Roger explained, "they're for the licensed physician you decide to see. He'll examine you like I just did, order some X-rays, an MRI, probably a CT scan. They might even run some routine lab work since your veins are handy. The whole workup will be exorbitantly expensive and probably unnecessary. You'll wait a while for the results to come back, then you'll go in again for your follow-up office visit. Chances are, the doctor will tell you that you have a frozen shoulder. The diagnostic procedure will cost a fortune, but the treatment itself is only a few bucks."

"What's the treatment for a frozen shoulder?" Jeffrey asked.

"If it was me, I'd take some pain medicine and stretch out the shoulder muscles once in a while," Roger said.

"Why can't a licensed doctor just tell me to do that in the first place?" Jeffrey asked.

"He's got to run all those redundant tests first," Roger said, "because he's got a license to protect. He's got to rule out the unlikely, the implausible, the iffy, the dubious, the doubtful, the highly improbable, the rare exception, even the near impossible. I'm not qualified to do all that."

"But you're saying I should take some pain medicine and stretch out my shoulder muscles?" Jeffrey confirmed.

"No, I'm saying that's what I would do," Roger corrected. "Of course, you can do that too, if you want. Just don't tell anyone I told you to do it."

Jeffrey thanked him for his help. Next, he asked, "What do you know about a company called InfinitiCare? They provide nursing services to older people in their homes."

"I've heard of them," Roger said with a nod. "They actually do a lot more than that. New-baby care, weight loss, even some kind of program for teenagers. I was on their advisory board for a while, and I remember Arthur Geegan gave us a big presentation about all the new things they were going to offer."

"Geegan?" Jeffrey repeated in surprise. "How is he involved? I assumed they were a privately owned company."

"They are," Roger affirmed. "Geegan was a stockholder, or an investor in some regard. I was there only as a medical advisor, so I don't know about the financial part of it. It's an easy guess that somebody's making money from that operation, as busy as they are."

"Are they competent from a medical perspective?" Jeffrey asked.

Roger paused for a moment before saying, "This may sound strange, but I think they focus too much on illness and aging. They're an aggressive bunch, and they like to screen the patient for everything as early as possible, ordering every test allowable under the insurance. Of course they don't do anything the patient might actually have to pay for, because then the guy starts asking embarrassing questions like, 'Do I really need this?' They're in the business of finding problems to treat. If you look long and closely enough, you'll see that nearly everyone has some developing illness or debility. Sometimes it's just part of the normal aging process. People become overly focused on what might be wrong with them instead of just enjoying their lives. I mean, if you're truly sick or in pain and it's keeping you from doing what you want to do, by all means get it treated. But don't keep digging until you find something wrong. None of us would get out of bed in the morning if we thought about all the things that could go wrong that day."

"I think that's what's happening to a friend of mine," Jeffrey said. "He's in his early eighties, living alone. Up until a year ago, he was active and independent, always busy with hobbies and freelance work. Now he's scared, obsessed with his own mortality. He's given up playing the tuba, which he always loved to do. He sits around all day taking his blood pressure and trying not to do anything risky."

"Remember, I'm not licensed to order redundant tests," Roger said. "If you're asking me what your friend should do, I would say he should do what his nurse tells him. After all, he signed a contract with that outfit. But if you're asking me what I would do in his situation? I would play my tuba."

CHAPTER 22

Jeffrey made a point of sitting between Fern and the door when he told her she would be playing a special solo at the band concert. As he expected, she immediately resisted.

Her face grew pale and her eyes widened. In a trembling voice, she said, "All those people will be staring at me."

"They sure will," he affirmed, "because I'm going to ask you to stand up in front of the band while you play."

They were sitting at the Turcotts' kitchen table. Fern had come for her weekly tailoring session with Terri prior to taking Jeffrey to rehearsal. He had been tutoring her for several weeks, and her playing had steadily improved to the point where she had replaced Steve in the first chair position. Jeffrey knew it wasn't going to be easy to sell her on the idea of performing a featured solo at the concert, but after having seen her remarkable progress so far, he wanted to push her toward ever-greater achievements.

He watched her facial expression as she wrestled with his request. She had begun wearing a headband to keep her hair back, revealing a face that was diamond-shaped with prominent, firm cheeks. Along with her improved musicianship had appeared a corresponding blossoming of self-confidence in small but noticeable increments. She smiled more easily now, and when the light was just right, her small, blue eyes looked like sapphire chips. She was becoming quite a nice-looking girl, he thought.

A sudden realization occurred to her. She looked at him and said, "I'm going to be the only one wearing a uniform, aren't I?"

"Yes," he admitted.

Her shyness instantly returned. It was like watching the petals of a flower closing up in a time-lapse film. Fearfully, she said, "Jeffrey, I don't think I can do it."

"Oh yes," he said with quiet conviction, "you can do it. I need you to. A lot of people do. This whole town needs you to play that solo."

Her fear was momentarily forgotten as she now looked at him in puzzlement.

"Please don't back out now," he said. "It's not just me that's counting on you. Many people have dedicated their time and effort toward making this concert a success. You've seen the new gazebo going up in the park. That's volunteer work, all of it. Additionally, the music we're playing was donated by someone in the community, a member of the composer's family. She believes that this music needs to be performed for the people it was written for, the residents of Baxter. Several businesses in town have bought ads in our program booklet in hopes that the band concert will help improve their sales. Everyone is counting on you to make their investments pay off."

She gave a shaky laugh and said cynically, "Try putting a little pressure on me, why don't you?"

"That's not pressure, Fern," he said. "That's support."

He had put his hand on the back of her chair and now leaned forward to look into her face. She could feel his nearness. He wasn't touching her, but the air between them seemed to be vibrating from his speech.

"What you're feeling is the support of countless people who

are behind you," he said, "people you don't even know, but who have placed their complete confidence in you. I know you can do this. I wouldn't be asking you otherwise. We have more work to do together, but I am willing to help you. More than that, I am determined to help you. I won't give up on you, no matter how long it takes."

She blinked a few times and appeared genuinely moved by his declaration. Yet her fear predominated. She pleaded softly, almost begging, "Couldn't I play the solo sitting down?"

He shook his head. "Not emphatic enough," he said. "I want everyone looking at you, listening to you, and saying to themselves, 'What a marvelous thing that young woman is doing for us. She's playing for the whole town.'" He sat back in his chair then, giving her a little space, and continued, "When the composer wrote that music 150 years ago, he had something in his heart that he wanted to say to the people of this city. Think of what that composer's message might have been. He had just come home after fighting in a terrible war, one that had torn our country apart for a while, and not everyone was convinced it had been a worthwhile effort. You and your cornet are going to give voice to that message. In doing so, you also will be affirming the trust of everyone who has backed you."

She lowered her eyes again, but this time she appeared more thoughtful than afraid. "Hope," she said at last. "That's what his message would have been. 'Have hope for the future. Don't give up or else all of our efforts up to this point will have been wasted.'"

"I think you've got it right," he said, smiling. "Will you do it? Will you at least try?"

"You really think I can?" she asked, stunned.

"I'm sure you can," he said definitively. "You've already gotten immensely better. Are you practicing daily?"

Giving a little nod, she smiled and confessed, "I used to sit in my rocking chair and watch old movies at night, and now I'm using that time to practice. It really cuts down on the popcorn." She laughed.

It was evident that she had lost a substantial amount of weight. She had begun wearing successively fewer sweaters, too, and this evening he could see that she was using a belt to hold up her pants.

"You've come far in just the past few weeks," he continued, "but I think you need to keep pushing yourself. You're not done yet. I think you're going to amaze everyone, including yourself, when you live up to your full potential."

She had been looking at him in wonder as he spoke, and now she suddenly pressed her eyes shut. He thought she might be holding back tears, but when she opened her eyes again, he saw that she appeared hopeful, even a bit excited in her own soft-spoken way. "No one has ever had that kind of confidence in me," she said. "How can I say no when you're so committed to helping me? Of course I'll do it, Jeffrey. If you think I can do it, then I will do it. I'll start working on it tonight when I get home."

"Don't your neighbors complain about you playing your horn late at night?" he asked.

"I live on River Street," she explained. "The trains run by my apartment building all night. Nobody notices a dinky little cornet."

"River Street?" he said worriedly. "That used to be a rough neighborhood."

"It still is," she said. "My apartment is on the third floor, though, so break-ins aren't as likely as on the ground floor." With a shrug, she added, "It's the best I can afford on my salary." Earlier in their acquaintance, she had told him she worked as a nurse's aide at a convalescent center. She had wanted to become an RN but had run out of money for nursing school. Seeing his continued expression of concern, she assured him, "I keep my door locked, and I'm careful when I go out after dark."

"I'm very glad to hear that," he murmured. While riding with her to rehearsal every week, he had learned a little more about her and found her to be a pleasant conversationalist. He could honestly say they had become friends.

At Terri's beckoning, Fern went upstairs for her fitting session. Watching her go, Jeffrey realized that if she continued to lose weight, she was going to look pretty good in a band uniform.

Later, as he helped her into her coat prior to leaving for rehearsal, she asked, "What are you going to do about finding a tuba player?"

"I don't know," he admitted. "My friend Bob was going to ask his visiting nurse if it was all right for him to play, but I haven't heard anything from him. Maybe I ought to remind him." He shrugged into the secondhand overcoat he had bought recently for himself. Suddenly, he asked her, "Could you and I go visit him now? I'd like for him to meet you."

Fern said she would be happy to go. Jeffrey gave her directions as she drove and also told her what he knew about Bob's condition. She parked at the curb in front of the big Victorian house. Jeffrey asked her to bring in her instrument case.

Bob looked about the same as the last time Jeffrey had seen him. Although happy to see Jeffrey again, he was apprehensive about the stranger accompanying his former tenant.

"Bob, I'd like to introduce you to my friend," Jeffrey said. "This is Fern."

Bob meekly invited them in. Fern stepped through the doorway and stood while holding her instrument case in front of her with both hands, smiling and scanning the room with interest as if touring a museum she had always wanted to see.

Jeffrey took their coats, folded them together, and laid them on the floor, out of the way. "We were just on our way to band rehearsal and thought we'd stop in," he said to Bob. "Did you ask your nurse if you could play tuba?"

The old man looked embarrassed and mumbled, "No, I meant to do that, but I haven't just yet. I don't think I'd better—"

"Bob, are these your grandchildren?" Fern asked. She gestured toward a row of small, framed photographs that were displayed on the mantle behind Bob's recliner.

After a moment, Bob answered, as though just remembering, "Why, yes. Yes, they are." He shuffled over to stand next to her and carefully recited the names and ages of his youngest progeny.

Watching the two of them, Jeffrey wondered if it was because he had been spending so much time with Fern that he had begun to notice a surprising attractiveness about her.

Now Bob was telling her about the wooden puzzles he used to make.

"You made puzzles?" Fern exclaimed softly. "How clever of you!"

"I think I've got one around here somewhere," Bob said and began rummaging through a drawer.

Fern glanced discreetly at Jeffrey, who nodded at her with approval. He thought her kind attitude toward the old man spoke well for her character.

"Here's one," Bob declared as he handed her a lidded oval box. After she had admired its polished beauty, he explained, "The idea is to get the lid off."

"Oh, can I try?" she asked eagerly. She fiddled with the object, twisting and pulling every which way, and laughed at being stumped at every turn. At last, she declared the box a complete mystery and handed it back to Bob. When he opened the lid with a simple push from his thumb, she burst into hearty laughter. Jeffrey marveled at the delightfulness of the sound.

This was the first time he had heard her laugh so openly, and it impressed him with its musicality and goodness.

Bob sniffed a little, and suddenly he was weeping.

"I'm all right," he assured them as they helped him into the recliner. While they hovered around him worriedly, Bob dabbed at his eyes with a tissue and explained, "I can't tell you how pleasing it is for me to hear a woman's laugh in this house again. After my wife died, I was alone here for a long time. Even after Jeffrey moved in, it was just us two guys." Seeing Fern's surprised expression, Bob said, "Oh, didn't he tell you that he used to live here? He rented a room from me while he was in college."

With a little smile, Fern asked, "Didn't any of Jeffrey's girlfriends ever laugh when they were here?"

Bob hooted at the ridiculous notion. "Girlfriends? Jeffrey? Now that's a good one!" he said.

Jeffrey stood to one side of the recliner with his hand on Bob's shoulder, while Fern sat in a chair close by. "It was good for me, having Jeffrey around," Bob admitted. "I get such joy seeing young people like yourselves. You're just starting along a road I've already traveled. I know some of the landmarks you're going to see. Getting an education, choosing a career, finding a partner."

Jeffrey looked at Fern and was very pleased to discover that she had been looking up at him.

"Courtship," Bob said warmly, "that beautiful love dance of wooing and learning all about each other. Meeting each other's parents."

Jeffrey raised his eyebrows inquisitively at Fern. She gave an eager nod.

"Then the engagement," Bob said, beaming. "All the planning for the wedding, friends and family coming to celebrate the joyous day."

Although it was a highly speculative possibility and far in the future, Jeffrey could picture himself standing alongside this woman, maybe in that colonial-era meetinghouse in Cold Harbor. The place would be filled to the rafters with all their relatives and friends. And K, of course, would stand as his best man, pigtail hanging down the back of his tuxedo. Fern seemed to be preoccupied with her own internal vision, and pleasantly so. She hadn't mentioned to Jeffrey anything about her parents, but he knew she would tell him about them in time.

"The honeymoon!" Bob cried exuberantly.

Fern appeared to have developed an itch on the bridge of her nose. She partially hid her face with her hand as she scratched it. Jeffrey had never known a half-lowered eyelid could be so alluring.

"Children, of course," Bob went on.

When Fern looked up questioningly, Jeffrey raised two fingers and, when this brought no objection, a third. Seeing no reason why he shouldn't, he raised a fourth. She looked startled, then shrugged and nodded as if to say, *Why not?*

Jeffrey decided he had better speak up before Bob made him into a grandfather. "Fern," he said, "before we go to rehearsal, why don't you show Bob what instrument you play."

She placed her instrument case on Bob's lap and raised the lid, allowing him to marvel over the silver cornet. By the time Jeffrey had rounded up a pair of Bob's shoes and an overcoat, the old man had decided that he wanted to go to rehearsal to hear Fern play.

As the two young people escorted him out to the car, Bob said, "Jeffrey, I really like your girlfriend."

"I'm very glad to hear that, Bob," Jeffrey said, looking over at Fern. During their short visit, he had become convinced of the exceedingly good heart and potential compatibility of this woman. He wanted to continue and deepen their friendship. A warmth had begun growing inside his chest, and he recognized it as the coal of romanticism he had buried in ashes long ago. However, there was something else he felt too, an aching of despair, as he knew he would never be able to support Fern and the family they might have together if he continued to direct the Baxter Band. The playful pantomime they had enacted in Bob's living room would remain just a dream unless Jeffrey could somehow augment his meager salary with more substantial employment.

During the drive, Bob sat in the backseat of Fern's car and stared through the window in fascination. "Been a while since I was out," he confessed. "Oh, look at that! The city is building a new gazebo in the park. Is that for your band, Jeffrey?"

"It sure is," Jeffrey affirmed, pleased to see Fern smiling proudly at him from across the front seat.

Bob's surprise appearance at rehearsal was hailed enthusiastically by his fellow band members. Someone brought out a tuba from the school's storage room, and Bob sat with it in his usual back-row seat. He rattled the valves to loosen his fingers, played a few notes, and then sat back in his chair, swinging his feet and beaming.

Fern was shocked to see Jeffrey's uncharacteristically grim expression. Worriedly she asked him what was wrong.

Jeffrey whispered to her, "If he has a heart attack while he's here, I'll never forgive myself for bringing him."

She assured him that Bob appeared to be handling the outing just fine.

"I'm sorry we missed your lesson tonight," Jeffrey said.

"Visiting with Bob was more important," she said. "Don't worry, I'll practice when I get home."

In spite of his shoddy potential as a husband and provider, he asked, "Fern, would you like to be my girlfriend?"

She said she would.

"Don't expect me to go easy on you during rehearsal," he warned.

She said she wouldn't.

❊

The next day, Jeffrey thought it was time he checked with his bank in Hawaii about regaining access to his account. On the way home, he had Terri stop at an ATM so he could try his debit card. To his amazement, cash came out. With the failure of Andrew's attempt to charge him with embezzlement, his account had been unfrozen at last.

Five time zones away, Andrew Quigley watched a man who was sitting at a computer, tapping the keyboard, and scrolling through the list of ATM transactions displayed on the monitor. Upon finding the entry he had been seeking, the man turned to Quigley and smiled. "He's in Maine," he said.

CHAPTER 23

Prior to the next budget committee meeting, Jeffrey sat alongside Terri's desk while the two of them reviewed their department's budget report.

"This report is wrong," he said, frowning. "It shows zero revenue for our department last month. I know we received several donations for the gazebo project, but they don't show up anywhere. What could have happened to them?"

"All departmental revenue goes into the city's general fund," she explained. "The accountants pay the city expenses first. Anything left over is allocated to individual departments for authorized expenses."

"But those donors were supporting the rebuilding of the gazebo," he argued. "They weren't agreeing to pay for piping Muzak into the administrative office, or to buy coffee and pastry for the budget committee."

"All donations are handled that way," she said with a shrug. "It's specified by the Activity Funding Ordinance."

He remembered that this had been Andrew Quigley's reason, a year ago, for donating his money to the college instead of to the Baxter Band. Studying the budget report again, he said, "Since your salary is still coming out of the secretarial pool budget, my department's only expense is my salary. Are you saying that I'm being paid by all the city's taxpayers, even those who may be opposed to the idea of a municipally funded band?"

"You got it," she said.

"This is what I don't like about the city underwriting our band expenses with tax dollars from people in the community," he said. "That money is their own sweat—hardened and durable. They themselves should be the ones deciding what to do with it." Getting up from his chair, he said to Terri, "I need you to come with me to the budget committee today. I want you to hear everything that goes on in that meeting so you can understand what I'm about to do."

"Bring us back some pastry," Randie urged. Seeing Jeffrey's disgusted look, she offered in her defense, "Hey, they throw away the leftovers. It's a city ordinance."

As Terri headed down the hallway with Jeffrey, she said to him, "If I do take pastry back to the office, I'll make sure they understand that Mrs. Roosevelt bought it for them."

Jeffrey gave her a proud smile. As they reached the conference room, he paused before opening the door. "Terri," he asked, "do you trust me?"

Surprised, she said, "Of course I do. Why are you asking me that?"

"I'm going to give you an opportunity to prove it," he said and opened the door for her.

There being no crisis of the day to announce in his usual dramatic fashion, Arthur Geegan was available to start the meeting on time. Members reviewed the previous meeting's minutes and then listened to a financial report given by the Adjunct Deputy Assistant for Information Delivery, who advised them that the city's revenues were continuing to drop, with many vital services going unfunded. This news was met with the gravest of head shaking and the conclusion that taxes would have to be raised.

Cap came in quietly. Seeing there were no vacant chairs at the Round Table, he leaned against the wall at the back of the room.

Geegan then asked if there was any new business to discuss.

Jeffrey said, "Yes, I have a budget request for the Baxter Band."

With strained patience, Geegan said, "Mr. Bowden, we just heard a report explaining in great detail that the city is sorely lacking in revenues. I trust that you were paying attention as it was being read to us?"

"Oh, indeed I was, Mr. Geegan," Jeffrey assured him. "In fact, my budget request is very much in sympathy with the city's current financial condition. I am asking this committee to eliminate my salary from my department's budget."

Everyone around the table looked at him with expressions ranging from puzzlement to amazement to horror. Even Darla, who usually focused her attention strictly on taking the meeting minutes, interrupted her stenography to look up quizzically at him.

Cautiously, Geegan said, "Let me be sure I understand you, Mr. Bowden. You want your salary eliminated completely? In its entirety?"

"Completely, in its entirety," Jeffrey said, "and permanently."

Beside him, Terri murmured worriedly, "I hope you know what you're doing."

Geegan looked at his copy of the departmental budget report and said, "That would leave your department's budget at zero."

"Yes, it would," Jeffrey agreed.

"What about your secretary?" asked the Commissioner of Housing, Family Planning, Utility Subsidies, and Dog Control.

"Mrs. Turcott's salary falls under the secretarial pool budget," Jeffrey replied. "She would not be affected by what I'm proposing."

Mrs. Roosevelt, who had been gazing steadily at Jeffrey, now said, "Mr. Bowden, functions that are not funded by the city are dropped from the budget altogether. You essentially are asking us to fire you and to dissolve the Baxter Band."

"To dissolve the band as a function of the city, yes," Jeffrey clarified. "I plan to continue it as a private endeavor. And, yes, I am asking to be fired as a city employee."

"Will you please tell us why?" she asked, clearly baffled.

"I don't think any citizen should have to pay for the band or for my directing it," he said, "unless they wish to donate directly toward those things."

"That viewpoint is admirable but very worrisome," Mrs. Roosevelt said, "given the large number of private businesses that have failed in this city." Her noble face had become gravely shadowed with distress. She looked at him intently and asked, "Jeffrey, are you sure you can assume the risk?"

It was the first time she had addressed him by his first name, and this action conveyed to him the depth of her personal concern. "I assure you," he said to her, "I would not take that risk if I weren't committed to the success of the Baxter Band. I regard its supporters too highly." To the membership at large, he said, "I want to point out that the bottom line of my proposal would be a cost savings to the city, which in previous meetings of this committee has been sufficient reason for granting approval for the request." He looked at the faces around the table. Most were nodding in agreement, if reluctantly.

Arthur Geegan had kept his steely gaze on Jeffrey throughout his statement, as though trying to read his underlying motive. Slowly and emphatically, he said, "If we do what you are suggesting, Mr. Bowden, your band will never get another dollar of tax money again."

"That would suit me just fine," Jeffrey replied.

Greatly perplexed, the Advising Facilitator to Environmental Processing said, "But I don't see how your band can continue to operate without city funding. How exactly does that happen?"

"A group of people will get together and play music," Jeffrey told him simply. "Any material needs would be paid for through donations, like with any charity."

The Chief Implementation Officer of Goals Planning turned to his Assistant Chief and said, "Just what this city needs, another charity."

"You'll have to change the name," Geegan said. "You can't call it the Baxter Band if it's not a function of the city."

Surprised, Jeffrey pointed out, "Plenty of private businesses have *Baxter* in their company names. That is, they did, up until those businesses closed."

"They all had to pay for a licensing privilege from the appellation board," Geegan said.

Incredulous, Jeffrey asked, "You have a board just for naming things?"

"Of course," Geegan said. "You can't just stick a name on something. Most of our positions and programs are new concepts. We don't use outdated terms here. They carry all sorts of preconceptual baggage."

"Such as expecting people in those positions and programs to perform real work?" Jeffrey asked pointedly.

Geegan ignored this slight and continued, "Here at the Muni Building, we use fresh, new verbiage—creative descriptions with poetic flair."

"But how do people know what they mean? They don't describe what you actually do," Jeffrey said.

"No, but they describe the essence of what we aspire to do," Geegan said firmly, "It allows people to use their imaginations. We can fulfill all sorts of different expectations then. That's how we satisfy everyone. So if you want to keep running the Baxter

Band on your own, you'll have to seek approval from the appellation committee to retain the name."

Jeffrey considered this option for a long moment. At last the temptation proved irresistible. He cleared his throat and asked, "Tell me, what exactly is involved if I decide to follow the appellation trail?"

Darla emitted a noise that sounded like a tiny sneeze, although it might have been a muffled laugh.

Oblivious to the joke, Geegan shrugged. "You pay a licensing fee," he said.

"One time, or annually?" Jeffrey asked.

"Annually, of course," Geegan said with impatience, as though this should have been obvious.

"Are you saying that all the businesses in this city are required to pay an annual fee for the privilege of using the name of the city in their company," Jeffrey asked in exasperation, "on top of all the other taxes and fees and penalties they have to pay?"

"I have to fund our public programs somehow," Geegan blustered defensively. "People in this city demand programs and services, and it's my job to give them what they want."

"But you're killing the businesses in this town," Jeffrey protested. "Why can't you be more prudent in the things you offer?"

Geegan gave an abrupt laugh and said, "That's easy for you to say. I'm the one on the hot seat. Do you think I want to look out my window and see protest signs? TV cameras filming people in need, reporters interviewing all those unhappy citizens? Mothers with sick children and no health insurance? Homeless people blocking the sidewalks? Teenagers whose parents can't afford school supplies and sports equipment? It's perfectly acceptable for me to stand up to a banker or a store owner and say, 'You have to pay more taxes so that I can give the people what they want.' On the other hand, I can't stand up to an unemployed single mother of five who smokes and uses drugs, and say to her, 'You should have made better decisions in your life.' I can't stand up to the family of an eighty-year-old demented woman and say, 'She's your grandma. It's your responsibility to take care of her.' They would drive me out of office for doing that. When people ask me for a program, I have to say yes. That's the only option I have. In public office, the rule is that certain people in this town will ask for help and they will get it from their elected representatives. That's the reality of it."

"You're appeasing them in the short run," Jeffrey conceded, "but over time you're making people dependent on your programs."

"That's not dependency; it's security," Geegan replied.

"Security for whom?" Jeffrey asked.

An embarrassed silence fell over the table.

Abruptly, Geegan got up from his chair as if he had been stung by an insect. "You don't get it, do you?" he demanded with a belittling sneer. The mayor walked over to the arched window and gestured toward the glass. "Those people out there need me," he said. "Even though I don't help them in any practical sense, they need someone they can turn to for assistance, someone to beg favors from, and, yes, someone they can blame when things go wrong. Why do you think so many countries have royalty? The Brits love their queen; the Dutch, the Danes, and on and on. A surprising number of people in Russia wish they had their tsar back. What do you think would happen if kings abdicated, if governments disappeared? Half their countrymen couldn't feed and house themselves. They don't know how to protect themselves or educate their children. Without government to advise them, they are phenomenally ignorant of how to stay alive. And that is the function of government, to take care of ignorant people."

Geegan circled the meeting table, gazing with pride at each of his department managers and appointed minions. "If the people cannot govern themselves, then we are exactly what they deserve," he declared. "People sometimes complain about the bureaucracy, as they call it, but it is those same people who created it. There was no military coup here. No invading army took over this city. The people who live here asked for this. City officials were elected. Constituents voted. Referenda were passed."

Geegan continued to stroll about the room. His suit had been perfectly tailored to showcase his beefy torso. His lapel fluttered with the colored ribbons of various activist groups. Besides the pink ribbon signifying breast cancer awareness, and the green one for environmentalism, there were many that Jeffrey didn't recognize. He suddenly realized that the ribbons were not awards but were brands of sponsorship signifying a special arrangement of political support in exchange for financial consideration. As private donations dwindled, each of these groups had lassoed Geegan and burned their brands into him, and now he was their cash cow. Jeffrey wondered how much these alliances influenced the mayor's decision making.

For a moment, Geegan stopped, having spotted a smudge on the table where someone had carelessly touched it. He pulled out his handkerchief and briskly rubbed away the offensive spot before continuing his circuit of the room.

"You're right," Jeffrey said as Geegan approached him, "people sometimes don't know what is in their best interests, but you're taking advantage of their ignorance when you should be trying to correct it. You're appealing to their fear and neediness, encouraging them to be dependent while keeping them uninformed as to who is paying the cost for the thing you're giving them. Those are simple human beings out there, frail and wrongheaded at times, and some of them are downright brutes. But you shouldn't regard them with contempt. You should be using your influence to correct their thinking, to lead them toward self-government and personal responsibility."

Geegan scoffed, "You think that's my job? Where did those homeless men come from? Those teenaged mothers? Those gangs of wayward boys? Did they just drop out of the clouds like human raindrops dotting the sidewalks? Every one of them had a flesh-and-blood mother who had attained some degree of maturity, who could have taught those miserable people when they were children how to feed and clothe themselves; how to cough without spreading their germs to their fellows; how to care for themselves in sickness, to prepare food in a sanitary way, and to handle sharp-bladed instruments; how to bear children and educate them and raise them properly; how to take care of their aging parents and comfort them in their last hours on earth. Every one of those wretches had a father who could have taught them a trade, who could have instilled in them some feeling of responsibility for their own existence, the understanding that, in exchange for being given the gift of life, they were expected to maintain themselves throughout that life, to earn a living, to discover their talents and contribute their unique gifts to society, to learn to weigh the risks of an action before taking that action and later regretting it and having to call for someone's help. They all had two parents who could have taught them the skills they needed to get through life as independent, capable human beings."

Geegan was standing squarely in front of Jeffrey now, blaring his message directly into his face. "But those people out there did not learn those lessons," the mayor went on, "and we here in this room are what they have gotten as a result. They put us in this position. And as miserable as we have made them, we are exactly what they deserve. Do you wonder why I find them contemptible? They can't find their own way in this world. They can hardly wipe their own noses."

Now Jeffrey stood up, and Geegan had to take a step back in order to avoid a collision.

"That's not true!" Jeffrey declared. "They do know how, but you intimidate them into thinking that they are helpless. Those lighted billboards all over town, the ad campaigns and brochures, they're nothing more than propaganda and scare tactics appealing to their weaknesses, all for your gain. If you're going to appoint yourselves as surrogate parents of this city, at least try to be good ones. You should appeal to a man's better nature, not his lesser one. When someone has to make a choice between right and wrong, you have a responsibility to help him make the right one. But it doesn't take a committee or a task group to do that. All it takes is another human being who cares enough to get involved, someone who has the good sense and morality to know what to do and the courage to do it." He looked over at Cap for a moment to be sure his meaning was understood.

One of the committee members spoke up in objection, saying, "That is not always possible."

"It's taking place right now," Jeffrey argued. "For years, the Baxter Band played its concerts in the gazebo in the park. People came to listen and brought their families, and they had their picnic dinners there on the lawn. Neighbors visited with each other; children played together. It was a communal event. Habits changed over the years, and the park was abandoned and ultimately condemned. Now the only people who gather there are gangs of kids looking for entertainment or escape, something to fill their idle time. But a small group of citizens have begun reclaiming that park, and now there's a new building going up, a gazebo."

"Which we paid for," Geegan said.

"No you didn't, Arthur," Cap interjected. "The city didn't pay for any of that new gazebo. The proof is in black and white, right there on the departmental budget report."

"Materials were authorized, I believe," Geegan said, turning to his executive secretary for confirmation. "Isn't that right, Darla?"

"Authorized," Darla confirmed, "but no invoices were submitted. No monies were paid by the city."

Cap threw an accusing squint at Jeffrey as if to say, "I knew it."

"What about Cap's overtime?" Geegan asked, looking at the maintenance man.

"The only overtime you paid me was for athletics," Cap answered. "I never charged the city for gazebo work. Did it on my own time."

Geegan fell silent, thinking about all this and trying to find some loophole he had overlooked.

"The gazebo project was started, and has continued," Jeffrey said, "solely by individual effort and without city involvement." He remained standing as he addressed everyone at the table, including Geegan, who stood alongside him. "You all sit at this table, and when you look at that window, all you see is the sky," Jeffrey said and gestured at the arched window. "The sky," he repeated for emphasis, "which apparently you perceive is the limit of your power. But down below the windowsill, where you can't see while seated in your comfortable chairs, are the people whose lives you are affecting." He put one foot on the seat of his chair and stepped up onto the Round Table.

Every mouth fell open. All eyes bulged in disbelief and followed his towering figure as he strode across the diameter of the huge table.

Standing before the window, he declared, "Each one of you needs to come up here and look at the city from this viewpoint. That's where you should be looking," he said, pointing, "down there, at those boarded-up storefronts, the empty office buildings, the uncollected garbage bins spilling trash onto the streets, all the people in line for welfare because they think that's the only way they can survive. You need to see all that, because that is the wreckage you have caused.

"By contrast," he went on, "you also need to see, far over there in the corner of the park, one of the rarest sights this city has seen in years, that of a new structure being built, the new gazebo, not built by the city but by volunteers. Before a few concerned citizens took the matter into their own hands, the city allowed the previous gazebo to disintegrate until it had to be condemned." He turned and looked down around the table at the faces still frozen in surprise. "I don't want the same thing to happen to the community band. The only reason that new gazebo is being built is because individuals like Cap and others thought it was important enough to do themselves, and they didn't need an official task force to bog down the process with regulations and committee meetings. It should be apparent to you, now, why I'm firing myself. I have decided that the community band is too important to be entrusted to the city. I love that band, and I want it completely out of your inept hands. I personally am taking full ownership and responsibility for it. With its removal from the city's budget, the Baxter Band no longer exists. From now on, it is Jeffrey Bowden's Band!"

Still goggle-eyed, the committee members watched as Jeffrey walked back to his chair, stepped down onto the floor, and strode out of the room.

Then they all sat in silence and looked at his footprints on the table.

CHAPTER 24

Finding himself with an open schedule, Jeffrey invited Fern to accompany him to Cold Harbor for a weekend visit with his parents. Their friendship had deepened significantly over the past few weeks. In addition to his giving her weekly music lessons, they routinely chatted on the phone after she got home from work, and she had come to the Turcotts' house for dinner a couple of times.

The coastal weather was on its best behavior for the occasion, offering a bracingly cold breeze, with shards of sunlight tossing around on a light chop in the bay. After warm greetings and introductions, Jeffrey's mother absconded with Fern, and he didn't see her again until hours later when, after digging fence-post holes with his father, Jeffrey collapsed into an Adirondack chair on the porch and catnapped in the sun.

The aromas of chowder and baking bread brought him awake slowly and by degrees. With his eyes closed, he listened to the music of the seashore: a chorus of crying gulls accompanied by distant, clanging buoys and the rhythmic slap of water, and he knew, even before recognizing his parents' voices coming from the kitchen, where he was. Then his eyelids opened slightly, and there was Fern lying in a chair beside him, with her cheek against the pillow, looking at him.

His brain cells began nudging each other awake,

murmuring, "Hey, look who's here," and for a while, he just lay there, utterly relaxed, all extraneous muscular activity suspended in the torpor of his drowsiness, able only to breathe and to look at her, which was all he wanted in the world, for now. He visually caressed her apple cheeks, her tidy chin, the little curl of hair resting on her temple. He felt certain that this was what he wanted to wake up to, every day for the rest of his life.

Her hand lay on the arm of her chair, just waiting for Da Vinci to come by and paint its portrait: small, tapered fingers, short nails, no polish, exactly Jeffrey's preference. While making the transit from her face to her hand, his gaze had lingered on notable features in between. The word *voluptuous* came to his mind repeatedly. She wore a knitted pullover, a long denim skirt, and lightweight ankle boots that had showed just a bit of leg as he helped her out of the car earlier. It was a mere representative glimpse, though an impressive one that invited speculation about what lay beneath that skirt. He didn't want to rush that aspect of their relationship. They had the rest of their lives for that, and he wanted about that much time for it, with her.

That morning as they drove down to the coast, he had explained to her just what kind of Neanderthal he was, saying that early in adulthood he had decided to limit his physical experience with women to his one chosen life partner and that he regarded his wedding night as the ideal threshold for this sacred tryst, believing that this would strengthen their marriage bond. It was his way of tactfully saying that she, in agreeing to journey through life with him, was getting a model with essentially no mileage on it, and that he wouldn't be looking for any test drives before signing the contract. She had been surprised, though not unpleasantly so—that he could tell—and his admission hadn't seemed to dampen her excitement about their weekend excursion.

Now, lying drowsily next to her on the sunny porch and

looking at her hand, Jeffrey extended his index finger and brought it toward hers, half the distance and then half again, proving Zeno right every time, leaving the smallest possible gap between his finger and hers, until at last he pushed away the last molecule of air that separated them. He felt the faintest pressure of her finger against the tip of his, and he raised his sleepy eyes to meet her alert ones, seeking her concurrence. Yes, that would do for now. They had the rest of their lives for everything else.

"Jeffrey," she said as soft as a sigh.

"Mm."

"I made a mistake once."

Still slowly breathing, still looking at her, he gleaned the meaning of her statement. The questions of who, when, where, and why failed to rouse the least amount of curiosity in his mind. Looking into her eyes, he opened his mouth and whispered, "I don't care," swearing by his unwavering gaze that it was the truth.

Then it was his turn to confess his mistake. He told her about the Pacific Wind Symphony, all of it, beginning with Andrew Quigley's recruitment of him a year ago, moving on through the disappearance of Helen and the trust-fund money, Quigley's initial sympathy for Jeffrey followed by the older man's sudden obsession with charging Jeffrey as an accomplice in the embezzlement, and ending with the worst part, the part he hadn't told his parents yet, the possibility of some ugly business with hired thugs.

Fern's eyes widened in distress. Incredulous, she whispered, "Do you mean to say he's so angry that he would physically hurt you?"

"I think Andrew knows that I didn't steal the money. He's just frustrated because he can't find Helen," Jeffrey said.

"Shouldn't you go to the police?" Fern asked with growing desperation.

"There's nothing to arrest anyone for," he said. "No one has threatened me directly."

"Maybe you should hire a bodyguard," she said. Fearfully she looked out at the choppy water of the bay, as if expecting a submarine to surface there and discharge a landing party of armed frogmen with AK-47's, ready to deliver the ultimate in body piercing.

Jeffrey had already faced and conquered his paranoia; he wasn't going to lead her down that dark alley of constant fear and overly diligent precautions. He said her name and had to say it again before she finally looked at him, and when she did, he said, "Please don't think about all the bad things that might happen. We face countless risks every day just by getting out of bed in the morning. But ultimately each of us has only one future, one that we create for ourselves consciously by pausing at every crossing and electing to follow one route or the other. God can help us along from time to time with a nudge or the occasional volcanic eruption, yet it is up to us to make the actual steps and to take responsibility for them."

He remembered the afternoon he had stood in his room at the Turcotts' house, packing his suitcase, convinced that he had to go to San Diego, desperate to go there. If he had gone to work for Ray Greenleaf, then he never would have fallen in love with this woman sitting beside him. Tracing back through a tenuous yet clearly linked chain of events, he could accurately say that he had met this lovely woman because a little boy died a long time ago.

"I brought this danger upon myself by accepting Andrew's invitation to direct his symphony," Jeffrey said. "I see now that it was foolish and overreaching for me to expect to go directly from college to such a phenomenal career without having to work my way up to it. As a result, I put myself in the middle of a domestic money-grab, and now I am a handy scapegoat for

Andrew. The reason I'm telling you all this is so you can decide whether I'm worthy of sharing your future. You need to tell me whether you want to continue associating with me now that you know my predicament."

"Oh, I do, Jeffrey, I do," she said, gracing his ears with the most thrilling of words. Then she continued, "It's just so scary. I don't want to think of anything bad happening to you."

"Believe me, neither do I," he said, "but the truth is, I have never yet come across a guarantee saying that I am entitled to survive without incident to the age of seventy-six and a half years—or whatever the average life span is for a man nowa-days—and I have looked carefully through all my paperwork trying to find such a document." He paused to relish the gift of her smile, then continued seriously, "I may have to pay dearly for my mistake. But let's not allow that possibility to ruin our time together now. This is our courtship, part of the sequence that Bob described for us on that first night when we took him to band rehearsal. I don't want to rush through this step, because we're building the foundation for the next, the one where you throw your bridal bouquet to someone and then we check into a very nice hotel somewhere as Mr. and Mrs. Jeffrey Bowden, followed by candlelight and a hot tub and any other sensual pleasures that might strike your fancy, any at all." He was wide awake now, blood coursing, all systems go, thinking what a joy it would be to discover by what various methods he could please her, and he cherished the knowledge that he would con-duct this investigation in an utterly moral and rightful manner, not sneaking around a duck pond at twilight, but living as two lawfully wedded people and letting those intimate experiences create a lifelong bond between them.

The worry disappeared from her face. With a little smile, she said wonderingly, "I've never been in a hot tub before."

Jeffrey's pulse was battering his eardrums with a triple-f

dynamic worthy of a Sousa march, the grandioso part where the piccolo player stands up. Putting his steamy imagination on pause, he brought his feet to the floor, stood, and then helped her up. "I think we'd better go inside and have dinner with my parents now," he said.

⁂

Unemployed, Jeffrey worked harder than ever. He helped Tommy with his catering business and worked on the gazebo every afternoon. On Wednesday evenings, he tutored Fern before band rehearsal, and then the two of them drove to Bob's house and took him and his tuba to rehearsal with them. The old man had decided that the benefits of playing music again far outweighed any health risks. Also, he had chosen not to renew his contract with InfinitiCare.

The Jeffrey Bowden Band had picked up another member. Cap's grandson Bud had appeared at the door of the rehearsal room one Wednesday night and asked to speak with Jeffrey.

Seeing Bud's uneasy expression, Jeffrey feared the boy was about to confess some new wrongdoing, but Bud merely asked in a low, hesitant voice, "Mr. B, do you think I could play in the band?"

"Sure, Bud," Jeffrey responded. "What do you want to play?"

Bud pointed toward the reed section and said, "I was thinking maybe the clarinet. There's a lot of them, and I could just sort of blend in. It wouldn't matter if I wasn't any good."

"I expect all my musicians to play well," Jeffrey told him. "Nobody just sits there faking it."

He assigned Bud to the bass drum and showed him how to strike the head with the lamb's-wool beater. Bud thought it was a thrill to be able to hit something that didn't break and that didn't result in his punishment. He learned fairly quickly how to get a good thump out of the big drum. Jeffrey gave him a short lesson every week before rehearsal and quickly noticed an improvement in his technique. Bud later admitted that his grandpa had rigged up an oil drum in the garage at home for him to practice with.

"Goes out there every evening," Cap confided to Jeffrey with a huge grin when the two were working at the gazebo one afternoon. "Really whales away at it. I think it's the best therapy he's ever had. My daughter finally took him out of that InfinitiCare program. It sure wasn't doing him any good."

"InfinitiCare?" Jeffrey repeated in surprise. "I didn't know they provided therapy to teenagers."

Cap snorted in disgust. "To me, it looked more like babysitting with some brainwashing thrown in," he said. "Lectures on anger management, and anti-aggression videos. What that kid needed was a way to blow off some steam, and playing the bass drum with your band seems to be doing the trick."

What Jeffrey noticed in Bud at band rehearsal was an emerging confidence and self-control. Having been given the responsibility of playing the biggest drum in the band, Bud seized the opportunity to prove himself worthy of the privilege. He worked hard to live up to Jeffrey's expectations, much in the same way that he had become a responsible youth captain on his grandpa's work crew.

The gazebo reconstruction was coming along on schedule. One of the members from Tommy's neighborhood support group had been hired for the part-time maintenance position with the city, relieving Cap of his athletics department responsibilities and leaving him free to work on the gazebo project every evening. The ground had thawed enough to dig holes for the posts, which now were fully installed along with the floor frame. Under Cap's direction, the work crew nailed down some floor planks and had gotten about halfway done when they decided to call it a night.

Walking out with Jeffrey to their cars after the work session, Cap looked with remorse at the darkened restaurant
across the street. The facility had closed its doors recently, owing to continued poor business. "I sure miss complaining about
that coffee," the maintenance man lamented before getting into
his truck.

For his part, Jeffrey missed hearing Cap complain about the
coffee. He would have suggested going somewhere else to visit
for a while, but it was late and he wanted to get home. He had
begun studying the R. B. Harte manuscripts a few hours every
night, wanting to get a sure grasp of the historic pieces before
rehearsing them with his band. As Cap started up his truck,
Jeffrey bid him good night and then watched the older man
drive out of the parking lot.

A hot shower and some aspirin for his aching shoulder were
the next items on Jeffrey's agenda, but something caused him to
linger there in the parking lot. He took one last look at the gazebo, admiring the work they had done so far. As with any large
construction project, there was something hopeful about the
unpainted assembly of wood; it stood as proof of men's ability
to come together with a plan and build something useful in an
orderly way. He wanted to remember to tell Cap to find a good
supply of flags and bunting for the band's opening-day concert,
enough to really dress up the gazebo. He was just about to head
home when he noticed a forgotten spade stuck in the ground
at the perimeter of the work area. He retrieved it and had just
stowed it in the back of the VW when a small car pulled into
the parking lot.

Bearing Maine plates, the vehicle drove directly up to him.
Two men, strangers to him, were in the front seat. The one on
the passenger side rolled down the window and asked, "Jeffrey
Bowden?"

"That's me," Jeffrey said.

"Special delivery," the man said. He tossed a small object at Jeffrey's feet, and the car drove away.

It looked like a centipede two or three inches long, but it wasn't moving, so Jeffrey picked it up and examined it in the streetlight. It was a small, black braid with a ragged-edged tab of fabric or leather a few inches square holding it together at the end.

He almost dropped it when he realized what it was.

※

Tommy and Terri were waiting up when Jeffrey got home that night. They had been worried about him being out so late, and their concern worsened when they saw his ashen face and grim expression.

"We thought you might have had car trouble," Tommy said. "What happened?"

Jeffrey had to sit down. It took him a while to answer. "I had to go to a funeral," he said.

All this time, he had worried only for his own safety. During his phone calls with K, they had discussed the danger posed only to Jeffrey, never the potential risk that K faced as a source of information whom Andrew's thugs might squeeze as a way of locating their intended victim. Why had Jeffrey never thought to warn his friend? Earlier that night, standing in the deserted parking lot after the two strangers had driven away, he had looked down at the gruesome object in the palm of his hand and had been appalled by his own self-centeredness. The braid of hair with its attached piece of scalp was all he had left to apologize to.

"Anything you need, ask me," K had told him the night of the car accident. "Anything."

But Jeffrey never would have asked for this.

He didn't speculate how irreverently the killers might have disposed of K's body, nor in what cruel manner they had taken the life of this man who had done nothing but help Jeffrey throughout their all too short friendship. He only wanted to treat these paltry remains with due respect.

It took only a few thrusts of the shovel to dig the hole, but how much more effort it took for him to cover up the little black braid. He buried it underneath the exposed section of the floor frame, directly beneath the place where he would stand while directing his band. At the next work session, Cap and his crew would finish installing the flooring over the tiny grave. No one else would know it was there, but Jeffrey would think about it every time he climbed those steps and took up his baton.

Sitting with him in the kitchen, Terri and Tommy begged to hear what had caused him such evident distress, but he couldn't talk about it just then, not even to his surrogate parents. He only wanted to go up to his room. At last, they let him go and watched him slowly climb the stairs.

He closed the door to his room and lay down on the bed, but he found it impossible to sleep. With a smoldering anger billowing inside him, he struggled to understand the arrogance that could inspire someone to orchestrate an act of such barbaric cruelty. At last, he set that matter aside for now. He wanted to say goodbye to his friend.

Against the blankness of the ceiling, he envisioned snippets of his yearlong acquaintance with K, going all the way back to K's picking of Jeffrey's pocket and ending with his last glimpse of K, now Kenneth, gradually shrinking at the foot of the escalator at the Honolulu airport, looking up and smiling as the conveyor carried Jeffrey to his new future. Then Jeffrey thought of all the images he had wanted to see, most notably, K wearing a tuxedo and standing with him as best man at his wedding. He would have liked to have shown him the Atlantic Ocean, bought him a lobster dinner, maybe a parka; lost opportunities now, all of them, leaving him without so much as a photograph.

He remembered then that he did have one souvenir of Hawaii. On the windowsill of his room sat a ridiculous-looking monkey made from coconuts stacked one on top of the other, snowman fashion, with crude limbs and a garish, painted smile. K had mailed it to Jeffrey at the Money Building shortly before Jeffrey had quit working there. It had arrived carefully packaged and with no note, just the Hawaii postmark and the return address of K's grandmother's store. Jeffrey had almost thrown it out, seeing it as useless and silly, but he had been waiting for K to call again so he could razz him about sending such a quirky object.

Now he picked it up and looked at it again, wondering if he might have missed something. It wasn't like K to be so frivolous. After fiddling with the monkey for a while, he discovered that the coconuts unscrewed. He persuaded them to do so. Once they were apart, little green rolls of currency fell out onto the floor.

The Benz. K had sold it.

Jeffrey thought of the money has his and Fern's first wedding gift.

CHAPTER 25

People at the Money Building were still talking about the Round Table incident weeks later, and Arthur Geegan knew he had to do something about it.

Initially the mayor had shrugged off the importance of Jeffrey Bowden's abdication of his position with the city. The loss of a community band seemed to be no big deal at first. Now, however, the mayor saw that he had a growing problem on his hands, what with an apparent rallying of support behind the citizen-directed gazebo restoration and the growing anticipation for the upcoming Jeffrey Bowden Band concert on Memorial Day. He didn't want anyone thinking that the way to get things done in Baxter was for some renegade to take things into his own hands and do whatever he wanted. There was a hierarchy in this city that people like Jeffrey Bowden needed to learn about and be reminded of from time to time.

He promptly called a meeting in his office with his two personal aides, O'Malley and Franklin, to propose ways they might subtly redirect public opinion and slow down the momentum behind the newly privatized community band.

"I'm starting to see changes I don't like," Geegan said. "Things like falling enrollment in the InfinitiCare programs. Some of the dropouts are saying they don't need the services anymore, and I think it's because of what this guy Bowden is doing with his band."

"Maybe we need to scare him a little," said O'Malley, a big, red-haired man with a little mustache. He was the thinker; Franklin, an even bigger man who now sat cracking the knuckles on his melon-sized fists, was primarily a man of action and few words. Geegan thought the two made a nice combination, with himself in the middle holding their two leashes, as if walking a pair of mastiffs. "He won't be able to lead that band if his arm is in a sling," O'Malley went on. "There are lots of places he could have an accident in this city. The roads are so poorly maintained. Guardrails are loose in places."

"Nothing lethal," Geegan warned, "or we risk making a martyr out of him. I was thinking a good place to hit him would be in the pocketbook."

"Did he get a license to rebuild that gazebo?" O'Malley asked.

Geegan nodded. "Cap Ordway took care of that. Cap's been around long enough to know all the hoops he has to jump through."

O'Malley tried again. "How about imposing a public-impact fee for putting on a private function in the park? At the very last minute, of course."

Pressing the intercom button on his desk phone, Geegan said, "Darla, bring me the regulations on permits and user fees for city property."

When Geegan had settled back in his chair again, O'Malley said to him, "We also should find out where he's getting the money for those construction materials. He sure couldn't afford them on the peanuts you were paying him, and since he's not patronizing my hardware store across the border, he's got to be paying top dollar for that stuff." Along with a thriving market in retail hardware supplies, the state of New Hampshire had

O'Malley to thank for a profitable shirt manufacturer, now in its fifth year of operation.

"Probably he's got a stash of his own money somewhere," Geegan said with distaste. "He seems the type to hoard his wealth."

"Yeah, but where did he get it?" O'Malley persisted. "We might dig up some useful dirt on him if we can find out his history."

Geegan nodded in agreement. When Darla came to the door with the regulations he had requested, he asked, "Darla, where was Mr. Bowden living when we sent him that employment offer?"

"Hawaii, I believe, Mr. Geegan," she replied. In order to place the documents on his desk, she had to circumnavigate the sprawled legs of Franklin, who simply watched her with interest.

Geegan said to her, "Start reading the archives of the local newspapers there. I want hard copies of any references to him, details about anything he was involved in—names, dates, photographs, the works. This takes precedence over whatever else you're working on. I need everything you can find out by this afternoon."

She gave a slight nod and left the room.

"Doesn't she ever smile?" O'Malley asked.

"I don't want her to smile," Geegan said.

⚓

Jeffrey and Bud routinely worked the early shift on the gazebo, with Cap joining them directly after work. They were shingling the roof now, and the project was drawing to a close. The concert was only a couple of weeks away.

It was heartening for Jeffrey to see how Bud had

straightened himself out with the help of Vince, Cap, and a few others. Despite his size, Bud was still very much a child, but he wasn't afraid to ask questions or admit his ignorance about some aspect of how the world worked. Jeffrey thought this spoke well to the boy's potential. Given a little more experience in thinking through moral dilemmas, the youngster was bound to improve his decision making.

During an early shift at the gazebo one afternoon, Jeffrey worked on the roof laying up shingles while Bud brought him materials by stepladder. "I just figured something out, Mr. B," the boy said to him. "If I don't do anything illegal, I won't get arrested."

Jeffrey was glad he had a roofing nail in his mouth to bite down on so he didn't laugh. After he had driven in the nail with his hammer, he asked, "You figured that out all by yourself, Bud?"

"Yeah," Bud said, clearly exhilarated by his insight.

With genuine admiration, Jeffrey said, "Some people go through their whole lives without making that connection." He stopped to rub his aching shoulder and looked up as the first sprinkle of raindrops fell from the darkening sky. It would be a short work session for them that evening, as heavy rain was forecast.

"I know I shouldn't have messed up that old gazebo," Bud said ruefully, "but the money was just too good to pass up."

Jeffrey briefly pondered the meaning of this statement, then looked down at the boy and asked, "Are you saying that someone paid you to write that graffiti?"

With a bit of persuasion, Bud revealed that Mr. O'Malley, a big, red-haired man with a little mustache, had paid him and his friends to deface various structures around town so the city's graffiti-abatement team could stay in practice, as Bud put it.

"Sometimes he had us do other things, too," the boy added, "like break windows and stuff. It seemed kind of weird, being given permission to do that, but he said we were helping the city workers keep up their repair skills. But don't worry, Mr. B," Bud hastily added. "Nobody's going to lay a finger on this new gazebo, not if I can help it."

As soon as Cap pulled into the parking lot, Jeffrey walked over to meet him and said, "I need to talk to Geegan right now. Was he still at the Money Building when you left?"

Cap affirmed that he was. Seeing the intensity in Jeffrey's eyes, he said, "If you're going to walk on his desk, I want to come watch."

"Bud just told me that he and his pals were getting paid to deface the old gazebo," Jeffrey said. "It sounds like job insurance for Graffiti Abatement. Who's O'Malley?"

"Geegan's right-hand man," Cap said. Gravely, he added, "You don't want to walk on his desk."

Jeffrey drove Tommy's little sedan to the Money Building, parked it in the visitor's lot, and sprinted through the rain to the main entrance. Upon reaching the administrative wing, he discovered that all of the staff had already left for the day except for Darla, who had stayed behind to close up the offices.

"Mr. Geegan has gone home for the evening," the executive secretary told Jeffrey. "Do you want to make an appointment with him for next Monday?"

"I'd like to speak to him now," Jeffrey said with polite firmness. "Can you tell me where he lives?"

She opened her mouth to decline the request, but she hesitated, clearly torn between allegiance to her boss and her desire to help Mr. Bowden, whom she had come to regard as an admirable and honorable man. All afternoon, she had downloaded images and newspaper articles from her computer describing his involvement in a financial scandal in Hawaii. It was a sensational account of infidelity and betrayal, with millions of dollars gone missing, yet Darla could not believe the outrageous claims against the man standing before her desk now. To her, the media attack looked like slander. Mr. Geegan had been exultant at her discovery and had taken the evidence home with him. Now she was regretting having possibly caused trouble for this former city employee who seemed to be making some good changes in her city.

Faced with her evident reluctance, Jeffrey said, "Of course, if you're not supposed to give out that information, I understand. I won't ask you to violate any office rules."

Darla blinked her stiff lashes like a doll about to say "Mama." With wooden professionalism, she said, "Mr. Bowden, I regret that I am not permitted to give out Mr. Geegan's personal address. Only with his authorization can I read it to you from my Rolodex there." With a sideways glance, she indicated the file of index cards on her desk. Then she looked up at Jeffrey again and gave him a little smile before turning away.

Leaving him standing alone at her desk, she walked across the room to close the shades in the waiting area. The pull cord seemed to become tangled in her fingers. Patiently she fiddled with it, looking thoughtfully out at the rain. At last she heard the click of the administrative door closing. Turning, she saw that Mr. Bowden had departed.

With a benign expression, she returned to her desk and straightened the cards in her Rolodex. Then she finished closing up the office and went home.

⁑

It was safe to assume that no one shoveled snow on Hillcrest Avenue, where Arthur Geegan lived. The city snowplow always made its first pass of the day there, and the neighborhood homeowners' association employed people to run snow blowers along the driveways and sidewalks in order to keep the place looking its best for its well-connected residents.

The drive there took Jeffrey up a series of switchbacks climbing a steep rise of land that overlooked the river and the downtown area. He drove slowly with his headlights piercing the rain, which was really coming down now.

Geegan's house sat at the top of the hill and faced away from the city, offering its occupants a picturesque view of the wooded hills to the west. Jeffrey parked along the curved driveway and walked up to the covered entryway of the house. The door was answered not by Geegan but by a big man with red hair and a little mustache. Another man stood silently behind him, his hands jammed into the pockets of his size-XXL warm-up jacket. Jeffrey asked to speak with Geegan. Instead of asking Jeffrey in, the red-haired man told him to wait outside and then closed the door.

Just as Jeffrey thought he was going to have to ring the bell again, the door opened. Geegan stood there, smiling as if he had a nice surprise in store for his visitor.

Jeffrey said to him, "I'm out of work right now, and I was wondering how much you pay graffiti artists to deface buildings in the city."

Geegan hadn't expected this. He hid behind his professional smile while combing through his file of stock answers to surprise questions. At last, he said, "I don't know what you're talking about, Mr. Bowden. That's an absurd idea."

"One of your recruits told me he had been paid to deface the old gazebo," Jeffrey said. "Someone named O'Malley paid him and his pals to do it. It sounded like a good way to be sure your graffiti-abatement team had enough work to keep them on the city payroll."

Smiling a bit less now, Geegan said, "Only a fool would take the word of a hoodlum over that of a city official, Mr. Bowden. Now I think you had better leave."

Jeffrey quickly delivered his parting shot, saying, "If it happens again, I'll bring a newspaper reporter up here so you can describe the whole operation." At that point, Geegan abruptly closed the door. Jeffrey turned and walked back to his car in the heavy rain.

Geegan's men were on Jeffrey's tail before he got to the end of the street. Stubbornly, he maintained a safe speed, refusing to let them rattle him with their high beams flooding the car interior and blinding him when he tried to use the mirrors. Every raindrop reflected the glare of his pursuers' headlights. Soon they began nudging his bumper, jolting the car and causing the tires to lose traction on the wet roadway. Jeffrey repeatedly pulled his car out of its fishtailing as he negotiated the countless switchbacks leading down the steep hillside. As the other car continued to butt the little sedan, crunching metal each time, Jeffrey realized he was going to owe Tommy some bodywork.

At last, the pursuers dropped back a short distance, as though finished with their bullying. Jeffrey concentrated on the road ahead, desperately looking for the turnoff leading him back into town. Suddenly he heard a bang as one of the tires blew. Gripping the steering wheel with both hands, he struggled to maintain control over the car through the next switchback. He had picked a bad place to have a blowout; there was no shoulder room to pull over and put on the spare. Upon hearing another bang, he realized that the men behind him were shooting at him. This wasn't a good place for that to be happening, either.

He lost control of the vehicle and broke headlong through the guardrail. Crashing through small trees and bushes, the car bounced roughly down an embankment that would have made a good model for a roller coaster. Fortunately, the windshield had shattered into a mosaic of fractures, so he didn't have to watch what was coming at him. At last, the car landed on the driver's side at the bottom of the incline. Hurriedly, he struggled out through the uppermost door.

His descent had brought him to the edge of a deserted train yard. Desperate to get to a populated area and put himself in the company of people who didn't want to shoot at him, he ran across the train yard toward the buildings lining the tracks. All the railroad offices were closed, their windows dark and their doors locked. Slogging through a muddy field, Jeffrey headed for a row of grimy brick buildings that looked like abandoned factories. By now he was thoroughly drenched and cold, having worn only his windbreaker. The company of some hoboes with a campfire and a bottle of something to drink sounded pretty good to him. His right shoulder didn't seem to bother him quite so much now that he had banged up the other one.

He hurried through an alleyway, looking for any signs of habitation in the buildings or doorways. The isolated street-lights reflected off shards of broken windows that revealed darkened rooms within, but he noticed a few illuminated ones farther down the street. This was River Street, he realized, Fern's neighborhood. He would have called her and asked directions to her apartment, but he had loaned Tommy his cell phone for the evening.

As he hurried down the street, he saw homeless people huddled shoulder to shoulder inside the modular Plexiglas vestibules the city had erected to keep them out of the bus terminal. They stood there out of the rain, with the glowing red tips of their cigarettes rising and falling like drugged fireflies. Jeffrey had heard that a welfare agency in town provided them with free cigarettes as a benevolent gesture to make them more comfortable in their indigence.

He had reached the row of apartment buildings and now

looked up at the array of lighted windows, wondering which one might be Fern's. The first door he came to was unlocked, so he stepped inside and began to look for anyone who might be able to help him find her, but the hallways were vacant. From behind the apartment doors came the familiar clamor of late-night television, crying children, and family squabbles. He tried knocking on a few doors, but he realized that no one in his right mind would answer at this time of night.

Outside again, Jeffrey squinted up through the rain at the side of the building. Fern had told him that she lived on the third floor, and now he studied the many lighted windows at that level, wondering how he could find hers. A train had just rumbled by, reverberating off the brick structure. As it Doppler-shifted off into the distance, he heard the sound of a cornet.

Keep playing, Fern, he silently urged her as he let himself into the central hallway and headed for the stairs. His clothing was so sodden with rain, it was an effort to climb to the third floor. With each step he took, he could hear the cornet more clearly. She was playing one of the R. B. Harte marches they had been rehearsing and had reached the breakup strain near the end of the piece; he would have to hurry and locate her apartment before she finished playing. He noticed she was rushing the tempo a little, and he made a mental note to coach her on that during their next lesson.

At the top of the stairs, he discovered that the third floor hallway led to either side. The music had stopped, so he waited there, unsure which way to turn, hoping she wasn't going to quit now. After a moment, she resumed playing, bless her little spit valve. The music was coming from his right. He followed the sound, pausing to listen at each door, and at last he located the source. He pounded his fist on the door, and when she stopped playing, he called to her, "Fern, it's Jeffrey."

Immediately, she opened the door. The expression on her

face told him how bad he looked. Drenched, muddy, bloody, shivering violently, and weary to his bones from his exertions, he asked humbly, "Can I come in?"

She sat him in a kitchen chair with a space heater blowing on him and a blanket over his shoulders. While a teakettle heated on the stove, she looked at his eyes—making sure they both were still there, he presumed—and she asked him if he thought he had broken anything. He said no. She gave him a washcloth to hold against his bloody lip, which apparently he had bitten while bouncing around in the car as it careened down the hillside.

"They were paying those kids all along," he told her, "rewarding them for breaking the law. Fern, I don't understand it. I can't comprehend people who think that way. Those kids are being taught that money can buy the worst kind of behavior, that unattended property is free to be used in whatever despicable manner they wish, that their actions carry no consequences because somebody else will clean up after them. It was all a way for Geegan to ensure that his graffiti-abatement team had plenty of work to do."

He stopped in deference to a shiver that seemed to rattle his bones, like a thousand tiny drumsticks ruffling the underside of his skin. When the tattoo had ended, he continued, "I've heard of firefighters doing a similar thing, starting brushfires when business was slow just to keep themselves employed. It's one thing coming from an individual who might be wrongheaded and maybe desperate for income. But coming from elected officials who have sworn to carry out their duties with the community's interests uppermost in their minds, it's intolerable. I can't fathom that degree of cynicism and exploitation of human nature." He looked around for Fern, wanting to make sure that he hadn't been babbling to the space heater, and was reassured to see her doing something at the stove.

"People wonder why we have so many problems in this city," he said. "I'll admit, I'm just a band director, and for me the world doesn't get much more complicated than six-eight meter. But this is not nanotechnology we're talking about. It's simply the question of how to maintain a decent, cohesive society, and we already know how to do that. We live honorable lives. We marry for life. We have children and raise them to live honorable lives. Da capo, go back to the first measure and repeat. The whole thing goes on and on for generations, the eternal human canon. It's not easy to do; there are plenty of pitfalls and temptations, but we can help each other through those difficulties. And the whole thing is pretty straightforward, in actual fact. Fern, enough of us have to remember how to do the right thing or else our city will be lost, maybe even our society."

A cup of something hot appeared on the table beside him. He picked it up and sipped on it, and this shut him up for a while. In his fury, he had been rambling for some time, telling her about his confrontation with Geegan and the subsequent chase down the hillside. Now he sat quietly with his toddy and watched her as she bustled about the small apartment, apparently going to do some ironing in the adjacent room. He noticed his windbreaker hanging on the back of a chair, although he didn't remember taking it off. It felt as though his brain had stopped functioning on its own and he was having to use the hand crank to keep it going. The little heater in front of him felt good. He wasn't quite done shivering, but the legs of his trousers had started to dry, and the blanket over his shoulders helped to preserve his remaining body heat.

"I heard you practicing," he said when she came back into the room. "Your tone is good, but you're rushing the tempo. Set your metronome at sixty, and I'll rehearse you at that rate on Wednesday."

She took the empty cup from him and set it down on the table, then took him by the arm and said, "Come on."

Trailing the blanket behind him, he accompanied her into the next room to a twin bed with the blanket and bedspread folded back. She had plugged in the iron and now ran its heated foot over the sheets on the bed. "Jeffrey," she said over her shoulder, "take off your clothes."

Seeking clarification, he asked, "Whaat?"

Once she had pulled the bedcovers up again over the warmed sheets, she turned to give him a reassuring smile. "Don't worry," she said, "I'm completely trustworthy. I can even give you references." She took the blanket from his shoulders and spread it over the bed. "I'm going out for a while," she told him. "That will give you some privacy. I want you to take off all your clothes and get into this bed and cover up completely, even your head. Do you understand what I'm saying?" Gravely concerned, she looked closely at his face and waited for him to nod. After he did, she explained, "You are very cold, and you need to get warm. Get in that bed, cover up, and get some sleep." She left him alone in the room and closed the door.

He fumbled with his clothing, baffled to have suddenly lost the knack of manipulating such simple objects as buttons and zippers. Eventually he got everything off and left it in a soggy pile on the floor. He then hurriedly sandwiched himself between the sheets, which graciously imparted their warmth to his chilled skin. *What a smart girl, that Fern,* he thought, *what a find I have made.* Wearily, he settled his head onto the pillow and reviewed the instructions she had given him, wanting to make sure he had done everything. Get in bed. Cover up, even his head. What else? Sleep.

Oh, that last part was going to be easy.

CHAPTER 26

Jeffrey woke up at midnight, according to the clock on the nightstand. He had no idea where he was, but he was happy to find that the proprietor had supplied him with the world's most comfortable bed. Clouds dreamed of being as soft as this bed. The whole thing was a pillow from head to foot, and he lay there with his feet hanging over the end, feeling weightless and perfectly content to be here, wherever here was.

A photograph on the nightstand served to reorient him. It showed him and Fern standing with his parents in front of the bay at Cold Harbor. He remembered now that he was in Fern's apartment and that she had put him to bed to get warm. Various aching places on his body reminded him of the car crash earlier that night.

It was time he got home. He attempted to push back the blankets but discovered they had undergone an alchemic transformation during his nap and now seemed to be made of lead; though perhaps Fern had gotten a bargain at some outlet store on bedcovers made from a nice wool–plutonium blend. At last having gotten himself uncovered, he sat up and looked at the place on the floor where he had left his clothes. They were gone.

This was the second time that this had happened to him: a girl told him to get naked and then ran off with his clothes. Would he never learn?

In spite of the late hour, the light was still on in the kitchen. Before heading in for a visit, he stumbled into the bathroom and looked in the mirror at the picture-perfect shiner he had acquired under his left eye. There was an accompanying bruise on his forehead just to balance things out, and the gash on his lip was still seeping a bit. He dabbed it with some tissue and then used a washcloth to do a general mopping up of his entire face.

After wrapping himself in a couple of blankets, he shuffled out of the bedroom and saw her sitting in a rocking chair next to the kitchen table and reading the newspaper.

"Excuse me," he said, fulfilling the responsibility of any person who found himself wearing a makeshift toga, "can you direct me to the Forum?"

She looked up at him and smiled. "Your clothes are in the dryer," she said. "They'll be done in a few minutes."

Strangely, sunlight was coming through the window. It wasn't midnight, he realized; it was noon. He had slept for sixteen hours. "Don't you have to work?" he asked her.

"I'm doing a little private-duty nursing today," she explained, putting down the paper. "Sit down. I'll feed you."

He sat down and carefully crossed the loose ends of the uppermost blanket over his chest. No doubt K could have instructed him on the proper method of wrapping the rudimentary garments in Polynesian sarong fashion. As it was, Jeffrey was pretty sure he had figured out the basic idea, since everything seemed to be properly covered. Of course the woman was a nurse, so she wouldn't be squeamish if he had a wardrobe failure. But she also was his intended betrothed, and he thought that a certain amount of decorum was in order here. He was looking forward to their wedding night as being an occasion of rapturous discovery, and he knew that its sheen would be dimmed somewhat if either of them got a preview of what lay in store for the other beyond knowing in general the contents of their respective packages.

Discreetly, he studied her as she stood at the sink across the room. A frugal lass, she was wearing a lightweight turtleneck sweater with a cable-knit cardigan over it. Her tapered slacks had a nice shape, with a practical but not excessive maximum beam and a pleasing amount of tumblehome.

"I should call Tommy," Jeffrey said, looking around for a phone. "He and Terri will be worried about me being gone so long."

"I called them last night," Fern said from the stove, where she was scraping something into a bowl. "They're relieved to know that you're okay, and they think it's a good idea for you to stay with me for a while. The police found your car and are doing a criminal investigation to find out who shot out your tires." She came back to the table with the bowl and a spoon and set them both down in front of him.

She had brought him a bowl of cooked cereal: oatmeal and some other grains, studded with raisins. There were walnuts and brown sugar in it too, he discovered, and it went down pretty easily. She had sat down to watch him eat. "Where did you sleep?" he asked her in between mouthfuls.

"In my rocking chair," she answered, waving off his immediate apologies for putting her out of her own bed. "Terri told me you've been putting in some long hours," Fern said. "I wanted you to get a good night's rest. She said you've been spreading yourself pretty thin, not eating much, and staying up late to study the Harte manuscripts." She regarded him with concern stemming from both the clinical and emotional perspectives. "You can push yourself only so far, Jeffrey, before the machinery begins to break down," she said.

His spoon settled into the empty bowl. She began to cook him bacon and eggs next, and while she was at the stove, he reached for the paper. Helen Quigley's photograph was on the front page of a slick magazine insert. So was his.

The Hawaii debacle had caught the interest of the *Baxter Daily News*. But this article wasn't just about the disappearance of the symphony's treasurer and the trust-fund money, he discovered. The writer was suggesting, with all the subtlety of a bugle call, that Jeffrey had been romancing Helen behind her husband's back and conspiring to help her steal Andrew's money.

There were photos of Jeffrey and Helen sitting together in restaurants, attending promotional events, driving around in her car or his, and appearing in other public places, but there also were shots of him carrying her through various doorways in her home, hovering over her as she lay on her sofa, even one of him brushing her hair the night he took her to the fund-raiser. He knew the benign nature of all those situations, and yet even he was a bit shocked to see them all pictured here, accompanied by suggestive captions and columns of speculative nonsense, including quotes from people he didn't know but who claimed to know certain aspects of his character, which he himself would have taken issue with. The photos taken in public were understandable; anyone could have snapped those shots easily without their knowledge. But he wondered who would have set up cameras inside her house, and whether this had been done as an attempt at blackmail. The article also showed pictures of him working with clients at the detox center, and these puzzled him at first, until he saw that the writer was implying something unsavory about Jeffrey's association with the illegal drug trade.

He looked up at Fern, who was now bringing him the second course of his breakfast. Of all the people in this city who might be affected by that newspaper report, she was the one whose opinion he cared the most about. He pushed the paper away and waited with a growing sense of dread for her judgment.

She set the plate of food in front of him and said, "Jeffrey, you must know that I don't believe any of that. Anybody who knows you won't believe it."

"You think they won't believe photographs?" he asked.

She sat next to him and rested her elbows comfortably on the table as though indicating that she was going to be there for a while. "I have complete confidence," she said, "that you could explain what you were doing in every one of those photos, and in each case it would have been something completely honorable. The woman looks drunk."

"She was," he admitted. He picked up his fork but found his gaze drawn to the newspaper again. That would be on kitchen tables all over town, he realized. What would Terri and Tommy think? Would Bud see that as an example of appropriate behavior between two unmarried people? Would Mrs. Roosevelt demand the return of her great-grandfather's manuscripts from Jeffrey's unscrupulous hands? Even his parents could get wind of this, he realized. Despite their knowing the truth, they nevertheless would suffer the embarrassment of the strongly slanted implications against their son.

Fern looked at Jeffrey with a gaze as steady as a cat's. "As far as I'm concerned," she said, "you don't have to explain anything to me. That article is clearly nothing more than a shameless attempt to sell newspapers."

With growing certainty, Jeffrey thought it also could be a tactical move by Arthur Geegan intended to discredit him before the band concert.

Having brought the article to his attention, Fern now folded it within the rest of the newspaper, putting it out of sight. "All of that, the photos and the slander, does nothing to change my opinion of you," she said. "I still think you are the most trustworthy and good-hearted man I have ever known."

"I am relieved to have earned your confidence," he said.

Unable to ignore the eggs any longer, he met their wide-eyed stare and attacked them with his fork.

"The only good thing about the article is that they mentioned the band's concert on Memorial Day," she said. "At least we got a little free advertising."

He reserved comment, being too busy delivering bacon, eggs, and toast to his grateful stomach. Discreetly, he studied Fern. *Single female, plays cornet, heart of gold, a figure that won't stop, and she cooks too,* he thought. What had he done to warrant such good fortune? "Don't you eat?" he asked before filling his mouth again. She just sat there and smiled at him, so he looked around at the orderly kitchen. Just the basics, no elaborate coffeemakers, no specialized appliances requiring an inordinate amount of counter space and attachments to make fondue or some other rarely consumed item, no ostentatious display of cookware—not that she could afford it on her meager salary. He doubted she wanted anything flashy and modern; look who she was considering for a husband.

"That newspaper article described the symphony that Andrew Quigley was putting together for you in Hawaii," she said. "You gave up a lot to come back to Maine."

"I used to think so, too," Jeffrey said, "but I'm finding a surprising amount of fulfillment here. Directing a community band is not anything I ever thought I'd want to do, and yet now I feel compelled to get this band pulled together in time for the Memorial Day concert. It's not an interim job for me anymore. I'm committed to seeing that it happens." It struck him as a sudden realization how attached he had become to his little group of amateurs. "I have tried very hard to leave this town," he told her, "and yet I can't seem to do it. I've got to think that this is the right place for me and that this is the job I need to do."

She didn't seem at all surprised to hear him say this. "The weekend we were in Cold Harbor," she said, "your mother told me she thought you seemed happier in Baxter than when you were in Hawaii. She said you never were one to seek ready-made success; that you had always wanted to make your own way in the world. I think your band here in Baxter is more challenging and meaningful for you because you're doing a lot of the work yourself."

"I'm hardly doing anything," he argued. "Terri did all the organizational work early on. Cap is leading the gazebo project. Mrs. Roosevelt donated the music. What did I do?"

"Jeffrey," she gently admonished him, as though it should have been obvious to him, "those people never would have done those things if you hadn't motivated them. You inspire people to do things they never knew they could do."

Humbly, he asked, "Can I inspire you to accompany me as I march steadily into poverty? I'm not even employed now, you know. I've gone from low salary to no salary."

With a smile, she asked, "Do you think I would only marry a rich man who would give me a ready-made life? I don't want that any more than you want a ready-made symphony." She looked at him in awe, almost in fear, and continued, "I have to wonder what else you could motivate me to do. You inspired me to keep playing in band and to drop six dress sizes, something I hadn't been able to do on my own through InfinitiCare, even after years of trying."

There it was, that company again, he thought. It was everywhere, it seemed, the one thriving business in town. Could Geegan's personal investments have influenced the administrative decisions he made on behalf of the city? "Why do you think the InfinitiCare program didn't work for you?" he asked her.

She gave the question some thought before answering. "Having seen what did work for me," she said, "I'd say their approach was far too complicated. They had me thinking about food all the time, and all I really needed to do was to start focusing on other areas of my life, such as practicing my horn. They gave me reading assignments, logbooks and diaries to keep, workbooks to complete, nutritional charts and menus to study. I had to buy their sugar substitutes and diet sodas and frozen dinners. Their logo was on everything. My diet coach kept coming up with different approaches for me to try rather than letting me stick with one routine long enough for it to work. I almost think she didn't want me to reach my goals."

Job security, he thought, just like Graffiti Abatement, Bob's home-care service, and Bud's youth counseling program.

"Why did you stay enrolled with them for so long if it wasn't working?" Jeffrey asked.

"I tried to drop out a few times," she admitted, "but they always talked me into signing up again. They were very persistent. Even this last time when I did quit, my diet coach called me for weeks afterward, telling me what a mistake I was making, even though I was actually losing weight on my own."

"Do you know any other people in the program?" he asked.

She nodded and said, "A few people from work, and one or two others. Why?"

"You might tell them about your success," he said, "how you achieved your goals on your own. I think that program is a failure." To be honest, he thought it was worse than that; he thought it was actually harming its enrollees by making empty promises and creating a sense of dependency that kept them hostage to the program.

After he had cleaned his plate, he said, meaning it as a compliment, "I could do that all over again," so she gave him the chance to prove it. Watching her take the carton of eggs from the refrigerator for the second time, he said, "I'll buy you groceries someday."

"I believe that you will," she said.

After Jeffrey had cleaned his plate once more, Fern

suggested that he go back to bed for a while. He did, and he slept through the night.

※

At six the next morning, Jeffrey awoke and discovered that his clothes had been folded, stacked, and placed handy to the bed. He found a shower in the bathroom and thought that was a good place for it. The cut on his lip had stopped bleeding, and his various bodily injuries all had settled down into a tolerable collective throb. Clean, dry, and dressed in clothing of a similar nature, he strode into the kitchen feeling better than he had in a long time.

Fern was still in her robe, tousle-haired and beautiful, pouring coffee into two cups. He walked up to her and said, "I just want to practice," and then kissed her. It was just a quick one, not enough to call out the Sousa Band again.

Judging by her smile, it was pretty good for a beginner.

"I'll be checking out today, and you can have your bed back," he said. With sincerity, he added, "I am immensely grateful for the way you helped me."

"I was just repaying a favor," she said. "Did you hear me practicing last night?"

"That was you?" he asked. "I thought it was Wynton Marsalis. Leonard B. Smith showing off for Herbert L. Clarke." He sipped his coffee, which seemed sweet enough without sugar since he had her to look at while he drank it.

In her eyes, he caught a glimpse of worry or, perhaps, of a confidence she wanted to share with him. Curious, he stood patiently before her, breathing in the steam from his coffee, while she gathered the courage to speak. It didn't take long.

"I almost made another mistake," she said, "last night, with you. I took your clothes in to lay them on the nightstand. You had your face buried in my pillow, just your arm and shoulder exposed. You looked so vulnerable, so available. It would have been so easy to slip under those blankets with you." Her apple cheeks turned briefly from Pink Lady to Red Delicious.

He forgot all about his coffee, savoring the words of her confession.

"It was only your shoulder," she said with an amused smile, "but it was incredibly enticing. For the longest time, I couldn't stop looking at it. I put the clothes down and started to touch you. My hand was inches away. But on the nightstand, there was that photograph of us and your parents. It felt as if you all were watching me, so I stopped. I walked out of the room and closed the door, and when I came in here I had to sit down, thinking how close I came to ruining it."

He thought of the night he had looked at Helen's back and nearly taken her into his arms. What a disaster that would have been, all of it captured by those hidden cameras, adding substance to the newspaper's otherwise baseless attack on his character. What fine pictures he would have made for the *Baxter Daily Sleaze* had he done as Helen had suggested, blown off the fund-raiser and taken advantage of the weak-willed, emotionally crippled Mrs. Quigley IV. And how would he have explained those pictures to this most precious woman standing before him, his future life partner to whom he wanted so desperately to prove himself worthy?

Fern continued, "I realized last night, as I stood next to you and looked at that photograph on my nightstand, what I want for myself. That picture of the four of us illustrates it perfectly in two generations. I want the same kind of marriage your parents have."

Jeffrey set his coffee cup on the countertop, thinking he might be needing both arms in a moment.

"That weekend when I met your parents helped me

understand what I want for myself in a marriage," she said. "Your mother and father still love each other, perhaps as deeply as they did when they were first married, perhaps more. It was apparent in the way they talked to each other and in a hundred little things I saw. While you were sleeping on the porch, the three of us were in the kitchen. Your mother had been cooking and had sat down to rest on a stool near the sideboard. Your dad brought over a cup of tea for her. He set it down with one hand and then put his other hand on the back of her neck. It was the tenderest gesture, yet there also was an element of possession. No—" Fern corrected herself, saying, "I think *privilege* might be a better word, the knowledge that he could do that and that she welcomed it, even relished it as an expression of their closeness. I think if I hadn't been there, he might have kissed her." She smiled a little at the memory and continued, "I want that kind of bond with someone, the kind that can make me feel that way about my husband when we are their age. The kind that can produce someone like you as a son."

She paused to give him a chance to say something, but he was utterly speechless, savoring her words as they resounded in his mind.

"You see," she said, "I didn't grow up in that kind of family. Mine was fractured and disjointed, all over the map. My father was a free spirit who didn't like the idea of being tied down by marriage, and my mother was too weak to decide for herself what she wanted. She went along with whatever strong personality happened to be in her life at the moment. They weren't cruel or neglectful as parents, but they didn't help me much when I needed guidance. My uncle took me in for a while just to give me some stability while my parents floundered around. Then I got involved with a man whom I thought I loved, but I realized pretty quickly that I was going down the same path my mother had taken. I knew I didn't want to end up the way she had, so I moved out of there and then rented this place, which was all I could afford. I thought it was important to be by myself for a while and figure out what I wanted. And then meeting you and your parents helped me discover it."

At last summoning his voice, Jeffrey said with profound admiration, "Fern, you are a marvel. That decision you made last night speaks volumes for your strength. Sometimes people need help in making decisions like that. Sometimes they need a maintenance man with a flashlight." Seeing her understandable confusion, he hurriedly continued, "I'll explain that to you another time. For now, just be assured that I want the same thing you do." He was speaking primarily of his parents' being a role model for them, of course, but it thrilled him to know that she found him physically attractive as well—and it was pretty exciting to imagine the two of them sharing that bed, or maybe one with a bit more legroom, at the appropriate time. "I know exactly how we can achieve what you want," he said, now seeing the simple construction of her robe and thinking that a few layers of clothing between them was not enough, that there needed to be a wall or two, "and one of the ways is for me to get out of your apartment immediately."

He declined her offer of a ride, saying that he felt like walking. She went downstairs with him to street level. In the safety of the open doorway, with the whole world looking on as a chaperone, he pulled her into an embrace. With her head against his shoulder and his mouth in her hair, the two of them stood pressed together in a fully clothed, whole-body kiss, a promise as well as a commitment to abiding by their principles.

Reluctantly, he pulled away, needing to look at her as he spoke. "You have that gorgeous solo to play at our band concert," he said, smiling, already proud of her, as if he were standing on the podium watching her take her bows, "that cadenza which showcases your playing ability. The composer knew precisely where in the score that solo belonged. The whole composition builds up to it, and when it occurs, the listener is ready for it, begging for it. It's the perfect climax to the whole piece. I am going to lead the band up to that point in the score, and then you are going to play that solo and knock everyone's auditory socks off. But you can't play it too early, or the effect will be ruined. You've got to wait until the right moment for it to be meaningful." He gave her hands a light squeeze, then he turned and walked away.

The rainstorm had passed. Jeffrey found the clear morning to be cold but tolerable once his windbreaker was zipped up. He followed River Street to Central, stopping to slip a few dollars into the palms of some panhandlers along the way. Then he walked uphill to the business district, never realizing there were so many newspaper vending machines in this town, each of them filled with copies of those images he wanted to forget.

A car pulled up to the curb beside him, and he was surprised to see it was Terri's VW. "Fern told me you were walking home," she said, evidently in a state of agitation. "Get in."

He did and saw that she had brought along the leather satchel, which now lay on the front seat between them.

"Mrs. Roosevelt has been calling the house, trying to reach you," Terri told him as she drove. "She is furious about yesterday's newspaper article about you and wants you to help her put together a counterattack. She said for you to come to her house and bring the Harte manuscripts. I've got them all there in the satchel for you." She dropped him off at the Roosevelt mansion, where a late model minivan was parked at the curb.

The maid escorted Jeffrey to a study just off the main hallway. Evidently the central heating was still on light-duty; Mrs. Roosevelt was wearing a turtleneck sweater of serious proportions and doing it elegantly. In response to her immediate gush of concern over the cuts and bruises on his face, he dismissed his injuries as the result of a minor car accident and assured her that he was fine.

She led him over to the long, polished table where she had been sitting with a red-haired, alert-looking young chap whom she introduced as Wilson Bean, reporter for the *Star Tribune* out of Portland, Maine. He stood up and offered Jeffrey a polite greeting along with a firm handshake. His demeanor could accurately be described as jaunty. Undoubtedly, the minivan outside belonged to the young reporter, but Jeffrey could easily imagine Wilson Bean wearing a touring cap and motoring about behind the wheel of a Model A.

Jeffrey placed the satchel of manuscripts on the table, out of the way but within reach, and took a chair opposite Mrs. Roosevelt. After he had sat down, she said, "Mr. Bowden, it is time to fight fire with fire. I have no doubt that Arthur Geegan was behind that disgraceful attack on you in yesterday's newspaper. Wilson here has expressed an interest in your collection of R. B. Harte manuscripts. I have told him about your band's anticipated performance on Memorial Day, and he thinks he can put together a timely feature for the historical arts crowd in Portland as well as Boston and possibly New York. He has in mind something splashy but with a far more dignified effect than our local paper's tawdry interests. I thought you might be willing to talk to him."

Jeffrey certainly was willing. Before starting the interview, however, he said to his hostess, "Mrs. Roosevelt, I want to thank you for giving me the chance to reclaim my reputation."

"Mr. Bowden," she assured him, "you never lost it with me."

He carefully took the fragile manuscripts out of the satchel and spread a few of them out on the table so Wilson Bean could see what a 150-year-old original composition looked like. Then the reporter started his recording machine.

Jeffrey started out by saying, "This is music for warriors."

CHAPTER 27

Jeffrey, Wilson Bean, and Mrs. Roosevelt sat at the long, glossy table with the fireplace blazing behind them. Over the next two hours, Jeffrey gave the newspaperman a crash course on military bands. "Musicians have been an integral part of the war effort throughout human history," he said. "Trumpets and kettledrums were commonly used for signaling the troops, of course, although the Janissary bands—"

"The what?" Wilson interrupted. "Spell that, would you?" He had found it necessary to augment his audio recording by applying pen to notebook. He scribbled furiously as Jeffrey continued speaking.

"Janissaries," Jeffrey said, "were the Ottoman bands of the thirteenth century. They carried instruments that were unfamiliar to the enemy: crashing cymbals, jangling crescents, and bellowing horns, which amazed and terrified the enemy soldiers with their strange sounds." He went on to discuss the Etchmiadzin priests of Armenia, who, as their countrymen fled, stayed behind to ring the church bells to inspire courage in the Armenian soldiers confronting the invading enemy. Then he talked specifically about the military bands of New England, many of which had been formed during the Civil War.

"No doubt you've seen photographs of that era," he said. "They're grainy and sometimes faded with age, but you can see the faces of the soldiers, which are grave in spite of their youth, scared but also stubborn. They wore thin boots and ragged uniforms, and they were going off to fight an enemy that looked just like them, that could have been their cousins. Each unit would have had a drummer who played a steady beat to keep them marching along over the miles, so they didn't lag behind and fall prey to their fears. The bugler played patriotic songs to remind them why they were out there risking their lives. He played brass fanfares meant to inspire them, and to assure them that they were warriors, as vital to their generals as the bravest of ancient Greeks, to compel them to make the charge into battle, especially when they were short of ammunition and outnumbered by their enemy. The drummer kept them going, playing robustly and magnificently as only a field drum can sound: a deep, grumbling roar like machinery—before they knew what machinery was. It was just a reverberating cowhide drumhead beaten by wooden sticks, but when played by a skilled drummer, it was enough.

"Music influences us in a primal and instinctive way," Jeffrey said. "A scholar could point out examples in the tribal music of Africans and American Indians, where drumming and singing were used to instill courage in the hearts of young men preparing to go out and hunt dangerous game or to fight their enemies. Religious people, such as in Haiti, drum and chant themselves into a hypnotic devotional fervor. People hear these rhythms, and they can hardly keep from tapping their feet. Get them off their chairs and they're marching."

Finally, Jeffrey spoke about the Baxter Band and R. B. Harte's significant role in it, impressing upon the young reporter the social value of the music lying on the table before him.

"Some people think there is no role in the modern world for a band with a military history," Jeffrey said. "People hear old marches like these and they think they're quaint and irrelevant

to our time. Though it breaks my heart to say so, I liken it to the
way some people think the notion of a representative republi-
can government is quaint, an outmoded idea whose importance
becomes lost behind a costumed facade. To them, the name of
George Washington brings to mind a funny-looking guy with
a powdered wig and wooden teeth, not a military leader who
exhibited extraordinary personal bravery and then followed it
up with public service of an astonishingly humble nature. Not
long ago, the Baxter Band was in danger of becoming another
quaint item in a scrapbook. A number of concerned people decided they didn't want that to happen, so they used their individual skills and resources to begin its revival. I don't want this
city to become endangered, either, and that is why, this coming
Memorial Day, it will be my supreme honor for my band to introduce these works to the people of Baxter."

Wilson Bean recorded it all. At an appropriate lull in the interview, he asked, "Why did you take on full financial responsibility for the band? Why not let the city continue to support it?"

Jeffrey exchanged a meaningful glance with Mrs. Roosevelt
and saw that she was leaving it up to him to answer. He said, "I
think the community band is far too important to be included
on a municipal budget report along with road repair and garbage collection. It should be supported directly by people who
value it. Doing so gives them ownership, even if they own nothing else." He paused for a moment, trying to decide whether to
deliver his last volley, then he realized that everything he had
said up to this point would be wasted if he didn't throw in the
stinger.

"A lot of Maine boys died in the war to end slavery," Jeffrey
said, "and I fear that we are seeing a recurrence of slavery, not
only economic enslavement but also slavery of the human spirit.
I'm not just talking about the taxpayers beholden to hand over
a percentage of their income to their government. I mean the

spiritual enslavement of impoverished people who depend on government handouts for their very survival, even at the expense of their dignity and ambition. The elders of this city will tell you that we didn't always have welfare here. We used to have tradesmen, merchants, bankers, hoteliers, artisans, craftsmen. All those people worked for themselves, not out of selfishness but out of a sense of responsibility. They took care of their families so no one else had to, sometimes enjoying such success as to sustain their heirs for generations and to enable them to leave generous endowments to colleges, arts institutions, hospitals, orphanages, homes for unwed mothers, every kind of charity. Now we have a few powerful individuals, elected officials and their appointed cohorts, controlling that stream of money, doling it out as they see fit and only after taking a generous cut for themselves. History has shown us that such an economy never results in prosperity, only in a dictatorship of some degree."

"Mr. Bowden, are you encouraging the people of Baxter to take over their government?" Wilson Bean asked.

"Not at all," Jeffrey asserted. "I'm encouraging them to take over their lives. I've seen amazing examples of small-scale success in this city. I hope to see more of it. Come to my band concert and you'll see vendors, advertisers, benefactors. All of them are individual success stories, every one worthy of a newspaper story. These R. B. Harte compositions have an importance to this community that I believe surpasses their musical value. They were intended to inspire soldiers in wartime, but we don't just fight uniformed armies. People go to battle every day with their own personal enemies. This music does not advocate war; it advocates courage. And that is why I want my band to play it. I want these marches to awaken people to their potential as individuals, to inspire them to fight for something they want or against something they don't want. Every citizen in this town needs to get up every day and fight his battle and to help his neighbor fight hers, not just sit back and ask, 'Who's going to help me?'"

At the end of the interview, while Wilson Bean packed away his recording equipment, Mrs. Roosevelt came over to Jeffrey to thank him for his participation. "You were magnificent, by the way," she added, "walking on the Round Table as you did. King Arthur couldn't get the housekeeper in there fast enough to buff it clean again. But all the polishing rags in the world won't erase your footsteps from the memory of everyone who watched your performance."

"You're very kind," he said humbly.

"You didn't save the taxpayers any money by quitting, either," she said. "The budget committee promptly moved your salary into another department's account for some new program or an extension of one that already exists."

He shook his head in dismay, then told her, "After the city officially took me off their employment records, someone tracked me down at home to offer me unemployment benefits. They wanted to give me a monthly check, medical coverage, and food stamps for the privilege of not working."

With a nod, she said, "I understand their agents work on commission. The incentive is to sign up every individual they can." A smile lurked behind the drapery of her eyes. "I would like to have been there to hear your response to that offer," she said.

"I'm glad you weren't," he declared. "I wouldn't have been able to use all those colorful words." He was pleased to get a chuckle out of her. Then he turned serious again and asked, "Mrs. Roosevelt, how are we ever going to change things in this city?"

"Just the way you're doing it," she answered, squeezing his hand and walking with him to the door, "little by little."

Jeffrey walked out to the street with Wilson Bean and complimented him on his minivan. He was remembering that he owed Tommy a car, since the sedan had been deemed a total loss by Tommy's insurance company. This one seemed just right for use as a catering van.

"It's a smooth ride," Wilson said, "but it's more than I need. I bought it a couple of years ago when I was doing freelance work for nature magazines, and it was great for hauling my camping gear. Now that I'm working out of Portland, I'd rather have something smaller."

The two men struck a deal, and Jeffrey test-drove the vehicle to the bank, where he withdrew the necessary funds for the transaction. He then drove Wilson to a halfway point between Baxter and Portland, where Wilson's wife would be picking him up in her car.

"Will you be covering our concert on Memorial Day?" Jeffrey asked as they headed south on the interstate.

"Without a doubt," Wilson said. "Likely you'll get coverage from all the major publications in New England once they see this feature I'm doing. My editor has wanted to break into this region for a long time. Traditionally, the media in Baxter have been pretty insular. The people running the town keep a tight rein on the type of news that gets reported. Some of our reporters have actually been warned off of stories they were investigating."

While Jeffrey drove, he told the reporter what he knew about the Graffiti Abatement scam. Wilson made copious notes and said he was pretty sure his editor would be interested in that story too. He would seek approval to do some undercover work, and in the meantime he urged Jeffrey to keep him updated on any new occurrences.

Later that afternoon, Jeffrey drove into the Turcotts' driveway and honked the horn. After Tommy came out, Jeffrey handed him the keys and said, "I always thought it would be a sign of achievement to be able to buy my dad a car."

Terri hadn't gotten home from work yet. The two men stood next to the minivan, which Jeffrey had parked about halfway up the driveway so as to allow room for admiring the vehicle from all sides.

"I hope you'll still ask to borrow it from time to time," Tommy said, beaming with pleasure.

Jeffrey was about to joke that he should buy a couple of spare tires first, in case he got shot at again, when a small, familiar car pulled into the driveway behind the minivan. The occupants looked like the same two guys who had made the gruesome special delivery at the gazebo. In a stern voice, Jeffrey said, "Tommy, go inside the house. Now."

Tommy obeyed. Jeffrey watched the two men as they got out of the car. They had left the engine running, as if this job wasn't going to take long. The one from the passenger side carried a baseball bat. Jeffrey hoped that if they were going to hit him, they would choose someplace that already hurt and thus preserve his few remaining uninjured body parts. On impulse, he decided to move away from the car; he didn't want it to suffer body damage so soon after its purchase. Before the men got too close, he called to them, "Which one of you is the butcher?"

The question didn't slow them down any, but the guy carrying the bat was curious enough to ask derisively, "What are you talking about?"

"That special delivery you made at the gazebo," Jeffrey said. "Was that your handiwork, or do you outsource that kind of surgery?"

"That thing I threw at you?" the batter asked. "I don't know what it was. I was just told to deliver it."

"Who's paying you? Quigley or somebody else?" Jeffrey asked. The two men had split up and were getting into position for the attack, the batter coming straight toward him, the driver moving off to his right to block any escape. While keeping the other guy in his peripheral vision, Jeffrey kept talking to the batter. "I know you're not supposed to tell me that, but I want to know anyway. How much is he paying you? What kind of a living can you make delivering severed body parts? Is the job market any better in the criminal underworld than it is on Main Street?"

"Will you shut up? I'm trying to do a job here," the batter complained.

"Can't you find a real one?" Jeffrey taunted him.

Another car pulled up just then, and two more guys got out. Jeffrey wondered if this was Geegan's team coming on deck. *They're lining up to get at me,* he thought at first, but he soon discovered that the latest arrivals were Don and Levi, members of Tommy's neighborhood support group, no doubt coming to discuss the sandwich vending booth they planned on setting up at the band concert. Jeffrey had participated in their recent planning sessions, and he had come to know both men fairly well.

"Jeff, that newspaper article about you is bull," Levi declared while climbing out of his car. "I know you, and I can't believe any of that stuff they were saying about you. I canceled my subscription to that paper."

"I'm doing the same thing," said Don, who also had stepped out onto the driveway. "Why should I pay to read stuff I know isn't true? I got better things to do with my money." A formerly athletic man who was now a bit paunchy but still active, Don gazed with sudden interest at the two hired thugs. "Are these your friends, Jeff? Hey, how'ya doing? You guys lose a ball? I've been thinking we ought to organize a neighborhood softball league now that the weather's getting better."

Another vehicle arrived, this one being Terri's VW, and the men had to step aside to make way for her in the driveway. She parked in the garage, hopped out of the vehicle, and came over to join the group. "Hi," she offered as a general greeting. Her attention settled on the two unfamiliar faces and the baseball bat. "You guys lose a ball?" she asked.

Tommy came out of the house and looked worriedly at Jeff. "Is everything okay?" he asked.

"We could use a ball and some mitts," Jeffrey told him, "but other than that, yeah, everything's fine."

"Whose minivan?" asked Terri, wide-eyed with admiration.

"It's ours," Tommy said. "Jeff bought it for us."

She exclaimed her surprise and happily climbed behind the wheel while Tommy showed her the various features.

Jeffrey turned to the guy with the bat and asked, "You want to reschedule this for another time?"

Both of the hired men looked disgusted and seemed stymied with so many witnesses hampering what was supposed to have been a hit-and-run job.

"You got us blocked in," the batter complained to Levi, who apologized and went to move his car.

Jeffrey walked to the car with the two hired thugs. As they got in, he said to them, "You tell Quigley I am insulted that he would hire someone to do his fighting for him. Tell him I said he's a coward if he can't face me directly with his complaints. I'll be at the gazebo in the park on Memorial Day. If he has anything to say to me, he can say it to me then. Otherwise, he needs to stop bothering me with these petty distractions. I'm busy putting together a band concert."

"Are we gonna get paid, Phil?" the driver worriedly asked his companion. "We didn't do the job."

Phil set the baseball bat down on the floorboard beside his feet. "Shut up, George," he muttered, but he didn't appear confident that a paycheck was likely.

"Are you guys any good?" Jeffrey asked. "I might need some protection from another couple of guys, but I don't want to hire just anybody. Your entrance today was pretty effective, but you really lost impact there at the end. I need somebody reliable."

"Yeah, we're good," Phil snapped defensively. "Your friends just got in our way, that's all."

"How much is Quigley paying you?" Jeffrey asked.

"A hundred each," Phil answered.

Jeffrey scoffed, "Tell him I also said he's a cheapskate. Do you know how rich that guy is? He leaves that much for a tip at lunch. Listen, until he starts paying you a decent wage, you're welcome to help us out with the gazebo. We'll start painting it pretty soon, and we could use some extra hands."

"How much does the job pay?" Phil asked.

"Nothing," Jeffrey said. "It's all volunteer work."

"Why should we work for nothing?" Phil demanded.

"Because you won't get arrested for doing it," Jeffrey replied. "Because volunteering will go a long way toward mending your broken character. Because you'll get to eat the best sandwiches you've ever had in your life. Because, if I like your work, I'll hire you for protection on Memorial Day, and at better rates than what Quigley is offering you."

"Let's go, George," Phil said, uneasy with being on the brink of legal employment.

After the car drove off, Jeffrey turned to see Tommy waiting for him by the minivan. Terri was shepherding Don and Levi into the house, the three of them chattering excitedly about their plans for the concert.

"I called the police as soon as I got inside the house," said Tommy, wide-eyed. He still seemed a bit shaken by the averted violence. "I don't know why they haven't come."

"It doesn't look like we needed them after all," Jeffrey said.

"Did you know those guys?" Tommy asked.

Jeffrey began explaining their connection with his former employer in Hawaii when a police cruiser pulled up.

"Everything okay here?" one of the officers asked.

"What took you so long?" Tommy asked. "I called a half hour ago."

"We were told another unit was responding to the call," the officer said. "We just were passing and thought we'd follow up."

Tommy explained that no other assistance had shown up, but said that everything seemed to have worked out. After the cruiser left, he said to Jeffrey, "Could things be that mixed up at the police department that they don't even know who's responding to a call?"

Jeffrey was wondering if they had just seen an example of how far Geegan's influence extended.

CHAPTER 28

On the day of the band concert, Jeffrey woke up with a sore right shoulder but was determined to ignore it beyond taking some aspirin. After breakfast, he helped Tommy load the back of the minivan with boxes of freshly baked rolls, insulated buckets of sandwich fillings, and packages of napkins and wrapping material.

"Maybe you ought to take it easy on that shoulder," Tommy cautioned. "After all, you've got a band concert to direct later today."

Jeffrey assured him he would be fine.

Don and Levi arrived with folding tables and a load of ice. The four men prepared to transport everything to the park, where they would begin setting up the sandwich booth. As they were loading the ice into the minivan, Terri came out and fussed at Jeffrey for doing too much heavy lifting. "You should be resting your shoulder," she said.

"Bring me my jacket," he urged her. "My music folder and baton, too. I'll take them with me to the park now." After having completed Fern's uniform, Terri had sewn a jacket for Jeffrey to wear. A handsome construction of white gabardine, it featured military-style epaulettes, gold braid, and brass buttons salvaged from the band uniforms.

"You're not putting that jacket in the back of a minivan full of ice bags and food and folding tables," she declared, promising to bring the jacket to him later along with the other things he needed for the concert. "Why are you going in so early?" she asked.

"I want to help Cap with the bunting," he explained. "There's a lot of it to hang, and we've got dozens of flags to put up too."

"Don't wear yourself out before the concert," she warned, but he waved off her concern.

It was promising to be a nice day, with a mostly clear sky and enough breeze to unfurl the flags but not so much as to blow the ladies' sun hats away. Jeffrey was heartened to see people beginning to trickle into the park with still a couple of hours to go before the concert. Some early birds were using their lawn chairs and picnic coolers to claim front-row seats around the gazebo. Residents from the nearby houses, having opened their doors and windows, were taking note of the activity in the park. A few came over to see how the concert preparations were going, and several stayed to help hang bunting and put plastic liners in the trash barrels.

Jeffrey had feared a lingering effect from the slanderous newspaper feature, but as he helped the volunteers with various tasks and exchanged pleasantries with some of the attendees, the only comments he heard were supportive ones.

"You're the band director?" one local resident said to him in surprise. "I thought you were a construction worker, the way you were out here working every night."

"Is that the guy they smeared in the paper?" another man asked, then scoffed. "If he really took that money, what would he be doing in Baxter leading a community band?"

One of the members from Tommy's neighborhood support group who had come to help hang bunting on the gazebo assured him, "Jeffrey, I know you ain't no millionaire. I only ever seen you wearing one shirt."

With the privatization of the band, the city's truck and equipment were no longer available for Jeffrey's use. He was impressed by his band members' ability to coordinate a fleet of private vehicles for transporting dozens of folding chairs from local churches and community groups, as well as music stands from the school where the band rehearsed.

While helping to assemble everything inside the gazebo, he was astonished to see Cap and Bud carrying in the bass drum with "BB" painted on its head.

"How did you manage to get approval to use the city's property?" Jeffrey asked the maintenance man.

"It's my property now," Cap declared. "I told Geegan I needed that storage room, and since the Baxter Band didn't exist anymore, I offered to take this drum off his hands. I bought it for Bud to use at home. As long as he's playing, we can bring it to your concerts."

Fern was there, appearing statuesque and regal in her exquisitely fitted uniform, and displaying an astonishingly confident attitude. A pair of white gloves added the perfect finishing touch to her outfit, and she had gotten a new haircut for the occasion. Jeffrey had much to say about her appearance, but when their paths crossed, he was busy carrying an armload of percussion equipment to the gazebo, so he packaged his hearty approval into a simple nod and sent it by way of a glance that promised a more expressive and detailed discussion on the subject sometime in the future. The emerging radiance on her cheeks indicated that she received his message.

Jeffrey's parents had driven up for the day, and he stood speaking with them briefly. His mother looked proud, whereas his father appeared a bit in awe of the mass of activity that his son had orchestrated on behalf of a simple community band. Jeffrey himself was beginning to feel as though he were riding on the crest of something much larger than he had expected. He had set all these wheels in motion, and now the whole vehicle was beginning to take on a momentum all its own.

He was especially pleased to see that Mrs. Roosevelt and her mother had chosen to attend the band's opening-day concert. The dutiful housemaid pushed the wheelchair bearing the blanket-swaddled old woman, who appeared happy as a child on this special outing, while two more staff members trailed along carrying a picnic basket, folding chairs, and tote bags. Jeffrey made his way over to them. From his conversation with Mrs. Roosevelt, he learned that they were staying in town for the summer.

He said to her, "Terri told me that Geegan imposed a public-impact fee for this event at the last minute and that you took care of it for me."

Mrs. Roosevelt raised a hand to silence him and said, "Now don't argue with me, Mr. Bowden, the deed is done. I wasn't going to allow that man to ruin this concert with such a sneaky technicality as that. It's as much our day as yours, this being a community band." She pressed a receipt into his hand and said, "If anyone asks you about it, just show them this. Darla assured me the transaction would be recorded in time for today's concert, but you can't be too careful with that bunch." Her facial expression betrayed a nagging worry and she said, "I can't help thinking you're not in the clear yet. You'd best be on your guard for more tricks."

Tommy's sandwich stand had begun attracting customers as soon as it was set up for business. Jeffrey had wanted to ask if there was anything he could do to help out, but Tommy was too busy to speak with him. Over the past couple of months, the fledgling caterer had developed a steady following of customers by taking phone orders and using the minivan for deliveries, even making a daily run to the Money Building. He and Terri were looking into the possibility of leasing the vacant restaurant across from the park as the next step in developing their new enterprise.

Terri caught up to Jeffrey just then and told him, "You'd better go get ready. Everything you need for the concert is in the VW. And once you get that jacket on, be careful not to get it dirty."

He promised he wouldn't, and then asked where she was parked.

"In the very last row," she said. Her eyes grew wide as she added, "That lot is almost full. I saw license plates from Massachusetts and even New York!"

"Thanks to Wilson Bean's newspaper article, no doubt," Jeffrey said, greatly pleased.

"Go on, go on," she urged, giving him a push. "Everything's ready but you."

As he headed for the parking lot, the full meaning of her words struck him as a sudden realization. Everything was ready. All of the work they had done these past few months was paying off, and now it was time for the actual event that had been the purpose for all their activity.

He had to stop and just look at it all. Up to this point, he had been wrapped up in the details of the preparations, but now, for the first time, he could stand at the perimeter and see what had been accomplished. There it all was in front of him.

In one sweeping glance, he saw the crowd with their lawn chairs and blankets, the musicians inside the gazebo, instruments and music all ready. The structure itself, larger than the one it had replaced, stood resplendent with its fresh coat of paint, patriotic drapery, and boldly flying flags. He could hear Bud thumping on the bass drum, Bob on his tuba, Fern showing off a little on her cornet. A short distance away, Tommy and his sandwich crew were feeding a crowd. And Cap would be around somewhere, bustling at the perimeter of everything, taking care of details that no one would notice unless they weren't done. For a moment, Jeffrey marveled at the scene, and then he wondered why it should seem such a rare occurrence that people had come together and applied their individual talents toward a common goal and achieved something worthy. *This kind of thing should be happening all the time, all over the country,* he thought. Perhaps it was and he simply didn't know about it.

They were waiting for him. He hastened through the parking lot toward Terri's VW at the far end. In the back of the vehicle, he found his jacket on a hanger, looking immaculate beneath a dry cleaner's plastic bag. Slipping off the bag, he saw what a marvelous thing she had done for him. He put his arms through the sleeves and felt the garment's perfect fit as it settled onto his shoulders. Then he fastened the brass buttons and picked up his music folder and baton. He wanted to remember, as he mounted the podium, to say a brief prayer in honor of K and of Jeffrey Turcott, the little boy who had played an invisible yet significant role in bringing all this about. He understood now the momentousness of a seemingly minor decision, such as choosing whether or not to pursue a girl across the marsh alongside a duck pond and whether or not to stroke the exposed back of a woman who had placed hidden cameras in her home to record the actions following his decision. This was how God was in the details, he thought; not in the clouds, as Michelangelo had portrayed him, but in a pair of rolling dice whose statistically driven outcome could change the trajectory of a person's life; in the decision of two mothers to independently and unknowingly give their sons the same name; in the fortuity of a city maintenance man deciding to take one more pass through the municipal park with his flashlight; in the mind of an Army retiree teaching his niece how to play cornet.

The sound of shouting drew Jeffrey's attention to a group of men standing at the far end of the parking lot near the trees.

Closest to him were a couple of teenaged boys. At the perimeter of the group, he recognized Cap's distinctively crooked figure and saw that he was talking agitatedly to a heavily built man with red hair. Jeffrey watched in astonishment as the man suddenly flung his arm forward to connect his fist with Cap's jaw, snapping the old man's head backward like a punching bag. A fraction of a second later came the sickening sound of impact, and the maintenance man collapsed onto the ground.

By then Jeffrey was in motion, his arms pumping as he found himself propelled by an explosion of outrage. He ran straight toward the man, and as he got closer, he saw it was O'Malley.

Coming in fast and at an oblique angle, Jeffrey took O'Malley by surprise and tackled him to the ground. He gave the man's face a brisk polishing in the gravel to make sure he had his attention, and then he said, "Don't ever hit an old man like that. Not ever."

"I'll hit anybody who talks to me like he did," O'Malley said, lying on his stomach with his face turned to one side. He looked like he had taken a bad fall off a very tall bicycle.

"Nothing he could possibly say would make him deserve to be hit," Jeffrey said.

O'Malley began to squirm beneath Jeffrey's knee. "Get off of me," he said, adding a few personal insults that Jeffrey found offensive.

But Jeffrey had more to say, and he wanted O'Malley to hang around to listen to it. He put his knee in the man's back a couple of times with vigor, and then he yanked one arm so far back that it hurt just to look at it. "Those boys you're recruiting to keep Graffiti Abatement in business are winding up in the criminal justice system," he said. "Tell me, do you and Arthur Geegan have some particular interest in that happening?"

O'Malley declined to comment, choosing instead to

demonstrate his fluency in foul language. The boys writing the graffiti must have learned their phraseology from him, Jeffrey thought.

Jeffrey had two more points to make: first, his objection to having been run off the road coming down from Hillcrest Avenue, and second, the question of whether O'Malley owned any hardware stores in New Hampshire. Before he could get to either of them, however, something that felt like a pair of boulders struck him from behind, one each at the top and bottom of his spine, and suddenly he was looking at the treetops against the sky as they went flying beneath his feet.

He came down on his side against an automobile tire, a whitewall with a good amount of tread still on it. The crunching of approaching footsteps on gravel told him his attacker wasn't done yet. Jeffrey rolled over to see another man, not O'Malley but the XXL-sized partner, swinging a foot at his head. Jeffrey got his arm up in time to shield his face, which nevertheless suffered damage as his forearm was driven into it by the force of the man's shoe, thus damaging two body parts with one blow. He grabbed the man's leg to trip him, and the two men rolled around on the ground for a bit. Jeffrey got in a couple of solid punches before the other guy slammed the back of Jeffrey's head against the side of a car. Stunned by the impact, he fell forward onto his hands and knees with his head down. Then he found himself being helped to his feet, a kind gesture, although it was done more quickly than he would have liked, the sudden change in altitude sending his internal compass spinning. Before he could focus his eyes on what was coming at him, something that felt like a freight train, a loaded one, settled into his midsection. It seemed like a good idea to lie down for a while, so he did.

CHAPTER 29

Fern looked at her watch and wondered what was keeping Jeffrey. It was time to start the concert. She had seen him earlier, so she knew he was at the park. Sitting at the front edge of the gazebo, she scanned the crowd for his tall figure and didn't see it. What she did see was a waiting audience and, behind her and to one side, a waiting assembly of musicians. It took her only a moment to realize what needed to be done and who needed to do it.

With a calm and determined air, she stood up and walked to the podium, taking her cornet and music folder with her. Although she had never stood on the director's platform before, she stepped up onto this one now as though this had been the plan all along. A few butterflies flitted around in her stomach, but she determinedly ignored them.

Standing erect, she faced the audience squarely and cast a brave smile out at the sea of faces looking up at her. Then she turned back to the musicians and gave them a smile as well. Her fellow band members quickly overcame their surprise at the sudden change in leadership. They readied their instruments.

There was no baton at the lectern, but Fern quickly decided she didn't need one. Using her white-gloved hand to arrest the players' attention, she gave them the downbeat.

⅛

The band led off the concert with "The Star Spangled Banner," of course. Jeffrey could imagine the audience standing, all of them, perhaps, except for Mrs. Roosevelt's mother. He would have stood, too, but he had to take a pass on it this time because it felt as though his leg was broken.

His attacker had left him alone after a while, perhaps having grown bored with his opponent's lack of participation in the scuffle, and now Jeffrey could lie on his back on this nicely stationary parking lot and just listen to that superb music wafting from the park.

He had chosen an old-fashioned version of the national anthem, a nineteenth-century arrangement by Grafulla that was charmingly simple and that featured—of all things—a lovely little cornet flourish. While serving admirably as the traditional opening piece for the concert, it also was remarkable for its unusually humble nature. He hadn't wanted anything grandiose. This wasn't the US Marine Corps Band; it was the Jeffrey Bowden Band, and he hoped to direct it himself one day. He couldn't imagine who was doing it now.

Soon, in just a minute or two, he was going to get up and call for help; he just needed to open his eyes first. This was something he had managed to do every morning of his life, but he was finding it difficult this time owing to some swelling in that general area. But at last he did open his eyes, and there he saw, sitting there on the ground next to him, a crippled old man wearing a fisherman's cap.

"That guy flipped you like a coin toss at the beginning of a football game," Cap said admiringly.

"Which way did I come up, heads or tails?" Jeffrey mumbled.

At first, he thought there was gravel in his mouth, but it turned out to be a loose tooth.

"Couldn't tell," Cap said. "You landed behind this car. Took me a while to get over here. I tried shouting for help, but nobody heard me on account of the band playing."

They sounded wonderful, and Jeffrey thought it was primarily by focusing his attention on the music that he was able to remain conscious. His eyes wanted to close as badly as a bartender about midmorning on New Year's Day, but he forced them to remain open. He didn't want to pass out again; he was afraid he wouldn't wake up. Yet moving around didn't seem like such a good idea, either. He was hurting in a lot of places, especially in his head, and a lot of tiny flashbulbs were going off behind his eyelids when he blinked.

"I've been meaning to get one of those cell phones," Cap said wistfully.

"I think you'd like one," Jeffrey told him. "They're not as complicated as you might imagine. If you do get one, don't loan it to people the way I do so often with mine. What were you and O'Malley arguing about?"

"I caught him trying to recruit those two kids into setting off firecrackers in the audience," Cap said with disgust, "panicking everybody and ruining the concert. The kids, God bless 'em, wasn't keen on doing it, so he kept raising the ante. I finally figured out what was going on and told him what I thought of his plan." He rubbed his jaw and concluded, "He didn't like what I had to say, but I'm glad I said it anyway."

In frustration, Jeffrey asked, "Cap, how do we protect the kids in this town from influences like that?"

"You got any more bass drums?" Cap responded. "It sure worked on Bud."

"If I thought that's all it would take," Jeffrey said, "I'd put together a whole band of boys with bass drums." Speculatively he looked up at the side of the automobile and considered pulling himself up by the door handle, but his arm wouldn't hear of it. "Do you think you could climb inside that car and honk the horn?" he asked Cap.

"I already thought of that," the maintenance man said. "It's locked. I'd try another one, but I don't think I can drag myself much further. I wrenched my back going down." Resting on one hip with his legs to the side, he appeared a likely model for a painting entitled *Christina's Grandpa's World*.

Jeffrey was determined to sit up. His left arm was useless, so he used his right arm, which cooperated but complained mightily all the way. "Boy, that Bud is sounding good," he said, concentrating hard on the music. "Trombones: not so loud now or else you won't be able to knock their socks off with that triple-f that's coming up." Pushing with one arm and one leg, he managed to gradually raise himself. At last, he was partially sitting up, leaning sideways against the car, which made it easier to keep his eyes open. Now he could rest his head against the car and just listen.

Oh, the music! It was a joy. That was his band playing, his musicians whom he had drilled and coaxed and bullied and seduced into playing their best, and now they were playing for him. Through a break in the trees, he could see the power lines forming a pendulous music staff across the sky. As he watched in amazement, a long train of migrating birds, hundreds of black dots, starlings and grackles and red-winged blackbirds, flew over the staff in an undulating rush of visual chords and arpeggios, a composition of marvelous complexity with impossible fingering, a sonata for piano twenty-four hands that Rachmaninoff could only dream of putting his name to. But Fern was playing it now on her cornet. It was her solo.

"Listen to Fern! That's my girl," he cried. She was hitting all the notes just right, and her tempo was perfect. This was the moment every musician lived for, he thought; this was the payoff for all the years of basic instruction, the tedium of playing scales and rudimentary exercises, the diligent sessions late at night and on sunny afternoons when all your friends were outside having fun. This was every musician's goal, to perform with enough control and grace as to make it seem easy, and to lift the heart of anyone listening, even someone who was badly banged up and sitting with another fellow, similarly debilitated, between two cars in a parking lot.

One of them, either he or Cap, was going to have to go for help, and Jeffrey seemed the better candidate. In a minute, he was sure, the world would stop spinning, and then he would see what else he could do.

※

The two boys had watched the fighting in wide-eyed horror, first as Mr. O'Malley punched Bud's grandpa for telling him he was causing Baxter's youth to grow up into the same sort of worthless, despicable crook that O'Malley was, and then as Mr. B, the band director, ran over and jumped on Mr. O'Malley and started giving him some of his own medicine. Then Mr. O'Malley's friend joined in and things got scary-ugly, so the boys ran and hid behind some trees. When it looked like Mr. B was going to get the worst of it, the youngsters decided they had better tell somebody.

"Let's go get Bud," said the oldest, a fifteen-year-old who went by the name of Hawk. He liked being called Hawk because his last name was Hawkins and his first name was Norwood.

The younger one, thirteen, was named Mason, and he didn't mind people calling him that. "There's a police car at the other end of the parking lot," he said. "I think we ought to go tell them."

Hawk was used to running away from the police. It seemed unnatural to approach them voluntarily, especially when bad things were happening, because that was usually when he got into trouble. "I'm going to tell Bud," he said assertively so that Mason wouldn't know he was afraid to go to the police.

"Bud's playing with the band," Mason protested. "He can't just leave while the concert is going on."

"So I'll wait until the concert is over," Hawk said. He ended the argument by heading through the parking lot and walking toward the gazebo.

Mason started to follow him, then stopped uncertainly. The fighting was over. Mr. O'Malley and the other man had gone, and now Mr. B was just lying there in the parking lot. It could be a long time before the band stopped playing, and even after they did stop, what good would it do to tell Bud what had happened? Mason thought he should tell somebody now, in case Mr. B needed help. Bud had said that Mr. B was a real good guy. Mason had been thinking about asking if he could play in the band too, or maybe just carry their instruments since he didn't play anything. He thought it might be fun to hang around with the band, like Bud was doing, instead of roaming around with Hawk and getting into trouble.

Mason looked again at the far end of the parking lot. The front end of the police car was just visible behind another car that was pulling in. Hawk had taught him always to run from the police, but now Mason thought about Mr. B lying there not moving and maybe even dying, while the man who had beat him up was getting away. He thought a policeman had to be the right person to go to in a time like this. What else were they for?

CHAPTER 30

Jeffrey heard the crunch of gravel, and for a moment he feared that he was in for another round of injuries, but then he realized the sound was that of a car coming in his and Cap's direction. Joyously he watched a big, white SUV, a high-end luxury model, rolling slowly toward them. Weakly he raised his arm to flag it down. The car slowed and then stopped. The passenger window rolled down, and Andrew Quigley stared out at Jeffrey, no doubt looking as surprised as Jeffrey did at that moment.

He had aged badly, poor Andrew. The loss of Quigley Enterprises had turned this once robust and propulsive figure into a haggard old man. His skin had taken on a sickly gray pallor, and what remained of his hair was a filthy, matted skirt hanging over his shoulders. A strange wildness had settled into his eyes, clearly showing the prolonged strain and torment of his unsuccessful quest. "Where is she, Jeffrey?" Quigley demanded. His low, raspy voice sounded like something out of a nightmare.

"Helen?" Jeffrey said sharply, then wished he hadn't, because the effort made his ribs hurt. With diminished vigor, he asked, "How should I know?"

"Because you two planned it together, that's how you should know," Quigley said.

"I had nothing to do with her pathetic scheme," Jeffrey

insisted. "She ruined my career and yours all on her own. Why did you set me up to look like an embezzler? You told me to get off the islands, but as soon as I did, you started telling the newspapers I had skipped town."

"That was our plan," Quigley said, "Helen's and mine. I never intended for that project to follow through to its grand opening. I put just enough gears into motion at the beginning to make it look real so that people would buy into it. It was a tax shelter for me. The three and a half million private donation was my own money. Helen funneled it into a second account, and we were planning to run off together to South America. The hidden cameras were supposed to lay the blame on you." He lapsed into a fit of coughing and pressed a handkerchief to his mouth while he cleared his throat of something that sounded horrible, perhaps terminal. After a moment, he continued resentfully, "But she tricked me. She began having second thoughts about our plan. Didn't think it was fair that poor Jeffrey should have to suffer the consequences, he being such a nice boy and all. She wanted to call it off, but I refused. So she disappeared with the money. I've been looking for her for months. Now tell me where she is."

"If I knew where she was, believe me, I'd tell you and the police as well," Jeffrey said. "I would love nothing more than to see both of you go to jail for what you did. You cheated all those investors out of their money."

Quigley gave a cynical laugh. "They got plenty for their money," he said. "For a while, they had the thrill of thinking they were contributing to something great. So what if they lost their investment in the end? The same thing happens every day in Las Vegas and at every casino in the world, and people call it entertainment." His arm came out of the window, and Jeffrey saw there was a small pistol at the end of it. In a shaky voice Quigley said, "Now tell me where she is, Jeffrey. I'm getting too old to wait much longer."

For the moment, Jeffrey was unable to say anything, being entranced by the muzzle of the gun as it wavered around in Quigley's unsteady hand, pointing first at one region of his body and then at another, as if trying to decide on the best target. Jeffrey found it hard to make a recommendation and instead silently willed the pistol away from one vital organ after another, thinking that now would be a very good time for somebody—anybody—to come by and intervene. Somebody did, but only after Quigley had fired the gun.

"How'd a nice guy like you get so many people mad at you?" Cap asked just as a police car pulled up behind Quigley's SUV.

※

Countless places in Jeffrey's body were hurting, and at first he couldn't tell where he had been shot. He felt the impact in his upper torso, but beyond that, he wasn't sure exactly where the bullet had penetrated. While the police were busy wrestling with Quigley, Jeffrey sat leaning against the car and thought of the different cinematic effects he had seen when people got shot in movies, none of them pretty, and here Cap was going to have to look at him while he did it, whatever it turned out to be.

He felt bad about that, but most of all he felt bad because he had failed so miserably to live up to the rarity of this day. All of his plans and efforts were wasted as he sat here, bruised and bleeding in his ruined jacket, such a wretched and utter failure. He thought that if he was going to die now, he deserved such a pathetic ending after having let everyone down: Fern, the whole band, his parents, everyone, he had let them all down. And how would he ever atone for it? A band had only one opening-day concert, and now the music had ended, the concert was over, and he had missed it all. Even his reaction to the gunshot had turned out to be subdued and impassive, just a tiny red hibiscus flower blooming near the right shoulder of his jacket.

The parking lot had gotten crowded suddenly, with the police officers as well as some other people who had come over from the park, he assumed, all of them crunching around on the gravel and talking about getting an ambulance in there. A couple of men helped move Cap out of the way, and then Jeffrey saw a boy, whom he didn't know but who apparently knew him, crouching alongside him.

Appearing to be about thirteen, the lad was wide-eyed and clearly scared by the gravity of all the activity surrounding them, but he seemed determined to be part of the rescue effort in his own small way. "Don't worry, Mr. B," the boy said, "I told the police you needed help, and now they're bringing an ambulance. They'll take you to the hospital and get you fixed up." He offered a brave, slightly trembling smile.

Jeffrey found the words to be beneficial and moving, even as they were comically altered by the modulations of burgeoning manhood—and perhaps because of it. "Thank you," he said, giving the boy's hand a squeeze of gratitude. Then he closed his eyes and thought what a lot of good people there were in this town.

❦

Everyone who came to visit Jeffrey in the hospital brought him a newspaper so he could read the headline "Lady Cornetist Steals the Show." He gratefully accepted each copy, spreading it open against the cast on his leg. While the visitor helped him turn the pages, he read the article again and again, feeling a thrill each time he read the description of how Fern had stepped up to the podium and directed the entire concert. Repeatedly, he gazed with awe and pride at the photo of her in uniform, standing with her cornet and directing the musicians with her white-gloved hand exactly in the manner of the early bandmasters. The newspapers accumulated on the foot of his hospital bed, on the nightstand, and in the visitor's chair, but he wanted them all, and he made sure the housekeepers knew that they were not to be thrown away.

Mrs. Roosevelt had news of her own to deliver to Jeffrey, news that she considered to be equally momentous. Standing before him, she said with genteel exuberance, "Mr. Bowden, you have done what no other person in this city has been able to do, and that is to inspire Arthur Geegan to unbind his personal checkbook from the rusty iron chains that have secured it for so long. He has offered to pay for your complete medical treatment, not with the city's money, but with his own. No doubt he realized it would be less expensive, financially as well as politically, if he paid outright for the damages caused by his hired men. That way, he can avoid any embarrassing questions from the press about his association with the unsavory people who are being charged with corrupting our city's youth." She beamed with pleasure as she concluded, "And it didn't take nearly as many lawyers as I thought it would to help him make that decision."

Jeffrey thanked her for spearheading that effort on his behalf. Then he said, "The high attendance at the concert was the result of Wilson Bean's newspaper article, for which I also must thank you. We received a phenomenal amount of donations at the concert. It's wonderful to see that kind of support from the community at large."

"I hope you also realize the income potential of those manuscripts," she said. "You can publish them, you know, and collect royalties for as long as you hold the copyright."

Struck with a sudden realization, he said, "That's why you didn't want Ben Hennessey to have them. They would have become the property of the city by virtue of that ordinance pertaining to donations."

"That is correct," she confirmed.

"I am happy to tell you that I've found a secure home for those original documents," Jeffrey informed her. "In the fall, I'll be starting a new job at Baxter College. The manuscripts you donated will be housed in a special archival vault, whereas the music itself will be drawn upon as instructional material for the concert band I'll be directing."

Professor Wilmot himself had come to offer the position to Jeffrey, who had gratefully accepted it and could hardly wait to tell Fern about it.

Andrew Quigley had been arrested for the shooting and was deemed incompetent for trial, resulting in his confinement at a private long-term treatment facility somewhere in rural New York State. The endowment he had given to Baxter College, however, was far more stable and durable, as was the career it engendered for Jeffrey. Being funded in perpetuity, the new position went far toward atoning for the year Jeffrey had lost in Hawaii while playing the pawn in the Quigleys' scheme.

A second Quigley endowment had arrived as well, this one in the form of a sizable check signed by Helen Quigley, who had enclosed a note addressed to Jeffrey. Written on stationery from a chemical-dependency treatment center in Boston, the message was simple: "Maybe it isn't too late after all."

⁂

Fern came to see Jeffrey on the day of his release from the hospital. She had been helping Terri and Tommy adapt their home to accommodate the needs of a temporary invalid.

Jeffrey gave her his written discharge orders to read and

said, "The doctor didn't mention anything about the curative benefit of hot tubs, but I'm sure it was just an oversight."

After scanning the list of discharge instructions he was to follow, Fern looked up at him and said, "You need a private-duty nurse."

"Yes," he acknowledged, "and, by coincidence, I have one in mind that I'd like to hire. It's a lifetime appointment, by the way."

Smiling, she returned the paper to him, then knelt and began wriggling a sock onto the foot of his uninjured leg. "Is the pay good?" she asked.

"Very competitive wages for a volunteer position," he said.

"Benefits?" she asked, now fitting a shoe over the sock.

"There will be additional responsibilities galore," he promised. "You'll find yourself in constant demand, with interruptions at every possible moment."

Having finished dressing his foot, she sat back on the floor and hugged her knees. She had taken the day off from work on his behalf and was dressed in jeans and a blazer over a plain T-shirt. He liked not having a clever slogan or sports logo getting in the way of what he really wanted to look at. "It sounds like the perfect job," she said in wonder. "People must be lining up to apply for it."

"Surprisingly few," he said, then admitted with a shrug, "You're the only one I'm offering it to."

"I'll dust off my résumé and see if I can come up with a few good references," she promised.

"Everyone who was at the band concert should be able to speak well on your behalf," he said. "Fern, I can't tell you how proud I am of what you did. You saved the concert, and you did it in such an exemplary way. Were you nervous?"

Her newfound confidence appeared to have taken root.

With a shrug, she said simply, "There was no time to be nervous. I saw a job that needed to be done, and it seemed as though I was the right person to do it." Her eyes shone with pleasure at the memory. "I was so grateful for all those hours you spent with me at your house, helping me learn my solo. You made me play it over and over—a hundred times, it seemed. I didn't think I would ever get it right. But you convinced me to keep trying. 'Just once more, Fern,' you said in your gentle way. 'Try it one more time,' you said, until finally I got every note right. Thanks to you, I did something I hadn't thought was possible."

He remembered lying in the parking lot while listening to her and thinking how he had failed everyone by not being on the bandstand to lead his musicians. "The most significant thing for me," he said, "is that you redeemed that event in my memory. I'll no longer think of that day as my failure, but as your triumph."

Terri and Tommy arrived to carry Jeffrey's collection of newspapers out to the car. Fern pushed him in his wheelchair to the hospital exit, where the minivan was waiting. They got him arranged in the backseat, making room for Fern to sit with him, and then started for home. Although one of Jeffrey's arms was in a sling, he used the other one to take Fern's hand, the left one as it happened. As he caressed it, one of the fingers felt terribly empty. "Fern," he said, "I have a question for you."

"Yes?" she asked curiously.

He glanced at his surrogate parents in the front seat and admitted, "This may not be the best time."

"It's the perfect time," she said with a straight face, though her smile wanted to bloom as urgently as a forsythia cutting on a sunny windowsill. "Never better, in fact."

They had stopped at a red light. Ever indulgent, Terri and Tommy appeared to have become fascinated by the idea of mechanized traffic control.

"Fern," Jeffrey said at last, "will you continue to direct my band this summer?"

Her smile burst into full bloom as she said, "Jeffrey, I would be honored."

"I should add that we'll have to change your name first," he said, "because the 'BB' on the bass drum stands for Bowden's Band."

"I always suspected that it did," she said.

%

Jeffrey was still using a cane when the fall semester came around at Baxter College. He and his new bride were renting the upstairs of Bob's house as an apartment. Walking to work was part of Jeffrey's physical therapy.

Halfway down the street, he began to hear a low, muffled roar which grew steadily louder as he neared the college. At last, he saw them on the athletics field: twenty boys beating tapered wooden sticks against a battery of drums in disciplined synchrony. The newly formed Baxter Drum Corps was one of the educational programs funded by the Quigley endowments, a joint endeavor with the city's juvenile corrections division.

It was enough to warm Jeffrey's heart through the coldest winter.

ABOUT THE AUTHOR

Jan Tenery began learning about community bands while living in Maine. Her love for their music sparked a self-guided study of the rich history of community bands that ultimately led her to Arizona, where her new husband, a retired band director, taught her to play percussion. Those experiences inspired her to write this novel. She has performed with several ensembles in Yuma and Oracle. *Brass Roots* is her first novel.

Printed in the United States
By Bookmasters